before the gods

The Chronicles of Fate and Choice
Book One

before the gods

K. S. TURNER

RUBY BLAZE PUBLISHING

Published in Great Britain in 2009 by Ruby Blaze Publishing

Copyright © 2009 by K.S. Turner

The moral right of the author has been asserted

A CIP catalogue record for this book is available from the British Library.

ISBN 978-0-9562242-0-0

Typeset by Hewer Text UK Ltd, Edinburgh
Printed by Cromwell Press Group, Trowbridge, Wiltshire

Ruby Blaze Publishing
Ruby blaze Limited
Somerset, UK

www.rubyblaze.com

For you, who forget.

Acknowledgements

My heartfelt love and thanks go to my mum, for her love, faith, indomitable will, encouragement and support, far beyond the call of duty. Mum, you inspire me. Thank you to my brother James, for being a brilliant light in a dark world, always shining with his genius, and for being interested in everything. And to my sister Jenny, the wild flower, for her mad humour, rock-solid trust and superb meringues. You all, above all else, have kept me sane while I have been engrossed in my writing.

Love and thanks to Tonka for his love, support, tenacity and wit, and for doing all those 'dad' things most superbly.

And a big heap of thanks and love to my friends for their encouragement. To Niko, for also making me laugh so much my sides hurt, and for being able to make my mind slow down occasionally. To Amanda, for being totally crazy and totally sane at the same time, and for making me participate in her latest mad ideas. To Zoe, the soul sister, for being able to talk with her about everything. To Johnny, for his enthusiasm for the story and for his conviction that I should start writing.

A huge thank you to my editor, Jeremy, for his subtle guidance, intelligence, honesty and encouragement. Everyone should know a Jeremy; what a brilliant mind.

Thank you to my agent, Leslie, for having the faith to take me on and for guiding me through all those early awkward stages.

And thanks to those whose songs and music inspire me, filling the silence while I write through the night: Switchblade, Dead Can Dance, Carl McCoy, VNV, P J Harvey, and Vivaldi, to name but a few.

I have heard them called many things:
Strangers, gods, angels, visitors.
Do not forget their real names,
Because they know our pasts are not as we've been told.

ONE

A steady trickle of sweat irritated Chia's brow, almost breaking his concentration.

"Focus, focus, focus," he instinctively chanted his mantra.

He almost had it. Just a fraction more.

There was no time to check his team behind him, no time to give them warning and to rally their strength. Chia would have to assume they were ready. This was the closest he had ever been, and it had to be now.

Mustering every part of his remaining strength, Chia ignored the pain of fatigue and surged forward, disconnecting all but the finest thread of his chi from his flesh and sending it deep into the metal of the craft's hull.

His chi directed him further into the craft, where Chia knew he had drawn close to it. Then, just as he thought that he could finally touch it, it moved, slipping away from the range of his senses as if repelled by his presence. He quickly scanned to find its new location. But there was nothing; all trace of it eluded him. He searched again. It was definitely gone. Gone from his grasp. Gone from his senses. Simply gone, as if it had never been there.

For a moment, Chia felt paralyzed from the emptiness that consumed him. This time he had been closer than ever. That same unknown energy had coursed through this ship, strongly this time. But once again it had seemed to vanish, as if it knew his intent to capture it. No other kutu sensed it, and he still could not find any evidence of its existence, let alone contain it.

Feeling suddenly drained, he slowly drew his energy back into his flesh. He pulled his forehead back from the cold metal he'd been pressed against and glared accusingly at the vastness of the craft in front of him.

"Damn," he whispered to himself. "It was there. I know it was. It's as if it taunts me."

He placed his palms on the cold metal and pressed with his fingers, as if he had the strength to pierce the indestructible alloy and pull out the elusive substance.

"Come on. I know you exist. Show yourself!"

Suddenly, Chia's frustration burst.

"Damn you!" he cursed, pounding his fists hard against the side of the craft.

A bolt of angry violet energy shot from his fists, slamming into the metal with such a tremendous force that sparks of violet showered down and the immense ship began rocking precariously.

The ground crew behind Chia moved backwards a step, as if sensing what was coming. From beyond their silence, a low rumble vibrated. The air became filled with the metallic taste of angry power, and the floor began to tremble.

"Stand down," a voice called from behind Chia.

"Only I have authority here," Chia replied, without turning.

The footsteps came closer and a large hand touched Chia's shoulder, making the nanos on his black body armour ripple down his arm with a golden hue.

"I know," a voice said calmly. "But I'm sure you'll not find answers by using your skills to rip this craft apart. Let's just say I'm saving you the trouble of filling out another damages report."

Chia turned to see Stanze: a friend, a fellow kutu of similar height to him, though three times his width. Stanze was clad, as usual, in the formal golden uniform of an Anumi warrior. His radiant golden energy wings were fully extended, casting light all around him, and his luminous blue eyes showed only the genuine concern of friendship.

Chia felt his anger subside and the floor immediately ceased vibrating and calm resumed. Suddenly conscious of his own dispersed energy, Chia refocused to form his wings and show the customary sign of respect to the Anumi warrior.

"Stanze," Chia bowed, as his vibrant violet wings stretched out behind him.

"Preserve your strength, my friend," Stanze smiled, returning the bow.

He moved closer, lowering his tone so that only Chia could hear, "You've been doing this for three days straight without a rest. Your crew needs a break. And you need a break too."

"You've been monitoring me?"

"Not monitoring," Stanze replied, "Just keeping an eye on your progress, while ensuring that news of your extra-curricular activities go no further than these docking bays."

"I thought I'd had very few interruptions." Chia considered Stanze's remark. "What did you do?"

"Nothing much: just stationed some of my available Anumi to this location. A standard procedure, but one with the added bonus of deterring prying eyes."

"Shursa?"

Stanze nodded. "Officially he is stretching his legs. It's funny, though – unofficially they always seem to want to stretch this way."

Chia laughed, making a sprinkle of violet light stream from his mouth.

"It is not because you are my friend that I do this," Stanze said soberly. "Despite how Shursa discredits you, I know you well enough to believe the things you claim."

A wave of relief and gratitude swept through Chia, but at the same time, the gravity of Stanze's remark fell heavily. Yes, Shursa discredited him at every opportunity, but there were many more that still questioned his stability and even sanity since the 'incident' he'd suffered when first discovering planet Earth. Until he could prove his claims about this unknown energy, his reputation would be damaged.

"My friend, I would not want you to put your rank or honour in jeopardy by openly agreeing with me or helping me," Chia nodded.

"My honour will only be in jeopardy if I do not do what I consider true. And as an Anumi, my rank is awarded for honour as much as for skill," Stanze stated.

"Then I will simply say, thank you," Chia smiled.

He saluted the large warrior in the Anumi manner.

Clearly satisfied that the situation had been placated, Stanze returned the salute and left the bays.

Chia immediately turned to his crew. Twenty-seven strong, they stood straight, alert and resolute, awaiting their next orders. Yet despite this, they were clearly exhausted. Three sleepless days of supporting their captain with their own chi had taken its toll. Their normally vibrant energy no longer bristled around them in various hues; their skin lacked any radiant shine; their eyes, although focussed, had lost their illuminating glow; and all, without exception, had deactivated their wings in order to preserve energy. Chia had not only pushed himself to his limit, he had also pushed his crew to theirs. They needed to be fresh and rested, as did he, especially if they were going to try again.

Once rest rotas were arranged, Chia dismissed his crew before returning to the main flight deck. The bays were unusually empty, with only a few smaller crafts and one harvesting ship currently occupying the vast space. The only movement came from the small cleaning drones silently manoeuvring around the floor, maintaining the purity of their surroundings, and the only sound came from the muffled echo of Chia's own footsteps and from the air against his wings. Around him, the shining black stone walls seamlessly spanned towards the gaping opening, with the tiny planet Earth perfectly placed as a central blue spot in the distance.

Chia launched the remaining harvesting ship back onto its automated flight pattern around the blue planet and scheduled the next batch of landings. This done, and with the docks wound down to an agreeable calmness, he stood at the edge of the huge launch window watching the stars, savouring the rare moment of solitude. It was the first time since being stationed here on the XLS substation that the bays had been silent.

And what am I to do next? I have pushed my capabilities to my limits without success. Am I missing something? Chia pondered, toying with the pendant around his neck, an unconscious habit whenever deep in thought. He had contemplated the same questions many times recently, and still seemed no closer to an answer. He knew he needed to clear his mind, to rethink from a new perspective, but he was able to think little else.

Suddenly aware of his unconscious habit of toying with the pendant, Chia unlaced it from around his neck and held it up: the small recording crystal, storing an unplayed symphony, glinted in the starlight.

A smile spread across his lips. In his hand was the perfect solution to help clear his mind.

Chia's unusual pendant had been a gift from his greatest friend, the renowned composer Orion, just before departure to this new Earth substation, the XLS. Orion had handed him the crystal, and had simply said, "My new composition. You'll know when it's the right time to play it." Chia had not found *any* time to listen to the recording, yet alone the right time. Eventually he had laced it around his neck, rather than carry it about, and it had become a mere ornamental pendant. Until now.

The crystal pendant was of a standard data format, and any port on the station would have the capability to play it; every ship had the facility, too. Chia strode towards the closest pod and climbed in.

Unlacing the crystal from its cord, Chia placed the recording in the pod's reading slot and settled back into the pilot's seat. Directly in front of him offered a perfect view of the launch window and the stars beyond. It was a beautiful sight. Knowing he had a rare moment of free time, Chia decided to take the opportunity for a spontaneous flight. He loved flying. He activated the pod and eased the little craft out of its hold.

The timing was perfect: as the pod cleared the base, the composition began to play. The hum of engines faded into the background as music rumbled through the ship, its intense rhythms building up and rolling together into complex harmonies and sounds. It took Chia's breath away. He stopped focussing on sending the pod co-ordinates, and the ship abruptly halted.

"Replay from beginning," Chia instructed.

But the music continued and, despite Chia's repeated commands, the recording would not stop. Eventually he tried prying the crystal from its reading slot. It wouldn't budge.

Crystal cannot be ejected until data has completed sequential output, the pod's information display blinked.

Touché, Orion, Chia laughed to himself. It seemed Orion had finally done it: successfully encoded a recording so that it had to be played from start to finish. Chia knew how much he detested his compositions being interrupted.

Chia gave in to the machine and relaxed back, closing his eyes while the recital continued. He couldn't pinpoint what emotion the music was trying to induce. Something potent, definitely, but what he couldn't quite tell. The moments evaporated; it was entrancing, beautiful.

The music stopped and Chia remained seated, drifting deep into thought. Suddenly, a high-pitched vibration shot a pain through his head and he doubled over, clasping his temples.

As if from the vibrations, Chia's mind became filled with a barrage of gruesome images: kutu in pain and anguish, faces contorted into expressions of betrayal and torture. And eyes: thousands of black eyes descending towards him in a cloud of black wings, all with the intent to kill, accompanied by sounds of hissing and screaming that no kutu should be able to make. His instinct said 'escape,' but he couldn't run away; his friends needed him. He saw his own hands in front of him, clasping daggers dripping with blood, and all around him was carnage; kutu slaughtering, being slaughtered, knee deep in the remnants of friends. Then there was a light - the brightest, all-consuming, blinding flash.

Another pain shot through Chia's head, burning the visions away. The blackness that followed was a dense nothingness full of something so terrible he could no longer see it. All he could feel was dread.

Forcing himself upright, Chia shook the images from his mind. *No, not again, not those visions. They're not real*, he told himself. *Empty them from your head.*

A burning smell tinged his nostrils, and for a brief moment, he thought he was imagining that too. As the ship filtered the pungent odour away, Chia located its source: by his right hand side, from where the recording crystal was embedded, dense, black smoke was streaming out.

Chia wedged his fingers into the reading slot and, disregarding the heat, pulled out what was left of the crystal. It came out easily this time, but as he picked it up it fragmented, creating a pile of fine black dust particles in his hand. Cursing under his breath, he gathered the dust into a small containment pouch and tied it around his neck.

The ship's displays indicated that the craft wasn't registering any malfunctions, yet something had disturbed Chia's psyche and made the crystal disintegrate. Perhaps the crystal was contaminated. If it was, then the ship could now be contaminated, which could spread to their entire fleet. This could be very bad indeed, Chia decided. He turned the pod around and sped back to the docking bays considering the best way to decipher this latest anomaly.

Meanwhile, back on the kutu home-world, Eden, Orion had stopped at his music console and pushed aside the ancient books that surrounded him. A smile spread across his lips. Yes, he felt it; it was time. It had begun. Chia had played the Summoning Song. Now all he had to do was wait. Soon he would know if there was anything left to summon.

TWO

Father was working fast and, even though it was only just midday, my fifth basket of Junir was almost full. I half watched his stiffly stooped, sun-browned back and strong arm swinging his long knife back and forth, as I collected the shafts from his trail.

Light reflected off his blade, off the sweat on his body and off the pale golden Junir crop. It was hot and bright, and I hoped we'd soon stop for water.

The birds didn't seem to be bothered by the heat, but left their shady perches to peck at the discarded grains. Their boisterous twittering, along with the swish of the blade and the rustle of the falling Junir, made a pleasant rhythm. I laid the shafts in my basket in a way that added its own cadence and entwined my thoughts in the sounds, moving in time to the rhythm and creating a smooth dancing motion.

As I worked to my imaginary tune, I began picking out unfamiliar, yet beautiful, sounds. They were more melodic than the birds, more rhythmic than father's blade, and full of the strangest, most wonderful noises all fused together.

I stopped, putting down my basket, and the sounds seemed to grow louder, filling my ears with a multitude of fascinating noises. I had never heard anything like this. This was not *his* voice, what I called the Earth-voice – the low rumbling calls that I usually heard in my head. This was something very different indeed.

"Father, do you hear that?" I said quietly.

"Oh yes, the birds are happy," father laughed, without halting the motion of the harvesting. "It seems they've a taste for Junir. It's a good job there's plenty for all."

"It's not the birds," I replied. "It's something else. It's beautiful."

Father stopped cutting, cocking his head to one side. "I can hear the birds, Tachra," he concluded, after listening for a moment, "and a faint breeze over the crops, but nothing else."

He turned his back to me and resumed his work, while I just stood and listened. By now, the rolling music filled my head with its enchanting sounds merging to form something beautiful, like a melody I had dreamt of, but couldn't remember. It was truly wonderful. It made the back of my neck tingle and my mind fill with glorious yet unfamiliar images.

Surely this cannot be my imagination, I thought. I could never imagine such a pleasing noise. But I didn't want to think about it; I just wanted to listen.

It seemed like only a moment had passed when father's call snapped me from my daydreams.

"Tachra," he shouted.

With an effort, I focussed on him. He was at the far end of the field, looking at me with his hands on his hips and a long line of neatly cut Junir spanning between us.

"Are you sure you cannot hear it?" I asked absently. "It's like music, but more . . . well . . . just more. I've never heard anything like it."

"I can't hear anything unusual, child," he replied, putting down his knife and walking towards me, looking concerned. When he reached me, he put his palm against my forehead. "You're not overly hot," he decided. "Still, you may have caught the sun. Go fetch yourself some water and, once you've rested, bring me some back too."

"Yes, I'll fetch the water," I responded vaguely, wishing he wouldn't talk over the melody.

"Go on then child, make haste," he nodded sternly.

Father crouched down and picked up my basket, gathering the shafts that I'd missed. I didn't even mind that he called me child – I'm past seventeen summers and normally I would have reminded him – but the music still played and everything seemed perfect.

Father looked up at me, but before he could hurry me on my way yet again, I turned on my heel and ran towards our hut.

I took the shortest route home, cutting across the field where it bordered Rew's orchard. I saw Rew with two of his youngest children, all heavily laden with baskets of ripe apples.

"Do you hear those amazing sounds?" I called to Rew.

Rew stopped and frowned, and the two little ones mimicked his movement. "Nope," he shook his head, "I don't hear anything."

I could tell by the look on his face that he really couldn't hear my music, so I just shrugged and continued running, leaving him staring in my direction. The music was still rolling through my head, but it was changing, it was as if it was coming to an end. I didn't want it to end. I wanted it to go on forever.

When I burst in through the open door of my hut, mother was cooking. She turned unhurriedly from her pots. "Tachra, it's too early for food. Is father coming too?"

I ignored her question. "You must hear it," I insisted, as the music played its final notes, "Those wonderful sounds."

"Hear what?" Mother asked, with the same look on her face as father and Rew. "The only noise is the bubbles from my pot and, pleasant as it is, I wouldn't call it wonderful."

I sat down heavily on the bench. The music had finished and I felt both sad and happy. How I wished someone else had heard it so that I could share it with them.

"It's stopped now," I sighed, burying my head in my hands. "But I did hear it; the most wonderful music. It was like birds and breezes and blossom and sunshine on water and movement and . . . oh . . . just wonderful things. Someone else must have heard it too, they must have. But you didn't and father didn't and Rew didn't either."

Mother frowned. I could tell she didn't think the music was real. She probably thought I was imagining it, rather like she used to think I was imagining the Earth-voice until I stopped telling her about it. She walked towards me and lifted my head, putting the palm of her hand on my forehead, just as father had done.

"You feel well enough," she said.

"I *am* well enough," I replied indignantly. "I'm better than well, and I did hear the most astonishing sounds, unlike anything I know. I just can't explain them; they were just wonderful. I feel . . . wonderful."

"You stay sitting. I'll fetch you some water," she decided firmly.

Moments later, mother handed me a pot of cold water. I gazed down. The water seemed to shimmer with a colour I'd not seen before, a colour which seemed to tell me things about the water. I knew instantly that the water was fresh, that it was gathered from the river only that morning, and that drinking it would be good. I didn't know how I knew these things, I just did.

I took a long draught and looked around the hut. I sensed many other things: the movement of insects in the wood, the fact that the wood was too dry, and that mother's stew would burn if she didn't stir it. Even the empty spaces seemed to have an invisible substance. I felt aware of something in everything my eyes perceived, and even more in the things that they didn't. These were not things I'd experienced before and nothing like the Earth-voice that I heard every day.

Surely, I am imagining this, I thought. *Yes*, I decided, *father must be right; I must have caught the sun.*

I was made to stay in the hut for the remainder of the day, even though I told Mother I was well. She took refreshments to father and, when she returned, insisted that I had a cold wash – not my favourite thing. The afternoon dragged, as she seemed intent on keeping me as still as possible, and then later that evening, once father had returned and I'd picked disinterestedly at my supper, I asked if I could retire early.

Mother and father agreed that a good sleep was just what I needed, so I gave them each a kiss on the forehead and went to my room, stealthily slipping two of the reddest apples in my pocket as I passed the food stocks.

I wasn't really tired, so I sat in my room, too restless to make any more of the carvings that I liked etching into the floorboards; in any case, I didn't think I could fit any more in the floor under the trunk in my room. So I sat by the window, just thinking. And although I didn't try to listen, I could overhear my parents discussing me.

It seemed that mother thought father had worked me too hard. Father said it was no different to any other day, and that I'd seemed fine. Mother then told him that the fairer skinned ones were more affected by the sun, and that he should take that into account. She also suggested that she should make me a bonnet. I felt bad that they were concerned, especially as I had repeatedly told them I was fine. I knew I'd been quiet, but it wasn't the sun's heat that had silenced me. I'd tried unsuccessfully to hear the wonderful music again, but instead had kept seeing things that shouldn't be there, feeling things I'd never felt before, and getting the strangest notions in my head. None of it made sense, and I didn't think a bonnet could possibly help.

My parents' conversation eventually dwindled until they retired, settling down for the night in the room next to mine. They shifted restlessly for a few moments on the crunchy grass mattress, and then fell silent. How I wished I could sleep that easily, I thought. But I couldn't, and never had been able to, although I'd tried. Instead, I sat looking out of the window, growing more awake as the moments passed, waiting, as I did every night, for the village to sleep and the Earth-voice to call to me.

Waiting made time crawl so slowly. My elbows grew numb from leaning on the ledge, and my limbs ached from inactivity, but trying to reposition myself was impossible: the rickety floor would only creak irritably in response and I didn't want my parents to wake. I eventually made do with an unsatisfying brisk rub to my arms.

From my raised viewpoint, I could see the entire village. Four lamps were still burning. I wished they would hurry up and be put out. As if responding to my gaze, three were snuffed out in quick succession. *Good*, I thought, *soon they'll all be asleep*. I fixed my gaze on the remaining lamp-lit window, willing the occupants to bed.

I knew the view before me so well it might have been etched on my eyelids. This was Threetops, my village, nestled into a large, shallow valley and surrounded by fields, berry groves and rolling green hills topped with tall trees. At night, the trees stood out on the horizon like men guarding the end of the land. The huts were almost identical, except for the irregular tufts of thatch that sprouted randomly, like fingers clawing for the stars. Mine was one of the last huts, part-built into the hill and on two levels, housing just my parents and me, now that my fifteen siblings had left to start families of their own.

I was not supposed to go out at night – nobody was – all the villagers were supposed to sleep. But, I'd never been able to switch to sleep as they did, so I would go out, letting the Earth-voice in my head guide me to new places. This was my secret.

The Earth-voice was growing loud tonight – louder than ever. I called it the Earth-voice because it seemed to come from everywhere, even the ground itself. I heard it every night; it was another of those things that no-one else seemed to hear. But tonight it sounded different – it was as if I understood its words. *Come and be free*, it seemed to call, over and over again.

The last lamp finally died, leaving the village dark and still. I waited a moment, drumming my fingers on the ledge, restless to be gone, but determined to ensure that all were settled. When I could be sure that they were, I wrapped my skirt around my thighs, and, putting the apples safely in my pocket, I swung my legs over the ledge and slid down to the ground. When my bare feet touched the soil, the whisperings from the Earth grew even louder.

Just being out of my hut gave me a sense of release. I wanted to run and leap and feel the wind against my skin, so I closed my eyes and gathered pace, letting the motion of my legs blindly carry me forward. I had no worries about where I would go, because the Earth-voice would guide me.

I ran silently, with the feel of the well trodden ground beneath my feet telling me where I was. First I was on the pathways between the huts, and then the foliage brushing my arms indicated that I was on the outskirts of the village, running through the narrow strips that separated the berry groves. The smell of ripe fruits filled the warm air, making my belly grumble greedily. I ignored the fleeting desire to collect berries, and continued into the dusty wheat crops, running through the fields until I'd passed the areas my people farmed. Eventually I had run deep into the uneven, clumping grasses of uncultivated terrain and the land grew more ragged. *I know this route*, I thought happily; I knew where my legs were taking me tonight: to my favourite place, the ravine.

I kept running until I could no longer smell the long grasses and until I started to feel an incline to the east, and then I halted. When I opened my eyes, a welcome sight greeted me.

Under the night's full moon, the ravine spanned out before me, the width of a thousand men, a giant crack running through the land. Its falling sides were covered in heavily leaved trees, creating a blanket of darkest green that shimmered under the moonlight. A breeze rose up and brushed against me, filling my nostrils with the warm damp scent of the earth.

I easily picked out the winding descent, memorised from my first visits, while my eyes struggled to adjust to the increasing gloom. The cool grass underfoot gradually gave way to soft warm moss that sprung back up behind me, making my path invisible once again. Gnarled branches reached down, touching my hair, greeting me as I passed. I held out my arms and returned their welcome as the increasing rush of the river drew me downwards. By the water was where the Earth-voice always seemed the loudest. Tonight, I hoped, I might be able to understand what it was saying.

By the time I reached the bottom of the ravine, my eyes had adjusted to the near blackness. Here was my hidden world. The huge contorted trees hung their lowest branches over the river, which glistened, spraying me mischievously as it rushed past. The ground was strewn with young trees of various heights, all competing to become part of the forest, and the clumps of vines strung above my head as if threading the whole place together.

I made my way to the mossy clearing by the water and inspected more of my carvings, which I'd left heaped under a Dean tree. Nothing had been moved since my last visit and, satisfied that nobody else had been there, I picked up my knife to carve some more.

I intended on working on my little collection of beads; the latest one only had a few of the tiny shapes that I liked to carve, but I just could not focus on making more. I stuck the knife back into the ground, removed my clothes, carefully hanging them over the branches, and plunged into the water, swimming to the centre where the protruding boulders made a welcome anchor against the current. The brisk water pummelled my body and mind to numbness, and then I pulled myself up to sit on the cool mass of stone and listen to *his* voice, the Earth-voice.

I had always heard him, and for many moons I'd followed his wordless call to see new places. It was as if I knew him, although I'd never seen him. I didn't even really know if 'he' *was* a he; his voice often changed, but it always had a depth and resonance and so, not knowing either way, I'd always thought of him as male. I didn't know what he looked like, and I'd imagined a hundred different figures over time, but none of them ever seemed right. I had so many questions that I had always wanted to ask him: Who was he? Where did he live? Why did I hear his calls when nobody else did? Did he make the music I'd heard earlier? I wanted him to come out and show himself so I could meet him.

I craned my head to view all directions, hoping to catch a glimpse of him. Nothing stirred, but I knew he was there.

"You're calling me again. I hear you clearly tonight. I'm here now," I said loudly.

His whisperings raged above the sound of the rushing water, making my skin prickle, but I couldn't make out any words and he didn't reply.

"The river's good. You could always come and swim with me." I suggested.

I waited a few moments, but still he didn't answer. It didn't make sense that he should call to me if he didn't really want to talk.

"Or we could just sit," I motioned towards the bank.

Nothing.

"I've bought you some apples," I offered.

Nothing.

"They're the best from Rew's new crop, the sweetest I've ever tasted. When you bite into them, they melt in your mouth. Come and try one," I suggested. "Please, just talk with me."

Still he didn't make an effort to reply, and I had run out of the things I had planned to say. I was actually quite irritated by his lack of response.

Maybe he doesn't like apples, I wondered. It had taken a great deal of planning to steal them, and I'd thought that everyone liked apples. He could at least just thank me for the offer. Perhaps he was being rude on purpose. Yes, I decided, he was probably watching me, hiding somewhere, laughing at me and my stupid apples.

"Why don't you come out? I heard you tonight and I know you're here," I demanded. "And I know you can hear me, so don't pretend that you can't. You've called me so let me see you. If not, well that's impolite. You are just rude!" I then fell silent, surprised at my own sudden outburst.

The breeze stiffened and swirled around me, chilling my wet skin, and I felt him closer than ever. It seemed I had a reaction.

You are not looking.

The voice drifted hazily around me as if part of the breeze, pulsing through my head like an ache, but with no pain. He was speaking, and for the second time this night, I understood his words.

I scanned the area, trying to find him among the shadows upon shadows, but nothing stirred except the usual rush of water and the flicker of leaves. It would just be so easy for him to show himself; now I was sure he was being difficult on purpose.

"I *am* looking," I stated indignantly. "But, unless you're a tree or a leaf, I cannot see you."

You can see me, always, he growled – yes, it definitely sounded like a growl – after a long pause. .

"Aah," I exhaled loudly. "So, now you're being funny. First I say I can't see you, and you tell me I do not look, and now you say that I can see you, always. Make up your mind."

All questions have many answers. You ask what you already know.

"Are you making fun of me? If you are, it's not funny and I'm not laughing."

I folded my arms and gritted my teeth. I would not say another thing. What a disappointment; at last I could make out his words, and then I found that they were nothing but self-contradicting nonsense. For so long I had wanted to understand him, and now it seemed he only wanted to ridicule me. There was no point listening to such unreason. He could go away for all I cared.

I sat unmoving on my boulder, refusing to speak, and gradually felt his presence recede. I knew he was still close, but his voice had left my head, leaving an emptiness that made a wave of dismay pass through me. Nevertheless, I was too annoyed to call him back.

Perhaps, I decided, he would want a decent conversation another night. If he couldn't be bothered to make the effort tonight, then neither could I. For now, I would just pretend that he wasn't there.

Before long, I dived back into the river and swam a little, pushing forward and letting the current take me back again. The water felt good and I soon forgot my annoyance, humming my recollection of the wonderful music I'd heard earlier while I swam. After a while, I pulled myself back up onto the boulder and sang at the top of my voice, kicking up the water in time to the loudest bits and waving my arms as if they were re-creating the sounds. It was not a very good rendition, but I didn't care because in my head I imagined I was singing it perfectly.

Suddenly, I sensed movement.

I spun around and stared into the darkness, listening while the music continued in my thoughts. But I couldn't hear anything, nothing at all, not even the moving water. I watched the river rush past my feet, and could see it throwing spray into my face, but couldn't feel or hear it. I kicked at the water – I could see what I was doing, but couldn't feel that either. In fact, I couldn't feel or hear anything. I wobbled, nearly falling off the boulder, and opened my mouth to make a sound, but no noise left my lips. I was mute, dumb and deaf.

I stared straight ahead. Keep still, I repeatedly told myself. Keep still and it will pass.

Then, as quickly as I'd realised that all sound had gone, my senses returned with a vengeance. From the distance, a mounting rumble filled the air and the boulder beneath me began to tremor. For a moment I was relieved, but the relief evaporated as soon as I saw the source of the vibrations.

In the distance, a huge, gleaming wall of water rushed towards me, rising above the river in a churning mass at least three men tall and spanning the width of the waterway. It looked like the river had come alive. It travelled at a ferocious pace, sucking in overhanging branches and small trees as it sped towards me.

I froze, knowing I couldn't make it to the rivers bank in time, and then the huge wall of water hit me with a force, throwing me from my boulder.

SILENCE! he cried out without warning.

The word exploded through my head, making my body scream in pain, and the water pulled me into its tumbling mass.

I flapped my arms and legs, trying desperately to reach the glinting surface that rotated around me, but the water's onslaught curled its fingers tighter and sucked me further down.

Then I heard him again, as if the grasp of the water was his grasp, and I could know nothing else.

You dare to stir me further with a song of awakening? his voice boomed.

He seemed angry. It scared me.

I tried shaking myself free from the grasp that held me. I knew I wasn't breathing and that I had to reach the surface, but no matter how much I pushed upwards, I didn't move. Ripples shuddered down my torso, forming a pressure in my back, and I knew the grasp was not just from the water. A suppressed power held me as if I were nothing but a small twig in its hands, ready to be snapped in two.

Who provokes me with the notes of awakening? he boomed again.

The music, I realised. He was referring to the wonderful music.

It's not me, I thought pleadingly. *I heard it too, the music was beautiful, but it wasn't from me. I'm just remembering. I thought it was from you.*

No! It is not from me, he roared. *And no,* he paused; *it is not you. But it fills your head. Silence it!*

I tried desperately to silence the music in my head, without success. It seemed that the more I tried not to think of it, the stronger it played.

I don't know how to silence it, I thought. *Please, I don't understand.*

Understand yourself! You have sight, yet are blind. You question, yet you understand. You heard it and now you make me hear it too. Are you not in control of your own will? Silence it!

The grasp on my back abruptly released, making a surge of weightlessness and tranquillity fill me, yet I didn't try to reach the river's surface. I knew I wasn't breathing, but it no longer seemed to matter, as all around me seemed timeless. I just stopped struggling, hypnotized by the movement of tiny air bubbles and bits of earth swimming gracefully past my face. I felt as if I had become part of the moving shapes, transfixed by the echoes of his growling voice. Amidst the haze, my thoughts faintly stirred, but they seemed dislocated, far away from my flesh. I tried again to repress the memory of the music.

Think of something else, I dreamily told myself. *You must think of something else.*

I struggled to concentrate on other things: father's crops, mother's hot Yute stew, the bees visiting the blossom, father laughing. Nothing was working. I could picture many things, but the melodic memories accompanied them all.

Then an image did fill my head that did not waver; a face with the blackest pit-like eyes set in ivory skin. They were watching me with such intensity that I could not look away.

Are you the Earth-voice? I asked.

The black-eyed one slowly shook his head, not dropping his penetrating stare. Suddenly, the word *focus* came into my mind with such clarity that every other thought stopped. I could think of nothing except that gaze. Even the music had stopped.

I've stopped it, I thought after a moment, still holding onto the image of the black-eyed one. *Although I liked remembering the music, it was beautiful, like something I remembered from my beginning.*

Beginning? the Earth-voice interrupted. I still sensed his anger. *Perhaps, little one, you do not have a beginning. If you do then you also must have an end. Perhaps **this** is your end.*

Why are you so angry? I just want to understand, I thought, hoping to reach him.

How can you understand, he seemed to sigh, *when you assume so much?*

His growl softened and a wave of defeat encompassed me. I stopped fighting, choosing only to stare at the black-eyed image in my mind as I tumbled aimlessly in the water.

I understand so little, I thought. *If I'm wrong to think these things, I'm sorry.* It felt as if I remembered things from my beginning, but how could I? I must be wrong. Nothing ends, does it?

Perhaps, he replied. *And perhaps you do have beginnings. Perhaps I shaped that beginning, and perhaps you must understand that truth if you are to break this link that binds me to you.*

I thought there was a moment's pause while his words drifted through my mind. I knew he was about to tell me something important. It didn't seem to matter anymore, but I heard it nonetheless.

I slept, he began. *I slept for a long time, until things crawled through my thoughts, disturbing my slumber. I awoke to terminate the source, but they were little things, pitiful; their existence mere ripples in dreams; no threat. Before returning to sleep, I passed through one who held new life inside her. I left an imprint. The creature adapted. That new life was you, little one. A mere brush from my thoughts became your shaping. You grew from that identity. Now you feel me and I feel you. But, though I shaped your beginning, your choices are your own.*

So choose, little one. Choose now: continue in your pitiful form and seek for yourself, or finish with that form, sleep in the water to remain with me and know all things. Join me in dreaming.

My muddled thoughts made me feel dizzy. Was he talking to me? Was I breathing? Did it matter? I could stay here. Wasn't this where I had always wanted to be? It felt so peaceful. Through the haze, images flashed through my mind, shaping themselves into a stream of memories: the crops when they flowered, my parents watching me protectively, father's laugh, my siblings' smiling faces showing me their newborns, and then nothing, a blank.

Blank? I didn't want my tomorrows to be blank; there were

so many things that I had not seen or done. Surely I couldn't be finished. Something, somewhere, tugged suggestively at my mind, and the peacefulness that made me want to sleep suddenly felt stifling. I mustered my strength, refusing the calm around me, though I knew not why, and pushed out my thoughts.

I'm not finished, I silently shouted. *I don't want to sleep. I am not finished! Let me go!*

I felt release. My head started spinning as I became aware of my motionless body. The numb comfort it had been drifting in drained away as every nerve awakened and I began struggling, thrashing with all my strength. The drag of the water fought against me like a dream in slow motion, and a muted rumbling tumbled around me. Then, all of a sudden, gravity was once more pushing down on my torso and the water around me was replaced by a cold, breezy darkness.

I found myself naked and wet, face down, and sprawled awkwardly over my boulder, fully aware of every unpleasant sensation and coughing uncontrollably as water spewed from my nose and mouth. Cold air painfully found my lungs again and so, exhausted and aching, I clumsily twisted around. After a while, I gathered enough strength to sit, shivering violently as his words sunk in.

No matter how much I wished to fight all that he had told me, I knew that I could not. I felt the truth of his words as if I'd always known them. *But*... my thoughts screamed, *what, how, why?* The questions were too big, so big I couldn't even form them; instead, they tumbled together aimlessly and fragmented into a blur of noisy activity in my mind.

I sat for a long time, not wanting to move, just keeping my eyes closed and trying to forget everything. I wanted to stop the whirring of my mind, to sleep so deeply that my thoughts would give way to silence. But sleep? Wasn't that what he had offered me, to sleep and forget? I'd refused his offer to sleep and here I was; I'd chosen this. He'd said my choices were my own.

I still felt his presence, as if he watched from a distance. I lifted my head, not caring to scrape the sodden hair from my face.

"So you are not human," I said hoarsely. Saying it aloud didn't feel as strange as I thought it should. No wonder I'd never seen him: I'd always looked for a person. "But you helped make me. Are there others made like me?"

No, he responded.

I ignored my shivering. I wanted him to keep talking. His voice was soothing now.

"Could others be made like me?"

Yes.

"How?"

Let me sleep so long, to the brink of eternal slumber. Annoy my slumber with dreaming, then, place a pre-life, ready to evolve, on my back as I arouse to stop the disturbance. Then there may be a chance.

His words took a few moments to understand and seemed to wake me up considerably.

"It's impossible, then," I stated indignantly.

The rock beneath me quivered as he roared with laughter. This was such a new and alien sound that I thought my eardrums were about to cave in. The roaring subsided.

Improbable yes, but not impossible, or how could you be?

I contemplated this for a moment.

"But why didn't you stop the humans if they disturbed your sleep?" I asked.

Perhaps I should have. Maybe I will. They merely cause movement, not change. I could return to sleep, but . . . he paused, *Now, little one, you give me dreams to keep me awake for an eternity.*

He laughed again to himself, a low, rumbling chuckle, and I

thought of my dreams. Did it mean he dreamt them too? My sleep was full of dreams. Although I knew the answer, I had to ask the question.

"Are you the black-eyed one?" I asked.

No, he replied. *No more than I am anything else that you dream of.*

"I didn't think so," I said, a little disappointed. "But I'd still like to meet you. Why don't you let me see you?"

You could and can, he replied.

Another wave of dismay filled me. "But I can't see you. I've looked for you often enough,"

If you do not see me, it is because you choose not to. Your choices are your own.

But I did want to see him, I thought. I knew I did, and I couldn't understand why I wasn't able to do it.

While I contemplated his words, my eyes were absently drawn to the tiny specks of sky glinting through the heavy foliage. Suddenly, I sprang up. The time! Surely sunrise could not be approaching so soon. Nevertheless, the skies were surely telling me that night was coming to an end. Without a second thought, I dived into the water and swam towards my clothes. I should be getting home now. I should be there already.

"Can I still speak with you?" I asked, whilst tugging my skirt over my wet skin.

I can always hear you, he answered.

"That's good," I stated. "I wish I could stay, but I must leave now."

He didn't reply, although I felt a strange sensation from him; a mixture of sadness, disappointment and amusement. I felt him recede completely and the ravine became just another beautiful yet empty place.

Without a further pause, I tugged on my bodice and started frantically climbing the bank.

It was the fastest ascent I'd ever made out of the ravine, and once I'd reached the top, I stopped to catch my breath. The dwindling darkness confirmed that I had stayed far longer than usual. It was almost sunrise. *I must run*, I thought, unenthusiastically, as every part of my body seemed to ache. I must reach the village and find my hut before daylight fully breaks. I must get home before anyone awakens. I must keep this place my secret, lest I be forbidden from coming here again.

So I ran as fast as my legs would carry me. I ran to suppress my spinning thoughts and focussed on the need to return to the security of my bunk. I didn't concentrate on the journey, only the destination, watching the sky grow paler with every passing stride. It seemed to take forever before I saw the familiar mounds that indicated the start of the farmed land, and I joined the winding dirt track into the village, heading home.

As soon as I could see Threetops, I knew I could reach home in time, just. Mother was always one of the first to rise and there was no smoke emitting from our chimney; a good sign as building a cooking fire was always her first task of the day. I finally reached my own hut, clambered up through the window into my room, and stood breathing deeply while my heartbeat calmed. I'd made it.

I wanted to climb into bed and sleep, but I knew there wasn't time. In the meagre moments I might have until my parents woke, I had to erase all signs of my trip. I tiptoed to the washroom, washed the visible parts of my skin, and refastened and straightened my clothes.

"It's good that you've dressed early," mother said, as I heard her emerge from her room.

She walked past me into the washroom and splashed her face with water. She was fully dressed, but her sleepy eyes told me she was only just awake. My heart quickened with the thought that she may have heard me enter my room through the window.

"I didn't finish my chores yesterday, perhaps I can do more today," I quickly offered.

"Father will be glad of that," she nodded. She didn't mention my damp hair, and made no reference to undue noises from my room, she just stepped past me again, making her way towards the stairs. "Come then child, father is readying," she said, stopping at the top of the stairs. "There's no point in being up early if you're just going to stand there. You can help me with breakfast."

I nodded and followed her, saying nothing.

Father and I got to the fields earlier than usual. I was well aware that we were already behind with reaping the Junir, but my mind wasn't on the task. I had so much to think about, and the call of the Earth seemed to reach me even though it wasn't night. I tried to work fast, but felt clumsy and slow.

At father's insistence, I gladly stopped before midday and ate a good meal of bread and dried fruits under a tree at the edge of the field. Father had brought supplies with him and made me drink more water than I wanted. He commented that from now we would eat at high sun, in the shade. I knew he'd decided this for my benefit; father could always eat while he worked and never seemed to need a break. Instead, we both reclined against the broad trunk, polishing off the last of mother's dried plums.

"Am I different?" I suddenly asked father, turning to observe his reaction.

Father looked at me for a moment, and then burst out laughing.

"Oh child, you haven't uttered a word all morning, and then the first thing you say is, "am I different?" Surely that answers your question?"

"Father!" I declared. "Don't tease. I want to know. Am I different?"

He contemplated a while, chewing steadily. "Everyone is different," he finally decided.

I offered him the last dried plum. He declined, so I popped it in my mouth and sat back with a smile.

Yes, I thought, everyone is different, not just me, so surely differences can't matter. What matters is all this: father, mother, the crops, the sun, and eating plums in the shade on a hot day. Yes, I determined, it doesn't have to matter what I'm told or what I find out, everything can just stay exactly as it is.

And at that moment, sitting under the tree, I truly believed it.

THREE

As soon as Chia had docked the pod back at the substation, he made his way towards the research laboratories on the upper levels, concealing the dust filled pouch. He didn't have anything to hide; he just didn't want to raise a false alarm if the ship hadn't malfunctioned. On the other hand, if it turned out that the crystal was flawed, and he'd introduced it into the pod's systems, he knew he'd be even less popular with the substation overseer than he already was.

Outside the bays, the normal flow in the corridors had become unusually hectic. Streams of kutu hurriedly emerged from their chambers, all heading in the same direction. Something, it seemed, had set them into a state of harried activity.

Chia spotted a senior technician whom he vaguely knew, a wiry kutu named Gattal who wore his insignia as an intricate glowing crystal tattoo all down one side of his face. He was correcting his robes, as if he'd just been sleeping, and was striding towards the nearest travel point.

Chia manoeuvred through the crowd, finally catching up with him.

"Gattal, what's going on?" he asked, matching Gattal's frantic pace.

"Don't know yet. An inexplicable surge from Earth. All analysts have been called to their posts. Sorry Chia, have to rush."

Before Chia could question him further, Gattal pushed forward, just making it into the crammed travel point before it closed.

Within moments, more kutu had arrived to use the travel point, none seeming to know any more than Gattal had, so Chia opened his senses, but their anxiety to get to their posts overrode anything else that he could determine. When the next travel pod arrived, Chia allowed his colleagues' entry first, but, much to his frustration, the portal only took a fraction of those waiting. He was again left waiting. With more kutu arriving, and all in an urgent hurry, Chia decided to return to the docking bays. He'd use their lesser, but adequate, research rooms where he'd be free from the commotion. How he longed to be back on Eden; space and amenities were never a problem on their home-world.

The small laboratory linked to the docks was usually empty. Chia strode in, pulling the pouch from around his neck, and then stopped. All the consoles were on, and various reports, data crystals, and portable modules lay strewn on every available surface.

A head popped up from behind one of the consoles, vivid green eyes flashing and long jet hair splayed out from its usually neat pony-tail. It was Kraniel; or simply 'the Genius,' as most people called him.

"I know," Kraniel pre-empted, seeing Chia's surprised expression. "I'm not supposed to be here. I hope you don't mind me using the docks' facilities; the main labs are packed out and these are good enough. Something rather . . ." he glanced away, nodding to himself as one of the readouts, flashing lines of text, distracted him. " . . . yes, sorry. Something rather unusual has emitted from Earth. I just have to pin point what . . ."

He stopped again, noticing Chia clasping the small pouch. "Ah Chia; the look on your face tells me you may have something interesting in your hand. What have you there?"

"I was going to analyse it," Chia replied.

Kraniel thrust out his hand.

"You look very busy already. I'll manage," Chia smiled.

"You should know I'm never *that* busy," Kraniel tutted. "I could do a hundred things at once and still feel under-utilized. It's quite a curse really."

Chia had to acknowledge that Kraniel was right. And he was undoubtedly the best kutu for the task. He handed the pouch over.

"A short while ago this was a recording crystal. The black dust is all that's left of it. It was either faulty or the 7A pod has malfunctioned and destroyed it."

"That's unheard of," Kraniel remarked.

"Exactly," Chia replied. "I don't want the ships interfered with unnecessarily. And if possible, I'd like the crystal reconstructed." He held out his hand, indicating that he wanted to feel some of the fragments, and Kraniel carefully poured a few particles of the black dust onto his palm, then another amount into an analysis field.

"I sense wholeness, even through these fragments. It doesn't make sense," Chia said.

"It does," Kraniel replied after a pause as he studied the fragments. "It's good news; the pod didn't malfunction, and you are right; the crystal is not flawed. It's pre-programmed to disintegrate once played. Take a look at this," Kraniel moved aside so Chia could view the results. "It's well done and quite innovative. Every molecule holds a command to destroy itself, erasing all data in the process. It's impossible to reconstruct because it undoes itself as soon as I try to recombine it."

Chia nodded. It wasn't what he'd expected, but did confirm what his senses had told him. Before he could reply, his direct com-link indicated someone was contacting him.

"Yes?" he responded.

"I've been trying to locate you. Are you suffering from an inability to answer communications too?"

"Councillor Shursa," Chia replied, knowing that his embedded comms link had been constantly on and unwilling to let Shursa's words ruffle him. "What can I do for you, Sir?"

"Have you sensed any energy abnormalities in the last hour?"

"No. Although I've been on an official rest break. I was out flying."

Shursa made a short derisory snorting sound.

"The one time you could be useful and you're elsewhere. Typical. Organize an extensive energy sweep of Earth, using all available ships, immediately. I want the full report on my desk the moment it comes in."

"Understood. ETA for the . . ."

Shursa terminated the connection before Chia could finish responding, leaving him mouth ajar and repressing a feeling of annoyance.

Kraniel shot Chia a look, eyebrows raised. "It sounds like you're not in our charming councillor's good books, my friend. I do not envy you that. Don't let it ruffle you; everything and everyone has become chaotic in this last hour."

"It's not an issue," Chia replied.

Kraniel's eyes glazed over and he covered his ear, tilting his head to one side as if he too was receiving a direct communication.

"Yes . . . Yes . . . Understood . . . Immediately, very good."

Kraniel stopped talking, quickly glanced around the room at his scattered reports, and then looked at Chia and smiled.

"I have been summoned. I must present my reports, then it's back to Eden with me. It seems I am needed everywhere. Well, what would we do without me?"

He returned Chia's black crystal fragments to their pouch, gathered his findings, flicked the display ports back to neutral, glanced over the area once again, and then gave Chia a hearty slap, handing back the pouch.

"Come visit me soon on Eden, Chia; we'll go feasting. This substation isn't exactly built for social activities – there's not even one recreation area. Perhaps you should ask Shursa to sort that out." Kraniel started laughing to himself again and, like a short, tunic-clad whirlwind, marched from the area.

Chia tied the pouch back around his neck. The fragmented crystal and Shursa's disagreeableness – he knew he was not the root cause of either issue. No, there was one common factor in both: Orion.

Orion was still on Eden, too far to speak to using personal comms, so Chia activated the communication port within the research room.

"Contact Orion, Eden," he instructed, placing his hand on the identification panel.

The port indicated the connection had been successful, but the receiving end showed no response. Chia impatiently rapped his long fingers against his thigh, making the little nanos ripple on his body-suit.

"Cancel live connection. Record and send," he decided.

"Orion," Chia continued. "If you're listening, log in . . ."

He waited a moment for Orion to collect, readying himself for the imminent energy sweep of Earth. Suit buckled down.

Protective fields activated. He glanced at his reflection in the console, his long violet eyes shone brighter than ever; his chi was good. He pulled his eye-piece down to cover them. He was ready.

"My friend," Chia continued; he had no more time to wait. "I must ask; your crystal recording . . . did you program it to erase itself intentionally?" He paused, realising the point that was really bothering him. "Is it linked to Earth?" he asked. "There's been an energy surge from the planet and I've had the same visions as the first time I went there. I know they're not real, but the timing . . . I don't believe in coincidences. Contact me."

With that, Chia closed the port; he had a sweep to oversee and hundreds of ships to organize. Time was, one again, of the essence.

What an interesting day it was turning out to be, Chia thought. It was as if he could smell change in the air. He just wasn't sure if he liked it.

FOUR

Father's words that everyone was different had eased my spirit. I'd gone back into the field with a renewed vigour and toiled well, even though I was tired. By the time we had returned to the hut, eaten supper, and I had helped clean the pots, I was pleasantly exhausted. With all the chores done, I excused myself early, knowing that sleep would be good, and went to my room.

I lay down on my bed and closed my eyes. I couldn't remember the last time I'd wanted to sleep so early in the night. Ever since I'd been able to run, I'd been creeping out of my room as soon as the village was quiet. I decided that thinking made me tired, and thought that banning as many thoughts from my head as I could was the best solution – that, and sleep.

I'll sleep tonight, all night, I decided, *just like everyone else does.*

But, although I lay on my bed, and as much as I wanted sleep, sleep didn't want me. I fidgeted, tossed and turned, and, even though I shut out as much of the Earth-voice as I could, my head still spun with thoughts crowding in on me enough to make me dizzy. I heard mother and father retire and the village grow quiet, but still I didn't find sleep. Eventually I sat on my bed, annoyed at my own body's refusal to comply with my wishes, and gazed out of the window.

The lamps in the village had already been put out, and the moonlit surroundings looked more like home than my own room.

Perhaps I had grown too used to going out at night, I thought. Perhaps I'd sleep more easily outside. It was worth a try; I certainly wasn't finding any rest in my room. I stood, bundled up a blanket, wrapped my skirt around my legs, and slid out through the window.

I headed to the mounds just beyond the farmed land and, once there, spread out the blanket, found a comfortable position, and then spoke to *him*.

"Can you hear me?" I whispered.

Always. A breeze fluttered around me.

"Everyone is different. Not just me," I told him.

He didn't reply.

"I don't want to run tonight," I said, as if that wasn't already obvious. "Or talk. I don't understand everything you said yet so there's no point in telling me more."

Your choices are your own.

"Yes, you said that yesterday," I replied. "I'm tired. I'm going to sleep."

He didn't reply, I felt him leave, but not entirely, and I was happy about that because it made me feel like I wasn't alone.

"I'm glad you're still my friend," I thought aloud and closed my eyes.

The first time I awoke, the night was still in its prime. It was warm and a scattering of clouds had brought a steady drizzle of rain, wetting my blanket. I pulled the blanket tighter around me and kept drifting into sleep as quickly as I drifted out of it, until I gave up and sat, huddled, staring at the stars.

I must have fallen asleep again, as I awoke with a start, overwhelmed by a horrible feeling that it was daylight. It wasn't. Reassured by the darkness, I closed my eyes again, but was instantly bothered by a sense of unease. I looked around, but only the usual trees and plants looked back, and so I stood up, holding the blanket around my shoulders, and wandered around the mound.

As I passed the muddy hillock, I could see that the sky in the direction of the village seemed to be alight. The sun always rose in the other direction, and the rest of the sky was still black, so the light wasn't coming from the sunrise. My uneasiness grew.

"Is that you?" I asked him. "Making that light?"

I felt his presence as if he was looking through my eyes.

No.

"What is it?" I asked.

It is nothing to me.

It certainly feels something to me, I considered, and I didn't like it.

I dropped the blanket and began hurrying towards the village. As I neared Threetop's valley I climbed one of the larger mounds to gain a better view, and then stopped dead in my tracks. The huts seemed to have light coming from them. Surely it was too early for the villagers to awaken.

I strained my eyes to detect the source of the light. I could see most of the huts, but the light didn't come from them; their windows were still dark. The light appeared to be all around them – not the familiar soft amber glow from a flame, but a pale blue light. It was not bright, but it still hurt my eyes. The more I concentrated, the more the hairs on my arms tingled and stood upright, my heartbeat doubled and an uncomfortable hum shivered through the back of my head. My mind was alert. I sensed danger.

Cautiously, I crept towards the village, consumed by an overwhelming need for caution. The bushes gave me cover as I crawled through the mud, descending the mound. I aimed towards a broad, concealing tree and, as soon as I'd reached it, crouched low and watched.

Now I could see the light clearly. The immense blue glow highlighted a broad clump of huts. At its centre was an even brighter core, the width of a large tree trunk, shining with a mass of fine multicoloured lines, blending and twisting into a pillar of brightest blue. The central core pointed to the middle of just one hut. The light seemed to come from the sky, but looking up the brightness dazzled my sight too much to see where it might be coming from.

Suddenly, the core of light moved, swinging to the neighbouring hut. It lingered for a moment, and then moved again to the next hut, and then again, travelling west towards the edge of the village, each time pausing over someone's home. It didn't make any sound, yet my eardrums itched with a vibration that told me I should hear something, and my hair danced around my head as if it were alive.

Initially I had thought this was coming from the Earth-voice, but he'd said that it wasn't him. It didn't feel like him anyway. This was something else; the forth strange occurrence in less than two days, and none of them made any sense to me. The wonderful music hadn't been him; in fact, it had made him angry. Then, for the first time, his voice had found words, telling me the strangest things about beginnings. And there was the face that came into my head with the black eyes; he was not the Earth-voice, but it seemed as if he knew me. Now there was this, and again the Earth-voice said it wasn't him – this time he seemed not to care about it at all. But I *did* care. And although for some unknown reason I didn't like it, it stirred my curiosity beyond anything I had known.

I watched the blue core continue moving west, and held my breath in fear when it shone on my hut. The light paused for a moment, just as it had with the others, and then swung to the next abode until it was on the last dwelling at the edge of the village. Then *nothing*: it was gone. I hadn't seen it pass over the hill or fade out. It had simply vanished.

I rubbed my eyes to rid them of the outline still imprinted on them. Threetops now looked the same as it always did. The only thing different was a harsh smell that made a bitter taste in my mouth. I hadn't liked what I'd seen. It was wrong. The pounding of my heart wouldn't decrease, and my limbs were still shaking. I tried to still them but my body refused. An indignant rage welled through me, making my flesh throb, consuming me more with every heart beat. Something was happening in the pit of my stomach: it was growing, pushing upwards, threatening to engulf me.

I stood up, arched my back, threw my head back to the sky and screamed.

I came to, moments later, flat on my back in the mud, with a thumping head and the smell of burning filling my nostrils. Just above my face a large branch dangled by a thread from the tree, its end a smouldering stump where healthy twigs had once been.

I groggily pushed myself away from the hot branch. Had something hit me? I looked around, but couldn't see anything. My head spun with thoughts and images; nothing made sense, yet my senses felt alive. What had happened to me? What was that light, and what had it been doing to the huts? Were mother and father awake and watching it with wonderment too? What if it had stirred their sleep and they had come to my room to wake me?

I must get home.

I staggered to my feet and, brushing myself down, stumbled towards the village. Through my daze, I could see that all appeared calm – nothing stirred. No one was looking out of windows. The blue light hadn't seemed to rouse anyone. The huts looked the same, the ground looked the same; in fact, everything looked the same. But I knew I hadn't imagined that blue light. I was perplexed and exhausted, and nothing made any sense.

I was grateful to find my hut looking exactly as I remembered, and I climbed the ledge to my window. I waited a while to confirm that my parents hadn't stirred, and then, too tired to do anything else, I fell onto my bunk to sleep.

Everyone was always ready for the daily routines an hour after sunrise. I was awoken by my mother calling my name; I woke up with a start, aware that in last night's tiredness I had clambered into my bunk fully clothed.

I had dreamt a great deal through those meagre moments of sleep. I had dreamt the dream I always had, of the black-eyed one holding out his hand. But, this night I had also dreamt of the blue light over my village. I had tasted the bitter taste and felt my body throb with the strange pulse of anger that burned with physical force. I lay wrapped in my blankets, thinking of everything until all my thoughts jumbled together into a mixture of reality, dream and imagining. My sense of unease had not dissipated with sleep; instead, it had manifested into something far greater.

"Tachra," mother called again.

I sat up sharply and my body cried out with stiffness.

"I'll be through in a minute," I shouted, trying to sound fully awake.

Getting out of bed was a chore, as every piece of me seemed to complain. I noticed the state of my grubby and ripped clothes with dismay. Then with horror, I noticed that I'd bought smears of dark, gritty mud to my bed. My bedding was filthy. I was filthy. I had to clean up. I carefully covered the stains and dirt on my bed with a clean blanket and peeked around the narrow entrance of my room; the passageway was clear. I ran into the washroom and closed the door behind me. I had to think quickly.

"Tell father I'll join him shortly," I proposed loudly through the washroom door.

"Very well, but make haste, he's leaving now," mother replied in her usual calm tone.

I stripped off and scrubbed myself roughly with a brush and soap before jamming my clothes into the wash pail; they were filthy and had so many tears they would take a week to repair. How could I have been so careless, crawling through mud and grass as if I had a dozen sets of clothes? I only had two sets and these were clean on yesterday. It would be unthinkable to request the others so soon, even if they had been washed. I needed an excuse for fresh clothes and bedding as well as for being so late up, and it had to be good. There was only one reason I could think of that might be acceptable.

I draped one of the large scratchy drying cloths around myself and tiptoed back to my room with my wet garments, making sure I hung them over the end of my bed in a way that covered their damage. The bed's top blanket was clean, so I pulled off the two under blankets and bundled them together to conceal the mud. Mother was busy in the kitchen. She would be cooking for some of the mothers who had new offspring today – perfect.

I took my spare knife from under my bed, braced myself against the bed-stead, and slowly cut into my right foot. I had to cut deep, as the skin on my feet was thick and hard, and the pain brought a sickness to the back of my throat. I bit my lip to make myself focus on something else, and smeared the dripping blood over my bundled bedding.

I knew what was supposed to happen when a girl came to childbearing age – the women talked about it a lot – and I was already a good two years past that age, but my body had shown no signs of obeying the biological urge yet. I'd decided to make use of that.

Once I was satisfied that enough blood had been squeezed from my now-throbbing foot, I lit my lamp and leant the blade of my knife into the flame. I didn't have much time and was anxious that mother may come in at any moment so, after only a minute, I took the hot blade and pressed it against the wound. It hurt. I bit my lip harder, distracting my senses with one pain for another, and pulled the knife away. It was sealed enough to hold.

Mother was busy at the stove when I walked into the kitchen, wrapped in the scratchy drying cloth and concentrating on hiding my limp.

"You are so late," mother stated casually with her back to me. She turned, "and not even ready to leave."

She sighed, shaking her head, and turned back to her pots.

"Your father will be working single-handedly on the Junir crop until you get there," she stated disapprovingly. "You know it's barely manageable with just the two of you now, yet alone one."

"I've started my bleeding," I blurted out, eyes to the floor, ashamed at the deceit. "I didn't realise until I was clothed; now my skirt is marked too, so I've washed it."

My stomach churned. It was my first lie.

Mother turned again and this time she smiled. "That is good, and not untimely," she nodded as she dried her hands on her skirt. Then she lifted my chin until my eyes met hers, she looked concerned and then smiled encouragingly.

"Oh, do not fret, Tachra, it is natural; all my girls fretted for a few days, but then they found contentment in becoming a woman, just as you will," she stated.

It seemed that mother mistook my shame for worry; that made me feel even worse.

"You must stay here and help me today," she decided.

She left me standing in the kitchen and bustled into her room, the swishing of her skirt the only sound above the bubbling pots. She returned immediately, clutching a package wrapped in papyri.

"You'll be needing these," she instructed, handing me the package. "Go and get dressed; your clean clothes are dry. Then you can help with preparing the vegetables. Your place is at home now."

She returned her attentions to the stove, and I stood looking down at the package for a few moments before scurrying back to my room, grabbing my clothes on the way.

Once in the safe confines of my room I threw the package into the depths of the wooden trunk in the corner and got dressed. My deceit had worked, but instead of feeling relieved, I felt terrible. I ashamedly lingered as long as I could in my room, and then quietly returned to the kitchen where mother had already started the vegetable preparations.

The kitchen smelt particularly good. Mother turned when she heard me and nodded towards one of the pots. She was making my favourite Junir stew. I hadn't thought I could have felt any worse, but now I did. Still, I mustered a smile. She handed over a long chopping blade, indicating towards a pile of vegetables, watched me slice the first one and, once satisfied I could perform the task, she rustled away in the direction of my room. As I continued chopping, I could hear her collecting my bedding and taking it to the washroom.

Later that afternoon, before father returned home and while mother was out washing the linen, I took the opportunity to repair my damp clothes. I worked quickly, using scraps of fabric from mother's trunk, and also took the opportunity to make a rough pair of slippers with ties to secure them over my feet. They looked quite peculiar on – I was only accustomed to bare feet – but they would help stop the dirt from rubbing into the cut.

Mother returned late that afternoon having spread the linen to dry and delivered food to the new mothers. She looked tired.

"The nights can be cold," I said, "So I made coverings for my feet." It was the only thing I could think to say as she stared at my new footwear.

"Yes they can. Would you make me some also?" she replied, to my surprise.

Grateful that she did not make me discard my slippers, I set to the task immediately, while mother stocked the fire in preparation for the evening. When she had finished she sat in the nearest chair, watching me stitch the final ties on her slippers.

"You are nimble with a needle and thread," mother observed. "You will make a good mate."

I held up the finished articles and she nodded in approval. It was the first time mother had said I was good at anything. It was the first time I'd heard her say anyone was good at anything. I leaned over and handed her the items. She carefully placed them on her feet and wiggled her toes.

"These are good. Thank you child," she stated as she fumbled awkwardly with the ties.

I took the ties and secured them around her ankles. She was very cold, and I touched her hand lightly.

"Are you alright?" I asked quietly.

She nodded, and then as if suddenly aware of herself, sat straighter. "But of course," she said. "It is your time now, Tachra. A suitable mate will be selected, and we have preparations to make."

She got up abruptly and returned to the kitchen, leaving me with a sinking feeling.

I followed her and helped finish the day's cooking, washing and scrubbing of surfaces, ready for father's return. It was a tedious task that never seemed to finish, and I was glad when I heard father approaching, for it meant I could stop doing chores for the day.

Father was back later than usual. The table was already set and he moved straight to the bench while mother slopped generous portions of Junir stew on top of large flat breads. Mother and I joined him, settling down to fill our bellies too.

"I had to ask Tulu to help me with the crop," father stated, giving me a look of disapproval, and then held up his dripping bread. "This is fine stew."

"And we will help Tulu when his wheat is ready," mother intercepted. "But I have fair news Dannel. Our youngest is ready to be paired."

Father put down his bread and stood up, his tired face instantly breaking out into a broad smile.

"That is fair news indeed. Tachra, my last child, now ready to pair," he smiled. He pulled me up, clasping me tightly to his chest for the first time in years. Then, holding me at arms' length, he studied me. "We will find a good mate for you, my Tachra. You work well and your mother has shown she can bear many children, as you will."

Mother smiled proudly, "Sixteen."

"Then from my youngest I expect at least seventeen," he exclaimed jovially. He let me go and sat back down, readdressing his cooling stew with renewed vigour.

"Tomorrow I will arrange the hunt," he spoke through mouthfuls. "Mother, arrange the choosing for five nights from now; we will hunt then."

"The choosing?" I asked. I didn't know of this choosing.

"Yes, choosing," mother affirmed as she watched father eating with satisfaction. "Just as we had with Dac's third daughter. It is the new way, what with the village expanding and many in neighbouring Watersedge, Longplain, and Whitehill ready to pair now. To have a choosing makes finding a mate more timely and suitable."

"And we have a good hut here," father smiled. "As our youngest, this home will become the home of you and your mate. There is plenty of space here ready to be filled with your children, so you'll not even need to devote time to building. And the crops spread of their own will; there is much land we can add to our tender with more hands to help."

He stared at my gawping expression and indicated towards my plate.

"Come, child, eat your fill and get some colour in those cheeks," he smiled. "No man will want a pairing with one who eats like a bird."

And I did eat my fill, although it was more because every time I put down my spoon father made me eat a little bit more, than because I was hungry. And I was sure there was a great deal of colour in my cheeks as my parents continued their talks of the seemingly imminent new babies, the preparations to be made for my pairing and the forthcoming hunt, which was only five days away. *Five days!* It was so soon, and it scared the thoughts from my head. What was my untruthfulness leading me into?

At the earliest opportunity, I faked yawns, made my excuses and left my cheerful parents to their talk. I hoped to find some solace in my room. But my room offered no comfort; just a lumpy bed I could not find sleep in, a large trunk with its latest storage items produced from my lies, and a window giving views of a fading day that made me think of the blue light again.

At this hour the village was still awake, with little ones still running around and women continuing their endless chores while there was still some natural light remaining. It was too early to venture out, but my mind raced so much that it could hold no thoughts, so I picked up my knife, quietly shifted the heavy trunk, and stared down at the carvings in the thick wooden floor.

I didn't know what they meant, or why I did them, but making carvings always quietened my thoughts, so I huddled down and continued boring out shapes in the wood. The shapes somehow echoed my hopes and fears, and I filled some of the little gaps between the carvings I'd already completed, taking care not to extend beyond the trunk's concealing area.

That night I did not have the heart for adventure or mind to concentrate, so as soon as I sensed stillness in the village I repositioned the trunk and clambered out of the window, ignoring the whispers of the Earth and the guilty nagging of my conscience.

I crept out of the village, collecting the blanket that I had discarded the previous night, and made my way to a well-concealed area just beyond the village. This position, where tall grasses grew around an old tree, offered a good view of Threetops. I had decided that, as much as I didn't like it, I wanted to see if the blue light came again. I lay the blanket out to dry and settled down to wait. I did not have to wait long.

The night wasn't even a quarter of the way through when the distasteful vibrations once more stirred my thoughts. I stared toward the huts as a patch of sky at the nearside of the village lightened with the same blue core of light at its centre. My anger rose again, but I gritted my teeth, pushing against the force that welled in the pit of my stomach. Managing to keep restrained, I concentrated on discovering the source.

I couldn't decipher any more from the glowing blue core than I had the previous night. I counted the rhythm of the movement, noticing that it lingered longer over some huts than others. It shifted over the village as before, and then it left, as quickly as it had come, with no breeze following its departure and with no tangible sign that it had been there.

Why should it linger longer on some huts than on others? I asked myself. All the huts were made of the same Lana wood, thatched with the same branches, and of a similar size to one another. I knew my own hut so well. I'd lived there all my seventeen summers, and by day, there'd never been any indication of a blue light – but my hut had not been exempt from its presence. There had to be something causing the light; it had to be there for a reason.

I thought about what I'd seen over and over again until eventually, devoid of answers, I curled under the tree and shut my eyes. Perhaps if I slept the answers would come to me. Even if they didn't, perhaps I'd dream of the black-eyed one, and in tonight's sleep I'd reach that outstretched hand.

I slept lightly, anxious that the blue light might return. But it did not. Instead, I drifted in and out of brief dreams of the black eyed one, dreams of wanting to talk but not having a voice, until this dream eventually wakened me. I didn't know the black-eyed man, and so why would he appear in my dreams as an uninvited guest? Was he linked to *his* voice, the Earth-voice? Yes, somehow, although I knew they were not the same. I wondered if this black-eyed man could hear the Earth-voice too. But these were all just more questions without answers.

Eventually, and still dreadfully tired, a cool dawn drew me back to the village and into my hut. I climbed stealthily back into my room and lay down in my bunk. I was sure I wouldn't get back to sleep, but I did, and mother let me sleep late into the morning for the first time in my life.

When I eventually rose, greeted by a bright sunny day, I found mother in the kitchen, as usual, making enough food for the entire village. Father must have been back at least twice already, as mounds of fresh vegetables piled up in every available space.

I picked up a large spoon and started stirring the pot on the fire. Mother came over, put down a second large pot of uncooked stew beside me, inspected the almost cooked pot, and nodded in approval.

"What is that tune, Tachra?" she asked. "I heard you humming it yesterday too."

I stopped abruptly. I hadn't realised I was humming. I must have been doing it without thinking. It was that tune again, the one that had made *him* so angry.

"It's just music I have in my head," I replied, feeling anxious.

"Don't stop, I like it," mother smiled. "It sounds even prettier than the morning birds."

I started humming again, cautiously observing if there were any changes around me, but all seemed as it always was. I certainly didn't want to make *him* angry again, especially in front of mother. As I hummed, my mind kept drifting to that pale blue light over the village.

"Mother," I paused casually. "Have you ever seen a blue light around our hut, or anywhere around the village?"

"Have I seen a blue light?" she repeated my question, looking confused as she sliced potatoes. "Light is more yellow than blue. There is no blue light."

"But perhaps there is," I said carefully. "If there is, have you seen it?"

"No," she replied, and then laughed. "Come child, surely you are not thinking of the sky; it is the sun that lights the sky to make it blue. Everyone knows that."

"Yes," I replied. "I know that."

Clearly, she hadn't seen the blue light. But there again, it only came at night, when she was sleeping.

"At night, do you ever dream of a blue light?" I asked, trying to re-angle the question.

She stopped and turned to me with her head tilted to one side, as if thinking. I could see she had no idea what I was talking about, and that she was perplexed in trying to understand what I was saying.

I manoeuvred the subject again. "Do you dream, mother? When you sleep, do you have thoughts and pictures of things you haven't done?"

"Oh yes. Last night I dreamt of the hunt – that I was there, running with them, and the wind kept blowing my hair in my face. I could see a fat boar and I was going to catch it."

"A boar!" I laughed. "Are you joining the hunt then?"

"Of course not," she huffed at me. "Men hunt."

"I see no reason why only men hunt. You could hunt too, if you wanted to."

She turned around, frowned, and then broke into a smile.

"Oh Tachra, you do like to play, but you are not a child now. Women do not hunt. You will have strong sons to hunt. Now help me with these potatoes; your father said there are many suitable pairings coming for the choosing and we have much food to prepare to make them welcome."

She thrust a bowl of water in my arms and pointed me towards a large pile of dirt-encrusted, freshly dug potatoes that had been piled in the corner of the room. I took the bowl to the corner, made myself comfortable on the floor, and began scrubbing.

"So you've not dreamt of a blue light over the village?" I prompted again.

"No Tachra. That would not make sense, would it?"

Her tone told me that I should drop the issue. I kept my silence for as long as I thought necessary, and then started again, this time with questions of a different nature.

"Mother, can you remember how you came here?"

"You have asked that before," she answered. "We were just here."

"But you must remember something," I sighed, exasperated.

She thought about this and after a long pause said, "We were here. I had Dannel and he had me, and there was Shawn and Gurl, and Rew's father Linn, and Mina, and the other first ones in the village; but you know them all, Tachra."

"Were there any children?" I asked.

"You know there were not," she replied. "We were the first, and when we had children, they were the first."

"So you were suddenly just here one day? How did you get here?" I asked again. "I'm here, sitting on the floor scrubbing potatoes, because I walked here and sat down. So how did you get here, right at the beginning?"

Normally she would say 'we just were'. I looked at her expectantly, trying to pluck the thoughts from her mind.

"We just were," she said.

My heart sank. It was what she told me every time, as if she had no more thoughts on the subject.

It must be strange to be my mother, I thought, *one of the 'originals.'* My parents were both originals. They would tell me that they were just here, paired off and contented, with fruits and vegetables growing in abundance in the area where they decided to build the huts, and with no children until they made some.

"Do you wish you had been a child?" I pondered aloud.

"Why would I?" she shrugged. "You ask many questions Tachra; I hope they are not slowing your chores."

"No, I can talk and clean potatoes." I shrugged, knowing it was mother's way of telling me to be quiet. I wanted to ask her how she and the others had known how to build huts. Had someone shown them, or was it another thing they just seemed to 'know'? How did they know how to weave cloth, carve wood, or sharpen flint into blades? It seemed that those questions would have to wait until another time – not that it mattered, because mother never answered them anyway.

"Do I speak too much?" I asked yet another question, but this time I was hoping to soothe her frustration with my earlier ones.

"You speak less than any of my other children," mother replied thoughtfully, "yet you ask more questions than anyone I've known."

I had to admit she was right, however reluctantly. I had always asked questions, ever since I could remember, and often the same ones over and over again.

Perhaps, I thought, *I wouldn't ask so many or so often if I actually got an answer once in a while*. Still, mother had always looked after me; it wasn't her fault that she didn't know the answers.

"Tell me more about the choosing." I said, knowing more questions would be pointless.

"Ah," she smiled, obviously liking that subject, "that will come soon enough."

"Then tell me what I need to know," I smiled.

"Well, the choosing is a good thing. Soon you will have your mate," she replied. "You will be content and everything will happen just as it should."

"How does it work?" I asked, wondering how, if there were more than one suitable mate, they would select one.

"Each time is different; what will be, will be," she shrugged.

"So, how can you say everything will happen as it should, if each time is different?" I asked. I'd begun with only a vague interest in this choosing; now I wanted to know what I was letting myself in for.

"Because soon you shall have a mate," she replied sharply. "And I hope you do not fill his time with as many useless questions as you do mine."

Useless questions! I wanted to scream, but I took out my frustrations on a potato instead, scrubbing vigorously.

The choosing cannot be too bad, I thought; everyone else goes through it, after all. Everyone leads that life and seems content with it. But my stomach churned for no apparent reason, making me feel most uncomfortable.

I scrubbed potatoes for a good part of the morning, during my attempted conversations, and the scrubbing water soon became filthy. I got up to dispose of it outside and replace it with clean water from the well, but mother insisted on performing this task herself, regardless of my protests.

"You cannot leave the hut," she said, and was not prepared to hear of me venturing outside. "It is your time, and you stay indoors for the duration."

Neither reason nor protest, and I did a great deal of both, would change mother's mind. I was so exasperated that I almost let the truth spill that it was not 'my time,' but I bit my tongue and eventually let her take the grubby water from my grasp. I sullenly sat back down and awaited her return.

Shortly after mother had left, father's boisterous approaching shouts lifted my mood. He strode into the kitchen, placing a small sack in front of me.

"Your favourites," he beamed.

He pointed to the small sack, and I carefully peeled back the flaps to reveal a neat pile of perfect Kathi berries. Kathi berries were difficult to cultivate, and preserved in apple juice they're a rarity to savour. They had always been my favourite. I forgot my pout and leapt up to hug him.

"Where did you find these?" I asked.

"Ah, and where did you think your nose for Kathi berries came from?" father laughed. "I've been trying to grow them for many moons, knowing that sometime soon my Tachra would be ready to find a mate. And here they are, ripe and ready for the occasion."

"Thank you father, they are wonderful."

"Indeed they are," father nodded. "And tell me, how are your new chores going?"

"I would rather be in the fields with you, but mother says I cannot go out," I sighed, taking the opportunity to protest, hoping father would say otherwise.

"Yes. As much as you are my youngest and last child, you are a woman now, Tachra. You know that a woman does not work the land when it is her time."

"Mother did when she had me."

"Tachra, you know mother was thought to be past childbearing," father said sternly. "She would not have worked the land if we'd known otherwise."

"But I am not asking to work, just go outside. I can peel potatoes outside," I appealed.

"No."

"But, I do not . . ."

Father held up his hand, cutting off my argument abruptly.

"Tachra, it is the way. I have never even heard of any woman thinking otherwise."

It wasn't mother returning that made me drop the subject. I couldn't bear the look of uncomfortable disappointment that spread across father's brow.

"Very well, father. I'll stay indoors and make the best Kathi preserves in Threetops."

I smiled up at him, and kept smiling until his face lightened. Father relaxed, ruffling my hair the way he used to when I was a child, and then turned to speak to mother. But, before he could engage in conversation, a high-pitched shout piped in through the open door, calling for his attention.

"Dannel, Dannel!" a small boy shouted, calling out my father's name.

Father looked up:

"It's Rew's boy, Sparrow," he said, moving out to meet the child running towards our hut.

Moving to the doorway, I watched my father greet the red-faced child

"It's my father," the small child gasped in loud rasping shrieks. "He's fallen, fallen from a tree. He won't wake up."

"Where?" my father asked as he reached Sparrow, bending down to him.

"He's fallen," the child stammered, struggling to speak.

"Sparrow, look at me and take a deep breath," father said calmly. "Where is your father?"

The child gasped out something I couldn't hear and pointed towards the orchards. Father called to mother, mother went to fetch the child, and father ran in the direction that Sparrow was pointing, towards the section of Rew's orchards that bordered our crops.

"What is it?" I asked mother as she walked back towards our hut carrying the sobbing child.

"Something to do with Rew," mother answered. "Father is tending to it. I'll take Sparrow back to his family."

She turned and left with Sparrow clinging tightly to her, his little face buried in her shoulder. I knew mother would be gone for some time. Rew's hut was quite a distance away, on the other side of the main orchard. So, as she turned the corner from my view, and although I knew I was supposed to remain indoors, I slipped out of the hut.

I followed the direction that father had taken, tracing his easily visible route through the long crops which were now bent from his passing, making a darker trail through the gold. It wasn't long before I found myself bordering Rew's orchard and could hear father talking.

I moved slowly, making sure I wasn't seen or heard, and then I saw father. He was with another man, Rew's father, Linn. Linn was breathing heavily as if he'd been running. Both he and my father had their backs to me. Father was bending over Rew, who was lying silently on the grass.

Rew looked as if he was sleeping, except for the streak of red blood that ran from his nose and another, finer line from his mouth. Then I noticed that his head wasn't creating the long shadow I could see, it was laying in a large pool of dark blood that had mostly seeped into the soil but which still stained the grass. I took a deep breath and smelt his blood in the air.

Something with Rew was not right. I could sense that he was breathing, barely, and I could see his chest rising and falling in ragged bursts. I could sense he wasn't in any pain; he had been, but he wasn't now, and his hands twitched spasmodically as if he couldn't control them. I had no idea what he was doing, lying on the ground. If he wasn't in pain, surely he should just get up. The apples can't pick themselves. But the look on father's face and Sparrow's panic told me that this wasn't a game.

Then something happened instantaneously: if I had blinked, I would have missed it. As Rew lay, limbs twitching, a shimmer of light emerged from his torso. It hovered above him for a brief moment, then gathered into one point in the centre of his chest and quivered down his arms. I saw it drip from his fingertips, lighting the blades of grass around his hands before disappearing into the soil. Then his shuddering stopped. He was motionless.

Father and Linn didn't seem to notice the light, but they did notice that Rew had stopped twitching and that his chest had stopped moving. Father crouched, putting his ear close to Rew's mouth and then on his chest. After a moment, he shook his head and looked solemnly at the other man.

"He has ceased. Tell his mate," father said to Linn in a low, grave tone. "I'll put him in the forest before the sun causes a stench."

Ceased, I thought. *Ceased means finished. How can Rew just cease? People don't just cease.* My head screamed the question, but I stood mute, with my hand clasped over my mouth as my every sense told me that Rew had indeed ceased.

This thing, this body, lying on the ground that looked like Rew was as an empty shell, devoid of any essence. It did not feel as though it was Rew any more, but where was he? I took a deep breath and concentrated, scanning around the area with my mind, but I couldn't find any trace of Rew the orcharder anywhere. The trees and grass around him seemed to have a greater substance than his flesh now had. My eyes told me he was still solid, but my head pictured a translucent outline and I felt nothing from it, nothing at all. My last sense of Rew had been from the glowing light that had left his flesh and trickled from his fingers as he stopped breathing. It has disappeared into the soil and the grass around him, becoming part of them, of everything.

In horror, I realised that Rew really had ceased. That lump on the ground wasn't Rew; Rew was no more.

But, I thought, *if Rew can cease, then other people could cease. People can just stop being!* I pushed my hand harder over my mouth to stop my gasps being heard, turned, and crawled frantically through the crop, away from the terrible scene.

Mother was still away when I got back to our hut. I ignored the potatoes, ran to my room, closed the door, and slid down to the floor. I wanted to scream or cry, but felt mute and tearless. *This is not right*, I kept telling myself, *how could anyone simply cease to be? It's just not right.*

59

I eventually had to venture from my room, beckoned by mother's calls, and I faced the world with stunned silence. The silence lasted the rest of that day and the next. Suddenly I couldn't look at those around me in the same way. All of them – everyone, even my parents – had the potential to become nothing. How could we be so fragile that a mere fall from a tree could snuff us out, and just make us cease? From what I learned by eavesdropping on my parents' conversations over the following day, it seemed that people could do just that. I heard this was the third ceasing my father had seen, and he had heard of others, but neither my father nor my mother seemed at all perturbed. Their only concern seemed to be that Rew's mate would bear no more children until another mate had been found, and that finding her another mate would take time because there were so many younger ones ready for pairing. And yet their acceptance of Rew's ceasing only made it seem even more wrong.

On the second evening after Rew's ceasing, father sat me down and explained it to me. Of course I knew that people could hurt themselves, and even break parts of their body. I had always assumed that people mended following such accidents, such as when my brother had worn strapping on his arm after falling from a horse, but father said that sometimes people were hurt too badly to mend. Then they ceased. And as people grew older, mending became more difficult. It sounded horrible. I didn't want to accept it. But what else could I do? I could watch people to try to make sure they didn't have similar accidents, but I wasn't even permitted to leave the hut to watch father work, yet alone make sure he kept safe. I begged him not to help with the apple picking, but he just laughed and told me that he could always climb better than Rew anyway. When mother slipped over I bolted to her assistance, but she had no more than a scraped shin. Suddenly my world seemed frail and temporary.

Regardless of my mood, the bustle of activity around our hut continued with the preparations for the hunt and the choosing, and my parents seemed content. People both familiar and unfamiliar brought food, goods, bowls and blankets in abundance, and more unusual items, like a low bench and a long harvesting blade. Strangers came; some left after having donated items and some stayed. Many, it seemed, were parents of sons coming for the choosing. I greeted them all politely as they critically noted my stature. I felt as though I was constantly being evaluated.

I kept busy, helping with chores while mother instructed me at every opportunity. I learnt a multitude of new tasks, from darning woollen tunics to preserving unusual fruits; 'all things that a good mate should know,' or so I was told.

Each night I took to excusing myself at the earliest opportunity to sit in my room making carvings in the boards under the trunk. I liked the way that carving clarified my thoughts; how mixing lines and curves could make a picture in my head. Then I could come back, look at them days later, and remember those pictures. I drew shapes to help me remember how I felt about ceasing, about the Earth-voice, and about the black-eyed man from my dreams.

In between my careful scrapings, I overheard some of what my parents were saying before they slept. Their talks revolved around the hunt and the crops, but more predominantly about their desire to find a suitable mate for me. Once they slept, I crawled out unseen and slept amidst the trees. Sometimes I talked to *him*, the Earth-voice, but not often. He had already given me so much information I had yet to understand. He seemed to beckon me less, as if he understood my dilemma. Mostly, I spent my time watching and waiting for the blue light to pass over the encampment. It appeared at different times, but always during the night. My apprehensiveness about it grew, yet my inquisitiveness grew faster. I had to find out what it was.

The five days from my first lie went quickly, and the eve of the hunt and the choosing was soon upon me. Our hut teemed with people that day, whilst immediately outside, various young men set up camp. Many had come with their fathers, and I watched as they gathered wood and arranged small fires. I acknowledged each new face as they arrived, smiling politely, hiding my disappointment that none even vaguely resembled the black-eyed one.

As the final day before the ceremony drew to a close, the mothers came into our hut, helping to scrub and sew, making bedding, or so it seemed. My stomach constantly felt as if it was jumping into my mouth, but I paid little notice to their talk as they sat around the fire, choosing to bury myself in each small task they gave me.

Mother had been sitting with the other women, sewing for hours. She called me over.

"Go and bathe, Tachra. It is almost time," she instructed, holding up a long draping dress, nodding in approval.

My stomach performed another jump.

"Mother," I bent forward and whispered closely in her ear so that no-one else could hear, "what if I do not wish for this choosing? What if everything could stay just as it has been? I do not need a mate. Or could we at least just wait until I want to have one?"

She stood up and looked at me stonily. "Tachra, tonight you will have a mate. It is the way things must be."

"But what if I don't want one?" I asked bluntly, no longer caring any more if the other mothers could hear. They stopped their talk and stared.

"Nonsense, of course you do," mother's tone softened slightly. "You are just nervous. Everything will be fine. You'll have your mate and be happy, just wait and see."

I tried to object further, but she wouldn't listen, and my protests kept finding the same answers. Eventually, she ushered me towards the washroom, telling me not to come out until I had cleansed myself.

I did as I was told while my mind turned itself in circles, trying to find a good excuse to call off the choosing. I could think of nothing, and it seemed no time at all before mother was telling me to make haste. I returned to the main room, my skin freshly glowing from an abrasive scrub, clutching my favourite towel around me.

As I entered the room, some of the women stood up, holding blankets between them to create a small circle. Mother chivvied me into the enclosure.

I felt as if I were in a strange dream as she pulled off my towel and began dressing me in the newly sewn gown. As she fastened the last ties around my shoulders, my fingers couldn't help caressing the fabric; it was the richest golden brown and the softest weave I had ever felt.

Finally, mother stood back and stroked my hair away from my face, bringing it around one shoulder. It matched the dress perfectly. The women around me looked on, seemingly with approval, as a loud horn blew from outside.

"You must stand in the doorway," mother whispered in my ear, flattening the folds against my accentuated hips. "They will decide if they partake in the hunt."

She guided me forward and opened the hut door.

I moved into the open doorway, where at least twenty sets of eyes, lit up by the light of the lamps, greeted me.

Nobody moved. Was I supposed to do something?

"To those who hunt!" I heard a shout. It sounded like father.

The eyes turned and with yells, the men ran towards his voice.

I felt a hand grab my wrist and pull me back from the doorway. It was mother. She closed the door and smiled, taking my head in her hands and kissing my forehead.

"They all stay to hunt for you Tachra. It is a fair life when my youngest has none who would turn from the hunt. I will sleep and dream well this night."

I looked at her confused. "Why so many?"

"They've had several young women cease in childbirth, especially in Longplain, and there have been no such counts in our line; we are strong. And of course I must say that your stature would stir the loins of any young man," she replied.

"And the hunt?"

"Now they hunt for the greatest game. Your father will only choose the one who can hunt an even greater game than he can. It shows he will provide well for your children."

I nodded. I knew who would win. He was fast and strong and my father had already singled him out, helping him prepare a fire earlier that day. The lucky winner would be Hoc, the sandy haired eighth son of a vegetable crop harvester from Longplain. If picked, he would share my bed tonight before returning to Longplain to finish their harvest. Then, with his harvest finished, and hoping I were already with child, he would return to make this place, and me, his own for good.

"What do I do now?" I asked.

"We wait," mother replied. "Tomorrow you will have a mate, and soon this house will be filled with the sounds of your children. Then I will sit by the fire, warming my toes in the evenings, with a smile to carry me through my last days. You, Tachra, have been a child to make me smile above anything I have known."

Her last days? Her words revolved in my mind. How could she accept 'last days'? How could she accept that everyone would cease at some point – even my parents, even her? I hadn't accepted it. There was so much to think about, and this was all happening too fast. In the midst of my muddled thoughts, one sentence kept repeating itself: *your choices are your own.*

Tears started rolling down my cheeks and mother cupped my face in her hands.

"Are you hurt?" she asked.

I could not speak, but shook my head so she knew that I was well. I embraced her, holding her tightly, hoping she could hear the thoughts that poured down with my tears. *My mother, I love you so, but I must leave. Please do not be disappointed with me.*

I knew I had to leave. That was my choice, although I felt like I had no true alternative. I could not go through with this choosing and not just because I had lied about my bleeding and all its implications; there was simply too much I didn't know and too much that I was looking for.

I let go of mother and wiped my wet face as I looked around. This night, the hut – none of it seemed real anymore. The fire still burned bright and warm, the group of women still sat around the fire sewing and talking of their sons and of their son's sons who roamed the hunt, food was still loaded on the tables and the pots still bubbled on the cooking fires. None of it seemed real, it faded into a dulled slow motion around me, but it was real. This was the reality of the making of a life for me that I didn't want and had never asked for. I knew what I had to do. I did have a choice.

I stretched, declaring that I needed rest while the hunt took place, and then went quietly to my room.

In silence I gathered my bale, a bundled array containing my knife, my spare clothes and several large pots of preserves that I had plundered, all collected and wrapped into my spare skirt. I left the jar of preserved Kathi berries, because when I looked at them I imagined my father's troubled face. I just needed some time to think, I decided – time to think about why I didn't want my choosing, why people ceased, where the blue light came from, who *he* was, and who the black-eyed one was. Just a little time to understand, that was all.

In the distance, I could hear whelps and shrieks; the hunt was almost finished. Soon the men would be returning. Squeals of a wild boar vibrated above the shouting and I thought of my mother; she should still be there, hard at work. From my window, I could make out the flicker of hand-held torches in the distant trees, but the village itself was quiet.

Clasping my bundle tight to my chest, I swung my legs over the window ledge and slid down to the ground for the last time.

FIVE

Six days had passed since Chia had listened to Orion's composition, and still he suffered flashbacks of the horrific visions. It had also been six days since the Earth substation, the XLS, had detected a huge power surge from Earth. It seemed as if the flashbacks and the power surge were linked in some way, but the source of neither could be determined.

The inexplicable energy surge had propelled the substation into frenzied activity, with most personnel reassigned to analyzing the unknown power. Because results weren't immediately forthcoming from the Earth substation, the task now consumed their home-world too. A new source of energy was a bounty that only came along once in a millennium. Discovering its source, and then harvesting it, was of the highest priority.

Chia had officially logged the disturbance he has felt in his chi, but had omitted the finer details of the visions, and the council had concluded that the disturbance was no more than a manifestation of his acute skill, as a Sensitive, to an energy surge.

Chia however, believed it was more than this. The timing of the composition playing itself, the visions, and the unknown energy surge: in his opinion, the coincidences were too many.

As Head Sensitive, Chia's skills were now more in demand than ever. The last six days had become a repetitive blur of sensing and analysing, with so many reports to read that they now stacked up in piles along one wall, more useful as seating than as reference material. Chia needed sleep, but this had become a luxury.

Chia was deep in conversation with his captain, Nirrious. "All that data is distracting us from the primary facts. Just give me your conclusions and a summary as to these energy surges."

"I have to conclude that the two small surges are the same unknown energy as the first one," Nirrious stated. He removed his eye-piece to rub his brow. They were all tired.

"And your conclusions?"

"Determining the reasons why is exactly what all these necessary facts are for. Let me run through them one more time."

"Please, Nirrious," Chia held up his hand, "Do not give me even one more figure to store in my head. I trust your accuracy. Just a summary, or outline, or pointers . . . even draw it out using stick-men if you like – whatever; just no more numbers."

Nirrious laughed, breaking the strain of the complex discussion.

"Very well . . ." he paused, re-evaluating his procedures. He walked away, returning with a basic 3D model of planet Earth and started spinning it. "The first energy surge – the huge one – was emitted from the entire planet. We couldn't miss it," he said, waving his hands around the globe, trying to indicate something large.

"Agreed."

"And since then, you've personally examined every harvesting and sweep ship that returns from the planet."

"Again, agreed."

"You've sensed this unknown energy in every ship. But you logged particularly strong levels of it in 4 out of the 427 ships you analysed."

"No figures please. But, yes, agreed."

"No figures at all is easier said than done," Nirrious said good humouredly.

He stopped the globe, indicating to a wide segment spanning from pole to pole.

"Those four ships were all coincidentally allocated to this area. And the dates they were there coincide with the dates immediately after the small surges. I think the two subsequent surges were localised, not planet-wide."

Chia sensed they were on the right track. He sat straighter. "Can you pinpoint a more specific location?" he asked.

"Only a little. Two other ships were also worked around the poles, the Arctic and the Antarctic, at the same time. They came back with just standard levels of energy present, so we can discount those areas. These would be the parameters." He indicated to an expanse of the continent and their seas directly above and below.

Chia thought about this, "I think that your theory may have substance, Nirrious. Submit it to the council for immediate review."

"I submitted it earlier today. It was rejected," Nirrious stated matter-of-factly. "Admittedly, it's based merely on loose facts and supposition. They said that the smaller energy surges are most likely to be the planetary equivalent of sun-spots. The intensity of the first surge has convinced them that the planet itself is the source, something in the soil or water, or something at its core. Although most theories suggest this is correct, I do not allow myself the luxury of assumption, and so I also look elsewhere."

"As do I," Chia agreed. He liked Nirrious' theory; it felt right to him. He too sensed that the first energy surge was not entirely the same as the subsequent two smaller ones. But he also sensed that they were somehow inextricably linked. Nirrious was the first to think along the same lines. Maybe, just maybe, he had the right idea.

"I cannot rule out your theory as easily. And my role is to work with intuition," Chia decided. He suddenly stood up, invigorated by the strategy forming in his mind, and immediately summoned his crew. They came to the deck within moments.

"We shall set up new working grids for Earth's harvesting ships. We want this segment, from here to here," Chia indicated on the globe the same section of continent, "with more ships, on shorter runs. And the remainder of the globe must be allocated whatever ships are left equally, on longer runs if necessary. This smaller section is now our key focus. Split it into a grid with one ship allocated to each area. We'll start with a five by five grid; twenty five ships at a time. And then we'll narrow it down further once we have more information. Any questions? "

Nobody spoke: all were ready and willing to initiate any new strategy Chia suggested. He sensed they trusted him, despite his compromised reputation. They were a good team, and Chia allowed himself a rare moment of pride and respect.

With the crew dismissed and beginning their tasks immediately, Chia was left with his captain. Nirrious gathered his stack of reports in his arms, and then looked at Chia solemnly.

"You do know that if we do this, the tally from the regular harvesting will be reduced significantly. And because that will adversely affect our energy stockpile, it is most likely that you will be called to council for disciplinary procedures."

"I know," Chia replied.

"And you must also know that, in your position, I would have made exactly the same decision," Nirrious added.

"Yes," Chia nodded. "Hopefully we'll have results to show quick enough to convince the council not to take any disciplinary action. If not, then I'll suggest that I stand down and hand my authority to you."

Nirrious went to object, but Chia halted him.

"And Nirrious?" he added. "Take some rest time, please. It's not escaped my notice that you've not stopped working for six days. The crew can manage the reconfigurations, so go to the lounges, or your quarters, or anywhere quiet, and get some sleep while you can."

Nirrious didn't object this time; he too knew that his psyche would suffer if he went too long without sleep. He left Chia and walked towards the exit, stopping to add his reports to the accumulated stack along the far wall. He considered the – now thigh-high – pile, and then, instead of leaving the docks, placed his satchel on the make-shift bed of papers and, using it as a pillow, lay down to rest.

Chia himself set about the necessary but unpleasant task of forwarding the new strategy to the council. Shursa would undoubtedly review Chia's report before forwarding it to the board of council, and his feedback would undoubtedly be unfavourable. It seemed that Shursa's methodical approach was just too different from Chia's instinctive style. Nevertheless, Chia made a particular effort with his analyses and the use of supporting data on this occasion, hoping it would buy him the time he needed to test the theory.

With the strategy logged, and the first fleet of ships aligned for launch, Chia tried, yet again, to speak to the one kutu he had been trying to contact without success: Orion. The fragmented remains of the little crystal still hung around his neck, and he still had no answers as to its purpose. The communication port blinked repeatedly as he made the call, and Chia let it run for a considerable time, but still Orion did not pick up. His silence was unusually prolonged.

Back on their home-world, Eden, Orion leaned back from his console and shut his eyes, letting his wings trail back behind him. Did he just hear his communication port again? He opened one eye, glancing towards the communications module. It showed over three hundred unread messages. He shook his head and shut his eyes again; they could wait until later.

He'd just finished composing the follow up to the Summoning Song, which he had simply named 'The Dream.' It had been written in less than a week: he'd had to hurry. Once he had sensed that Chia had played the Summoning Song, and that it had invoked a force far stronger than Orion anticipated, he needed something to open the minds of his fellow kutu. He needed a composition that would hopefully help their receptiveness to new possibilities. That something came within the hidden keys of music.

Orion focussed, withdrawing in his energy wings, and then rose and stretched his stiffened body, causing his energy to ripple around him satisfyingly.

Running his hand over the workings of his composing unit, he instructed it to send the composition to Una, the Supreme. The unit bleeped, confirming that the new composition was now dispatched. It was Orion's first contact with anyone in the outside world for many weeks.

Deciding that he really should peruse his backlog of communications, Orion headed to the communications port and began scrolling through the long list of messages. There were three from Chia, as he'd hoped, and too many from Shursa to count – even more than the previous time he'd checked. He listened to the last message from Chia, and then tried contacting him straight away. Chia wasn't in his chambers.

"Record and send, Chia's quarters, substation XLS," Orion said, and the unit confirmed the instruction. "Well my friend, I have not heard all your messages yet, but I know we have much to discuss. It would be more appropriate to talk in person. Could you request leave? It would be good to see you. Until then."

The remaining messages would take an age to scroll through, and Orion had no desire to deal with them all right now, so he closed the port. He felt both exhausted yet alert, not a good mixture to do anything with. His rooms seemed quiet – too quiet – and so he opened his mind to sense any movement beyond his walls. Peniva's quarters to the left seemed equally silent – he was probably on duty – but Kraniel's, to the right, were a bustle of activity; he was probably amidst another social gathering. Orion momentarily considered joining the party, but then regarded his huge recliner covered in a mass of pillows in the far corner of the room. He couldn't remember the last time he had slept on his proper sleeping recliner. Gratefully he slumped onto the mass of comforting pillows. *Just for a moment*, he thought.

When he came to, what felt like only seconds later, it was because the buzz of his communicator was beckoning him to rouse, and whoever it was, was clearly refusing to leave a message. Orion cursed to himself that he'd forgotten to reactivate its mute facility, but then saw that the call was from Una, the Supreme, and so dragged himself from the recliner and accepted the transmission.

Una started laughing. "Obviously a full day's rest wasn't enough, Orion."

"It's been a full day?" Orion was surprised; he felt as if he'd only been sleeping for mere moments.

"Yes, but this isn't urgent," Una continued. "My apologies for the disturbance Orion; contact me when you're ready."

"Really, now is fine," Orion assured. "What can I do for you, Supreme?"

"For us all," Una smiled. "The council would like to arrange a public showing of this new composition, 'The Dream.' It is exquisite, Orion. It lifts the spirits and produces a tremendous sense of well-being. Well done. We thought a live performance in the main arena, whilst broadcast live to the XLS substation."

"That would be good. When would you like this to take place?" Orion was secretly pleased. He had anticipated needing to apply for permission for a live performance. The request was welcome news.

"That's entirely up to you," Una replied. "Everyone is working particularly hard at this current time; a performance from our esteemed composer would be a beneficial interlude for all."

"So the sooner the better?"

"If possible."

"I'll need at least a few moments," Orion smiled, looking down at his crumpled attire.

"That's the spirit. Would tomorrow evening be too soon?"

"Tomorrow evening would be highly acceptable."

"Then tomorrow, at twenty one hours, in the main auditorium," the Supreme confirmed. "I'll arrange a grand feasting afterwards. Thank you, Orion."

Orion nodded in confirmation and switched off the communicator. He looked around his rooms, which were untidy even by his standards, and then back to the comfortable looking mound of pillows.

Tidying or sleeping? he pondered.

It really wasn't a contest. He set the rooms atmospherics and returned to his soft, well-padded recliner.

Orion's dreamless state was interrupted at the pre-set time, and rather more gently than before, as the atmosphere had been modified to wake him. He was greatly revived by his sleep, and jolted fully awake by the shock of seeing his own reflection. A full day embedded in pillows had made his hair knot into a single red clump; his face had distorted into a patchwork of indents from lying on creases of fabric; and he refused to consider how long he'd been wearing the same clothes. Nevertheless, he had a performance to ready himself for, and time was now of the essence.

By 20.5 Orion emerged from his room, transformed into the expected persona of The Composer. His gleaming crimson hair flowed down his back in ragged twists, his complexion was restored to its golden glow, his wings were fully activated, translucently radiant and casting a red hue around him, and he wore a fresh crimson gown rippling with reflective nanos. At his hip he wore the scarlet sash embedded with the symbol of his realm. In comparison to the attire of most performers it was understated, but Orion always preferred to let his music make the statement.

The main halls of Eden's central zone bustled with a steady stream of kutu, all heading towards the great arena. It seemed that tonight's performance was attracting a vast audience. They were all adorned in a simple finery of dark colours, and had darkened their faces to highlight their crystal tattoos. They bowed when they saw Orion, and Orion bowed back. Their respect made him feel humble – he was only a simple musician after all – yet it seemed they had not forgotten his time on the council.

Orion headed to the inner hall behind the stage: a vast white area full of equally white statues. The one geometric sculpture, a stark, carved pillar with a singular globe at its top, stood out rather markedly beside the entrance – it was far too large for the space. Una, the Supreme, was waiting at the entrance behind the stage. Orion sensed him before he saw him, because he was virtually camouflaged against the pale surroundings.

Clad entirely in white, with his long, fair hair unbound and framing his pale face, the Supreme walked forward, smiling. Even he had withdrawn his radiant wings for the performance, yet he looked as strong and unreal as always.

"Orion," he greeted the musician. "It seems as though every available kutu wishes to attend this performance. Never have I seen the arena so full. It has been too many years since you last played live; your insights have been missed. May I have the honour of introducing you?"

"The honour would be mine," Orion bowed.

"Very good," the Supreme nodded. "You have a few minutes. I have requested that this area be kept quiet for you. You'll hear your introduction from here," he paused, acknowledging something to himself. "You know the scenario better than I, Orion. I will leave you in peace to prepare yourself."

"Thank you," Orion smiled, and Una, the Supreme, bowed in return and left.

Orion knelt down on the polished marble floor and closed his eyes for a few moments of contemplation. Almost immediately, someone tapped his shoulder.

Orion opened his eyes, expecting to see that the Supreme had returned. Instead, crouching in front of him was a familiar figure.

"Shursa?" Orion stated, automatically standing back up, very surprised that he had not sensed him approaching.

"It's good to see you," Shursa exclaimed. He leant forward, embracing Orion, and then pulled back, although still grasping his arms tightly.

"I thought you were stationed on the XLS substation," Orion wondered aloud, pulling back from Shursa's grasp.

"I would not miss this live performance. I have travelled here especially for the occasion."

"Then I am honoured," Orion graciously bowed. "Is Chia here too?"

"Do you not have room in your life for more than one friend?"

Shursa did not return the bow and the contempt didn't escape Orion's notice.

"I have many friends, councillor Shursa," he replied calmly. "But Chia and I have worked on many projects together and have found many similarities in our outlooks."

"Then I can only assume that Chia did not want to come here, as he did not make the request," Shursa commented dismissively.

He held out a hand. "Here, I have a gift for you."

When Orion looked down, a length of yellow silk was draped over his palm.

"A sash," Shursa stated. "I had it designed for you. You should wear it for your performance."

Orion stared at the sash, dumbfounded. It was ornately embellished with Shursa's yellow emblem. It was a piece of beautiful craftsmanship, admittedly, but to be adorned with the emblem, or colour, of another was not the done thing.

Orion bowed graciously.

"Thank you for the gift. Although it would not be fitting to wear another's crest, especially during a public performance. I support the council as a whole, not one singular member."

Shursa's eyes flashed, clearly dissatisfied with Orion's reply, and then he smiled, masking his feelings.

"Then perhaps you will wear it to the feasting. I must return to the substation afterwards and I would hope to see you wearing your gift before I depart."

"I will give it consideration. But right now, I can only think of my performance. I must have some time alone, to prepare."

"Of course you must."

Orion waited for Shursa to leave, but Shursa didn't seem to be in a hurry to go anywhere, leaving Orion with the conclusion that he would have to be more forthright than he would have liked.

"I do not wish to be rude, and I thank you for the gift, but I must have time alone, to meditate, before performing. I am sorry, but it is necessary." He indicated towards the exit.

Shursa looked with disdain. "As you request," he nodded.

Finally, reluctant and disgruntled, Shursa departed, leaving the inner halls empty once again. Orion stuffed the unwanted sash into his gown pocket. Sinking back to his knees and closing his eyes, he barred the recent conversation from his thoughts to concentrate on the task ahead.

It did not take long for Orion to sense the energy emitting from the arena: thousands of kutu all waiting in anticipation. They longed for an evening of enlightened entertainment, and all were open to the prospect of learning something new through Orion's medium of sound. The composition to be played, 'The Dream,' was apt, as the audience was ready and open to embrace new thought. Orion relished their buzz of activity.

"Kutu," Orion heard the announcement. It was Una, the Supreme, making the introduction. A hush fell over the arena.

"It gives me great pleasure to introduce the greatest theorist among us – one who shares his insights through music. Tonight Orion performs 'The Dream.'"

A hum of anticipation rippled through the crowds, dying down to absolute silence.

The silence was Orion's cue. He entered the stage, the air against his wings and soft shoeless footsteps now the only sound, and took his place in the centre of a transparent, domed console. He stood for a brief moment, looking out at the thousands of kutu, savouring the occasion. There was no light in the arena, since every kutu had withdrawn their energy wings and wore darkened attire. The only luminescence emitted from the console on the stage and Orion himself, which lit up their crystals tattoos so they glittered amongst the audience like stars in far off galaxies.

Orion stretched his arms, making his rippling crimson energy move visibly through his body and down to his fingers. After taking a moment to consider the circular instrumentations around him, he began to play.

'The Dream' was an intense composition of dark undertones wrapped in sparkling suggestions. It was full of hope and the implication of change, expressed in ways that each kutu would experience differently. From the opening bars, Orion took them on a twisting journey of perceptions. Through his sounds he conjured images of possibilities, playing with all his strength and giving his energy to the music so that it touched the hearts of all. The composition crashed through their beliefs that they knew everything, by invoking unseen questions and a desire to understand. Through sound, they moved their thoughts in synchronized anticipation. Through him, they all became united.

The performance was a triumph. As 'The Dream' concluded, every kutu stood clapping in appreciation, cheering and making streams of multicoloured light flow from their mouths and fill the arena.

It was done. Exulted and satiated, Orion bowed.

As was customary, Orion left the stage via its front steps to join the crowds, allowing the audience members the opportunity to express their thanks.

Una and the councillors were the first to congratulate Orion before heading off to the feasting in the grand halls, ready to welcome others as they arrived. Shursa had gone with them, albeit begrudgingly, as Orion mixed with other kutu, thanking them for their attendance. Slowly the multitudes dispersed, and eventually

Orion was left, virtually alone in the grand arena. A few small groups lingered on, chatting amongst themselves on the upper levels, and dozens of cleaning droids whizzed silently around the seating, returning the great space to its usual immaculate state.

Orion had refused numerous offers of company for the banquet; he felt too animated to attend the feasting just yet. He needed to do something that would diffuse his excess mental energy first.

It'll have to be the flight chambers, Orion decided. "Perfect!" he cried aloud.

Feeling pleased with his decision, he strolled contentedly from the auditorium and headed towards the upper levels of Eden.

The hallway into the flight chambers presented many large, arched doors leading to various flying spaces. All the doors were slightly ajar, a sign that none was in use, so Orion headed towards flight chamber seven. It was neither the biggest nor the grandest, but it was his favourite; arranged to be tall and narrow, with a Mazium crystal spire that pointed to the stars.

Approaching flight chamber seven, Orion suddenly stopped; he could hear the most exquisite singing coming from inside.

The voice from the chamber was beautiful indeed, but it was much more than that. Orion felt a shiver down his back as he recognised the tune. It was a version of one of his own compositions, and not just any composition, but the one nobody but he and Chia should know. It was *that* song, the Summoning Song. How could this be possible? His mind spun: surely no one else had gained access to it? No, only Chia's signature could have played the recording. It should be impossible for any other kutu to know that song. Yet the interpretation being sung by the kutu in flight chamber seven was truly amazing.

Orion did not know whether he felt curiosity, horror or

enchantment. Either way, he felt compelled to see who could produce such wonderful sounds. He glanced through the narrow gap in the open door, slipped quietly inside and looked up.

There in the spire, right at the top, dancing to the sound of his own voice, was a raven-haired kutu that Orion had never seen before. His bone-white face pointed upwards and his immense black wings outstretched, as he flew and danced to his heartfelt song. The raven-haired one seemed unaware of his spectator. And Orion? Orion was spellbound.

Orion was equally entranced by the song, the dance and the kutu, with his unusual black wings and strong black and white energy. This was not an illusion, this really was a black and white kutu; something that Orion did not know could exist. How such an extraordinary kutu had not been noted before was beyond his comprehension. And the interpretation of his melody was full of truth and inspiration; the slow, swaying dance mirroring it like a reflection in space. The sound created white energy with black shadows that floated around the spire, following the raven-haired one's movements before shooting into the cosmos with sparks of darkness and light. And the dance moulded around the dancer, enveloping him in a spiral of poise and grace.

This dance, this song – Orion knew it held the potential for greatness. Never had he found a kutu so at one with the sounds he could invoke. There and then Orion decided this kutu must be his apprentice in music.

Feeling a pang of shame for his intrusion, and not wanting to interrupt, Orion quietly eased out of the chamber and made his way to the chamber records. Currently at work in Chamber seven, the logs revealed, was a kutu named Jychanumun. It was an unusual name, and one he had never heard before.

Orion was too sure of his decision to delay. There and then, he contacted Una.

"Orion," Una stated as he received the communication. "You're not at the feasting?"

"No, no," Orion said hurriedly, suddenly remembering that Una must be busy. "Sorry to interrupt. When would you have a moment for me?"

"In truth, I could do with an interlude from all this merriment," Una replied. "I'll be in my conference halls shortly; contact me there."

"I'll come in person," Orion replied.

Una nodded, closing the communication, and Orion hurried towards Una's halls.

When Orion entered the conference halls, Una and several councillors were standing behind the huge, sunken conference table, conversing casually.

"Una, Hytach, Shursa, Uriel," Orion greeted each one as he stepped down into the chamber. Shursa didn't look very impressed, and Orion remembered the sash he had stuffed in his pocket.

"Again, excellent performance tonight," Una smiled. "So, what can we do for you Orion?"

"I've found a kutu who would be the perfect apprentice. I'd like your approval so that the process can begin straight away."

"That's excellent news! We've been hoping for a long time that you'd find someone suitable. We all enjoy and benefit from your talents. Of course, this person must be transferred straight away. Well, do not keep me in suspense, Orion: who is it?"

"He has extraordinary talent. His name is Jychanumun."

Una glanced up, his eyes momentarily flashing.

"You must be mistaken," he frowned.

Orion pulled out a copy of the logs, showing the evening's flight chamber attendees, and then went on to describe the kutu he'd seen.

"You cannot mistake him if you see him," Orion stated. "For he has black wings! And he has pure white and pure black energy. I have seen no other like him. I did not even think that a kutu could be both black and white. Una, this is phenomenal; I can only imagine the scope of working alongside a kutu with energy such as his."

"It is Jychanumun," Hytach verified, whilst scanning the logs. "These records confirm his bio reading. It's definitely him."

Una looked perplexed. Shaking his head, he took the nearest seat and sat down.

"Orion, there must be some mistake." He cast a glance towards councillor Hytach.

Hytach nodded, and they all looked back at Orion, who stood resolutely waiting.

"This Jychanumun is considered quite mad from being solitary for so long," Una stated, as he rubbed his brow.

Orion waited for further explanation. The kutu he had witnessed looked far from mad.

"We found him, or rather stumbled across him, in his ship," the Supreme continued. "One of our trailblazers spotted his craft drifting far outside the boundaries of Eden. We took him in, thinking it must be a test pilot with a malfunctioning prototype ship. But it was clear there was something wrong; there was no record of his existence, his ship was outside our design parameters, his uniform was unknown – he even looked different. Have you seen his eyes? They are *black* – pure black."

Pure black, Orion thought. That was what Chia had thought he had imagined. So pure black eyes could exist. He snapped out of his thoughts to concentrate on Una's account.

"From the state of Jychanumun's ship, it was clear he'd been in it for a long time: his last log was over 80,000 years old. Eskah knows how he strayed so far, and for so long. From what we found, we assumed that he was perhaps one of our test pilots with a design that was never logged. Perhaps we had just lost all records of him over time. We kept him in secure convalescence here for years and, although we couldn't find anything actually wrong with him, he either could not, or would not, communicate. Eventually, we concluded he'd lost his mind from the prolonged solitude. We didn't want to keep him in convalescence forever; the poor creature still knew how to feed and dress himself and could perform the simpler tasks we gave him, so we allocated a room in the lower quadrants and gave him work to occupy his time, servicing the cleaning drones in the lower tunnels. He started work immediately, and after that nobody really saw him."

Una stopped, staring down at his hands, his fingers pressed together into a pyramid shape, contemplating.

"I kept trying to help him," Hytach added. "I visited him many times, but never found him in his rooms. It seemed as though he preferred to live in the tunnels. I sent him invitations to events, but he didn't socialise. After a while, I stopped trying. Admittedly, I forgot about him."

"Until now," Una stated. "Orion, I will be blunt. I put a great deal of effort into that creature, yet found nothing and got nowhere with him. You saw him: it was clear that he contains both white and black energy. I have never known a kutu to embrace both, but he did, and he was as blank as a void. Eskah knows what benefit his knowledge could have been to us, but all our efforts resulted in nothing. Now you too want to waste your efforts. I suspect that what you saw and heard was nothing more than a mindless imitation of something he'd overheard."

"I understand what you're saying, but I know what I heard and do *not* think it was mere imitation," Orion stated determinedly. "If I'm to have an apprentice, it must be this one."

Una sighed, looking suddenly drained.

"Then tell me how it should be done, Orion. For I was there watching all the unsuccessful attempts to communicate with this creature. I do not know how to grant your request."

"Just try and summon him to my quarters. Arrange a meeting as you would for any other kutu. I will take it from there."

Una considered this for a while. "Then that's what I'll do," he stated.

He rose from his seat and moved towards the door. "But I'd suggest that in the meantime you look for an alternative apprentice. You'll waste your efforts with this one, and I have much more pressing matters to concern myself with. Deciphering this new energy on Earth is taking most of my time and effort."

"You have sensed new energy?" Orion immediately asked him, his instincts jumping.

"Orion, do you not listen to your communications at all? It's all there." Una shook his head in disbelief. "You must be the only kutu oblivious to it. Every other kutu can think of little else at this time. In fact, I could do with your input on the matter. It would be time better spent than trying to make this Jychanumun your apprentice."

"You have my word that I will look into it immediately. Although I'd still like you to try and summon Jychanumun."

"Of course I will."

Una motioned the doors open and held out his arm, indicating that Orion should leave.

Orion bowed politely and left, his head reeling as he tried to calculate all the possibilities. A new energy? Could it be linked to the Summoning Song? It must be. It wasn't the result he'd expected, but there again, he wasn't sure *what* he'd been expecting. And Jychanumun? Had he lost his mind? From what he'd witnessed in the flight chamber, Orion thought not.

He hurried down the corridor, heading for his rooms, anxious to contact Chia to catch up with recent events and get a summary report on this new energy. But before he'd even turned the first corner, someone called him.

He looked around as councillor Shursa strode forward to catch up with him.

"Perhaps I will accompany you to the feasting now," Shursa stated.

"Apologies, councillor Shursa, but I'll not be attending the feasting."

Shursa abruptly stopped walking.

"Are you snubbing me, Orion?"

"No, of course not. I merely have much to think about and attend to," Orion replied.

Shursa seemed to consider this, "I see," he eventually stated with an air of disdain. "You would be wise to leave this Jychanumun alone. If you seek a kutu to work alongside in music theory, you should look elsewhere. A councillor with many skills, such as myself, would be more worthy as a protégé. I would even be prepared to start as an apprentice."

Orion took a step away, genuinely surprised at the request. "But you are an esteemed councillor."

"I would request reassignment."

"And you have no specific interest in enlightenment through sound."

"I could be taught."

"But it requires the sort of dedication only attained from genuine passion for the subject."

"I would be dedicated."

Orion took a long, deep breath.

"Councillor Shursa, we both know that you're really not interested in creative mediums," he sighed. "Creativity requires forward thinking in non-standardized ways and although you have many amazing talents, you are not a forward thinker. I have tried to skirt around this, but it seems I cannot. I'm flattered by your attentions, but this is too much, it's not welcome. I do not choose my friendships; they come about through a genuine compatibility that just happens. You're a good councillor, and you have my greatest respect for the work that you do, but that is all. You cannot force yourself into my life. I have no feelings for you other than the ordinary respect I hold for a fellow kutu."

"You think too much of yourself, Orion!" Shursa glared, his eyes flashing yellow, barely managing to control his voice. His face paled as he shook with contained rage. "You insult me. I can be creative and I am a forward thinker. Your rudeness is affronting and incorrect and you will regret it. So listen Orion, listen very carefully to what I say to you now . . . You *will* regret your words."

With that, Shursa turned and walked away. Orion called out to him, but he would not stop. He disappeared around a distant corner.

That was excessive, Orion thought. *Either that, or I did not choose my own words carefully enough.*

Nevertheless, Orion decided that Shursa's ability to display such rage should be made known to the council. Orion momentarily considered discussing it with Una, but then thought better of it. He didn't want to bring Shursa any unnecessary humiliation. He had said what needed to be said; now he must leave Shursa to calm down and regain balance in his own time. He would be fine. Orion congratulated himself for having handled the situation honourably. Now he had far more engrossing things to think about.

When Orion returned to his rooms, he immediately tried contacting Chia. As before, Chia was not in his chambers, leaving Orion with no other option than to record and send a brief message. Afterwards, he listened to every message stored on the communication port, gathering information on the energy surge that had been sensed from Earth. He absorbed the information restlessly, before activating his communication port and searching for Una's location.

The port showed that Una was in his chamber, alone.

Una sat deep in thought, enjoying the stillness around him. It was pleasantly quiet, with most other kutu still at the feasting. Ordinarily it was a time he would relish, but he felt a discomfort in his heart, something he didn't usually experience. At first, he put his unease down to Orion's request, which had caused old, unpleasant memories of failed hope to resurface. He thought he'd left those memories behind. There was so much they could have learnt from Jychanumun, but all they had discovered was his name and his rank. He could recall it even now: Jychanumun, 696DPW, whatever that meant. The only thing he had gained from the experience was a new sensation, of failing a fellow kutu.

Una cast his eyes around his chamber, allowing the tranquillity of the white stone to ease his spirit. Then he pushed his senses further out, moving through the layers of energy tunnels and storage tanks directly under the surface of the room, and then on, through the native remnants of Memorite stone, towards the feasting halls on the upper moon side.

The feasting halls were full of the laughter of kutu deservedly taking an evening away from their work. Una smiled to himself, feeling their enjoyment. Then he drew back and entered the heart of Eden, where there was still more of the planet's Memorite stone than there were facilities. The smoothly bored tunnels linking the multi-layered facilities were full of the lifeless movement of drones; he scanned through them, knowing he would eventually detect Jychanumun: he was the only kutu who chose to live down there.

As Una scanned the tunnels, he sensed life – a kutu, undoubtedly Jychanumun. As usual, Jychanumun gave off no emotions for Una to sense: he was an empty shell – either that, or his skills really did go beyond any that Una had encountered. He wondered if Jychanumun would even be able to read the request that had been issued to him earlier that evening, the poor creature.

Una sat back and closed his eyes. No, he realised, it wasn't Jychanumun that was troubling him. But what was it? There was something. It niggled his senses like an itch he couldn't scratch.

Orion sensed that the Supreme was alone, and the port confirmed that he was in his chambers. It was unusual that he hadn't rejoined the feasting.

Orion tried raising the Supreme on the comm-port, marking the communication as non-urgent, just in case Una didn't want to collect, but Una picked up immediately.

"Orion," Una greeted him. He seemed deep in concentration. "Do you have another bizarre request for me this night?"

"I do not," Orion replied. "Can we talk; as old friends, kutu to kutu, like we used to before there was such things as councillors and Supremes?"

"Of course," Una smiled. "It has been a long time, Orion. I miss our conversations."

Orion heard heaviness in his fellow Supreme's voice.

"Una, my friend. What bothers you?"

"I am sure it is nothing more than a mere moment of deep contemplation," Una considered. "I have felt a ripple of discord among some kutu, one that I do not recognise, and so I know not what it is or where it comes from in order to readdress the balance. The ripple unsettles me. It will be discussed at council tomorrow, but it's probably nothing more than my own sensitivity. We are all so focussed on harvesting on this new planet, Earth.

Anyway, take my mind off this matter, Orion. What did you wish to discuss?"

"I'd like to throw some ideas to you, like we use to do: the 'theories and possibilities' game."

"Ah, I remember that. Fire away," Una replied, smiling, sitting straighter.

"What if our myths are based on fact?" Orion began.

"Highly unlikely," Una responded. "I could make up a story now, and in a thousand millennia it would probably be considered a myth." He chuckled to himself. "In a thousand millennia even I would probably think it was a myth, even though I concocted it."

"Ah Una, you're not playing. Play the game," Orion smiled. "What if our myths *are* based on fact? Let's say, the ones in the oldest scripts."

"Those myths are ancient," Una contemplated. "I barely remember them being written, and even then they were just rumours, stories told to explain reality. But, to play the game, if they were based on fact then they would suggest that there is a very old, and possibly infinite, being in existence."

"Do you think we would sense it?" Orion continued.

"Very likely," Una replied straight away, and then paused. "No . . . definitely – sensing is fundamental to our existence."

"So, if we could sense it, do you think we'd be able to absorb it?" Orion prompted.

"No. How could one absorb something that is greater than it is? Ah Orion, I see exactly where you are heading, but you grow rusty my friend. Are you suggesting that this new Earth energy that we are detecting is somehow a great or old being?"

"Yes, I am," Orion said bluntly.

Una contemplated this for a few moments. "What makes you think this?"

"The chain of events hints at it. But more than this, I think I sense something, but it remains elusive – beyond my grasp. It is as if I cannot remember it."

Una went to speak, and then lapsed into thought again before remarking, "I cannot believe that I am even considering such a ludicrous suggestion. But I've not forgotten that many great things often stem from our mind-sparring. I will give it further consideration. I may even put some of our theorists onto researching it."

"Would you keep me informed of their progress?"

"I'll tell them to forward all reports to you. You are still the best theorist among us, Orion. You know we'd welcome you back on the council at any time."

"Thank you." Orion appreciated the sincere gesture. "But I must pursue my path from a different perspective. Theory is my passion, and music the love and medium for those theories. Through both I am, and will be, giving the current situation much thought."

"You have a unique position, Orion; as a past councillor who still holds an honorary position, and the only kutu granted free reign to direct their studies, your perspective is most valuable. You have my greatest respect."

"As you have mine," Orion smiled. "As a friend, as well as the Supreme."

"Listen to us! Enough of these sentimentalities," Una laughed. "Well, Orion, you have replaced my heavy thoughts with deeper ones. You keep that thinking cap on and I will keep you informed when I uncover anything of further interest. We will speak soon."

Una and Orion bowed in unison.

Over the next few days, Orion kept himself busy. He stayed in his chambers waiting for a response from either Jychanumun or Chia, who, it seemed, had a problem with his communication port, so that Orion only heard static whenever he tried to establish a connection. And Jychanumun? Una had issued the meeting request to him, as promised, but was convinced that he would not turn up. As the days passed, Orion started to accept that Una was probably right.

It was late. Orion didn't wish to rest, and so he sat messily sculpting a new art piece; he wasn't very good at the art, but enjoyed it nonetheless. He was sitting astride the small pottery table, focusing intently on an intricate area of his model, when his service lift opened slightly and a little drone whizzed through the gap between the doors and into his room.

The service drone dropped a tiny crystal in front of him, spun around, and then zipped out as fast as it had entered.

Wiping his hands on his gown, Orion picked up the crystal and examined it. It was a typical storage device, nothing remarkable. He slotted it into his port and a visual-only message flashed up.

'15 minutes' the notice stated, nothing else. There was no sign-off, but as it had been an impromptu dispatch by a service droid, and knowing Jychanumun had been allocated work maintaining the service droids, he hoped this was the communication he'd been waiting for.

Exactly 15 minutes later, a kutu stood outside Orion's chambers with his palm over the read-out for identification. It was, as Orion had hoped, Jychanumun.

Orion greeted the kutu into his chambers.

"Welcome," he smiled. "I was beginning to think you would not come."

"I was beginning to think you would not invite me," Jychanumun replied.

"You've been expecting my invitation?" Orion asked, surprised.

Jychanumun didn't reply, so Orion indicated towards the loungers and offered him a seat. He sat down stiffly, staring silently ahead.

Orion poured them both refreshments while discreetly observing his new guest. Jychanumun had arrived in a simple white sleeveless tunic and long black sarong skirt, neither bore any insignia at all. He had chosen not to arrive with his energy wings and his skin was a matt ivory, rather than radiant; it was as if he had learnt how to shield his energy. He wore nothing on his feet, a trait Orion had only seen among some of the Sensitives, and clad to each of his upper arms were very unusual, black metal armlets. Each armlet appeared to be inscribed with writing rather like their ancient script, although Orion didn't recognise the dialect. He handed Jychanumun a goblet and sat down opposite him, making a conscious effort not to stare at his black, pit-like eyes.

"My name is Orion. I'm a composer and theorist," Orion introduced himself.

Jychanumun did not return the formality.

"I have heard you singing. You have an outstanding voice."

Jychanumun did not comment.

"The detail on your armlets is very unusual. I have seen nothing quite like it. Is it old script?" Orion asked.

Jychanumun did not volunteer a response, but Orion was sure that this received a minor reaction from him. It was a very slight change of focus, or small change in his stance, he could not be sure as it was so discreet.

Orion searched for a point of interest to get some sort of response from the kutu.

"I understand that you are very good with robotics?"

Jychanumun remained silent, staring blankly at nothing, so Orion tried raising other questions, only to find that these, too, elicited no response.

Deciding that perhaps Jychanumun had been subjected to enough questions from others, Orion turned instead to discuss his work, the performance, and life on Eden – anything. He merely chatted on, leaving occasional pauses to allow for Jychanumun to respond, or even to give any indication that he was aware of Orion at all. But Jychanumun still remained silent, his exquisite yet expressionless face giving nothing away.

Time passed, and the one-way conversation grew more and more fragmented as Orion struggled not to repeat himself. He began to wonder if the black-eyed kutu actually understood what was being said. Perhaps, he thought, his first sentence really had just been an imitation of his own opening statement, just as Una had suggested. Perhaps this kutu really had lost his mind.

Orion tried again to motivate conversation. Again, he was unsuccessful. Eventually, fresh out of ideas, they both sat in silence.

But Orion was determined no to give up. He snapped himself out of his vacant thoughts, shaking his head and thinking, If *words do not work, perhaps music will.*

He swung around to his composing equipment, ran his hands over the workings, and began to create sound. He started with the skeleton of a new song, but it felt unsatisfactory, so he began to play the song he thought he'd never play again, the Summoning Song, changing it to be more like the rendition he'd heard Jychanumun sing.

Before long, Orion was nestled into his equipment, engrossed in the music, and had forgotten about Jychanumun's silent presence. The music pulsated to a dramatic crescendo and then finished. Orion fell back into his seat feeling exhausted, satiated.

"That," came a quiet voice behind him, "Is my favourite piece."

It was Jychanumun.

"I've never played that piece publicly," Orion stated, looking around and trying to hide his surprise.

Jychanumun glanced down.

"It is called the Summoning Song," Orion continued through the silence. "It developed from my research into the old scripts. It took me over two hundred years to write, because of its complexity."

"Every story is complex," Jychanumun stated, his face still expressionless.

Orion wondered whether to tell the direct truth or evade it. Somehow, he felt compelled to state the facts as they were.

"I spent years deciphering the old scripts until I found what I had been searching for: a concealed sequence," he explained. "When I unlocked it, I still could not understand it. I tried everything. I nearly gave up. And then, as a last resort, I fed the sequence into my music console. The result was, ironically, the very best of my compositions, although I had no hand in its outcome. I named it from the title of the old script it derived from, 'The Summoning' and simply called it the Summoning Song."

"A song to summon what?"

"I am not quite sure," Orion admitted. "The scripts mention the elder ones, stemming from the original consciousness, their existence beyond the limits of time, and these scripts are not referring to us as kutu, but something even older. Ah," Orion sighed dismissively, "It's probably all just a story. And even if there is a hint of truth in it, then there is no guarantee that I interpreted the codes correctly."

Jychanumun seemed to contemplate this.

"I am sure you did," he finally stated.

Now, having managed to overcome his shock that this strange kutu could and would talk, Orion would not let the conversation drop. He stayed focussed on the music, but at least now, the conversation was two-way. Jychanumun still did not have much to say – he seemed to prefer to listen to Orion and interject with the occasional question or reply. But Orion did not mind; he felt that he needed to show this strange kutu that he was trustworthy. He felt as if Jychanumun was evaluating him, although he sensed no negative motives in him at all.

At several points, Orion tried raising the same question as to how Jychanumun had come to know of the Summoning Song.

"I only made one copy of the recording, and then erased every piece of data on it. And even that singular recording was programmed to erase itself once played. Your rendition of the Summoning Song was beautiful, and yet I still do not understand how you could know of it at all."

"Some things belong to no kutu." Jychanumun spoke quietly.

"True," Orion agreed. "It never was *my* composition; it had been embedded in the old scripts for a long time for anyone to decipher. Had you read these too?"

"No,"

"Had you heard the deciphered music before?"

Jychanumun shook his head and looked down at his hands.

Orion nodded, sensing he would get no further on the matter and their fragmented conversation continued into the early evening, until, for no apparent reason, Jychanumun abruptly arose and said that he had to leave.

Just as quickly as the service drone had announced his coming, Jychanumun was gone.

Orion was left alone in his chambers with an abundance of unanswered questions. How he wished that Jychanumun had been able to talk more. *But he had talked!* That alone was far more than the council had told him to expect. And as much as the council had questioned Jychanumun's sanity, it had not taken long for Orion to discover that the black-eyed kutu was far from mad.

The following day, Orion told Una of the successful meeting with Jychanumun. The Supreme was surprised that Jychanumun had responded to the invitation request at all, and then became momentarily speechless when he heard that Jychanumun could and did talk. Orion wasted no time requesting that another invitation be issued.

"It will be done straight away," the Supreme complied. "Orion, if you can get though to this kutu you are opening more possibilities for information and new technology than I can imagine."

"But remember that he is still a kutu – please do not see him only in terms of what can be gained from him," Orion insisted.

"Yes, of course. My apologies, Orion: that was most unlike me. My days have become subject to a constant barrage of requests for answers and results. Sometimes I long just to sit in quiet reflection, knowing that there is nothing that I must do."

"As Supreme, it would be perfectly acceptable to take some leave," Orion suggested.

"Yes, although I will have no such rest until the problem of this new energy is solved."

"Are we any closer to harvesting it?"

"Unfortunately not – we still don't know what it is. We don't even know its source. Everyone seems to be taking the same approach, trying to analyze the composition of the planet right down to its sub-molecular levels. Although an interesting report did fall on the council's desk recently. It seems your good friend Chia has a different idea to the rest of us. He seems to think a link to the source may be rather more localized."

"Still on the planet?"

"Yes," the Supreme nodded. "The council wanted to reject the notion. Chia's past . . . ah . . . *extremes* have not been forgotten. But we are giving him leeway for a while to see what he comes up with."

"That's wise; Chia has insight, for all his past indiscretions . . ." Orion was thinking aloud. "Perhaps you could consider sending a research party to the planet to explore his theories."

"You know we cannot interrupt the growth of the planet; it could jeopardise the still delicate eco-system. The project would be too complex to implement a second time. We have one shot at setting up the harvesting tiers. There are too many other resources at stake to chance ruining it."

"It was just a thought," Orion conceded, acknowledging Una's tension. "Perhaps, Una, just for one evening you would like to hang up your Supreme's robe and join me in a game of sound throwing. We can be just two kutu, feeling unsocial, taking it out on the walls of the games halls."

"That may not be a bad idea," Una agreed. "In fact, it's a very good idea. Let me get back to you with available times. Meanwhile, I will dispatch this next invitation to Jychanumun."

Orion returned to his half-finished sculpture, deciding it looked rather more like a random series of stalagmites than an interpretation of their finest city. He pinched the tops off some of the great buildings. Yes, he decided, the sculpture would now have a new title.

Two days later, Jychanumun turned up again, followed by another impromptu meeting. The conversations between the two kutu gradually grew in depth and breadth, and Orion discovered that Jychanumun shared his interest in many arts and theories. Jychanumun often fell silent when he no longer wished to speak of what he knew; at such times he seemed content to listen to Orion.

During their fifth meeting, before Jychanumun made one of his quick exits, Orion took the opportunity to ask Jychanumun to be his apprentice.

"I would be most honoured if you would accept," Orion concluded his well-rehearsed speech.

Jychanumun looked at him, musing over the suggestion.

"Do you think any kutu here would appreciate any composition that stemmed from my thoughts?" He paused before continuing,

"There are too many shadows in my heart. Shadows of truth, yes, but they are shadows nonetheless."

Orion considered this. He wanted to object, but could not. From the little he had come to understand of this kutu so far, he knew he had to concede to his judgement.

"I see the truth of your shadow," Orion responded quietly, "but I see it as light. However, I understand."

"Thank you," Jychanumun nodded.

Orion looked at the reclusive kutu and silently reflected to himself. *This one has spent millennia upon millennia alone. He has had thousands of years with nothing to contemplate other than who we are and what we know, stand for, and believe in. He must have come to conclusions far beyond our grasp in a way that time alone can provide. Most would not see his truth, because it's too complicated.*

"You think very loudly," Jychanumun suddenly stated, intruding on his contemplations.

"You could hear me?"

"Yes," Jychanumun confirmed. "You think very loudly."

Orion was dumbfounded. There were many who could pick up thought, but only ever through touch. He himself had the ability, quite strongly. Because he was aware of his skill, he closed his thoughts to any who might accidentally touch him. It seemed that Jychanumun had breezed past those barriers without physical contact.

"I do not need to touch," Jychanumun interrupted. "Although touching makes it stronger – too strong, in fact. I hear thoughts through a kutu's energy too. It is not a blessing; I wish I could not."

Orion nodded, considering the implications of what the kutu had said.

"Is it a problem?" Jychanumun asked. He seemed concerned.

"Not at all," Orion decided, and then laughed to himself. "Well, what have I left to hide from you that you have not already picked up? You are very different, but I trust you."

Jychanumun looked relieved, "And you are right. Your thoughts . . . somehow you are able to translate my motives. You are the first I have found here who can do this. When I heard your composition I knew it would be so."

"Thank you," Orion smiled. "You would have been a good apprentice."

Jychanumun contemplated the floor for a moment, "We will work together, but it will not be with music," he said, almost wistfully.

"But I speak too much," he added, and then suddenly fell silent, as if correcting himself.

"Never," Orion replied, trying to appease him. "Please, do talk to me."

Jychanumun nodded thoughtfully and looked Orion straight in the eyes. It was the first time that Jychanumun had looked at him directly. Orion felt a shiver of energy surge through his back.

"I will only say that I have always known the tune you call the Summoning Song." Jychanumun said. "Is it possible to know of something before it exists? That is but one question; I have many more, as you do too. Our questions, although different, will lead us to walk the same path. It is something that fills me with both dread and joy. It is something that has already begun."

SIX

I walked slowly away from my village, looking back often, as if I hoped to see a reason to return running after me. I carried my few favoured possessions, along with as much food and water as I dared take, wrapped together in my spare skirt, and made my way to the only place that I could think of: the ravine.

I spent my first full night away from Threetops deep down in the craggy ravine by the river. It was not the momentous occasion my idle thoughts had anticipated. I didn't have a plan, and hadn't decided whether my leaving was temporary or permanent, but I had chosen to walk away from having a mate and all its inevitable outcomes. I was not joyous about this; instead, I dampened the moss with weeping until I had no more tears, and did not question why I wept.

Pushing through my weeping, the Earth-voice whispered all around me as if waiting for my response, but I was silent. I could think of nothing to say, and I shut my thoughts to everything, including myself. I blocked out my mind entirely.

When the sun rose after that long first night I started wandering along the mossy bank of the river and away from the populated areas that I knew. I still had no thoughts, and didn't want any. I just walked, slept, and ate as my body demanded, allowing my mind the detachment I wanted.

I don't know how long I wandered, but eventually my inner fever dulled enough to restore some clarity of mind. A muddled vision of my new mate coming to wake me, only to find an empty room filled with luscious green grasses, had made a pang in my stomach strong enough to rouse me from my apathy. And now these visions of green were no longer blurred extras from my hazy dreams, but a strange reality.

By now, I was no longer in the shadowy, damp ravine. The ground was a rolling mass of green pasture with small patches of trees and undergrowth scattered to the horizon, and above me the bright sky held long white clouds that concealed the high sun. I took great comfort that the river still flowed by my side, now a wide but shallow serpentine of water throwing tiny sprays from a jutting array of small rocks. Today, though, even the river looked different. All the scenery looked different.

Dozens of images flickered together to form a fragmented story of the countryside I'd passed. A good deal of time must have lapsed and I could remember little of it. I noticed that my cloth shoes had worn through, indicating that I had indeed travelled far, and a quick inspection of my foot showed that the cut had healed well. I checked my bundle, which was considerably lighter than I remembered – the water carriers were empty and most of my supplies were gone. As I bent to the river to refill my pots, the pale, sunken face that reflected back at me was as unfamiliar as my surroundings.

After hastily repairing my shoes, and not knowing what else to do, I gathered my bundle and continued walking. I sang my song to raise my spirits, and when my song finished I made up more. The Earth whispers also rose in response to my wakefulness, but I still didn't want to talk, and closed my head as soon as I felt *his* presence, which seemed to be all the time. I just wanted to keep moving. I didn't want my old life back. I wanted to get as far away from it as I could. I think I felt ashamed.

Purely by chance, I'd chosen a good time of year to leave. The days were full of sunshine and the nights were still warm. As my clarity of thought and common sense grew, I took to walking with the moon and sleeping with the sun. At first I did this to watch out for the blue light, but I saw no more of it. But soon I saw the added benefits of using the sun's heat as a blanket for sleep and the cool of the night to allow me to cover more ground. I followed this pattern unless the drizzling rains kept me moving during the day, and eventually the days and nights rolled together until I stopped paying attention to them. I just kept walking.

The river, my constant, speechless companion, twisted and wound through shallow valleys, its banks entwined with dense undergrowth and long-leaved plants that offered their vividly coloured blooms to the sky. I passed a particularly beautiful tall blue flower standing alone under a tree, its vibrant petals unfolded to the warm day. It looked similar to the irises near my village, and this thought made a twang in my chest. I picked that beautiful bloom and pressed it between papyri, carefully laying it in the bottom of my bundle. *Father would like that,* I thought, and then I felt another sharp, unpleasant twang in my chest. I didn't discard the flower, but I decided not to pick any more.

Without a route to guide me I continued following the water's trail, wandering often from my path to collect fruits and vegetables as the land offered them. The constant walking kept my appetite constant, too.

Every day was a continuous barrage of new sights and sounds, teaching me that the land was a vast and changeable place. The river narrowed and deepened as I walked on, its steep banks becoming encased in rambling masses of brambles that were covered in unknown, dark berries. The berries were delicious, but the tiny hostile thorns that accompanied them dissuaded me from attempting to collect many, although they seemed to be no problem for the small twittering birds. Gradually, the soil became increasingly visible between scrubby tufts of grasses and the land stopped providing as many edible fruits, so I braved the unfriendly berry bushes more and more frequently to keep my hunger at bay.

After navigating a particularly difficult expanse of prickly masses, which sprawled away from the river bank to cover a wide chunk of the land, and which offered more thorns than fruits, the area opened up to reveal the river running through a broad expanse of bare flatland. Shortly ahead, the water divided into three smaller offshoots, each one travelling in a different direction. The flatland seemed to go on forever.

I stood gazing at the river's three offshoots ahead of me. The river had been my only path, but now I had to choose which route to take. It was a complication to my simple journey that I hadn't expected, and it certainly wasn't welcome. How would I know which offshoot would be the best choice? The stark flatland looked barren in every direction, its bleakness stretching as far as I could see. All of the choices looked grim.

Choice? I wanted to scream. I didn't want choice. I didn't ask for choice. I'd never had choice before; now this was the third time I'd had to choose in as many moons. Feeling frustrated, hungry and tired, I broke down and wept.

My heart felt heavy in part because I realised that I would not be returning to Threetops soon, if at all. I had made choices and I now realised they had consequences. I had chosen not to be a farmer's wife. I had chosen to walk away from the place I'd called home. I knew that, whether I liked it or not, I was aware of choice, therefore, I must have it. I also knew that the choice before me now would not be my last.

My head throbbing, I wiped away my self-pitying tears, pulled myself up, and determinedly moved on. I would aim to reach the point where the river forked before the following day. Once there, I would choose which direction to go in.

The journey to the fork was uneventful, and when I reached it, I stayed there for two full nights and a day, mainly sleeping. On the second evening I watched the sun set while I contemplated what should be my next course. I could find no reason to select one stream over another: each was of a similar size; each travelled through the flatland before disappearing into the horizon. The only difference was direction, but direction meant nothing to me.

A red haze reflected off one of the offshoot streams that branched into the horizon under the sun's direct path, making a thin trail of rippling crimson through the land. It was like an arrow pointing westbound.

West, I thought: the sun's red line points west, just as did the movement of the blue light. It seemed that two great lights chose west as their paths. And so this would be my path too.

I will walk with the water that follows the sun and points to the home of the blue light, I thought. Perhaps one of my questions would be answered after all. If not, it was as good a direction to go in as any.

I gathered my belongings, packed my last pot of preserves carefully in the cloth, and headed in the direction of the setting sun.

From the fork, the river's offshoot narrowed to a rushing stream with shallow, exposed banks and murky water that tasted like dirt. The days rolled together, and seemed to grow hotter as I walked through the flatland. I took to fixing my sights on the sporadic markers on the landscape such as a tree or a twist in the stream, and would try to head towards it, but they always seemed to take too long to reach. If it weren't for the stream, it would have seemed as if I was walking without moving.

The ground around me became dryer and sparser every day – even the clumps of grasses by the stream had become brown and crispy to walk on, and the soil had turned to hard sand. With little other noise around me, the sound of my footsteps seemed deafeningly loud. I took to stopping just to get the rhythmic echoes out of my ears.

I had chosen to travel west; consequently I had the heat of the sun on my back in the mornings, and so I draped my spare skirt over my head so that it covered my shoulders. I'm sure it looked strange, but I only had insects for company, and their response was just to bite any flesh that was still exposed. They were horrible little things, and never had I been bitten so much or so often. They came regardless of whether it was day or night, and I entertained myself by swatting as many of the pests as I could, but they still managed to chew my exposed skin until it was a mass of lumps upon lumps.

Although the biting insects seemed to have found a good source of food, I had no such good luck. In Threetops food had never been an issue; now it was. The prickly berry bushes that had fed me, albeit meagrely, had ended with the start of the flatland, and now edible produce was limited to the occasional small sour fruits, which made my belly ache, and roots that were only accessible by digging, so that the effort of finding them expended more energy than the roots themselves replenished. I'd rationed the few preserves I had left wrapped in my bundle, but still there was barely enough for one meal. I tasted one occasionally, to savour something that wasn't sour fruit, but that only served to remind me of how hungry I was. So I drank as much of the muddy river water as I could to fill my belly.

It was not long until the hunger began walking with me, and my pace slowed with every new night. I knew I was growing weaker. The land ahead indicated nothing but more of the same and by now the land behind me was no better. So I just had to keep going. With only three tiny conserves left in the last pot, and my cramping belly keeping me awake so that I could not sleep, I kept walking.

After several days without food, and feeling nauseous at the very thought of another sour fruit, I knew I had to find something to eat, and soon. It seemed as though hunger had numbed my mind but sharpened my senses; I was sure I could smell maize.

I stopped and breathed in deeply. Yes, I could definitely smell maize, and not that far away. Maize meant people, and people meant food.

"Are there people close?" I asked aloud, without thinking.

So, the little one has found her thoughts, the reply came straight away.

"I know you've been watching me. This time, I chose not to speak."

I sensed amusement from him and was glad.

"People?" I repeated.

You *can smell them.*

He was right, I could.

I turned, breathing slowly and deeply, analysing everything I could smell. Yes, the maize was strong, but there was more, much more, and it seemed that if I emptied my mind I would know what those things were.

In my path, but just to the south, I saw that there were rocks, water, new plants, and even a few animals and birds, but no people. To the east, from whence I had come, I could sense many people, but very far away: I knew that this was Threetops, with all its surrounding villages. However, to the north I could smell them strongly: people. They were as little as two or three days walk away from the river.

My hunger guided my feet and I immediately set off north bound, in the direction of the closest people, memorizing the landscape around me so that I could return to the river if I wished. The anticipated taste of fresh bread made my stomach growl, and I scoffed my last preserve, knowing that at the very least I would soon find wholesome food. Perhaps, I thought, I might even find a new home where my choices would be my own.

Even though I was hungry, I felt happy, and as I walked towards new people and the prospect of food I realised I was humming. It was the tune that had filled my head; the tune that *he* seemed to dislike, but he wasn't asking me to stop it.

"You do not ask me to be silent anymore."

No, it is done.

"What is done?"

Much, he replied.

"Do you wish me to stop?"

It makes no difference, he replied, *unless you choose to join me in sleep so we can both forget.*

"I do not wish to sleep *that* sleep," I replied, remembering the murkiness my mind had felt in the water. "I wish for some freshly baked bread for my belly."

I felt him retract, but I sensed no anger from him and so I kept walking, trying not to sing to myself, although I probably did hum without realising it. In any event, he had said it didn't matter if I sang it again, and I had to do something to occupy myself; I'd given up counting footsteps once I'd got to numbers bigger than I had names for.

After two days' walking at an improved pace, fuelled by my eagerness to find food, my senses became confused as to which direction I should take to reach habitation. My nose told me there was more than one settlement, and I'd reached the point where two were clearly discernable. In one direction I could smell a small village close by, probably only a half a day's walk to the north-east. There was another, larger collection of people to the north-west, but this scent was much fainter and I estimated that they were four or more days' walk away. Either community would undoubtedly have food, so I chose the closest and continued walking through the night, knowing I could get there by sunrise.

The thought of the possibility of fresh bread or sweet plums made me refuse the sour fruits that now grew in abundance, and my instincts soon proved right. As daylight started to break, the smell and sight of a small sprawling village was laid out before me under the dawn sky.

I quickly changed into the clean outfit from my bundle and rubbed at my face, neck and hands until I was sure most of the dust had gone. Then, as soon as I sensed the people rousing from their slumber, I threw my bundle over my shoulder and hurried towards the dirt track that led into the village.As soon as I reached the track, I held my head high and smiled, sauntering, as if I'd walked that path every day. Well, if I wanted food, I had to make a good impression.

The trail into the village was well trodden, winding through tightly sewn fields of maize and Yute that looked ready to harvest. In the distance, a sinewy, red-haired man walked towards the fields, leading a large docile horse, its shoulders and back strapped with a heavy-looking contraption. A sprawl of half a dozen red-haired children ran behind him, trying to match his pace, all carrying empty sacks. It could have been a scene from Threetops.

What should I say? I couldn't just walk up to someone and ask for food. I had to have a reason, and I had to be able to give them something in return. Then my belly grumbled again, reminding me of how hungry I was. I'd just have to make it up as I went along, I decided.

"Excuse me," I called out bravely, as I approached the red haired man. "What is the name of the next village, the one to the north west?"

The man stopped and eyed me hesitantly, and then broke out into a wide smile.

"That'll be Hollow," he replied. "But you'll need to take water, it's a few days' walk and it doesn't look like rain."

"Thank you, that's good. Hollow is where I'm going," I lied, hoping he'd offer to provide refreshments.

"I thought as much," he nodded, and then bent to talk with one of the smaller children. "This one'll take you to Mags to get water."

I called my thanks to the man as the red-haired boy dumped his sacks on one of the larger children and ran skipping and jumping through the long maize towards me. The bobbing head of red, in a mass of yellow crops, eventually emerged and came skidding to a stop in front of me.

"I'm Ren, who are you?" he chirped.

The directness of one so young took me a little by surprise. "Hello Ren, I'm Tachra," I smiled.

Ren grabbed my hand and pulled me towards the huts. "Come on Tachra, we're going to see Mags. Tachra? That's a funny name. What does it mean?"

"Don't you have Tachra trees here?" I replied, surprised that they didn't have the type of fruit tree I'd been named after.

He shook his head. "Of course we don't – I'd know. I know all the names of the trees and all the plants. Father tells me, he knows them all. You don't get a Tachra tree."

"Well," I explained, "Where I'm from there is a Tachra tree. It bears sweet yellow fruits all the year around. So it means 'most fruitful.'"

"Oh, so that's why you're going to Hollow then," Ren sniggered and jerked me forward. "Look, there's Mags. Mags! Mags!"

Ren let go of my hand before I could ask him what he'd meant and went bounding up to one of the huts. Its door was wide open, and a delicious smell drifted from it, making my nose tingle and my mouth water.

Moments later, a pink faced and red-haired woman emerged, holding the boy's hand.

"Father calls me Mags, not you," she scolded the boy, as he smirked in my direction.

The woman looked towards me. "I'm Mags. I already know your name and where you're going," she laughed. "Our Ren can talk more than the rest of them put together!"

"He can indeed," I smiled.

Mags slapped Ren fondly on the bottom, to send him on his way back to the fields, but the child held on to her skirt.

"Mother, can't I stay here and talk to Tachra?" he pleaded.

"No child, father needs a hand with the Yute today," Mags replied.

"But I'm hungry," Ren protested, looking up at his mother appealingly.

"You've only just finished your morning meal, you can't be hungry again already," Mags shook her head.

Little Ren remained staring up at her, nodding vigorously.

"Oh well, alright then," Mags conceded merrily. "Come on – you too, Tachra. It looks like I'll not get away from the hearth just yet today."

She stood to one side, motioning me into her abode, and I went inside. The main room was clean but sparse, with doorways without doors leading into three other rooms. Rows of beds lined two of the rooms, and a large pail of water in the third indicated a washroom. The main area had two cooking hearths, both busy heating bubbling pots of delicious smelling food, and a large table with long benches on each side.

Mags indicated towards the table, so I took a seat on one of the benches. Ren plopped himself down beside me, staring up at me, grinning and swinging his feet so they banged the table.

"We've water and food if you want to stock up," Mags said, as she began stirring the pots with a large wooden ladle. "You'll be wanting to look your best if you've been sent to Hollow."

I opened my mouth to answer, but she started talking again.

"You must have come from Rainmouth," Mags continued. "Yes, they're too busy this time of year to send a guide. Did you stop at the in-between-huts? I suppose so." She twittered on, not allowing me to answer, for which I was extremely grateful. All the while, Ren sat beside me, swinging his legs, continuing to grin.

"You've got green eyes," the boy stated abruptly. "That's funny. I've never seen green eyes before." He stretched up, trying to peer as closely as possible.

"Oh yes," I remarked to the child, smiling. "That's because I eat lots of green vegetables."

"I've got blue eyes," Ren declared proudly, as if I hadn't noticed.

"Blue? Really?" I feigned surprise. "Does that mean you eat lots of sky?"

Ren burst into hysterics, "Ha ha, you're funny, Tachra! Mother, Tachra is funny."

"And you're even funnier, Ren." Mags ruffled his hair and plonked an ugly but delicious-smelling bowl of thick broth before him.

My pangs of hunger were almost too much to bear at seeing Ren's bowl of food, but thankfully, a large bowl was quickly placed in front of me too.

Mags sat down on the opposite bench and motioned for me to eat. Ren pushed his broth around disinterestedly, while I tucked in heartily and kept going until I'd scraped every last mouthful from my bowl. It may have looked ugly, but it was the best thing I'd eaten since leaving Threetops. Feeling slightly less ravenous, I thanked her.

"It's good to see a healthy appetite in a young woman," Mags approved. "My boy here seems to enjoy playing with his food more than eating it, don't you, Ren?"

Ren put down his spoon and continued smirking at me.

"Well, young Ren," Mags announced, "I think it's clear that you are not hungry. Off with you: father needs all the hands he can muster today."

Ren tried to object, but his mother was having none if it, looking at him with raised eyebrows every time a squeak passed his lips. Eventually, he pulled himself from the chair and dawdled to the door, disappearing at a snail's pace around the corner.

"Ren!" Mags commanded, and the boy popped his grinning face around the door, waved, and ran off.

"Thank you again. That was a fine stew. I am good at sewing and darning if I can do anything for you," I offered, hoping to repay the meal and wondering if I could prompt her into offering a comfortable bed for a short while. "It sounds as if you have a plump harvest, I could help in the field."

"Oh no," Mags responded hastily. "You get yourself to Hollow. Tell Huru I helped you on your way if he asks – that will be a fine thing. You could do with more flesh on you, but a good scrub and you'll be pleasing." She pointed towards the wash pail.

I was indeed very grubby, so I didn't object. I gathered my pack and walked through to the small washroom, where an assortment of pails littered the floor, some already full of clean, cold water.

The walls were lined with narrow shelves, offering piles of thin towels and a well-used assortment of mashed up soap leaves.

"There's no door," I called, as I searched for a curtain or screen.

"Of course not," Mags laughed. She brought a large pan of steaming water through and tipped it into the largest pail. "Don't mind me; you've not got anything I've not seen before."

I waited until she had left and awkwardly stripped off. I was standing on an area of already wet floor with holes bored through to the ground below. I carefully slopped handfuls of hot water from the pail onto my grimy body.

Mags came through with another pan of water and shoved the pail towards my feet, laughing heartily at my coyness.

"Didn't they ever wash in your birth home? You stand in the big pail of hot water and wash with this," she said, handing me a small sloppy rag.

Feeling highly embarrassed, I took the rag, got into the larger pail, crouched down, and began scrubbing.

When I emerged, feeling cleaner than I could remember, Mags turned and looked at me in the same way that the mothers of the sons at the choosing had done.

"You'll do just fine," she nodded. "Come and have more broth."

I didn't argue. Mags seemed nice, and the first bowl of stew had really just whetted my appetite. So I sat and slurped through another helping, while Mags told me about everything in her life, especially her children. Ren was the youngest of twelve; the oldest two had already paired and now lived in the same village, and the first of the fourth-generation babies was due at any time. She paused for only a moment to refill my empty bowl, and I surprised myself by finishing it before she could explain the lengthy workings of a new ditch they were digging to bring more water to their fields.

Satiated, I pushed my plate away and held my hand up to decline a fourth helping. A few days feeding like this and I would be back to my usual self, I thought. I decided to ask if I could stay a while and help with their over-ripening crops in return for lodging; they definitely needed it.

Eventually, Mags paused in her otherwise unbroken patter and I made my offer.

"Mags, you have been very kind," I began. "Surely you have some chores I can help with in repayment. Your crops are ripening quicker than the hands you have can harvest them, and I know Yute crops well. I could help here for a few days and really lighten your workload."

"No, no," she muttered quickly, "I would not hear of it."

I thought she was being kind. Harvesting was indeed back-breaking work; my parents had always refused the help, as they didn't want to hinder others.

"I would like to help," I appealed.

Mags looked across the table at me, but now her firmness was tinged with fear.

"You cannot stay here, Tachra!" she quickly exclaimed, shaking her head. "No, no, you cannot stay with us – not with any of us here. A healthy young woman who has been sent to Hollow and waylaid by us would not serve us well. No, that really would not do at all. There is a girl – Sara, bless her – from our village, who is off to Hollow herself tomorrow; we cannot have tales spreading that you were delayed here with us. You must leave, and soon. You must take the path and stay at the in-between-huts on your way if you have to; that's why they are there. And when you get there, you must tell them that I sent you on you way, and that I only gave you food and the chance to bathe as necessary, and didn't delay you."

She rushed around the hearth, clattering bowls and stirring the broths, casting uncertain glances towards me as she talked. Now she seemed hospitable no longer; in fact she seemed desperate to be rid of me. Whatever her reason, my welcome was over.

I stood up and collected my bundle.

"I must be on my way, then. Again, my thanks for the fine broth," I smiled. "Your kindness has been very gratefully received."

Mags stopped her clattering and walked over to me, trying to smile over the look of relief in her eyes. "Ren can walk you part of the way to the first in-betweener," she offered.

"That's not necessary," I said. "You are all very busy here. And anyway, I walk faster alone."

She conceded at that, breaking out into her jolly smile again; as I made my way towards the door, I thanked her again.

"Well, good walking young Tachra, and send Huru my regards." Her words had a ring of finality about them.

Scrubbed clean and with my hunger satisfied, I left. Young Ren saw me leave, and quickly caught up with my slow, full-bellied amble. He wanted to know why I was not staying to have dinner with them. I told him I was in too much of a hurry, but would try to visit, and then I sent him back to the fields to help his family. He seemed happy enough, and ran off without a fuss, leaving me to depart the village and set off in the direction of Hollow.

Once I had passed the huts, I veered from the shallow track and headed towards the bush land. My full belly had given me a contented weariness, and so as soon as I was satisfied that I was far enough away from the people not to be spotted, I lay down to sleep.

I awoke sharply to a dark, star-spotted sky and a familiar vibration scratching through my head. I leapt up, knowing instantly the cause: it had to be the blue light.

I was right. The village I had just visited was awash with blue light, and its familiar moving core spiralled over the huts. I felt the familiar wash of adrenaline, but I had now learnt how to smother it, and so I crouched down low to observe, hoping that the scrubby bushes would hide me.

The core within the light worked in the same precise way as it had in Threetops, moving gradually westwards and hovering over one hut at a time until it reached the edge of the village. And then it vanished, once again not leaving any trace except the imprint on my eyelids.

A few moments later, I felt the vibration again, but much weaker, and now behind me. I turned to see a small patch of sky lit up with the same silver blue. I was too far to distinguish if it had the same spiralling core, but I didn't need to see it; I knew it would be there. A fraction of a moment later it was gone, followed by four more rapid bursts of light, each time slightly further away. Then, further away still, a large patch of light filled the sky that lasted quite some time.

So the blue light was not unique to Threetops, I thought. *It appears wherever there are people.* There were five very short bursts; most likely over the in-betweener huts that Mags had spoken of. Then there was a long patch of light, which must have been over Hollow.

Why people? I wondered. Why would the blue light shine on people when they slept? Did the sky light up over me when I slept? How would I ever know? I always felt angry when I saw it, as if it was wrong, just as the knowledge of ceasing made me angry. Although I knew that people lived on after the blue light had visited them, without seeming harmed, and although I couldn't yet see the connection between the light and ceasing, somehow I knew there had to be one.

I didn't go back to sleep. Instead, my legs took me in the direction of Hollow. Both the blue light and Mags' references to Hollow had intrigued me enough to make me want to go there, and not just for the food supplies; I was simply very curious. Hollow sounded like a remarkable place.

As the day broke and I walked in my own long grey shadow, I saw a small ramshackle hut in the distance. It sat beside the vague dusty track that I presumed led to Hollow. I guessed it was one of the in-between huts, but it looked unkempt and not at all welcoming. I avoided it, making my own path through the dry land, but regularly watched the tracks for signs of other people.

By the time dusk came, I hadn't seen any other people on the path, and now a second small hut approached in the distance. An orange glow flickered from a window, indicating that they had a fire inside. It was already growing cold, and the thought of warming my hands against a stove was very appealing.

I'll just go and have a look, I thought, *there's still quite a while until nightfall. They may well have warm food as well as a warm fire.*

Mags had said that these huts were for the travellers going to Hollow; wasn't that exactly what I was? Surely I would get a welcoming response. I made my way across the sandy ground and joined the track that ran past the hut.

As the hut grew closer, I noticed it was even more dilapidated than the previous one. It was lop-sided – it had been damaged by a dead tree that had dropped a heavy branch onto its roof, so that one corner had caved in; gnarled bits of grey wood also hung off the walls, creaking in the breeze. And what I at first took to be shutters over some of the windows were actually permanently nailed up wooden boards. The hut didn't look habitable, and although I could definitely see fire light coming from inside, it didn't look appealing at all. Warm fire or not, I didn't want to go there at all.

I walked off the track and away from the uninviting abode when I heard the creaking of wood behind me and somebody calling out.

"Hey, you girl."

It was a woman calling to me from the hut.

I didn't really want to stop, but I didn't want to be rude, so I turned around and smiled.

"Hello, I'm not stopping," I called to the silhouette in the doorway. "I'm on my way to Hollow."

"But of course you are," she shouted back. She shuffled towards me, walking very strangely, as if one of her legs didn't work properly.

"Come on girl, stop and rest," she said.

"Thank you, but I'll not be needing to trouble you," I replied.

She laughed loudly, as if I'd said something funny, and kept shuffling towards me until she stood in front of me and I could see her unsightly features.

"That's what us huts are here for," she said.

As she talked, she smiled; it made her look even stranger, because her big grin revealed that many of her teeth were missing, and the ones that were left were misshapen and brown. I tried not to stare, but felt a compulsion to gaze at them. Her small face was covered in creases, and her nose looked huge in comparison to her gaunt features. Her wide eyes darted from side to side, as if there were many people around her instead of just me, and her face was framed by a mass of curly hair that stuck up in all directions. And as much as I thought I needed a good meal, she needed one even more; she was one of the skinniest people I'd ever seen. No, I'd never actually seen *anyone* as thin as her. Indeed, I'd go as far as to say that I'd never seen anyone like her at all. I think I must have stood and stared at her for quite a while.

"Come, girl," she said, taking my hand. "You need drink and a bed before you go on your way."

Despite my horror at her appearance, I let her take my hand. I felt strangely sorry for her, and knew she didn't mean me any harm. Her gap-toothed smile must have mesmerized me, for the next thing I knew, I was walking with her, towards her hut.

Her hut was surprisingly warm, with several large lamps burning on the dust-covered floor. The only furniture was a small bed, a trunk, a barrel and a chair, all in the one room. There wasn't even a cooking area. There were two doors to other rooms, but both were closed with wood propped up against them to keep them shut. I guessed it was due to the caved in roof; luckily, the main room had survived such damage.

"I'm Tachra," I told her.

"Girl, Tachra; makes no difference. Come, girl, sit," she said, pointing to the chair.

I could tell that she'd just been sitting on the chair, as a part-mended, raggedy shawl lay over the back, which she'd obviously been working on.

"I'll sit on the floor, you sit here," I smiled.

"No girl, you're guest. Here, sit here," she insisted, pulling her sewing off the back of the chair and standing over it, waiting for me to comply.

I sat down.

"Yes, yes, you sit," she said. "I'll get you something real nice to eat."

She went over to the large trunk, eased off the heavy lid, knelt down and began rummaging inside. As she fumbled noisily, I noticed a small arrangement of dried leaves and grasses in a cracked pot. It was very pretty and she'd obviously taken great care over it.

"Your plant arrangement is very nice," I said.

She looked around, grinning.

"Yes, we has to make nice things with what we can find," she said happily.

"It's pretty," I nodded. "You said 'we.' Is your mate here?"

"Oh no, he's no more. That's why I was sent here," she replied, turning her attentions back to the trunk.

"Oh, I'm sorry. Did he cease?" I asked without thinking, and then wished I hadn't been so tactless.

"Yes, almost soon as we got to Hollow. Hollow didn't like him, and me's past bearing children so they didn't want me," she replied.

She sounded sad as she told me. She must have liked her mate a great deal, I thought, and Hollow must be something very special.

"How long have you been here?" I asked.

She just shrugged. "Ah, this is good," she said enthusiastically, finally pulling something out of the trunk.

She held something up which vaguely resembled flat-bread. She examined it, blowing off something with deep, spittally breaths, and then dusted it down a bit more with her hands. She broke off a chunk and handed me the largest bit. It was very old and, if that wasn't bad enough, covered in grit and dust, compacted down by her spittle.

Now, I didn't want to eat that lump of bread, but she was looking at me as if she'd just given me her best treasure. I broke off a tiny corner, the least offensive looking bit, and popped it in my mouth, trying not to think about it.

She nodded, satisfied, then went over to the barrel, picked the mug off the top, lifted the lid, and peered in.

"Not much left," she said, shaking her head. "Have to go to Meadsins and get more tomorrow."

She bent right into the huge barrel so that her scrawny feet lifted off the ground and it looked as if she was about to fall in. Then I heard her scraping the bottom of the barrel; I assumed the scraping was from the mug and that she was trying to get water into it.

"Save your water," I said. "I really am not hungry, or thirsty."

She pulled herself out of the barrel and looked at me uncertainly.

I smiled and nodded as I tried chewing the rock-hard flatbread that was still in my mouth, trying to look as if I was enjoying it.

"And you should save this too," I said, offering her back the rest of the bread. "There's a girl, Sara, on her way from the next village. She'll probably be here tomorrow; keep it for her."

"Another girl? There is? Good, good," the old woman smiled her gappy smile, taking back the bread.

She looked at me curiously. "Are you not from Meadsins?"

"No," I replied, "I'm from a long way from here."

"Where? Who sent you?" she asked, her head twitching curiously.

"Sent me? What, to Hollow?" I asked.

She nodded.

"No one sent me. I'm going to Hollow of my own accord," I said.

"No one sent you, girl?" she asked, her voice going very shrill. "You sure?"

"Yes, I'm sure. No one sent me," I repeated.

This seemed to fill the woman with glee. Her face brightened up and she started doing a strange little jig on the floor. "No one sent her, no one sent her," she sang, lifting her feet up and down to her own off-beat rhythm.

She kept doing her strange jig as she repeated the words, then she suddenly stopped, rushed to the trunk and pulled out a small chalkstone and a knife. She quickly scraped three shallow 'v' shapes into the stone.

"You give this to Huru, in Hollow," she said, handing me the chalkstone. "Tell Huru that Tooth sent you."

I looked at the stone she had given to me. This Huru must be a great man, I thought – everyone seems to know of him. I wondered if he could be the one from my dreams.

"And you are Tooth?" I asked, trying not to smile at her name.

"Yes, give Huru that and tell him that Tooth sent you, and that Tooth wants food and cloth," Tooth said, scratching her chin. "And someone to mend the roof." She seemed to think about this for a while longer, and then nodded to herself and looked at me.

"Yes, you tell Huru that. You will not forget, will you?" she said. "Say that Tooth sent you."

"No, I'll not forget," I replied.

She made me repeat her request word-for-word anyway, and then became quite fidgety.

"Are you staying, girl?" she asked.

"No, I must be going," I said, noticing the darkness outside. "Thank you for your hospitality."

"Good, good. Good girl," she beamed.

Again, my welcome was over. Only moments ago she'd virtually pulled me into her hut; now she wanted me gone. This message to Huru was clearly very important to her, and quite urgent. But I was grateful of the opportunity to leave before nightfall, and relieved that she didn't try to stop me as I headed for the door. Instead, she shuffled ahead and opened it, making a breeze kick up the dust as she waved her hand around, encouraging me out.

"Do not forget to tell Huru," she reminded me.

"No, I won't," I said, as I walked out onto the sand outside the cottage, which was cooling from the day's heat. "Goodbye, Tooth."

"Goodbye, girl," she said, shutting the door.

I walked away, feeling strangely disorientated. How could she, Tooth, be happy living in such an awful place? She said that 'they' had sent her there, but why would anyone send somebody to such a ramshackle place? And she had said that Hollow didn't like her mate. That was also quite strange. Still, I thought, she was not quite right; she clearly wasn't looking after herself properly, and I could only imagine what extended periods of neglect could do to a person.

It struck me that many people wanted to go to Hollow, and that Hollow must be a great place. And this Huru must be a great man, as everyone seemed to know him. Curiosity about the place and the man occupied my thoughts. I quickly tucked the small chalkstone into my bundle, walked off the main track, and headed for Hollow with a new enthusiasm.

I walked through the night, with the pale blue light first appearing behind and then in front of me. I kept off the track, but stayed close enough to it to sense any other travellers. Meeting Tooth had been the oddest occurrence. I felt sorry for her, and didn't like the idea that the other in-between huts might house others in such a sorry state, and so I was reluctant to visit any more.

Before dawn had lightened the sky I sensed another hut parallel to my path, but. sticking to my resolution, I ignored it and kept walking, even though I'd almost finished my water. Then, at high-sun, I sensed yet another hut. I'd intended on ignoring it, but the sun was so intense that it was creating a haze in the air, and I had no more water left. I was already thirsty, and knew that Hollow was still at least a day's walk away. So, with a burning thirst, I made my way towards the hut with the intention of asking for water.

The hut looked hospitable as soon as I saw it. Unlike the previous huts, this had neatly battened windows and a tiny green area to one side, shaded by well-built wooden umbrellas. As I approached, I could see that the green area was filled with a selection of well tended vegetables and fruit bushes, all freshly watered and glistening. It pleased my heart to see something well cared for – it was a welcome sight in this barren land. Feeling certain that I would find water here, I approached and knocked loudly on the door.

"Jin!" I heard a man shout from inside.

"Jin! We've a traveller at the door," the voice shouted again.

There was a few moments' silence, and then a thud, followed by a rhythmic scraping sound.

"I'm coming," the same voice now called out towards the door. "You can just let yourself in if you wish. The latch is a little heavy, so just give it a good tug."

I put both my hands on the large wooden handle and pulled. At first it didn't want to move, and then it shot up, nearly crushing my fingers.

"Yes, come in, please," the voice said.

I opened the door and saw a young man, not much older than myself, sitting on the floor, pushing himself towards me with his hands.

"Sorry I was slow – legs don't work," he said, smiling up at me.

He had one of the most beautiful faces I'd ever seen, tanned a golden brown, with wide grey eyes and a mass of curly brown hair, and his smile was broad and genuine. I looked down at his legs; they seemed twisted and thin, and the feet pointed in the wrong direction – seeing their sorry state made my heart clamp with sadness.

"No, I'm sorry," I said, as I walked forward. I could see he had been sitting on a low chair and had dragged himself towards the door. "Here, let me help you."

"I'm fine. I can move, I'm just a bit slow," he replied. "Please, take a seat. I'm Jan."

"Thank you, Jan," I smiled. "I'm Tachra."

Jan nodded towards a second, higher chair, opposite his own. Before I moved towards it, I heard another call.

"Jan," the voice called, "were you calling me?"

It was another man's voice. A moment later, he walked in through a doorway at the back of the hut, laden with a huge pile of logs that obscured his chest and face, so that he could barely see where he was going.

"Were you calling me?" he repeated, as he lowered the logs by the entrance.

"Yes, we have a travelling guest; Jin – this is Tachra," Jan replied.

Jin immediately straightened and turned around.

"Oh, I'm sorry; did you manage the door alright?" he asked Jan. Jan nodded with a smile.

Jin turned to me. "Good-day, Tachra," he nodded.

Jin had the same type of beautiful face and brown curly hair as his companion. These two young men were obviously from the same family, but whereas one had damaged legs, the other stood tall and strong.

"You must need refreshment. May I fetch you some water and food?" Jin asked, while I stood staring.

"Water would be very good," I replied, quickly lowering my gaze, embarrassed that I'd been so obviously looking at him. "But only if you can spare any. I imagine water is quite precious in this heat."

He looked at me a little oddly before walking to a large barrel and filling a mug.

"Hollow's travellers are not usually so courteous," he commented, handing me the mug with a wry smile.

"I've not met any other of Hollow's travellers, so I can't comment," I replied. "I've only met Tooth along this path."

"Tooth," Jan started laughing. "Good old Tooth. How is she?"

"Strange. And without much food or water," I replied honestly.

"I will take her some tomorrow," Jin frowned. "I've told her countless times to pass a message to us when she needs anything."

"Is she family of yours?" I asked.

"Oh no, not Tooth, but nobody else seems to remember to provide for her," Jin replied. "No, Tooth is not family, but we," he indicated to Jan, "we are brothers."

"I guessed as much," I smiled, "You look so similar."

"Apart from the stupid legs," Jan replied, looking down.

"Will they take long to mend?" I asked.

Jan burst out laughing. "Mend? Oh no; they're quite useless," he replied, still chuckling.

I wondered at this. Father had said that people could break limbs, but I'd always thought that if someone didn't cease from an accident then the limbs would eventually mend. How terrible it must be not to be able to run and walk – I could barely contemplate it.

I think I must have been frowning as I thought about Jan's situation,

"It's alright," he insisted, "they don't hurt." He slapped one of his useless legs. "They used to work alright, so I'm told, but I lost the use of them when I was young, so I don't even remember."

"I do," Jin muttered under his breath.

"But that's terrible," I said. I felt tears trying to form, but blinked them away. "What happened?"

"He was a baby," Jin explained, as he fetched himself and his brother some water too. "I wasn't much older. A great storm pulled down our hut in Hollow. Jan was trapped, and no one even tried to get him out or help him, even though I begged them for aid. They said he was dead, or as good as. It took me two days to get him out. If only I had been stronger then, I might have saved his legs."

"Could they not have mended them?" I asked. "My father told me about the body breaking; he says there are ways to help mend things."

"I was too young to know such things. And if anyone around did know, they didn't act on it," Jin replied.

"Jin did his best, and it's only because of him that I'm here at all," Jan intervened. "I am happy to be alive and have a good life. Perhaps if we'd known . . ."

"Why do you go to Hollow?" Jin suddenly asked abruptly.

"I am looking for something, or someone," I replied. "I have heard Hollow is a great place."

"It is great for some; but not all," he stated.

"Did you once live there, in Hollow?"

He nodded.

"Then why did you choose to come here?" I asked, wondering about their lives. Did they not want mates, families, or at least to have their own families around them?

"We were sent here," Jin replied.

"Jin," Jan said quietly. "*I* was sent. You did not have to come here."

"But I am happy here," Jin said, looking at his brother with a shrug. "I like it here better than Hollow."

"I thought Hollow was a wonderful place?" I asked, wondering why anyone would wish to leave.

"I am sure it is, for some," Jin repeated. "Personally I prefer as much tranquil space as possible, so it is not so great for me."

I nodded in understanding. My father had been the same, and had often discussed taking the family from Threetops when I was young in order to begin a new encampment. He too had preferred as much open space as possible.

Jin asked me if I would like some food. I hadn't intended on staying for anything other than water, but I said yes, I would like that very much. So, as Jin prepared some wonderfully fresh-smelling vegetables, I talked more to them both. As Jin cooked, Jan wove a small basket, creating intricate patterns into a design using different shades of dried golden vines. It was fascinating to watch his fingers move with nimble, hypnotic precision to create a fine piece of work.

The day passed far too quickly, as I enjoyed our conversations: these brothers were two of the finest people I'd met, and in no time at all the sun began descending. As we sat and ate vegetables, we talked of many more things. The more we talked, the more I liked them, although they still couldn't understand why I wanted to go to Hollow.

When dusk did inevitably beckon, Jin showed me the spare sleeping room, assuming I would stay the night as all the Hollow travellers did.

"You hospitality has been appreciated and I've enjoyed being here, but I cannot stay," I said. "I prefer to sleep outside at night."

Jin looked at me with the same questioning smile.

"You are a strange one, Tachra," he laughed. "I may only have known you for half a day, but I already know that there's no point in arguing. So where do you sleep?"

"Under the stars, under trees . . . anywhere," I replied.

"Well then, we have a short while before night settles in, so perhaps you'll join us for some sweet fruits before you go," he said.

"I would like that," I replied, surprised and grateful that he didn't question my habits.

Jin went to cut some sweet-fruits from the area outside the hut, and Jan sat watching me with a concerned expression.

"You could stay here," Jan said eventually. "Jin likes you, I can tell."

"And I like Jin, and you," I replied.

"But," he stated. "It's more than that. Jin *really* likes you. I see his eyes smile as well as his mouth when you talk; I've not seen that for a very long time. He is a fine man; you would have everything you needed and I would not get in your way. You could both go somewhere nicer. I know he would provide for you well."

I looked at Jan and my heart felt heavy. I know he spoke the truth. Jin was beautiful, kind and strong. He would be the perfect mate. I wished, oh, I wished my heart could say yes.

"Jin is a fine man, the finest I've met," I sighed. "But – and there is a but – I am looking for something, I do not know exactly what that is yet, but I cannot rest until I find it."

Jan looked sad and shook his head.

"If you change your mind, or if you find what you're looking for," Jan considered, "you'll still be welcome here."

"Thank you," I said. "I won't forget either of you."

There was a slightly awkward silence when Jin returned with the freshly picked fruit, but in no time this awkwardness was forgotten, and conversation was once again pleasant and flowing. After the three of us had nibbled on small, delicious sweet-fruits, the brothers started yawning. Night was settling in. It was time for me to go.

I gave my thanks, bade my farewells, and gathered my bale. I could hear the two brothers talking quietly; Jan seemed to be scolding Jin, but his voice was too hushed for me to hear their words. There was another moment of awkwardness when I returned and Jin showed me out. He walked a little with me; I knew he was thinking of what to say, wondering how to ask me to stay. I decided to broach the subject first.

"Jin," I said, feeling oddly shy. "You and your brother are the finest men I have met. Jan has already asked me to stay, but . . ."

"He has?" Jin interrupted, seemingly surprised, then he laughed. "Yes, he knows me a little too well sometimes. Tachra . . ."

I put my hand to his lips to silence him.

"I cannot stay, although I wish that I could," I sighed. "I am not a whole person yet. There are things I must do and find."

"I will wait for you," he said.

"No, do not," I replied. "Find a better woman, one with a settled heart."

"I do not think that possible," he sighed. "I have met many while I have been here, yet none such as you. But I am not a fool; I know you will not stay, and so perhaps I will try to find someone. You have given me hope." He looked at me, frowning. "Tachra, do not go to Hollow. Turn back, go anywhere else but there."

His conviction took me a little by surprise.

"Hollow is not good to everyone," Jin added. "It controls its people, it doesn't care about them; it's not the sort of place where you choose where or when you sleep, or what you eat or with whom. You will not like it there, and in any case, they might not let you leave. Please, Tachra, don't go there."

I thought for a moment and looked into his eyes; they were genuinely full of concern. "Would you be living there if Jan had not hurt his legs?" I asked.

"Maybe, but . . ." he began to reply, but I cut in.

"Then I must see for myself," I added. "And please do not be concerned. I have come this far; I can look after myself."

"Is there nothing I can do to persuade you?" Jin said, shaking his head.

"No," I replied. I smiled at him. He was such a handsome man, his concern made him even more beautiful. "I'll go now, but I will not forget you, Jin."

"Nor I you, Tachra," he smiled.

Before I threw my bundle over my shoulder and turned away, he pulled me close and wrapped his strong arms around me.

Then he kissed me, my first kiss, not the hesitant pecks I had seen others give, but a passionate kiss, as if he was wrapping me entirely in him. I felt his heart thumping against my chest, and my whole body tingled in response. For a moment I considered staying in that embrace, in those arms, and that moment seemed to last an eternity, and yet no time at all. How I wished I had a settled heart!

He let me go and stroked my hair.

"Do not let Hollow spoil you," he said. "You are welcome back here anytime, as traveller, friend, or more. Anytime."

"Thank you," I whispered. I picked up my bundle – I must have dropped it during our embrace – and then threw it over my shoulder. I went to say good-bye, but this time he put his hand to my mouth to silence me, leaned forward and gently kissed my forehead. Without a word, he turned and walked back towards his hut.

I stood watching him until he got to the door, still with fleeting thoughts of running after him, even though I knew in my heart that it would not be right. He didn't turn as he passed the threshold of the hut, and I sensed both great sadness and great happiness in him. It was a strange mixture. As soon as he was out of sight, and the door had shut once again, I waited a moment more before turning and starting to walk away.

I didn't venture far, stopping a little way past a dune from where I could still see their hut. Although I was very tired, I couldn't sleep. Finally, when the sky was lit up with the familiar pale blue light in the distance, I fixed my eye on the hut, waiting. As I had expected, the core of light soon hovered over the brothers' hut, and this confirmation of my thoughts felt oddly calming. Now I knew for sure that the blue light followed people during their sleep.

I determined there and then to find the origin of that blue light: it was more than I could see, and I had to know what it was and why it was so interested in people when they slept. Finding the home of the blue light would be one of my goals.

As I started walking, I thought again of Tooth and Jin and Jan, and the blue light that fell over their huts too. I knew that I would find what I was looking for, even if I had to walk to where the sun fell from the sky.

On the third day of walking at a leisurely pace, having survived on the food that was already in my belly and a few of the sour fruits that inundated the landscape, and choosing not to stop at any more of the in-between huts, Hollow eventually came in sight. At last.

My elevated position gave me an excellent view of the settlement. Hollow was huge – at least twenty times the size of Threetops. The afternoon sun glaring down on the tightly packed huts made it look like a forest. It was laid out in an almost perfect circle, with huts arranged in rings, all facing inwards towards one central area that seemed to have no building in it at all. Even the farming land encircled the village in one slender band.

This is the place I sensed the strongest, I silently spoke to him.

I felt his presence move around me, but he did not reply. I knew that this place, just like any other human settlement, was insignificant to him.

Maybe you should be interested, I thought, *for if you are aware of existence through my experiences; does it not affect you what I do and where I go?*

Although he did not need to reply, I was sure that I sensed his approval of my reasoning.

I descended from my elevated position and continued towards Hollow. As I approached, a single path running straight into the dwellings came into view. I cut across the flatland and took to the well-trodden trail, clasping my bundle and adopting my familiar smile of greeting, as if I was pleased to be there. If Mags' suggestions were right, this place would not be surprised to see an unfamiliar face.

I passed through the outer ring of farmland, musing that such meagre crops could never feed the masses that must live there, and soon entered the outskirts of Hollow.

Hollow felt dim and sombre as soon as I moved into the shadow of the huts. All the dwellings were far smaller and made of darker wood than the ones I was use to. They were built so closely together it gave a gloomy feel to the otherwise bright day. There was little or no greenery around each dwelling; instead, a wide walkway ran towards the centre of the village with narrow tracks criss-crossing between them. The ground was pale and dry, kicking up dust as I walked, and the air was full of the stink of faeces. This was not an attractive place; it lacked the abundant blooms and grasses of Threetops and the general sound of children playing that I imagined you should hear in every village.

At that moment, two children wearing matching red tunics emerged in front of me, struggling with a heavy pail of water. They stopped to reposition their hands and glanced up as I approached. I smiled, but they didn't smile back. Instead, they picked up their pail and hurried on their way.

"Where is your well?" I called after them.

One of the children pointed without slowing his stride. Then the children turned a corner and out of my line of sight.

I headed towards the direction they had pointed in, passing a group of women wearing the same deep red robes, although theirs were longer, and covered their heads. Some of the women were feeding little ones; others sat busily pounding grain in large bowls. I received only a few glances from them, and I kept up my smile, but I could not tell if it was returned. Gradually, the path between the huts widened into a clearing, where people, still all dressed in red, were hoisting pails of water. I had clearly found the well.

I called out 'good day' to a man who passed me.

He flatly ignored me.

Feeling awkward, I walked up to the queue for the well and waited my turn. As I stood in line, someone came and stood a little too closely behind me. I shuffled casually forward, trying to move further away without drawing attention to myself, but whoever it was moved forward again so that their chin was almost touching my shoulder.

"Do you come to reside, or for the fire?" the person whispered in my ear.

It was a female voice. I had no idea what she was talking about, but thanked the skies that she had provided me – such an obvious stranger – with a reason to be there. And at last, here was somebody willing to converse with me.

"The fire," I nodded, assuming she meant a warm hearth. I looked around to find a slim woman dressed in the now familiar red.

"You cannot walk around without reds then," she stated flatly, moving a step back and clearly losing interest in me.

"I do not have any reds," I responded.

"But you must," she protested, tutted, and then hurriedly continued. "Well, I suppose you had better get your water and then follow me. I have spares."

I started to thank her, but she was already walking away, her hips swinging as she nodded to those who passed her by. Once my turn had arrived at the well, and my water pots were full, I looked around and saw her lingering in the distance. She nodded, turned, and started walking again.

I guessed I was supposed to follow her, so I did. She made her way to a hut and went inside, leaving the door ajar. I followed her in. As soon as I'd entered, she closed the door and unwound her head covering. She was pretty but sharp featured, and only a little older than I.

"If you come for the fire you cannot attend without reds," she declared again, looking me up and down. "You certainly can't walk around dressed like that."

She began searching through an orderly pile of linens heaped in one corner, scattering them all over the floor.

"Here," she said, thrusting a pile of red fabric into my arms. "I suppose you can have the reds of my sister. She ceased four moons ago. Although you'd best make sure you see Huru before the day is out to get other clothing to wear tomorrow. You cannot wear the reds then, it's not fire, and your clothes are ugly."

"Thank you," I said uncertainly, but not forgetting my manners. I didn't much like her attitude to me, but she was the only person who'd been willing to talk, so I felt as if I should be grateful. "I'll give you them back," I added.

"Don't bother. They're too small for me anyway," she shrugged.

"Do you not have children who could wear them in the future?" I asked, as I looked around. She was old enough to have several children, but there was only one bedding room and it only had one bed.

"Of course I have children," she rolled her eyes as if I should know better. "But they don't need those."

"Where do they sleep? With you?" I asked, trying to strike a conversation.

"Don't be silly, that wouldn't be practical," she said dismissively. "My children live with the old women somewhere around here. I wouldn't want all that disturbance. Anyway, that's all old women are good for."

I went to disagree, but bit my tongue and decided to be direct yet polite. "I came here for water and food. I don't know of any

136

'fire', but if it guarantees a full belly then please show me the way. My name is Tachra and I come from Threetops; it's a long way from here."

She snorted derisively, as if she was laughing at me. "It doesn't matter where you're from, you're here now," she replied. "I'm Rian. I thought you must be relative to Wirrel, perhaps from Rainmouth or Meadsins, but your words sound too strange. You've picked a good day to come here, Wirrel takes the fire test and everyone attends. And yes, you will find a full belly and a full bed too, no doubt." She laughed at her own words. I couldn't see what was funny.

"Come, we must leave now. We don't want to miss it."

I finished tying the long red robe and hastily wound the length of attached fabric around my head, not entirely happy to wear the garments of someone who had ceased. Rian nodded, leaned forward, and loosened the gown's belt whilst plumping up the fabric so that it stood away from my body.

"Is that right?" I asked, noticing the smooth, body skimming lines she had folded her own gown into.

"Of course!" she retorted, and hastily motioned me outside.

The dusty tracks were now a teaming mass of red, with women wearing the same long robes as me, men in short red tunics, and many children walking in clumps with older women, all dressed in the same red. I certainly would have looked out of place if Rian hadn't provided my outfit. We fell in with the crowd, passing the well and moving into an open area at the centre of the village.

The central area was a large circular space with a cobbled stone floor. Many people had already gathered and were sitting in three distinct groups: the largest group consisted entirely of men, the smallest group was all women, and the middle group comprised mainly of children sitting with a few unveiled older women keeping them orderly. A shallow pit filled with wood and dried bracken nestled in the centre; everyone faced towards it. Behind it, I spotted lines of wide tables, all piled full of colourful foods. My mouth watered and I wanted to go towards the food, but Rian guided me to sit with the other women.

As the last of the crowds settled down in their groups, a large man walked into the centre.

"That's Huru," Rian sighed fondly. He seemed to have caught everyone's attention, but not mine; this man was stocky and ugly, not the tall, black-eyed one I'd hoped he might be.

Huru bowed and smiled at the people.

"Today," he announced loudly to everyone, "Wirrel takes the fire test."

Everyone started smiling and clapping, and Rian nudged me as she whooped with delight, making me join in the applause. And yet as the crowds cheered I sensed a quiet gasp from someone nearby and quickly glanced around. A young woman sat at the end of the row, her head downcast, as if weeping.

While everyone clapped, busily watching Huru bow and smile to the crowds, I spotted a slim young man emerging from a hut on the far side. He was shadowed closely by two others and had his head bowed, his unruly mop of thick brown hair falling over his tanned face. He walked with difficulty, as if exhausted, and his arms were tied firmly behind his back with a thick piece of twine. I noticed he wasn't wearing red clothes like everyone else, and that his brown tunic was dirty and torn. The two men either side of him, dressed entirely in black so they looked like shadows, directed him towards Huru. They stopped, placing a pail before the captive man.

The crowd roared 'Wirrel!' jubilantly as soon as they saw the young man. The woman to my far side gasped again, but nobody paid any attention to her. Huru held up his thick arms and all went quiet.

"I call the fire-bringer," he announced.

The crowds strained their heads, all looking in the direction of the women. The young woman who had been weeping silently arose, pushed the hair from her face, and gathered herself.

"It is I," she stated calmly.

"Soul," Huru smiled and held out his hand.

Soul walked forward, and all eyes followed her as she took Huru's hand.

The bound young man, Wirrel, whimpered as though in pain as Soul passed him, but she threw him a look that silenced him.

In that instant, the silent communication that passed between made me realise that they knew each other well.

"We know how to quench Wirrel's fire, don't we?" Huru shouted, holding up Soul's arm.

The crowds cheered.

Huru paraded the young woman, holding her hand in the air and twirling her around.

"Soul the fire-bringer!" he announced at regular intervals.

With each announcement, the cheering grew.

Then Huru suddenly pulled Soul to face him. He pushed her sharply to the ground, making her fall hard on her back. She remained lying as Huru slowly kneeled before her and put his hands under the hem of her robe, unhurriedly sliding them up her legs until her skirt lifted to her thighs. He pushed himself up and leaned back on his knees, looking down at her. I didn't like his sneering smile, or what he was doing to this young woman, but the crowds were delighted. He fiddled under his own robe then and spread his knees, forcing her legs apart. Almost drooling, he bent over her, his large arms holding his face above her own, and then he lowered his hips, arched his back, and started rocking against her.

Wirrel had his eyes closed, his jaw held together so tightly I could see ripples moving in his face, clearly angered at what was taking place. I was similarly distraught, but everyone else seemed to approve. Rian especially seemed to be thoroughly engrossed, cheering and clapping louder than most.

Perhaps this is Hollow's equivalent of a choosing, I wondered.

Other than Soul's head banging against the stones as she rocked back and forth, she didn't move or make a sound. After a short while, Huru gave one last aggressive thrust, let out a long snarl and stopped. He slowly stood back up with sweat dripping down his face, smiling, and pulled the woman to her feet.

"I have faced the challenge and I have no fire," Huru announced. "Soul is cured."

The crowds roared even louder as the young man, still bound, fell to his knees. Soul moved to aid him, but one of the shadow men guarding him roughly pushed her aside, while another promptly dragged Wirrel back up to his feet. Barred from reaching Wirrel by the large man, Soul shakily smoothed her robes as she was ushered out of the centre. She returned to sit a few women away from me. I caught her eye, but she quickly looked down.

Huru walked towards the visibly shaking and bound Wirrel.

Wirrel lifted his head and his hair fell away from his large brown eyes. I saw a look in his eyes that I had never seen before. It was pure hatred.

Wirrel spat in Huru's face. Huru wiped the spit away, smiling, and leaned forward, whispering something in Wirrel's ear that made him thrash violently in response. He tried desperately to get to Huru, but the shadow men held him fast and Huru just laughed, turning from Wirrel to face the people again.

"Wirrel cannot be cured; he has the fire," he declared. "Wirrel still has fire!"

A group of four men had walked out of the largest hut, each carrying what looked like large barrels. They set these objects down and began punching the tops of them with their fists, creating a pounding rhythm that made the people yell even more. Huru grasped the neck of Wirrel's tunic and, with one swift motion, ripped it from his back. From a small pail that had been placed by his feet, Huru commenced painting him with a dark gloopy substance. Wirrel was still shivering, but he didn't utter a sound.

The two shadow men escorted Wirrel towards the pit in the centre of the circle, where they chaperoned him down a small set of concealed steps until only his head and shoulders protruded from the bracken. The shadow men bent down, did something around Wirrel's feet, and then walked out of the pit, leaving Wirrel and kicking the deadwood that they had dislodged back into the pit.

"To the fire!" Huru shouted, drawing my attention away from Wirrel. I noticed that Huru now held up a long stick, ablaze at one end.

The pounding of the drums increased, and Wirrel started wriggling profusely, but he seemed to be held to the spot – he clearly couldn't get out of the hole in the ground. I sensed his fear; I could now smell it so strongly that it blanked out the enthusiasm of the crowds around me.

"You will never burn out my fire for Soul!" I heard Wirrel shout. "Never!"

The people around me began standing up, clapping, yelling, and surging forward. I went to get to my feet, but their pushing and shoving kept me down as they stamped their feet in time to the rhythm of the pounding drums.

"No!" I shrieked, as I realised what was about to take place. They were about to set Wirrel on fire. They intended to put that torch to the bracken around him and burn him.

"No!" I shrieked again, but the rapturous applause of the crowds drowned me out.

I tried to stand, but a hand grabbed my skirt and yanked me so violently that I went sprawling to the ground, hitting my head hard. A pain shot through me and I felt warm blood seeping down my face.

I fought, pushed, and struggled to find my feet but everybody moved around me, standing on my sprawled limbs and pushing me back down. The shouts and cheering now almost drowned out the screams that had started coming from Wirrel. Although I could barely hear him, in my mind I heard his screams louder than the noise from all the others put together.

The smoke from burning wood wafted through the air, growing fiercer and more pungent as Wirrel's painful screams wailed above the crowds delight. I nearly found my feet again, but someone kicked me hard and shoved their foot firmly in my abdomen to keep me down. I kept screaming 'no', but nobody heard.

His pain! They are burning him! I thought. *They must stop his pain!* It was agony, and I felt it as if it was my own.

Wrong! This is wrong! I called to the Earth-voice.

But I could not hear his reply, if indeed he replied at all. I felt a surge of anger rise from my belly, far greater than the surges I felt at seeing the blue light. I could not contain it. I gathered as much breath into my lungs as I could.

"Stop! Stop the fire!" I screamed, as the surge of pain and fear welled up from my stomach into my mouth.

"STOP!"

The burning of Wirrel had created my own fire; it had sprung from my belly with words that had a vehemence I didn't realise I possessed. Then all my energy had gone, drained away while I lay in the heaving crowds with the foot firmly shoved into my belly, still pinning me down as I tried desperately to resist. I had to help Wirrel – he was in such pain – but the people around me seemed to take delight in what was happening to him, and nobody was listening to me.

The crowds above me still shouted and clapped in time to the beating drums, egging the terrible activity on, but I could hear the cheers changing. Jeers and boos and whispers of confusion took over as the clapping became slower and more sporadic, and then the drums stopped. I tried to push myself up again, but the foot still held me firmly down. My head throbbed, and the blood now trickled down my ear.

"The fire has gone out," I heard someone say above me.

"How could that be? He was well doused," another whispered.

"*Fire! Fire! Fire!*" the people chanted.

"No, stop! You must stop," I tried shouting again. But it only came out as a whisper.

Through the darkness of my mind I sensed Wirrel, although I could not see him. I knew that his pain was so unbearable that he could no longer scream. A picture came into my head that sickened me: that of a hairless blackened body in the flameless smoke. In my mind I saw that the flames had ceased, but now all Wirrel wished to do was cease also.

I heard a flame taken, once again, to the smouldering bracken and the terrible crackling of burning restarted as the crowds surged forward and the drums started beating once more. I felt the foot lift its weight from my belly, and then hands pulled me upwards. I tried to stand, but could not get my feet beneath me, let alone hold my own weight. I strived to open my eyes, but they had been stuck together by something. I felt myself staggering forward, leaning on a shoulder, and the sounds of the horde gradually grew dimmer.

The pain throbbed through me. And then I felt nothing. Suddenly everything went black

SEVEN

All the display panels lit up in the docking bays. At the same time, a shrill alarm started sounding in quick bursts.

"Prepare the ships to launch to the new co-ordinates as they come in," Chia commanded his crew, running towards the controls. "And all of you, keep your communications links open."

Deactivating the alarm, he started rapidly punching in codes.

"This is what we've been waiting for," he announced, "It's another energy wave. This is not a drill!"

The dispatch team were already sprinting around the ships while Chia worked as quickly as he could.

"Come on," he muttered to himself. "Feel it, Chia, you know you can."

He quickly focused his chi on Earth's imaginary grid; he felt the general direction of the energy surge and began drawing his senses in deeper. There: that was it. Stage one of five complete. The next grid appeared in his mind. Stage two; yes, it was clear – there it was. The energy was undoubtedly emitting from there.

Zoom in deeper still. Harder to detect; he had to search. Yes, stage three of five complete.

Suddenly he stopped and stared at the sensor readings; they showed nothing and he felt nothing. The surge had disappeared.

"Damn!" he cursed, thumping the controls, "Eskah and damnation! It's gone. It barely lasted a moment."

There hadn't been enough time to locate the exact position of the energy surge. He had failed.

"Forward findings," he called out flatly.

The display immediately responded: 'Flight and Sensitive Division; target analyses failed.'

"You can all stop and return to the standard rota. I didn't get the co-ordinates," Chia announced, rubbing his brow. "Set the ships back onto their automated harvesting sweeps as per our standard grid co-ordinates. Nirrious, see to it that the grid is reduced according to the new parameters. At least we have managed to narrow the boundaries a little. I'm taking a break."

Chia returned to his quarters, knowing that his energy levels had reached a hazardous all-time low. His chambers were cold and felt unlived in, with a fine layer of dust on every surface and the metallic smell of newness still hanging in the air. He ignored the supposed comfort zone – a solitary recliner – and the entertainment modules that still sat in their protective wrapping, choosing to sit on the floor by the portals, staring out at the stars.

By Eskah! he thought, curbing his frustration. He should be out there, trailblazing, sensing new bounties for them all, not stuck here on this confined substation performing one analysis after another. His discovery of Earth was becoming a curse. He'd recommended that they leave the planet alone, regardless of its resources. Instead, they'd requested him to act as Head Sensitive on the project. How could he refuse the position? He couldn't, and so he did his job, and did it well. And now he would be disciplined for the very skills that they had requested him for. He had one chance to locate the source of the surge, and he had failed. Everything he had tried in connection with this planet had failed. This was not good.

For a fleeting moment, Chia considered requesting a transfer from his current position. He would need a good reason, though. Perhaps he should tell them exactly what happened to him when he first discovered planet Earth. No, he reasoned with himself, they would take him off any project that utilized his sensitivity. They would want him to be numbed, and they wouldn't want him trailblazing again, ever. He couldn't bear the thought of that.

His thoughts were interrupted as his direct link with the docking bay called for his attention.

"I'm on my way," he announced before anyone could speak. Could he not even have a few moments' peace?

"Haven't you read your comms?" came the reply. It was the dock's captain, Nirrious.

Chia looked around at his communication port. It didn't show any messages.

"I don't have any," he said, getting up.

"You should have," Nirrious stated. "Everyone has had the same message from the Supreme, and I sent you another, immediately afterwards, saying that you wouldn't be needed back at the bays until morning. I'd not received your confirmation, so here I am."

Chia walked to his port and double checked its status. It was on, and there weren't any messages from anybody. He deactivated the screen, making the workings unfold to display the internal systems. The discrepancy was immediately obvious: the port's receiving crystal was missing.

"I'll confirm now. Contact me directly if I'm needed. And thank you, Nirrious."

Chia scanned the floor for the missing crystal, and then started moving furniture and boxes.

The missing crystal wasn't anywhere in Chia's room, nor should it have been. It should have been firmly lodged in his communication port, where any comms crystal should live. *Well,* he mused, *at least that explains why nobody has contacted me recently.*

He pulled out his flight case and selected a crystal used for ship-to-ship transmissions, adeptly modified it, and then placed it in the port. The connection wavered briefly, and then activated.

Chia's first transmission was to the comms division, who insisted his port hadn't been touched. The crystal would be tuned to his energy only and useless to any other kutu, they said, and no, they could not have made an error, and no, it had not been serviced since the substation had become habited. Chia eventually gave up grilling them, having to accept their assessment that the error must lay with him. Now he turned to deal with the problem in hand: his missing messages.

Chia knew that copies of communications were never kept, but that all messages held an energy print for a short while, and Chia was good with anything that worked with energy. He assembled a link to his port and pushed out his chi, passing through the connection and looking into the machine as if he were part of it. Little fragments of data floated aimlessly; some with strong definition, some now too faded to touch. He pulled together any he could grasp, channelled them into the new crystal, and disconnected.

Yes, that was good enough, he decided, looking at the results as they flickered onto the screen. He had managed to retrieve eighteen full and partial messages – three were complete and fifteen were fragments.

The first message was from Nirrious, as expected. He skipped passed it. The next was from the Supreme, marked as urgent and issued to all on board substation XLS.

"Salutations," the Supreme's voice began. "On behalf of the council I would like to thank you all for your efforts to analyse the new Earth energy. However, our usual methods have proved ineffective. As a result, we have re-evaluated procedures, and particularly revised the protocol guiding us not to take any action that could hinder planetary system establishment. In order to speed up our search for this new energy, which we are now setting as priority, we have selected personnel to be stationed on Earth's surface. These assignees will join the XLS shortly. I ask that you give them any assistance they require. Current procedures are on hold while new protocols are put into place. It's been millennia since we discovered a new energy; long may we enjoy reaping it once it's harvested."

Chia sat back with a smile; maybe at last he would be off the Earth project and would be able to go out trailblazing again.

The port moved onto the next message. It was from Orion, transcript only. Only the first and last lines were hand written; the rest was a copy of a document.

"Chia, my friend, please read," the first line stated.

Chia skimmed through the main body of text and then stopped, moving closer to the display. He read it again, making sure that what he thought he was reading was correct. It was. Orion was overseer of the new Earth project. His position was approved, his team selected, and they were on route to the XLS substation, due to dock tomorrow at 14.5.

Then the final line, in Orion's elongated scrawl, read, 'I hope to see you then.'

The message was already a day old. It was already 'tomorrow'. Orion's ship would be docking anytime now.

Chia just made it to the bays in time. The landing pod had already arrived and the pod's hatch was open. A huge kutu, clad in golden armour, waited in the entrance, his short golden hair and radiant golden wings making him easily recognisable as Stanze. Stanze noticed Chia and nodded discreetly.

A similarly adorned huge warrior emerged from the ship, his golden helmet unfolded to show that it was Peniva; head of the Anumi. Peniva was the only Anumi to have wings even larger than Stanze, and the two standing side by side made the side of the craft glow with golden light. It was a vision of contained might. Peniva exchanged a few words with Stanze, before they both exited through a door in the far corner of the bay.

Moments later, Orion emerged. Robed entirely in his customary red, his gown had creased and his long red hair cascaded in ragged twists around him, blending in with his robe. He wore his long Kathani at his hip. Chia had not seen a kutu wearing a Kathani blade for many years; Orion's glinted with the power of his pure red energy.

Orion's eyes flickered absently around the room. They illuminated as soon as he spotted Chia.

Orion strode towards him, smiling. "I'm glad you're here. You have been very difficult to contact recently."

"As have you, my friend. Much has happened since I last saw you," Chia replied.

"Indeed," Orion nodded. "We should go somewhere to talk."

Chia guided Orion from the bays, talking amicably about general matters until they reached Chia's quarters. Orion settled down cross-legged on the floor by the portals, while Chia poured them both refreshments.

"I see you have made yourself comfortable here," Orion laughed, looking around at the sparseness.

"I do not intend on staying any longer than necessary." Chia handed him a long goblet full of smoking Ochrah, Orion's favourite drink, and sat down on the floor opposite him. "Although the years seem to be fusing together without an opportunity to leave."

"Then my new mission may be of particular interest to you."

Orion proceeded to explain the mission summary. It sounded fascinating, and well planned, with five kutu going directly to the planet to track the elusive energy source and another team of five remaining on the substation to analyse findings.

"There should be ten of us," Orion disclosed, "I have nine . . . would like you to join us? It's already approved, if you will accept."

"I am already assigned here to analysis of this energy, and so I am virtually a part of your mission anyway," Chia stated.

"But I don't want you with the team that stays here on the substation," Orion paused. "I want you on the planet's surface with me and three others."

"Oh no, no, no. I don't think so," Chia laughed.

"Chia, I know of the trouble you had when you were there before, but you're the only one who knows what it's like. I believe that whatever we're looking for, you truly felt it."

"No, it felt me," Chia replied, "and it was not good."

"I do understand . . ."

"I don't see how you can understand. This force, this energy, whatever it is on planet Earth is as potent as it is elusive. It breezed into my chi so strongly that I lost all sense of here and now. Can you imagine what it is like to lose time, to see things that do not exist, to truly believe you are somewhere else, some*time* else – to think that you are losing your mind? What I saw was dreadful, full of things far beyond any imaginary horrors. And this was not for a mere moment, Orion, it lasted months. It almost broke me. And I still don't like discussing it, even with you."

"Chia," Orion said gently, "When you returned and stayed with me on leave, I felt it from you; it was terrible."

"I know," Chia sighed, rubbing his brow. "You helped a great deal."

Orion put his hand on Chia's shoulder. "You're my greatest friend; if I could have taken the pain for you I would have. But I do think that returning to Earth may help you to heal those wounds further. You could find answers and understanding."

"They are not wounds," Chia shook his head. "It *took* something from me. As a result, I've lost many of my skills. I'm burnt out. I feel like a shell of who I used to be."

"Perhaps your skills are not lost, just buried," Orion nodded. "Perhaps you have buried them to protect yourself. And even without them, you are still our most talented sensitive. If you came to Earth, you'd be prepared this time. You could put up barriers. You could re-tune to be pure flesh so your chi was less accessible. And you wouldn't be on your own; I would be there, as well as others I trust. Our well-being would be top priority."

Chia didn't reply. He didn't want to go back to that place, but Orion had a very valid point. Perhaps the only way to heal something was to fully understand it. And if that wasn't possible, perhaps returning to the place that almost destroyed him might rid him of the fear he now felt about his own skills.

Orion sensed Chia's hesitancy, and activated the mission outline to show Chia who else would be with them.

"They're all skilled in their fields and visionaries in their own right," Orion nodded, "One from each colour: Me, red; Kraniel, green; Stanze, gold, Jychanumun, black and white; and you; violet. You know most of them well. We'd make a fine team."

"Who is this Jychanumun? I didn't think you could get black and white."

"Nor did I. I've met no other like him. Chia . . ." Orion paused, "he has black eyes."

Chia's insides instinctively leapt, but as he thought about it, he felt a huge wave of relief.

"Perhaps that explains that part of my vision. Perhaps I had caught sight of him on Eden, and it was a subconscious addition to my delusions."

"Plausible," Orion nodded. "I would like you to meet him, regardless of your decision. He's been in virtual isolation for millennia. I did not think he would agree to join this mission, but he did, without question. It all started with the composition . . ."

"You must know I have many questions about that," Chia interposed.

"And I will answer whatever you wish to know," Orion smiled. "I called it the Summoning Song. It is, was, beautiful, wasn't it?"

Orion went on to explain his original motives for the composition. He spoke of the years spent trawling through all the ancient manuscripts, which Chia had often helped with when on leave from trailblazing duties. He told of the search for hidden theories, and of the recent detection of certain common factors running through their oldest text. Contained within the myth of the sleeping ageless one, within the text named the Summoning, was a code. It was so plain to see within the text that it had remained unnoticed, despite countless readings. It seemed impossible to decipher, at least until Orion, out of curiosity, and as a last resort, had loaded it into his music console.

"It was only because the script kept referring to the Song of Awakening that I even tried to decipher it. Once I heard it, I knew there was something in it, but I was not sensitive enough to know what to do with it. So my friend, you had the only copy, programmed it so it could only ever be played once, by you."

"You specifically chose me?"

"It had to be you," Orion smiled, "You are the most straightforward yet inquisitive kutu I know, a sensitive without preconceptions, a pure violet-blue; instinctively drawn to truth and change. You intuitively know the right place and time to do many things, including, I hoped, releasing the Summoning Song. In the past, you were drawn to discover that little planet, Earth; I believe the two are interlinked. I believe the song holds a link to the last of the Old Ones."

"It seems too incredible," Chia considered, drifting deep into thought. "Although the first energy wave did coincide with playing the music. And I had a momentary flashback . . ."

"So, knowing you are already part of this adventure, and knowing that your safety will be a priority, will you join my team?"

Chia had already made up his mind.

"I will."

"I have been counting on your acceptance. I haven't made my theories public yet, and won't until I know for sure; I don't want to appear like a dreaming fool. For now, we are merely tracking a new energy source."

"What preparations are required?" Chia remarked, his mind switching to practicalities.

"Arrangements are in hand," Orion replied. "We leave tomorrow. I took the liberty of sending Shursa a message regarding your reassignment. Nirrious is overseeing the set up of the receiving base here on the XLS, and is readying our ship for departure. Matters are in order. For now," he concluded, "as overseer of this mission, I decree that this evening is for friends. We are simply to enjoy ourselves."

Chia didn't object. That evening they sat on the dusty floor, drinking the last of Chia's personal supply of Ochrah, and talking philosophy that digressed into nonsense. Once the morning was close and Orion had succumbed to sleep, Chia set an alarm for him, prepared his flight case, and left his room.

The launching bay was relatively quiet, and Chia found the prepared ship, the 7A, low on the deck, full to capacity, with the crew appreciative of his presence after so much activity. As he entered the ship, he began the checks that the crew had already completed twice.

By the time Chia was finished, the 7A had informed him that the remainder of the team were waiting in the bay. He then scanned his future team-mates, allowing the 7A to adjust its settings to their energies.

Orion stood between Kraniel and Stanze. Kraniel was roaring with laughter and Stanze was glaring at him, clearly not amused, a fact that in turn amused Chia greatly; these two were obviously not yet very familiar with each other. There were several kutu standing in small groups who would be remaining on the XLS, and another, in an unknown uniform, standing apart from the others in the far corner. His black mouldings and black hair made his skin look translucently white. Chia couldn't see his face, as his back was turned, but knew it had to be Jychanumun.

As the 7A scanned him, Jychanumun slowly turned. Chia had been told of his black eyes, but seeing them, remembering his hallucinations, almost made him reel backwards.

Jychanumun walked forward, his abyssal eyes making it impossible to know whether he was returning his gaze or not, and approached the 7A, placing a palm on its gleaming exterior.

Suddenly, Chia's mind was filled with thoughts he knew were not his own. *Please, I have no malice*, the words reverberated through his head.

Chia didn't think he blinked, but perhaps he did, for the next moment Jychanumun wasn't standing next to the 7A, he was in the far corner of the bay with his back to him, exactly as he had been when he first saw him. It was impossible – only a second had passed.

"Has Jychanumun approached you in the last thirty seconds?" Chia quickly asked the 7A.

Negative, the 7A's display blinked.

Chia stood, momentarily stunned, and then gritted his teeth and gathered his thoughts. *Fight it*, he thought to himself. *You don't want to be pulled off the mission.* He took several long, deep breaths, focussed and composed himself, and then continued with the scanning. He was just finishing, and deep in concentration, when he felt a tug on his chi that made him jump. It was Shursa.

"So, you agreed to join Orion's team," Shursa commented.

"Yes," Chia replied warily, exiting the 7A and trying to avoid Shursa's bitter yellow energy before it affected him.

"I could have been too, if I'd requested it," Shursa said haughtily, following him from the ship. "Nevertheless, the council needs me here."

Chia didn't reply.

Shursa stopped, holding Chia's arm, making him stop too. Chia felt a shiver run up his back.

"For your vital part in discovering the planet, Una and the council wish to show their appreciation. This is for you," councillor Shursa smiled. He produced a small, ornately carved, marbline box, holding it out expectantly. "The Supreme has asked me to present this."

Chia looked at the box, then at Shursa, knowing Shursa usually took every opportunity to humiliate him and feeling slightly suspicious of his motives.

"From the Supreme?" Chia questioned.

Shursa nodded. He seemed to be genuinely smiling with pleasure.

Chia bowed. "Then please convey my thanks to Una and the council," he said, accepting the box. "And thank you for taking the time to present it."

Shursa returned the bow, and then turned and watched as Orion approached. "Orion," he nodded curtly. "I have been instructed to inform you to contact me directly for anything you need."

"Thank you, councillor," Orion bowed, and then turned to Chia. "I believe we are ready to depart."

The launch went smoothly and, once they were a safe distance from the base, Chia switched the ship to automatic. He would be the pilot, as well as the sensitive, on this mission. As a trailblazer he was well versed with the dual role.

"Flight time set for eight hours, as requested," Chia informed Orion. "Is there any reason why we're prolonging the journey?"

"To give us time to re-tune to the flesh," Orion answered. "If it's not done slowly we'll all feel very unpleasant when we reach Earth." He indicated towards the long benches. "I'll start now."

Chia nodded, and seated himself next to Stanze, with Kraniel and Jychanumun opposite them.

"I need to implant your communication device first," Orion stated, looking at Chia. "We already have ours."

He picked up an alarming-looking long implement and moved towards Chia, who flinched, thinking he was about to get the length of the tool inserted into his head.

Orion gently brushed his ear and then pulled back, smiling wryly when he saw his friend's startled expression.

"Done," he said, "Nanos will be implanting now. The communication devices are new: they are called HOTS, or High Organic Transmitting Screeners. They work with voluntary submission only, and each one is tuned to our individual pulses so that nobody outside our circle has access to our communications. You'll be able to communicate with anyone in the group from a reasonable distance."

Orion moved so that he could address the whole group.

"From now on we always communicate using these HOTS. You speak aloud as normal, the HOTS activate as soon as any of us talk and you use your chi or senses to direct that speech to one or more members of this group. Understood?"

The team readily assented: the technology followed a fairly standard procedure, with the exception of the screening nanos, which were designed for privacy. It seemed that Orion felt the need for a degree of discretion.

"Good," Orion continued. "We're going to re-tune to become high physical, low energy – that is, ninety percent physical and ten percent energy. None of us has been attuned to such an extreme ratio for long periods, and you'll feel very restricted at first, but the ratio is compatible with the Earth. From the information we have from Chia's previous visit, I believe this unknown energy will enhance our abilities, and so protection is advised. We're going physical to protect ourselves."

Orion opened a small carbon case and selected five retuning discs. Starting with Stanze, he meticulously worked the sensors, adjusting them for each kutu.

"So it is you I must blame for having to be fleshy is it, Chia?" Kraniel piped up. "Have I ever told you how much I disliked it?"

"No, but the story of your time working in flesh with the Tala energy is very funny," Chia smiled, knowing Kraniel hated that tale.

"You've heard of that?" Kraniel grimaced, "That was not funny."

Orion placed a retuning disc on Chia's forehead and moved along to Kraniel, carefully positioning another small, glowing disc on his forehead. Jychanumun was next, and then Orion sat down, placing the last disc on himself.

"Whatever we're looking for," he stated, "must have a source – we want to locate it. I've promised the council that we won't interfere with the harvesting bios unless necessary. I don't think it'll affect our mission anyway, as this energy is too powerful for humans to harvest. This energy is both potent and complex.

We know virtually nothing about it, so we must be prepared for anything. Once we're more physical we'll be more protected, but we must still be aware of everything we can and cannot see. Once we're there, you must inform me of any discrepancies or oddities."

"This retuning isn't too bad," Kraniel muttered to himself. "I had expected it would be worse."

"It hasn't actually started yet," Orion smiled. "I wanted to give you the basic outline first." He leaned forward, lightly touching the disc to activate it. "You all know the procedure: relax and flow with it. You can move about, although try not to get too active until it's finished, for your own comfort. Ready?"

As Orion touched the retuning disc on Chia's head, Chia froze to the spot as his energy began draining away. His limbs started to feel heavy and his flesh felt weighty and sore. He leaned back, closed his eyes, and tried to concentrate on other matters as the others fell silent too.

The silence lasted a long time, as each bore the discomfort of becoming more physical.

"Chia," Orion finally mumbled. "What did councillor Shursa want? He seemed pleased. I think it's the first time I've seen him smile at you."

"That's probably only because you were around, Orion," Kraniel commented. "Even I can see that he struggles with his obsession with you."

"He is a strong kutu," Orion replied. "He will overcome it. Do not forget the great work he does on the council; he's more organized and meticulous than anyone. Give him respect."

"As you wish," Kraniel shrugged. "So, Chia, what did you manage to do to make Shursa smile?"

Chia eased his increasingly cumbersome body forward and pulled out a small marbline box from the pocket on his shin. "He presented this token of thanks from the Supreme," he replied. "It's probably a Barillian pain spike, if Shursa selected it."

There was a seal on the box bearing Chia's emblem, next to the emblem of the council. He carefully snapped the seal. The box smoothly unfolded and the area lit up with a warm golden aura.

"An Orb!" Orion exclaimed, forgetting his aches. "Some token!"

The others also disregarded their discomfort and sat forward. Even Jychanumun showed interest, pulling off his torso moulding to lean over and examine the object. The aura from the sphere tinged their faces with gold.

"I've heard an Orb is the greatest token of all, although I'm not sure what I'm supposed to do with it," Chia admitted, dangling the item from his finger and thumb.

"That, my friend, is the beauty of an Orb," Orion declared. "It can do *anything*. You do with it as you desire. Time travel, distance travel, communication; it does them all," Orion explained, "But only once. Each Orb takes a millennium to construct and can open a doorway, although only temporarily. They're made from the residues we produce when we move; it's all collected, rather than allowed to disperse, and then compounded until it inverts. That, my friend, is a tiny piece of every kutu, housed in golden Uana to keep it contained. It is an honour to receive one."

"It is a fine piece of work. I am honoured," Chia stated, tying the object around his neck. "And I need a new pendant."

"It's fitting that your discovery of Earth should be recognised," Orion commented, leaning back and rolling his shoulders, "And thank you for finding something that took my mind off this retuning – you should get another Orb for that."

"I feel so heavy it's as though I'm stuck to the bench," Kraniel groaned flatly. "I'd almost forgotten what it was like to be so fleshy. I just remembered it was very uncomfortable. I can feel my insides, I'm sure they're moving."

"That's your organs kicking in," Stanze stated matter-of-factly. "You do not bear discomfort well, do you?"

"No, I don't," Kraniel replied. "And I'm sure you don't want me to go through all the by-products of flesh which, I'm sure, even you'll find a discomfort."

Stanze simply raised an eyebrow as Chia groaned at the thought of it. He slowly stretched his long legs, and his skin rippled with cleaning nanos while his limbs made the most peculiar noises.

"Why does becoming physical have to be quite so revoltingly noisy?" he asked. "And have you noticed how much we look like humans now?"

"We were the inspiration for the human bios," Kraniel nodded. "They're our best design yet."

Stanze was standing up, flexing his neck, glancing over his shoulder and rubbing his back against the wall. Chia was amused to see that he seemed to find some satisfaction in the action, and then he jumped up, as though startled.

"Everyone's energy wings have gone!" Chia cried in alarm, trying to see his own bare back over his shoulder.

"You've only got ten percent energy; you're just too solid. They've withdrawn," Orion explained in amusement.

A look of horror came over Chia's face as he tried to muster every part of his will to make his wings form. No matter how much he exerted himself, pushed, and strained in his body, he could not.

Kraniel started chortling. The bench vibrated as he tried to suppress his laughter.

"It hurts, don't make me laugh," Kraniel closed his eyes. When he opened them again, he looked again at Chia, who was still trying to force his wings to form. Kraniel grinned, took a deep breath, held it, and bloated his face until it became crimson.

"You just looked like that!" he spluttered as he exhaled. "Trying to make your wings form at ten percent; I've never heard anything like it!" He finally burst into laughter and doubled over, holding his stomach. His stomach gurgled, and a loud ripping sound suddenly blasted from his backside.

Kraniel howled even louder as the 7A's filters increased air circulation efficiency, and the others collapsed with laughter too. It took them a long time to collect themselves.

Orion eventually sobered, wiping the watery substance from his eyes.

"It'll take a while to get use to being so physical again, for all of us. The ship's environment is only synthesised, so it's not exactly right, but yes, the flesh is a noisy, messy mass, and yes, Chia, the wings are introverted."

"Then we'd better hope to Eskah that I can land the ship in this clumsy state, or it won't just be me wishing we had our wings back," Chia replied. "And please, Kraniel, control yourself."

"Sorry, friends," Kraniel chortled. "My insides do get rather active when physical."

"Mine do too!" Stanze interjected, "And I get so hungry."

The others nodded in agreement. It took a little while longer for the major changes in their bodies to be completed, and as they slowly regained their bodily and emotional balance, they wandered around the ship, experiencing the familiar environment with their newly changed senses. Once Orion was satisfied that their retuning was going well, he suggested to Chia that they could speed up the flight a little. Chia agreed, and settled into the task of piloting the final stretch of the journey.

Chia gave the 7A free reign to travel as fast as it wished, and the ship made light work of the remainder of the distance. Soon they were approaching planet Earth.

"Target in sight," Chia announced. "Activate your landing fields – mobile is fine. This should be a smooth descent."

As they neared the planet, the sun's brightness reflected off the clouds below. Orion and the others – Stanze, Kraniel and Jychanumun – all moved forward so that they could watch through the portals. The brightness around them misted as the voluptuous rolls of clouds peeled away from the descending ship, and then suddenly below them was the planet's surface.

In the far distance, an expanse of deepest blue shone with reflections of the sky, and beside it vivid shades of green rolled together in a disorderly patchwork. As the surface grew closer, they saw craggy pale rocks scattered with plates of dark growth rearing to the skies, the tips of the rocks gleaming white and casting deep shadows over lush valleys sprinkled with multicoloured flora.

The rocks and the water had always been on the planet, the kutu knew, but the plants and creatures: these were their designs. They had made an eco-system capable of refining the 30 known energies present on Earth. It was a grand scheme, designed exclusively for this planet, and one that excelled in its purpose. The species and colours were breathtaking, and the closer they got, the more variants burst into view. They were all beautiful to perceive.

As the ship came closer to the ground, they passed over a small human colony. Modest dwellings had been built and spaced in an ordered form, with walkways between each hut and an open area at the centre of the settlement. The square and rectangular buildings all had gabled roofs, and beyond the dwellings, regular squares of land were patterned with lines of growing produce. The kutu were amazed. In such little time their human bios had manifested an understanding of geometrics. Indeed, all the bios, created from the planet's resources, had flourished beyond their expectations.

"It's out there somewhere," Chia said, breaking the silence. "This energy source could be under our noses, right now."

"It could indeed my friend," Orion smiled. "And it's now our mission to find it."

EIGHT

From the blackness I heard a voice.

"I didn't mean to hurt you," the voice echoed as I started, seeing speckles of light.

I tried to bolt forward. A hand pushed me back.

"Stay still. It is too late, it is done."

It was a female talking. I could tell it was not Rian. My heart sank, but I was also relieved. Whoever it was, they were wiping my eyes with a cool, damp cloth.

She removed the cloth so that I could open my eyes. At first, everything was still black, but slowly my vision cleared and I could make out the basic features of a face. It looked like the female who had been part of the burning ritual.

"Soul?" I asked.

"Yes, stay still."

My vision cleared a little more and I could see her better now. She was leaning over me, looking concerned. She was broad-shouldered but slim, a dark-skinned girl around the same age as me, maybe younger, with a mass of curls framing her face. We appeared to be in a small, gloomy room. Then, I remembered what had just happened.

"They put a fire to him!" I cried, trying to rise as blackness filled my vision again and dizziness overcame me.

"Yes," Soul replied, pushing me back down. "But it does not matter now."

"Yes it does!" I cried, pushing against her hand to get up. "I have to stop it!"

"No. It is over now, finished," Soul stated, holding me firmly. "Therefore you have no need to go anywhere just yet."

"Finished?" I groaned, slumping back down. I knew she meant that Wirrel had ceased. "What they did was not right. I have no words for how wrong it was."

"It was my fault," Soul groaned, "Poor Wirrel. He could not stop his fire from showing, and so they burnt it out of him. Then I heard you crying for the flames to stop, and the flames did stop, but it was too late. You're different; I took you away before anyone noticed. Do not be concerned, though – nobody saw."

"I do not know your ways here," I said. I wanted to say that I did not like them either, but the poor girl looked too troubled to hear my condemnation.

"This 'fire' is not right; it's just not right," I thought aloud.

"It is Hollow's way," Soul frowned.

"Then tell me about it, because I do not understand," I sighed, closing my eyes.

"I came of age last year," she stated proudly, as she dabbed something cool to my throbbing forehead. "And although we must share ourselves, I only had eyes for Wirrel, and he for me."

"Share?" I questioned, "You do not pair with just one?"

She laughed, "Is there such a place for that? No. Here, there are many more men than women. When we women come of age, we are provided with a home. Each night any man can come to us – sometimes there are many; that way our children will be strong."

"That is terrible!"

"Oh, no," she replied defensively. "It is good, and our children are strong. And it means that all men have an equal chance. We women are treated well and we have everything we want."

"Everything?" I questioned.

She sighed and looked down. "Yes, I used to think so. But things changed. As Wirrel grew older I could not help wanting to watch him, it felt good. And he would watch me, and it felt even better. When I came of age, I only ever wanted to share my bed with him. Wirrel was kind and gentle, just seeing him smile made everything seem good. Then Huru came round one evening to take me, but I still had Wirrel in my bed. When he found out that Wirrel would only visit me and no other woman, that was the end – Wirrel admitted to having the fire for me. It was my fault, but I could do nothing to stop him. And then, just now, the test; Wirrel could not help but let it show. If only he had rejoiced in Huru's actions, he would have proved he didn't have the fire for me and he would have been saved. He should have pretended."

As Soul spoke, I wondered if the same had happened to the woman Tooth from the in-betweener hut. She had said that Hollow had not liked her mate. It all made sense now. I looked at Soul, her dark, damp eyes sparkling amidst the mass of her curly hair. I could see she had lost something very precious to her, but it had not dampened her own fire as it had with Tooth. I liked her.

"You have had something very precious," I said.

"Oh yes," she beamed. "And I carry the fruit of that with me now. If I did not, I would have leapt into the fire and joined Wirrel. But now I have someone else to think of." She rubbed the gown against her belly, which showed a small bulge. "And she will have Wirrel's strength; though sadly I will have no sons from him to see the resemblance of his face."

Lost for words, I just smiled.

She pattered off and returned with a small wad of fine fabric.

"I think the bleeding on your head has stopped," she pointed to my left temple. "But it is a long and deep cut. If it opens up, put this on it. Would you like some broth?"

"Thank you, but I don't think I have an appetite anymore. And as kind as you've been, I don't want to stay in Hollow," I replied frankly.

She nodded acceptingly. "You really should stay tonight, though. Wherever you're going, you'll not get far with a gash like that on your head."

I didn't think the injury could really be that bad, and so I prodded the area on my forehead that felt numb. As soon as I touched it, the pain soared through me and I quickly pulled my fingers away from the hot sticky area.

"You've made it bleed again," Soul tutted, pressing damp fabric against it.

"I cannot stay here," I stated. In truth, I didn't want to stay. As much as I liked Soul, I didn't want to remain in this awful village.

I held the cloth against my forehead and tried pushing myself up, swinging my legs around. A flash of blindness forced me to be still, and I eased back down. Yes, I thought, perhaps I would have to stay a little while, at least until nightfall, but I would leave as soon as my legs would carry me.

"If I am here in your hut, what about your men visitors?" I asked.

Soul leaned down and pulled a circlet of beautifully entwined corn flowers from under where I lay.

"As you are such an obvious stranger, I will tell you. This is my bloom. I've just finished making it. It means I'm with child. I hang it on my door and will not receive 'visitors,' as you put it, until after the child is born. I've not started hanging it out yet, but I'll put it on my door tonight. This will keep Huru, and everyone else, away."

She looked at the ringlet of flowers with satisfaction.

"Then I'd like to accept your offer to stay," I replied, "just until I can walk – until nightfall at the latest. Thank you."

"Don't thank me; it's my fault anyway," Soul replied. "I was the one who tried to prevent you from stopping the fire by pulling you to the ground. Huru wouldn't have liked it if he'd heard you. I had to quieten your shouting, lest you end up joining my poor Wirrel."

She paused, deep in thought, looking very concerned.

"How did you do that with your voice, anyway?" she asked. "It boomed out 'stop,' and then the fire really did stop. And now your voice is just ordinary, if not a bit higher than most."

"Are you saying I squeak like a mouse, Soul?" I smiled, trying to lighten her concern. "Why thank you. Eek eek."

"No . . ."

"Eek eek."

Soul's laugh brightened the room. "I don't even know your name yet," she said.

"Tachra," I replied. "I'm Tachra, from Threetops."

"Hello Tachra. Where is Threetops?"

"I think it's quite far away, although at the moment, the end of this room looks quite far too."

Soul nodded. "The bleeding has stopped," she said, as she peered at my head. "It really is quite a big gash. I'm sorry, Tachra."

"Right then, let's see if I can find my feet."

I slowly pushed myself up, and noticed that Soul had somehow managed to put me on the long eating table in the middle of the room. I swung my legs to find the floor, put down my weight, wobbled, and lost my balance. Luckily, I was able to guide myself, with Soul's aid, and landed on the bench beside the table.

"Maybe you should only move a little bit at a time," Soul suggested. "But at least we can eat at the table now. I just couldn't manage those last few steps to put you on the bed. Now, even though you said not to, let's get some food. That'll make you feel better."

Soul began stoking the small fireplace in the corner of the room. As she reheated the cooking pot, we talked about generalities while I attempted to put my weight on my feet and stumble around. She took the flower circlet, hung it outside the hut, and returned, frowning, after slamming the door.

"They are feasting to the drums," she stated flatly. "It will continue until nightfall. They celebrate my Wirrel's burning. When I think about it I have this awful feeling."

"Like a wound that will not heal? In my village, they called it an angry cut. Angry is a good word."

"Yes, I am that cut; I'm angry."

"I know it well, Soul. What will you do now?"

Soul sighed. "I don't want to join them, but I'll have to, even just for a while, before this evening has finished. If I don't go, they'll come looking for me, but I don't want to have to face that brute Huru again."

"Why do you have to? Why do you have to do anything?" I exclaimed suddenly. "There is so much here that doesn't make sense, and so much that feels wrong. Who is Huru, and why do the others so adore him? Why do you have to do what he wants? You should not be in this hideous place!"

"Be still, Tachra; you'll open the wound," Soul replied. "Me? I was sent here when I was very young, so where else would I go? Huru is a brute, but I'm the only one who seems to think so. He plagues me far more than he does the other women, but I know how to handle him, mostly. Tonight I did not like my test, but that is the way here. I would rather have Wirrel, but now I'll have to content myself with just his child."

"Before it's taken to be looked after by the old women," I stated thoughtlessly. "You cannot tell me that this is as you wish."

"I will find a way of keeping my child!" Soul answered fiercely. "And perhaps, Tachra, you should think about staying. You're too thin, and clearly haven't eaten properly for a long time. You would have a home and you would be well provided for here in Hollow. New women are always welcome. It's not as bad as you seem to think."

"Perhaps not," I replied, "but perhaps it's just too different from what I know. I would never want to watch men burning, nor have men forced upon me. Sorry, Soul, I know this is your home, but the ways here do not feel right to me."

"No, you're right," Soul agreed, after a long pause. "I don't think that you would like it here, and somehow I know you should not stay." She thought for a moment. "It's more than that; you must go before you're not permitted to leave, before Rian tells Huru of you and he welcomes you in his own way. I already like you, Tachra, and I would like you to stay – we could be friends. However, something tells me that you should leave as soon as you can."

I looked at her quizzically, but before I could respond, there was a loud pounding against the door.

Soul looked at me wide eyed and clearly alarmed. She put her finger to her lips, telling me to be silent, and then pointed towards a small closed door at the other end of the hut.

"Hide!" she hissed. "Now!"

From the expression on her face I didn't need to think twice. I snatched up my bundle and stumbled towards the door she'd pointed to, willing my legs to maintain their balance. I went through into a smaller adjoining room and quietly closed the door behind me.

I was inside a large bedding room containing little other than a huge square bed covered in several threadbare blankets. I stood quietly and listened as Soul opened the hut's main entrance.

"Huru, you come to me again so soon!" I heard Soul announce sweetly.

"Why are you not at the celebrations?" came the abrupt reply. The voice was Huru's. He pushed past Soul and into the hut.

"I merely returned here for a moment to wash quickly. I was just about to leave to join you all again," Soul replied, following him.

"Is that right?"

"Well, now that you're here, you can accompany me to the celebrations. Come along, Huru."

I heard Soul's lighter footsteps move further away – back in the direction of the hut entrance – and then stop. Huru seemed to ignore her suggestion, and his footsteps thudded as he walked around her room.

"I hear we have new blood in Hollow, but she is nowhere to be found. Have you seen her?" he asked.

"How could I, Huru?" Soul replied. "I came straight to my hut. Before that, you know only too well where I was."

Huru's footsteps stopped. "What's that on the table? Were you bleeding?"

Oh no, I thought. The cloth used to clean my head had been left on the table. I held my breath.

"Yes," Soul answered. I detected a definite quiver in her voice. "Well, you are such a strong man."

Huru's footsteps grew closer, and he paused by the door of the room I was in. I could see him through the joins in the wood.

He faced the door and took a deep, slow breath through his nose that seemed so close I could almost feel it. He knew I was here. I was sure of it.

"Oh yes, I smell blood, but I'm not so sure that it's yours, Soul," Huru said, without moving to face her. "And tell me, why do you cook when the celebrations are on and food is provided?"

"I ate because I was hungry," Soul answered. "Unless you hadn't noticed, I have my bloom hanging outside. I am feeding two now."

"Don't tell me that you bring one of that weakling Wirrel's into the world!" Huru moved away from the door, towards her.

"N-n-no. Of course not. It is yours," Soul stammered.

"You lie!" Huru roared. "You hesitate because you lie. Your firstborn will be mine!" I heard a thud of flesh against flesh.

Soul's groans stifled as I heard another thud. He had hit her!

I shot from the room, gripping my bundle, and tripped over Soul, who lay prostrate on the floor.

"Stop that! It's me that you're looking for!" I shouted, but my giddiness caused me to stumble. The sudden exertion made the blackness in my vision return in dizzying flashes.

Huru was poised with his foot back, about to kick a groaning Soul in the belly. He looked at me and smiled, putting his foot unhurriedly down and his hands on his hips.

Huru was a hulking beast of a man up close, with an ugly crooked nose and fat, shiny lips.

"I thought I smelt new blood," he said as he walked towards me, smelling the air, "And fresh, too."

"I am not staying here, Huru," I said as I held my ground. "I am just passing through. Soul is with child and I hear she cannot be touched, so leave her alone. You have hurt her too much already."

Soul was getting up. I glanced at the main door, indicating for her to leave.

"Aw, have you hurt your head, you poor girl?" Huru said.

He reached out to touch my face as I pulled back.

"There now," he cooed in a mock-gentle voice. "Huru will make it better."

"Huru, leave now," I stated firmly. "Soul cannot be touched and I am not one of Hollow's women – I do not follow your ways."

"Oh, that doesn't matter," Huru drawled. His tone changed as he eyed me up and down. "You're here now, aren't you? I'll give you a proper Hollow welcome."

"Don't touch me!" I barked, backing off. "I'm leaving now and I'm taking Soul with me."

"I don't think you're going anywhere just yet!"

Huru laughed, lunging forward.

As I turned to sidestep, he grabbed my arm and tugged me harshly, twisting and jerking the limb behind my back, making it crunch with pain. My head pounded as I struggled against his strength and tried beating him with the bundle in my free arm. But he was strong and held me from behind, dragging me towards the bedding room.

Soul ran forward to help me, but Huru kicked the door shut. The door hit her hard, knocking her off her feet and shutting her out of the room. I heard the muffled thud of her hitting the floor again as Huru slid a long piece of wood through a large loop to secure the door shut.

"Now, let Hollow welcome you properly," he slobbered.

I felt myself shoved forward with a hard punch. I fell on my face on the hard bed with my bundle beneath me. I thrashed as he pounced onto my back, pinning me down, with one of my arms trapped beneath me and the other taut behind my back as he held it tightly. I gave a good backwards kick and got him square in his back.

174

"What's this?" he roared. "You've not been prepared for a Hollow welcome? Good! It's about time I had one that showed a bit of fight!"

He punched my side hard and I felt the air suck out of my body. Struggling for breath, I managed to get another hard kick to his back, but he still didn't budge.

"That's more like it!" he snarled. "I can see that you and I are going to have a great deal of fun."

He eased his weight from my back, hoisting me, still face down, further up the bed as he held my painful arm up between my shoulders. With his other hand he started squeezing the flesh of my backside while he sat on the backs of my knees. I felt him quickly lift my robe and tug at my underclothes. I tried kicking backwards again, but his heavy weight on the bottom of my legs meant I couldn't move him. I was pinned down.

"Leave me alone!" I shouted. My yells came out muffled as he pushed my face hard into the blankets.

"Fight all you like, I don't mind, but be quiet," he sneered.

An anger rose in me; this time I did not want to restrain it. Frantically, I wiggled the hand under my body that still clasped my bundle. Arching my back with all my might gave me just enough space to move my fingers a little. I fumbled my bundle open. *I must find my knife*, I thought.

Huru's excited exertion only increased with my movement, and he shoved his free hand to find the waist of my underclothes. He grabbed the top, ripping them downwards with one hard pull and giving my thigh a hard slap, laughing. As he moved his weight to use his knees to spread my legs, my fingers worked blindly through my bundle beneath me. The cool blade scratched my thumb; I had found it, my knife! I manoeuvred the handle into my palm and gripped it tightly. Then, using the little space I'd made, I quickly twisted around to face Huru. The sweat on his hands allowed my arm to slip through his grasp with yet another crunching pain that I refused to feel. Then, with all my force, I drove the blade towards him.

"Listen! Stop!" I roared, as I thrust forward, aiming my knife at his neck.

Huru moved sideways and his hand shot up to stop the knife. It was too late; although I missed his neck, the blade sliced past his hand and embedded into his shoulder.

A small spurt of Huru's blood splattered my face. Then he stopped, his eyes wide open and his fingers almost touching the knife's handle.

I lay for a moment, my heart pounding, waiting for retaliation, but none came.

Slowly I let go of my knife, leaving it stuck in his flesh, and wiggled from under him, using my one good arm – the other was now unresponsive. Huru slumped over as soon as my body wasn't propping him up, his eyes wide open and his legs twitching in exactly the same spread-out position, but now he'd fallen onto his side.

I wiped the blood from my cheek, stumbled backwards, and fumbled with the heavy latch across the door. When I finally worked the latch free, I found Soul on the other side of the door, trying to sit up, cupping a bloody nose.

I ran to her side, helping her as she pulled herself up.

"Are you alright?"

"Yes, we're both fine," she touched her belly. "I told you she was strong. Are you alright?"

"Yes," I nodded, suddenly feeling very shaky. "But Soul, I've done something terrible. I've put my knife in Huru."

Soul looked towards the bedding room where Huru lay rigidly amidst splattered blankets, one knee raised into the air and one hand almost touching the protruding knife handle in his shoulder, in the same position as when he had been straddling me. She calmly got up and walked towards him.

"Are you sure you are well, Tachra?" Soul asked as she walked around the motionless Huru, staying well clear of him.

I nodded.

Soul stopped and stood gazing at Huru for several moments, and then turned and looked at me with a very surprised expression on her face.

"What have you done to him?" she said. "He's breathing; he's as alive as you or I, but just *there*, rigid. His eyes aren't even following me, even though they're open."

"I put my knife in him," I replied blankly. "He's ceased."

"No, he hasn't," Soul replied. "Come look, the knife is only shallowly buried in his flesh; it seems as though his jerkin took most of the force. He would hardly have felt it. The blood makes it look worse than it is. He's still breathing; it's as if he's just *stopped*. I did hear you tell him to stop, and it was the same voice you used when you made the fire stop. Tachra, I think you *made* him stop."

"That can't happen."

"I think it just did."

Soul cautiously prodded Huru and jumped backwards. Huru didn't respond. Then she gave a hefty kick to his one overhanging leg.

"Good!" she declared, giving him another kick. "And that one is for Wirrel." And then another. "And that one is for trying to hurt my baby."

"Soul!" I exclaimed.

"No," she insisted. "He takes from others; I have lost count of how many. Perhaps it's fitting that he stops because someone makes him. I've decided I've had my fill of his ways. We should gather tools to fend him off before he gets going again. How do you get him going again?"

"I have no idea," I shrugged.

"Well, let's get him out of here, and then you can do it. He's not going to be flailing around in my hut anymore."

It was a wise idea. I looked at Soul and nodded. "I'll move him outside somewhere, while you tend to your bleeding nose."

"I'll help you first," she replied. "You can still hardly walk straight from that bash on the head, and it's bleeding again. Even with the two of us he'll be heavy."

I had to agree; neither of us would manage carrying such a large man individually, it had to be done together. I cautiously walked over to Huru's paralysed body and prodded him, just to make sure he really wasn't pretending, and then pulled the top blanket around to cover him. Feeling much better now that I couldn't see his face, I gathered one end together, taking the weight with my one good arm, and Soul grasped the other, making a fat-looking cocoon.

"What have you done to your arm?" Soul asked, obviously noting that I was avoiding using it.

"It's the shoulder; it's not working anymore."

"Does it hurt?"

"Sort of," I replied, purposely underestimating just how much.

Soul let go of the blanket and walked up to me, gently prodding my shoulder.

"It's badly dislocated," she frowned.

Soul moved to stand behind me. Before I could ask her what she was going to do, she grabbed my arm and yanked it hard. There was a loud crunch and the pain made me yelp. I spun around to face her, furious, but not sure what I was furious about. Then I couldn't help smiling with relief; the pain had lessened significantly. I rolled my shoulder; it still hurt, but not nearly as much. It seemed she'd fixed it.

Soul apologised with a wry smirk, and motioned towards Huru. Together we pulled him off the bed. He was heavier than we'd anticipated, and hit the ground with a thud. We waited a moment to see if he stirred; he didn't, so we quickly dragged him across the smooth wooden planks and out of the room.

We were both cautious leaving the hut, although nobody was in sight; it seemed they were all still too busy celebrating over Wirrel's charred remains.

Thh-thump, Thh-thump, Huru's rigid bulk thudded down the hut's steps, and then made an unusual chafing noise on the dusty path as we pulled him along. It was slow work and we'd only passed a dozen huts when I thought I heard voices.

"Sshh," I said, suddenly stopping.

As soon as we stopped, a woman's laughter was clearly audible, quite close by.

Not wanting to be seen dragging Hollow's chief with my knife embedded in his shoulder, I quickly directed my step towards the closest raised hut, dragging Huru with me. Soul nodded – by now she'd heard the laughter too – and she immediately helped push Huru under the hut, with us both quickly climbing down to join him.

It was hot under the hut, it stank of waste, and there was an abundance of large, fat flies. I crawled forward, breathing through my mouth, and watched as a man and woman, arm in arm, came into view and merrily entered the opposite dwelling. My heart initially sank, as they left the door open, but then, as if in answer to my fretting, the man pushed the door shut.

As soon as the way seemed clear again, Soul and I crawled back out from under the hut. We had dragged Huru's body there without much difficulty, but after much fruitless pulling it was clear that getting him out wasn't going to be quite as easy. Not only was he simply too heavy, but his knees, stiff and sticking out at angles, kept getting caught on the slope, forcing him to roll back. I eventually crawled back down, lying on my back in the excrement, and tried pushing him up with my feet while Soul pulled. After several frustrating attempts, Soul crawled back under the hut and we tried shouldering him up. Thankfully, on the third attempt it worked. We scrabbled out, dragging Huru away from the huts as quickly as possible.

As we left the well-worn path the way became rougher, and dragging Huru became increasingly difficult. We reached the narrow strip of farmland at the edge of the village and pulled him into the long crops. The progress was very slow, as the ground was uneven and the stalks of wheat acted like barriers. And so as soon as we were far enough away from the path not to be heard, we stopped.

Standing amidst the wheat fields, I pulled away the blanket in which we had wrapped Huru. By now there were even more holes in it, as well as splinters of wood, bits of vegetation and rather a large amount of dried faeces. Huru hadn't fared much better, and was now covered with fresh grazes and smears of muck. His breathing was strong and sure, however: he was still very much alive. His big eyes still stared towards his shoulder in surprise and my knife still protruded from his flesh.

I inspected the knife. Soul was right: it had only penetrated Huru's flesh slightly. Somehow, I had missed my aim for his neck. I felt strangely relieved. I folded my fingers around the knife's handle and quickly pulled it out. Huru didn't do anything.

"Right, let's get him started again," Soul decided.

As I stood back, Soul pulled out a long chopping knife from underneath her robe. I looked at her questioningly.

"It's my fruit knife – yours gave me the idea," she reassured me. "It's not very sharp, but he won't know that."

Good point.

"Right Tachra, get further back in case he charges at us, and let's be ready."

She took a stance, bracing herself with the fruit knife poised between both hands. I took a similar position a few feet to one side of her.

"Are you ready?" she asked.

I nodded.

"Huru awaken!" Soul suddenly shouted.

We both waited a moment, watching Huru expectantly, but nothing happened.

"Start! Get up!" Soul shouted again. She lowered her voice so that it came out deeper.

Still nothing happened. She walked closer and leaned over him.

"Huru move! Wake up!" she growled in the lowest voice she could muster. "Go. Jump! Run! Dance! Anything!"

I started laughing. Soul started laughing too. We laughed so hard until we were both sprawled on the ground, clutching our bellies.

"I don't know why I'm laughing. This isn't funny," I spoke through my hysterics. I really didn't think it was funny, not at all; it was terrible.

"I know," Soul chortled, barely able to speak, "and we can't just leave him like this, he'll eventually cease."

"Yes, or they'll reap the crops and find him, or maybe just a Huru tree."

We kept laughing until we could laugh no more.

Soul sat up, wiping her eyes.

"You can make him move, Tachra. Just do that voice again. And make sure he's slow so we can get away."

"I can try," I nodded.

I started decreasing the tone of my voice, trying to make it as low as possible. "Aaa-aah-ahh-aah-aaw-oow," I hummed.

"No, lower," Soul frowned.

I tried again.

"I can't get it lower," I said eventually. "Actually, Soul, I don't know how to do the voice. I can't help it when it happens; it just seems to happen."

Soul stood up, looking at me, a little perplexed.

"Well this is something. What are we going to do? We really can't just leave him here. Others will come looking for him and someone will know that the last place he visited was my hut."

She tried to hide her concern, but it oozed from her every word. I sensed her worry that she might be forced from the only home she had ever really known. I stared at Soul, and when I looked at her it felt as if I looked *through* her, as if I could see who she really was. The ground around her seemed to shimmer and I felt as if I was part of it, just as she was, and as Huru was.

I felt a tingle running through me, but it wasn't fear, or anger, it was something beautiful. It was as if I had only ever seen a dream world before this, and now everything looked more real.

I stood without thinking, and then walked towards Soul. It felt as if I was gliding. I could sense the life in her. I put my hand on her belly. The child was fine. And it was a girl, Soul was right. *You will not come to harm*, I thought.

I turned and looked at Huru, his body rippling like the long grass around him. It was not his ears that needed to hear, it was his heart. I bent down to him.

"Huru, I'm going to talk and you're going to hear me," I said. My voice was normal, no roar or boom, but it felt detached, is if someone else were saying the words.

"If you can understand, blink twice."

Huru blinked twice.

Soul approached, indicating I should go on. "He can hear you," she said, almost in disbelief.

182

I knelt down beside Huru. I felt great empathy for him – his life had been difficult, but I knew his choices had caused pain to others.

"You will move again, but first you must listen. You must understand how your choices affect all else," I said. "It is not balanced to hurt another person or cause anyone to cease. It is not balanced to take a woman unless she requests it of you. It is not balanced to set yourself up above all others. You have no right to make choices for others; a woman can keep her child if she wishes; that is not your choice. If two people wish to be paired, that is their choice, not yours."

As I spoke, I felt the tingling in my body start to decrease, and the world slowly started looking flatter again. Whatever it was that made me tingle, and that allowed Huru to hear me, was going away. I had to be quick.

I looked at Soul for guidance. What else should I say?

"Tell him they should stop raiding the surrounding villages for food," Soul said urgently.

They do that? I thought, struggling to keep focussed. I did not have much time.

I spoke the words to Huru, adding: "Grow more crops here; your fields are pitiful. If you're going to be viewed as a person in charge of this village, you'll put their well-being first and help people when you can." Thinking of helping people made me remember the in-betweener huts. "And see what help can be given to Tooth. And let Jin and Jan live where they wish, and help them if they ask for it."

I looked round at Soul, aware that the tingling had almost gone.

"Are you ready?" I asked, getting to my feet and taking a step back.

Soul nodded, standing poised with her knife.

"Put the knife out of sight," I suggested. "But keep your hand on it ready, just in case."

She tucked the blade under her arm and I turned my attentions back to Huru.

"Huru, you don't remember anything after Wirrel's fire except that you fell and hurt your shoulder," I said. "We've come to help and you won't recall how you got here." It was the best I could think of on impulse. "You are not stopped, you just fell."

I stopped talking; the tingling had gone. My stomach churned. Suddenly I was filled with the dread of the situation again.

At that moment, Huru's raised leg fell and he let out a long moan, putting his hand to his shoulder. He rolled onto his back and slowly pushed himself to a sitting position. Soul and I took a few steps back.

Huru groaned as he slowly stood, rocking on his feet a little, and then looked at his blood-spattered tunic. "I think I've hurt myself. I must have fallen. I'd best find my hut and tend to this cut." He looked up at us. "Thank you for helping me. I'm fine, just tired."

He rolled his shoulder with a grimace, and then began stiffly walking back towards the huts. Soul and I followed a few paces behind him.

"It seems to have worked," Soul whispered in my ear, and then she looked at Huru and raised her voice. "Huru, I'm with child," she announced bravely.

Huru stopped suddenly and looked back at us. Soul and I came to a rapid halt.

"That's good news, Soul."

"It's Wirrel's"

"That's a fine thing. Can I do anything to help?"

Soul hastily shook her head, barely believing what she had just heard.

Huru walked on again, mumbling to himself something about planting crops. He made his way back into the village, with Soul and I following, and he didn't comment on the obvious noisy festivities in the distance. When we got close to Soul's hut, we stopped, watching Huru as he disappeared between the dwellings in search of his own abode. As soon as he was out of sight, we hurried inside and bolted the door shut.

Neither of us said a word. We just sat down at the table. I went to speak a few times, but stopped, while Soul just kept looking at me with a bewildered expression in her big eyes.

Eventually, she rose and went to the fire, prodding the dying embers enough to place a pot on them.

"Will your words last forever?" she asked.

"I don't know. I think so."

"But how . . . ?"

"I don't know how."

"Well, you did it. What *do* you know?"

I thought about it for a moment.

"At first I thought it was anger that made my voice change. It has only happened twice before, and both times I was angry. But out in the field, when we were trying to wake Huru, I was not angry; I sensed your need. It was a true need. It made me see everything with clarity, and the tingle started in me that makes the voice. It only lasted a short while. I remembered that when I'd told Huru to stop, I'd also told him to listen. So that was what I tried: to make him listen. I do not know yet how it is done, but I am going to find out. I don't know," I sighed, "maybe I just imagined everything."

"That was definitely real. I saw it."

"Then we'll have to leave it at that, because it's as new to me as it is to you."

"What are you going to do now? Would you like to stay here? I'd like you to."

"I'll have to leave tonight, before it gets dark."

Soul looked disappointed, but tried not to show it.

"I have things that I am trying to find," I explained. "And that I must understand. I'm looking for the home of the blue light. I'm trying to find out why we cease. And I'm looking for someone with black eyes – all black, with no white in them at all."

"All black? That sounds awful."

"And I want to find out how the first people, like my parents, got here. Unless you already know how?" I added.

Soul's brows knitted together into a frown. "That's a very good question. My parents' parents didn't have a mother and father; they didn't know why."

"None of them know why, or how." I stated. "I'd hoped Hollow might hold some answers. But I'm realising that there are many more different places than I'd thought."

Hollow is the worst by far, I thought to myself. Soul would probably have a better home in another village.

"Soul," I considered, "My journey can be tiresome; it may well be long, and I don't know where it will end, but would you like come with me? There may be better places than Hollow for you to call home."

Soul seemed to consider this.

"I think not," she decided. "I'm with child now. Hopefully there'll be better things here in Hollow now you've dealt with Huru, and this place will make a good home for my daughter. But if I had met you a moon ago, both Wirrel and I would have pleaded to join you."

I smiled, feeling sad.

"What weighs heavy on your mind?" she asked.

"You have lost Wirrel. Ceasing is terrible, and I almost made Huru cease," I replied. "My actions could have caused you a great deal of trouble."

186

"And what were you options?" Soul looked at me sharply. "I thought you were different, and now I know that you are. You couldn't end up like me, with nothing other than ugly memories and a hope that my child comes from the one person that I thought was right? You fought back; I wish I had learnt to before now."

"Oh Soul, I'm so sad for you," I sighed, without thinking.

"Don't be," she replied. "We'll both clean ourselves up. I will attend the end of what will be the last ever fire celebration. While others are joyous at Wirrel's ceasing, I will feast with the joy that he was mine and that nobody else will have to endure the same end that he did. And you, Tachra, you'll continue on your way, and I'll know that I had met someone, albeit briefly, that I loved more than a sister."

I nodded, staring at her bruised face, which now presented a greatly swollen blue nose and one cheek that was twice the size of the other.

"At least I can cover it," she laughed, touching her nose, having noticed my staring. "You look far worse."

I insisted I was fine, but Soul arose and found a piece of fabric anyway, carefully ripping and folding it into a particular shape, forming an impromptu but serviceable sling, indicating that I should put my arm in it and informing me that a dislocated shoulder shouldn't have too much exertion for a while. Having just dragged Huru the length of Hollow, her words made me smile, but my shoulder did hurt, so I lifted my arm into the sling and the ache reduced immediately.

I reached for my bundle, and after fumbling at it with only one hand, untied it. It contents sprang loose and I began rummaging through them.

"What's that?" Soul asked, pointing to the bundle. She was looking at pale blue petals sticking out from between the pieces of papyri.

"That," I stated, picking up the papyri and unfolding them so that she could see the contents, "is a flower I saw on my travels. It was so pretty, and standing all on its own. It reminded me of the irises I use to see back home."

"It's so beautiful," Soul gasped. "Could there really be blooms as beautiful as that?"

"Oh yes. Please, have it," I smiled. "It's dried out now, it should keep its form and colour quite well."

Soul shook her head. "I could not take it, it's yours."

"You could, you will, and you have," I said, handing her the flower. "It's yours now."

"Oh, thank you, Tachra," Soul gasped. "What was it called? Iris? Yes, Iris. It's beautiful. I shall call my child Iris when she is born. She will be beautiful too."

"Yes, she will be," I smiled. "She'll be beautiful both inside and out."

I continued rummaging. Then I found what I'd been looking for; it had fallen between the crumples of fabric. It was a small bead-shaped piece of wood that I had almost finished carving.

"Here it is," I said. "I made this. It's not anything much and doesn't do anything, but I've greatly enjoyed carving it. Please take it. If ever you need me strongly enough, somehow I think I will know."

She took the small piece of wood, studying it intently. "Thank you Tachra. You have a welcome roof here if ever you want one," she said, and gave me a long embrace.

"I must leave now," I said, awkwardly retying my bundle. I'd noticed that the sky had rapidly darkened to dusk.

"I too must go, before I'm missed," Soul agreed. "Huru may have changed, but the rest of the village is still the same; those changes may be long in the coming. We must leave separately, in case there are any wanderers. Take as much food from the kitchen as you want to, and when you leave, follow the straight road out; it's always quiet."

She wrapped her red cloth back around her face. We embraced again, and she left, smiling as she closed the door behind her.

I glanced around the empty room. Now it was time to leave here; it was almost night already.

I considered taking up on Soul's offer of food, and glanced around her kitchen. There was a dismaying array of the small, sour fruits that littered the flatlands, a frugal selection of flat breads and three long-dried vegetables. I had no heart to take any of Soul's modest supplies; I would manage without. But I did fill my water pots from the ample supply, added them to my bundle, and then quietly left the hut.

I followed the straight road out, not stopping until I had passed out of sight of Hollow and was back into the dry barren land. I kept wearing the red robes until far enough away from Hollow, and then awkwardly discarded them with my one good arm. I left them heaped behind a rock protruding from the sandy ground. I didn't need to, but I covered the offensive fabric with sand until I could no longer see it. This simple act made me feel better. Even in the current cool nights, I would rather go cold than wear them any more.

Re-dressed in my old raggedy clothes, I hoisted my bundle over my shoulder and cut across the land, heading back in the direction of my stream. I continued walking through the night, and didn't turn back to see the blue lights shimmering over the huts. I kept on solidly, at a determined pace, through another two days, and didn't stop until I had reached the water on the second night.

Relieved at the sight of nothing but the land itself spanning to the horizon, I sat down and opened my bundle. I took out the small square of gauzy fabric that Soul had given me and untied the soiled one from my head – it didn't smell too good anymore – and then I replaced it with the new one.

After drinking my fill from the stream, I lay down to sleep, ready for a fresh start with the morrow's sun. I would not be visiting any more unknown villages. I would continue west, the direction I felt compelled towards, the direction of the moving sun and the blue light; above all, the direction that didn't smell of people.

From now on, I'd walk the path that led to no man.

NINE

As the 7A descended towards its designated landing, it began shuddering. Something wasn't right. Chia glanced over his shoulder from the pilot's seat.

"Increase your landing shields to full," he instructed. "This should have been smooth, but the ship isn't recognising enough of the energies to block them out."

Changing the ship's settings to manual, Chia tried lowering their altitude. The craft recoiled, pushing against his commands. He tried again, pointing the ship towards its landing spot, but the 7A jumped violently, suddenly propelling them forwards and up. Crashes and bangs sounded from the decks behind him, but he couldn't look around as he struggled to regain his influence over the ship; it didn't seem to want to get close to the surface. It was almost as if the ship was *afraid*.

"It's alright, I'm here," Chia coaxed the craft, sending his soothing thoughts through the sensors. "Come on, we can do it. I've been here before, and I'm still in one piece. And I know you've been to far worse places than this."

Chia kept talking to the craft, gently calming it while keeping firm control, and gradually the 7A relaxed, levelling its flight once again. Cautiously, and still talking to it, Chia guided the ship lower. Finally, the landing area was in sight once again and the craft manoeuvred precisely, though hesitantly, towards it.

With the pod finally on the ground, Chia turned to the decks behind him to inspect the damage. Orion and Stanze were kneeling beside Jychanumun, who lay prostrate and unmoving.

"What's happened?" Chia asked, sprinting forward.

"He's out cold. I'll get some healing rods," Stanze replied.

"Stay back," Jychanumun groaned, trying to lever himself upright.

The others backed off a few steps as he clumsily pushed himself up, first onto his elbows, and then slowly into a sitting position. One side of his face was covered in blood from a gaping gash on his forehead; the blood had congealed in his hair and was dripping down his chest. Stanze had a healing rod in his hand and leaned down to aid him.

"Don't touch me," Jychanumun said, pulling away.

Stanze stayed where he was and pushed the healing rod across the floor towards him. "Then use this, and quickly," he insisted. "The cut is deep."

Jychanumun picked up the rod and began applying it to his forehead, clearly unwilling to accept any help. The expression on his face never changed, even though the quantity of blood suggested that it must hurt, and when he was finished, he picked up the lumi-cloth Stanze had put on the floor and wiped the blood from his face.

The healing rod had done its job – the cut was healed – but a long silver scar ran from the top of Jychanumun's forehead to the outside of his right eye.

"Are you all right?" Orion asked,

Jychanumun got to his feet, using the lumi-cloth to wipe the last of the blood from his body.

"Fine," he stated,

Orion briskly encouraged the others to stop staring, calling out, "We're here, we've arrived."

Chia set aside his alarm at the thought of the amount of blood that could come from flesh, and released the ship's hatch. Streams of sunlight flooded in, and a cool breeze drifted through the ship, bringing in strange, sweet scents.

The 7A had nestled comfortably at the centre of a large clearing, high on a flat-topped mountain. Thickset trees stood all around, partially obscuring the sheer drops beyond and behind them, where the mountain stepped randomly downwards in layers of loose grey rocks. In front of their position, an overhanging craggy drop overlooked rolls of emerald and yellow vegetation. It was a striking, even breathtaking view; they seemed to hang above the rolling landscape as if the ship were still hovering among the clouds.

"I'll go first," Stanze announced authoritatively. "Wait here."

He collected his de-activated headdress from the ship's hold and slipped the gold band over his head so that it encircled his neck at the shoulders. With a slight movement of his head, the headdress unfolded to cover his neck and head as a rippling transparent shield shimmered over his skin.

"Readings indicate that the area is free from aggressive bios, but I'll perform a land sweep anyway," he called out, before stealthily striding from the 7A as if the weight of the flesh was no problem at all.

Some sort of physical protection seemed like a good idea, so Chia selected his vapour daggers – they were fast and clean, and he'd mastered them well enough to make them practically extensions of his hands. After all, he was physical now and he wasn't intending on risking unnecessary discomfort. He held the daggers against his shin plates while the nanos embedded in his body armour wove around the blades, leaving only the thumb loops on the hafts visible. He straightened, rolling his head so that his neck made crunching noises, and a shimmer of energy rippled over his skin as he drew a deep breath.

"Do you sense that, Orion? We're virtually entirely physical and yet my chi is still being pulled."

"Whatever is causing that is what we're trying to locate," Orion replied. "You should all activate your cerebral barriers, especially you, Chia."

Chia nodded, and noticed Jychanumun standing in the open doorway. He was barefoot and weapon-less, and looking straight out from the ship. Then he jumped down to the ground and walked out of sight.

Within a few moments, the others had followed Jychanumun from the ship, although they were rather more suitably protected; finally, Chia stepped down onto solid ground. He stood for a moment, preparing himself to feel the same energy pull as he had the first time he'd been here, but then breathed a sigh of relief: the sensation wasn't so strong when in flesh. He was grateful of that.

The 7A had finished adjusting to its new environment and had activated a protection field, expanding its boundaries to provide an additional area for the crew. A virtually camouflaged dome, its presence betrayed only by the energy rippling in the sunlit clearing, now tripled the capacity of the ship. It was large enough for all their needs, having a wide opening at its centre, and the crew now placed five recliners on one side and moved a large rune table from the hold to the other in order to act as a conference area.

The group then automatically gathered around the table, knowing Orion would want to brief them straight away.

"We have so much to do, so I'll jump straight in," Orion commenced, once everyone had settled.

"We will begin with method one," he began, "being the one suggested by the council. We'll analyse any changes in the bios, to get some idea of what we're after. The first energy wave was emitted from the entire planet, but subsequent waves have only come from this continent, from within an area that, luckily for us, has been narrowed down by Chia's research, although it's still large. Jychanumun and Stanze, you'll gather a range of bios samples, focussing on the smaller varieties for the sake of expediency: plants, insects, birds, and so on. Screen them for energy anomalies, and send the data to Nirrious on the substation and to Kraniel here. Kraniel, utilize that data to design a variable containment sphere suitable for capturing this energy source. And Chia, after ensuring that the carry-pods are calibrated, start low-level sweeps of the land – we're looking for the precise source of this energy. Days will seem shorter with these sluggish bodies, so we'll work with the natural rhythm of the Earth and start at first light tomorrow."

Orion looked around at the team. "That's all," he concluded. "Let's figure out what it is, find it, contain it, and then deliver it to Eden. If this strategy doesn't work, we'll find a new one. Questions?"

"It all seems rather too simple," Chia commented. "I tried that strategy before. It doesn't work."

"I know. I don't think it will work either," Orion agreed, sighing heavily. "Nevertheless, it's the most obvious route, and the one recommended by the council, so it must be tried first."

One by one, the rest of the group agreed.

"And our alternative strategy . . . ?" Stanze enquired.

" . . . doesn't exist yet. I'm working on the assumption that now we are here, once we have started gathering facts an alternate plan will become obvious."

"One more question . . ." Stanze began. Chia expected that he was about to query such a loose arrangement. "Do we have adequate food supplies, or am I required to go and find some?"

"You must all be starving. I certainly am," Orion admitted. "We have flesh now, with stomachs that are empty. We have plenty of supplies, so tonight you'll all have to adapt to your physical settings and become more acquainted with each other. For that I recommend a feasting, which will fulfil all needs at once."

The team agreed; although no one enjoyed the side effects of having so little energy and such increased physicality, they knew that a short, sharp, shock to their internal organs was the best way to become better accustomed with their fleshy states. Feasting would certainly accomplish that. With no more questions about their assignment, they set about selecting their finest supplies and preparing a banquet inside the 7A's field.

That first evening, they tried to make the adjustment to their flesh as comfortable and pleasant an experience as possible. They talked and feasted until one-by-one they exhaustedly slumped against the table, too satiated and lazy to move.

Stanze's loud snoring woke Chia from his slumbers. The rest of the team were still draped around the table and the sky was starting to lighten. He stretched his aching limbs, wishing he had thought to sleep in a recliner, and stirred the others, informing them that the new day was beginning.

Once the others seemed to be rousing, Chia wandered towards the cliff's edge to stimulate his sleepy body. The others ambled to join him, and as the sun was about to rise, they sat down to watch.

The distant pale disc soon mounted the horizon, casting long shadows over the land.

"Well, it's not colourful like Eifassi's sun, or as vibrant as the Uriglipta," Kraniel remarked, obviously disappointed.

"There's much more here, though," Chia commented. "It's not just what we see. Being fleshy numbs it, but whatever it is, I can feel it. It's still strong."

"It must be, even I can sense it," Stanze remarked, putting his hands on the damp grass. "In fact, I can almost hear it."

Jychanumun shot him a glance.

"Growing; I can almost hear it growing," Stanze added.

Jychanumun placed his hands on the ground. "Perhaps it is not growing that you hear," he murmured.

Chia looked at him quizzically, but Jychanumun just shook his head, shrugged, and then got up to make his way back to the ship.

Their first day on Earth had begun.

Chia's first task was to recalibrate the two small travel pods to accommodate their new physicality. He manoeuvred the pods from the 7A to work under the warm sun. It was a surprisingly pleasant experience, feeling the warmth on his face, sitting on the cool grass as he worked, and having a soothing mouthful of Kiyala slipping down his throat whenever he felt a thirst. It allowed him to remember some of the nicer sensations linked to the flesh.

Over the next few hours, Kraniel worked through the growing selection of specimens arriving from Jychanumun and Stanze, and Orion busied himself with the menial task of sending data to the XLS, which Chia knew he did just to observe his team's compatibility.

Already, there was an abundance of information to keep the council satisfied for now, but the team knew that what they really wanted was specific information on the new energy. They'd even given it a name: 'Factor X'.

By the second morning, Chia had finished recalibrating the pods and was ready to start sweeping the continent for signs of

Factor X. He gathered a large ration of Kiyala, notified the team, and left the plateau.

The pod was automated to do most of the work, and Chia could eat and rest in the cramped space, knowing that the sensors would rouse him if they detected anything. He might have enjoyed watching the changing landscape if he hadn't been so anxious to hear the sensors confirm they'd found something. He stopped when his body told him it was necessary, and one day rolled into another, but the pod detected nothing. When he finally reached the far end of the land mass, with the pod trailing the long sandy reaches that indicated the end of the land, he turned the pod around to sweep yet again, on his return to base.

Five days later, having travelled both day and night without rest, the little pod had still detected nothing and the base was once again in sight. Feeling disappointed, but sure that Orion would have formulated a better plan by now, Chia landed back on the plateau beside the 7A. Without pre-announcement, he went straight to see Orion.

"This is not good, although not unexpected," Orion sighed, on hearing the news.

"I've tried every combination of equipment; they all say that what we're looking for isn't out there, even though we know it is." Chia explained. "Have we had any better luck here?"

"Nothing from the specimens," Orion shook his head. "Although it is still early days to have all the results from the team on the XLS. So far they have found nothing either."

"My senses tell me that Factor X is everywhere, even though I can't find a source. Perhaps it's simply undetectable to our mechanical sensors. I'm sorry to be the bearer of bad news."

"No, I'm sorry you've had such a tedious task. In truth I did not expect results, I just hoped for them," Orion shook his head and lowered his voice. "I'm struggling to compose a better plan, my friend. I cannot find inspiration. How can we find what we cannot see or detect with our sensors?"

"Do you have no idea what our next move might be?" Chia asked. He'd assumed Orion would already have a multitude of alternative plans ready to implement, as he always did.

"No, and that's strange in itself. The pull of this planet is oddly distracting. I usually have so many ideas, I lose track of them. But have confidence, I will find us a good strategy."

"Well, if we still only have the one plan, I'll just have to try harder to make it work," Chia decided. "Tomorrow I'll sweep again, disabling my barriers to use every sense of my own, too. If there's any way I can detect it, I will this time."

"Please be careful; bearing in mind the trouble you had last time," Orion nodded. "And I shall meditate on a new strategy out here on the land. If there is a solution, I will find it."

"Are you sure that meditating out here is wise?" Chia asked.

"I too can be courageous," Orion smiled.

Chia frowned, contemplating the potential risks to Orion's safety.

"Come," Orion nodded, attempting to assuage Chia's obvious anxieties, "You know I must become at one with something in order to understand it. It is the only way I know to go forward."

He directed Chia back towards the 7A. "Let us speak with Una. I value his opinions, and I'm sure you'll find his thoughts on the matter interesting."

Once in the 7A, Orion swiftly prepared a port and opened a link to Una. The port blinked, but the connection didn't activate.

"Unusual," Orion frowned. "I suppose he's even busier these days, although he always used to accept direct communications. He's probably engrossed in examining the data we've been sending. I know he's fascinated by this new energy. I'll speak with him later. Do not concern yourself, Chia, I'll make sure our way forward is made clear."

Chia left Orion deep in thought near the empty port, and, after restocking the pod and taking a short rest, he bid his farewells. He was determined that this time he'd locate Factor X.

And Chia did push his next sweep further and deeper, using every sense he possessed, scouring every known crevice, ditch, cave, and valley without rest. He pushed his own senses out as powerfully as his flesh would allow, covering the entire expanse of the continent. Still he found nothing. The days rolled into weeks. Eventually, Chia had to accept that this process would not bear fruit. Fed-up and drained, he set the pod to return to the base.

The pod navigated back into the confines of the 7A's field and Chia dismounted, jaded and ready to fall into his recliner and sleep. But Stanze was waiting for him, obviously restless and perplexed.

"What do you know of Orion's meditations? Is refusing sustenance and not talking normal?" Stanze asked, before Chia could say a word.

Chia assured Stanze that Orion was well versed with all levels of meditation, and Stanze seemed content with that. He handed Chia a crystal.

"This is from Orion. He left one for each of us before beginning his meditations," Stanze stated. "Strategy one is concluded. Until we know our next strategy, we've been granted free time. Kraniel and Jychanumun have both gone exploring. I shall also be away before sunrise; our supplies are low."

Chia nodded and relaxed into his recliner as Stanze left. It was pleasantly quiet without the hum of the pod filling his ears. He tuned into Orion's crystal. The message was brief; in it, he proposed that the team should have the freedom to do as they wish while he meditated. Other than ensuring that they didn't affect the harvesting bios, they could roam the planet as they wished.

Chia guessed the free time afforded to them was merely an interlude while Orion devised a second plan, although he was surprised that he hadn't asked them to continue searching for Factor X. Chia was exhausted, but after hearing his message he couldn't rest. He pulled his aching body from the recliner and went to speak with Orion.

Orion was sitting on the grass by the plateau's edge. When Chia reached him and saw him close-up, illuminated by the bright night sky, he was shocked by the composer's dishevelled appearance. Orion's skin was pallid and drawn, his eyes glazed, and there were several bowls of untouched food by his side. No wonder Stanze had been concerned.

Chia penetrated Orion's haze, asking him how he was, but the replies were fragmented and unspecific. He knelt down and held a cup of Ochrah to Orion's lips, making sure he swallowed some.

Chia didn't like what he saw, but applied logic to mollify his concerns: Firstly, given that he was subsisting on less energy, Orion's physical appearance would be bound to be affected. Secondly, whatever energy source was here must have heightened his awareness, and so his meditations would be particularly deep. And thirdly, Orion meditated regularly: he knew what he was doing.

Once Orion had consumed as much Ochrah as he seemed prepared to accept, Chia stood up, brushed Orion's hair off his face, covered him in a heat sheet, and left him to his meditations.

The following morning, after a good night's rest, Chia took Orion fresh food, and then sat inside the 7A's force field, fine-tuning his vapour daggers. He was exhausted, but his mind raced.

He was determined not to grow restless. With nothing else to occupy him, Chia's daggers ended up as finely tuned as they could be.

Early evening came, and, despite his determination not to succumb to restlessness, Chia was still fretfully trying to occupy his time. Then Stanze's call through the HOTS alerted him.

"Chia? Are you still at the base?" Stanze asked, sounding out of breath.

"Of course."

"Then set up some healing sheets for Kraniel. ETA, eight minutes," Stanze paused, making a strange grunting sound. "Damn rocks," he cursed, "ETA eight minutes, if these rocks don't take me with them first."

"What's wrong?" Chia asked, immediately readying the healing sheets.

"Kraniel's down," Stanze replied. "Body needs a bit of repair."

"Shall I bring a pod to you?"

"No. Nearly there. Can already see the plateau."

Chia sprinted towards the back of the plateau, where the collapsed rocks make a tricky and unreliable descent. He quickly detected Stanze's broad bulk, carefully navigating his way up through the rocks, with Kraniel hanging limply over one shoulder.

Chia lowered himself over the ledge of the plateau and started to make his way down. By the fourth footing, he had sent a slide of shingle tumbling down.

"Don't come any further," Stanze instructed, as he stopped to let the shingle pass him. "Carrying two of you would be considerably more difficult than carrying one."

Chia saw the potential hazard in going any further and carefully pivoted, climbing back up onto the solid ground. An agonizing few moments later, Stanze had reached a high enough position for Chia to help lift Kraniel over the ledge.

When they had carried Kraniel into the 7A and settled him on top of a healing sheet, it was clear that his body wasn't faring well. He was excessively hot, and his normally pale face was now redder than Orion's hair.

"He's been in the sun too much," Stanze frowned. "Typical Kraniel, he never listens. It seems he wasn't taking precautions."

He spread a second healing sheet over Kraniel, sealed the edges so that he was sandwiched between the two, and set the output to 'cool and repair.'

"That's all that needs doing," he said.

"What happened?" Chia asked.

"I'm not sure," Stanze replied. "I found him lying just beyond the plateau. He'll heal fine; the flesh is easily mended. He'll have a headache, but nothing a little Ochrah won't rectify. Watch him," he indicated. "I'm hungry."

Stanze got up, and Chia noticed a large patch of blood on his arm. He pointed it out, but Stanze insisted that it was merely a scratch, and went off to find food. After a few moments, Kraniel's healing sheet started moving, the outlined shape of his palms working up and down the sealed fabric, seemingly looking for a way out.

Chia went to undo the seal and release Kraniel, but then thought a little longer might be good to allow Kraniel time to reflect.

Kraniel continued his silent search for a way out from between the sheets. Eventually, his hands dropped back down and he gave up.

"Okay, how long do I have to stay under here?" came his muffled voice from inside the sheets.

"Until you learn the limits of the flesh," Chia replied firmly.

"That," came Kraniel's subdued reply, "may take some time. How long have you got?"

Chia couldn't help laughing.

"Chia, that's you isn't it?" Kraniel said. "Excellent, let me out of here. I'm fine now."

Chia unsealed the healing sheets and Kraniel sat, putting his hand to his head and frowning. "Eskah, what have you done to me?"

"What have *I* done?" Chia said, shaking his head. "What have *you* done? You should be more careful. If Stanze hadn't found you, you would have stayed out there until your body automatically re-tuned and your energy kicked in to heal you. That could have taken months or even years."

Kraniel managed a rather insincere apology as Stanze returned, handing him a goblet of Ochrah.

"I noticed that the 7A has a materializer," Stanze stated, putting down a sturdy pair of nano-boots and a full set of protective clothing. "These are for you, Kraniel. They're more suitable for the environment than your robes. I'm off again now."

"I'll join you," Kraniel said, hastily putting on the new attire. "I think you'll make an excellent travelling companion."

"If you must," Stanze frowned, but Chia could tell that it was said in good humour.

Stanze crammed an armful of supplies into his shoulder holster and started walking back the way he'd come. Kraniel hurried after him and, shortly later, the two disappeared from sight, over the edge of the rocky slope.

Chia and Orion were alone at the base once again.

Over the following weeks, the cooler weather came while Chia saw to Orion's needs. Activity around the 7A varied. Jychanumun continued to stay away, sending regular, albeit brusque, messages that he was well, and Kraniel and Stanze came and went, each time bringing new finds to the base, from fruits to spring water, and even horses. Chia took every opportunity to take out a pod to continue his search for Factor X.

At first, Chia didn't mind that he was the only one prepared to continue with the search, but every time he saw his team mates, with their latest tales of travel, he couldn't help feeling exasperated. It seemed they were no longer bothered about the progress of their mission, or about Orion's condition.

Orion remained in the same position, sitting motionless at the plateau's edge, his blank eyes staring out to the horizon. His communications had gone from sporadic to non-existent. He didn't eat voluntarily, didn't respond when shaken, and was deaf to Chia's calls. His condition concerned Chia greatly, and he'd taken to forcing water, as well as Ochrah, into Orion's mouth just to try to keep him sustained. It also concerned Chia that they were on an important mission without guidance: aside from his frustration with the rest of the crew, he was starting to think that Orion's meditating was becoming excessive.

It was early evening. Chia was preparing food for Orion, even though Orion would undoubtedly leave it. Stanze and Kraniel had returned from the rains and Stanze was busy building a fire while Kraniel sat playing a game of solitary sands, using plant specimens instead of crystals. It seemed they had finally run out of trivialities to discuss, and, quite frankly, Chia wasn't interested in their tales of wanderings anyway.

Kraniel started the habitual tutting and muttering that he did when he grew restless. Chia knew he was doing it to get a response.

"Would you like a game of something with me?" Kraniel asked.

"No thanks," Chia replied.

"How about horse riding?"

"No,"

"Shall we take a pod and go to the ocean for a swim?"

"No."

"How about some cliff jumping?"

The sarcasm didn't escape Chia's notice. He just raised an eyebrow.

After a long patch of silence, Kraniel slammed his fist on the table, making everything jump. "Look at you! We're supposed to enjoy this free time! Looking at you makes me think of this drooping specimen!" He indicated a particularly lifeless looking plant on the gaming table.

Chia ignored him.

"It's just like you," Kraniel stated, lifting up the wilting plant, goading him further. "You're no fun anymore. In fact, Chia, you've become distinctly boring."

"Boring?" Chia frowned, turning slowly and flashing his eyes warningly at Kraniel. "You mean you haven't noticed that there are more important issues here than your frivolities? Ignoramus."

"You accuse me of ignorance?" Kraniel growled, standing to face Chia. "Do not call me ignorant."

The conversation grew more heated until it escalated into a full-blown argument. Eventually, Chia and Kraniel stood shouting in each other's faces. It was unreasonable and Chia knew it, but he was so tense he felt as if he could explode.

Kraniel was in the middle of delivering a tirade of hostile insults when Chia stopped. Realisation washed through him: here he was, arguing with a good friend, and for what reason? None. It was their shared worries that were causing their tension. Kraniel was clearly just as anxious about their situation as he was. He cocked his head to one side and smiled at Kraniel.

Kraniel stopped shouting, his mouth ajar.

"You're laughing at me!" he roared.

Before Chia could explain that he wasn't laughing at him, Kraniel lurched forward, expelling his energy as he hit Chia, sending him flying.

Chia landed badly and turned just in time to see Kraniel lunge towards him once again. But, before Kraniel could reach him, Stanze appeared from nowhere, threaded a fine cord through both Kraniel's arms and yanked him backwards.

Kraniel thrashed to break free, but Stanze's hold was firm.

"I think," Stanze quietly growled. "You've said enough. I'm starting to feel something I don't like. And if this doesn't stop, I don't think you're going to like it either."

Chia pushed himself up to stand.

"We must stop this," he insisted. "Kraniel, I wasn't laughing at you. I realised that you were just as anxious as I was: I was smiling at you. You're my friend. I would not mock you. Our arguing was stupid; we're both concerned, just as you are, Stanze. I can see it now. Put him down. He's not going to hurt anyone."

Stanze slowly calmed, lowering Kraniel so that his feet touched the ground.

"By Eskah, I'm sorry Chia. Are you all right?" Kraniel asked, in a voice of genuine concern.

"Of course I am," Chia nodded. "It would take rather more than you to floor me completely."

He stood up straighter, activating the nanos to clear the dirt from his body-skin. "For a split second I saw it coming and knew you had to let it out somehow: I was just unlucky enough to be in the way. Stanze, Kraniel, I do believe we're suffering from some of the odd side effects of this damn planet and this strange energy. We can't find it, but it seems to find us."

"I should have voiced my fears," Kraniel nodded. "I'm worried about Orion. I'm concerned that we're failing our mission. But that's no excuse; I've behaved in an un-kutu manner. I'm sorry, and I was out of order to put so much emphasis on enjoyment."

"Perhaps not," Chia continued. "You've made me realise that Orion wants us to learn something from our 'free time' endeavours. Perhaps I should have participated more. And so, perhaps we should start the evening again?"

"I've built a good fire," Stanze nodded.

"Yes," Chia smiled. "It's a cold night, so a fire is good. And with the fire we could have music, visions, and feasting, all out in the open, close to Orion so he too can enjoy our merriment."

Kraniel and Stanze agreed, and it wasn't long before a huge bonfire illuminated the plateau. The three settled around the blaze.

Kraniel had set up a piece of soulful music to play alongside some illuminated art of the Sharm-Nhadarah. Both mediums were set to exude from the centre of the fire, which resulted in an intriguing three-dimensional display, morphed by the flames. Slowly, the recital soothed their spirits and the atmosphere eased a little as they watched the show, quietly contemplating the flickering shapes.

Nobody heard Orion's shambling approach.

"Is it not beautiful?" a voice rasped from behind Chia.

Chia came to with a start, aroused from the hypnotic incantations, and looked around.

Orion stood hunched and expressionless, his blank face directed towards the fire.

"Come sit; you should join us," Chia stated.

Orion did not move, and so Chia arose and guided him to sit. "Come," he coaxed. "You need nourishment, clean robes, and the company of friends."

Orion slumped down clumsily as Kraniel rushed to the 7A, returning with fresh robes, while Stanze ladled a platter high with food. Orion clumsily changed his robes and then slowly pushed around the food on his plate.

"Thank you," Orion nodded, putting the full dish to one side.

"Are you well?" Chia asked.

"I must speak."

"Perhaps you should rest first," Chia intercepted, thinking that Orion really didn't look fine at all.

"No. It has to be now. I have felt concerns. I've not forgotten my obligations."

As he spoke, Chia noticed that his hands were shaking and beads of sweat were forming on his face. He was clearly on the verge of exhaustive collapse.

"Discussions can wait," Chia interrupted. "You must rest."

Orion shook his head. "I will rest soon enough. I must speak first, for I may rest for a long time."

He drew in a deep breath and continued, refusing to be halted. "Can you remember our existence before we found the shadow Aurar or the solid Ferollih? I can. We are timeless, yes, but we are not perfect; we forget. I remember our world without many of the things we now take for granted. Sometimes I dream of things even older. Perhaps they are imaginings. Perhaps we've strayed so far from what we were, and still are, that we have simply forgotten. I believe that the answers are within us. This place is a key."

He paused, holding up his hand as if he was searching for the strength to continue.

"That is enough talking for now. You need rest," Chia decided.

Chia moved around to crouch behind Orion, putting both arms around him, and then stood, partially lifting him to encourage him to rise. Half way up, Orion's legs buckled and Chia jolted as he took on his full weight. Stanze leapt up to help. Together, they led Orion towards the 7A.

"And you think that rest might wait, but I think not," Chia said kindly as they laid him carefully on a recliner, covering his cool, clammy body with layers of healing sheets.

Orion extended his hand to touch Chia's arm. "Tell them what happened to you here," he whispered.

"Tell them? Tell them what?" Chia questioned, rather surprised at Orion's request, but assuming he was not thinking clearly. "Hush and rest. Once you've rested, we will all talk about many things."

Orion's grasp on Chia's arm tightened. "No, you must face what happened, it's important. You're not burnt out, Chia; I saw it. No, not burnt out, you're not."

"Ssh," Chia insisted, but he felt Orion's resolve on the matter. "Very well," he added.

Orion seemed to smile, and his grasp on Chia's arm loosened. Moments later his eyes closed, and he fell into a deep sleep.

Chia chivvied the others away from the 7A, to give Orion peace, before he laid yet another healing sheet on Orion's body. Seeing that Orion slept deeply, he returned to the fire. Kraniel and Stanze watched him expectantly as he stood toasting his hands in front of the flames, deep in thought.

"As you heard, there's something Orion wants me to tell you. About this place – about me – but it's personal."

"You don't have to tell us anything you don't want to," Stanze insisted.

"I don't want to, but Orion thinks it's important. But I want to say first that I didn't lose my mind. I've had full checks and there was, and is, nothing wrong with me."

"You're making us think it's something terrible. Whatever it is, it can't be worse than what I'm imagining," Kraniel added. "And you must know that the reports on your 'incident' were made public."

"As usual, your perspective is refreshing," Chia smiled wryly. He sat down. "When I was here the first time, on my own, I lost time; over three months just disappeared. When I came to I was in rags, emaciated, and I'd wrecked my equipment. Yet I couldn't recall any of it except the grim hallucinations that I suffered. I have no idea what really happened to me."

"Didn't anyone come looking for you?" Stanze asked.

Chia shook his head. "No – in retrospect I found this surprising. My comms were automatically transmitting to the Overseer throughout that time, but he later informed me that the transmissions had stopped. He said he'd assumed I was doing in-depth analyses that required quiet time."

"And you don't remember anything?" Kraniel asked.

Chia shook his head. "No, but I did have visions: those I remember only too well. They were just dreams really; albeit awful ones. Dreams of kutu dying, killing and maiming each other, torn in two, on fire, without limbs, and worse . . . much worse. I saw kutu I knew and cared for tortured; some visions seemed to last for years. And there were atrocities I didn't think I could imagine, yet I visualized myself willingly partaking in them. There were kutu fighting with humans, against humans, and against each other. And there were kutu the likes of which I have never seen before. Thousands of them with the blackest eyes, black wings, and the intent to destroy. And then there was emptiness, a seemingly endless emptiness; that was the worst bit of all. It was as if I no longer existed. It was as if I had . . . died."

"A terrible vision," Stanze agreed thoughtfully. "Nevertheless, kutu do not die and kutu do not war. Some are trained as Anumi warriors, yes, but we keep the peace, and protect, not harm, other kutu."

"It wasn't just the Anumi fighting, it was all kutu," Chia added, feeling uncomfortable. "Anyway, they were just hallucinations. I don't know why Orion wants you to know about them."

"Do you think there's significance to his words?" Kraniel asked. "I heard Orion tell you that you're not burnt out; what did he mean?"

Chia shrugged; he knew many of his skills were lost to him – it was a painful fact that he faced every day. He'd experienced many things on this planet that he couldn't understand, and he didn't like it one little bit. It made him feel vulnerable.

"I don't know," Chia eventually answered. "Perhaps Orion still believes I can locate Factor X. But I can't, I've tried."

Suddenly, a loud shout boomed through their HOTS, interrupting their conversation.

"*Team please!*" the shout vibrated loudly in their ears.

"Eskah, what is it?" Kraniel replied, rubbing the side of his head.

"It's Orion!" the voice boomed. The voice was Jychanumun's. "Go see. I'm on my way . . . running . . . please see to Orion . . . *now* . . . he's dying!"

Regardless of the fact that kutu could not die, Jychanumun's voice was filled with alarm. Chia was already running towards the 7A where Orion's pallid body lay on the healing sheets, his chest rising in irregular, ragged bursts.

"Orion?" Chia said, bending towards him to touch his skin and pushing out his thoughts.

Orion? he asked again, this time through thought-touch.

There was no response; Orion's mind was lost to him. Chia's mind encountered only a blank wall.

"I'm getting no response from him. Kraniel, re-tune him," Chia commanded. "And Stanze, take a pod and find Jychanumun; he seems to know something about this and may be able to help."

Stanze was already out of the 7A as Kraniel hurried over with an assortment of tuning discs. "Stand back," he barked.

Chia jumped out of his way. "Do you know what you're doing?" he asked.

"What do you think?" Kraniel snapped, as he arranged discs around Orion's body. "The healing sheets should have worked. Jychanumun said he was dying; kutu don't die. I need him less fleshy, maybe his flesh is weakened. We *need* to get him out of this state. And get me more healing sheets; these are completely drained."

Kraniel activated the retuning, and then stood scrutinizing the read-outs as they appeared. A perplexed look spread across his face.

"I've never seen anything like it," Kraniel stammered. "He barely registers, as though he doesn't exist. He's on reserve, but his levels are dropping, not rising as they should be, even though I'm constantly feeding him energy. This should be impossible."

"I have the Orb!" Chia declared, "Surely that will be potent enough to revive him."

He took the shimmering object from his neck. The outer shell of Uana had to be shattered to activate the power within.

Concentrating on Orion, Chia rotated the Orb in his hand, and then hurled it to the ground. As the Uana disintegrated, Chia braced himself to redirect the released power towards his friend.

There was nothing. No energy, no release of potent forces, nothing. Only fragments and splinters of Uana littered the ground.

"It's empty!" Chia cried in dismay, kneeling to the floor, brushing his fingers through the shattered pieces.

"Impossible!" cried Kraniel, joining Chia in sifting through the fragments.

"It is. It's empty," Chia repeated. He picked up a tiny crystal that glittered amongst the broken Uana. It looked like a communications module, but there was no power that could be harnessed from it.

Kraniel stood up and checked Orion's status again. "No, it cannot be; Orion has no readings," he whispered.

"No, no, that's impossible," Chia declared. "No!"

"Perhaps you can reach him, then?" Kraniel asked hurriedly. "Orion said you were not burnt out . . . Use your chi. Lend him your strength. Revive him!"

At first Chia backed away. The thought of trying to use a skill that he thought had long been burnt out petrified him. But then he looked at his friend's pallid flesh and knew he had to try.

Chia sank down and placed a hand on Orion's cool, glistening body.

"I'll try. Please, Kraniel, if you can help me at all, do so. Any energy that you have . . ."

Kraniel automatically moved forward, placing a palm on Chia's back to give him his strength. He was not a sensitive, he would not have the chi strength of Chia, but he could help.

Chia searched for the essence of Orion. Through the dullness of his earthly, physical senses he felt something faintly stirring. He tried with everything he could, pushing through the murky barrier until he sensed him, and the pain was almost unbearable. Chia fought through it, struggling to pull together the memory of his lost skill, and jumped into Orion's mind.

But Orion's mind was empty. Chia soared through, breaking through the already disintegrating walls, reaching out in search of his friend.

"Not so fast, Chia!" he heard Kraniel shout. Then he heard only silence. Around him, all was darkness. The darkness offered a peaceful release. Release. Then nothing . . . a seemingly eternal gap of nothingness.

Chia was lost.

TEN

And so, by chance or by choice I journeyed again. This time I walked, not just away from Threetops and my old home, but away from Hollow, with all its terrible ways, and away from any other signs of people and habitation.

I had headed west, following the river across the barren flatland. I hadn't seen the blue light since leaving Hollow, but my mind was often filled with visions of it, and of other things that I had seen. I talked to *him,* the Earth-voice, often now; communication came easily, and I always understood him. Yet, through all my travels, it still troubled me that I had tried to take Huru's life.

"How would you weigh a man's life?" I pondered deeply as I walked.

Does a man have life to weigh? came his reply.

"Surely so," I considered. "He thinks and acts and changes the course of events. Is that not life?"

Indeed, you have grown, he replied, seeming to approve my reasoning. *Does a man change the course of anything? As man was made, does he have a life of his own to weigh?*

I stopped and sat down on the grass.

"Man was made," I repeated his words. It was the first time he had ever said such a thing. It was as I had suspected: he knew all along.

"By whom? You?"

Why would I make man? he laughed.

No, I thought, *I know he didn't make man.*

You walk as a human; you should be telling me, he continued, still laughing.

"You do know, though, don't you?" I said. "You're being evasive again. Why do you never answer anything directly?"

I sensed a change in him. He stopped laughing.

Because you change, and with that, you find your own answers, child, he boomed.

I covered my ears as the ground rumbled and shook.

Could you hold an eternity of thoughts yet? No! Your destiny is your own.

"I am trying!" I shouted in frustration.

The ground stopped rumbling and calm descended around me.

You try my patience, little one, he seemed to sigh, *but you make me remember the weight of all life.*

"Is that a good thing?" I asked carefully.

Yes, you could join me and sleep, he whispered. *Eternal dreams for us both.*

"Perhaps, when you are ready to walk with me on two clumsy limbs, I will be ready to join you in sleep," I said.

That seemed to amuse him greatly. His chortles rumbled off in to the distance until my mind felt my own again.

So, I thought, *he knows that man was made, and yet he did not make man.* And yet the question of who did make man didn't seem to interest him at all. But he didn't agree or disagree with my thought that a man has a life to weigh. I put my head in my hands in exasperation. *Do I have to figure everything out myself?*

Yes, I decided, getting up, slinging my bundle over my shoulder and walking again, *it looks as if I do.*

I thought about it all as I walked, until a small, rodent-like creature, moving along the muddy bank of the stream, caught my attention. I'd made Huru stop through the power of my command: I wondered if I could make this creature stop, too. I slowed down and crouched close, making sure I didn't alarm it.

"Stop," I told it.

The furry brown creature startled at the sudden noise and stopped burrowing. At first I thought that my command to stop had worked, but then I noticed its head twitching from side to side and its little paws scrabbling nervously. It had merely stopped running to sense where the danger was.

"Stop!" I told it again, putting as much authority into my voice as I could, but aware that I did not feel the same tingling sensation as I had experienced in Hollow.

The little creature jumped and started running until it came to a hole in the bank a little further down, and dashed in.

Well, that definitely didn't work, I thought. In a way I was glad, because there was no need for the creature to stop. What benefit would it have been to me, especially as it wasn't doing anything wrong?

Then the revelation hit me. That voice only worked when there was real need. I couldn't just 'make' it happen, because the need wasn't there. It was my first understanding. Understanding felt good. Feeling smug, I continued walking.

I walked for days.

The days grew into weeks.

The weeks crept on until I stopped counting.

The weather around me changed as time passed, from warm and calm, to fresh, and then to cool and stark with cold rains. Then the days started to develop a chill that grew to an icy bitterness with the onset of winter's darkness, and my clothes became persistently damp. It had never been this cold in Threetops. I shivered constantly; I could never get used to it.

The scenery had also changed, growing ever more rugged and sparse, and mimicking the roughness of the weather with its harsh emptiness. I stopped seeing animals and birds, and the occasional tree that I did pass had lost its leaves to the winter chill.

My supplies had finished long ago, and so I coped from day to day, collecting anything edible, such as fruits and roots, wherever I found them. I always seemed to be hungry. Still, I kept following the trail of the river as the weather grew colder, hoping I would find shelter and real food soon.

My body grew leaner every day. I knew this because my hipbones were always bruised and sore from sleeping on hard ground, and my arms seemed to grow thinner and more sinewy before my eyes. I had to keep a cloth wrapped around my forehead, because the cut had not healed and now constantly seeped with an unclean smelly liquid that made my stomach churn. However, my arm and shoulder had healed well, leaving no sign of damage. For that, I was grateful.

For over two weeks I'd been raggedly negotiating a series of rocky inclines that grew steeper and steeper, gradually turning into mountains. The flat ground seemed so far away. The air was thin and crisp by both night and day, and when a frosty wind did blow, it persistently pushed against me, making my limbs feel as heavy and as cumbersome as rocks.

The constant chill made it necessary to wear every sturdy item of clothing I had. I'd ripped my spare skirt to make wrappings for my feet and lower legs; everything else was layered to provide the greatest protection against the biting, icy winds. At first the iciness was painful, but after a while I couldn't feel the cold on some parts of my body, just a pleasant numbness. I thought that maybe some parts of my flesh were growing accustomed to the cold. Nevertheless, no matter how often I stopped, I had become so weary and chilled inside that nothing would warm me. And sleep? That had become almost impossible.

I'd lost sight of the river before I reached the mountains, but I had kept on, telling myself that the water must resurface beyond them. My stores of water were already finished. I was thirsty, and hungrier than I thought possible. My eyes constantly roved for any sign of water and food and drawing breaths as deep as I could I searched for the scent of anything edible, but on these cold rocky slopes barely anything grew, let alone something that could fill my stomach. These rocks had not looked so daunting from a distance, and with each step upwards on the deceptively craggy slopes, the cold, my hunger, my thirst, and my weariness grew. But I pushed on, forcing myself to get beyond these mountains, and I doggedly refused to glance down.

At last, high up under a colourless bleak sky, the bitter wind dropped.

With this lull in the viciousness of the weather I thought that perhaps I could find sleep. I gratefully thanked the skies, and huddled down into a small but reasonably level crack in the mountain. I lay my head on my damp, lumpy bundle and pulled my clothes tightly around me. Ignoring my churning stomach and dry mouth, I closed my eyes with the hope that I might at last get warm.

I think I nearly fell asleep, but just as my body sank into a state of painless stupor, a strong gust of wind gathered, throwing my skirt up and tugging at the rags around my legs. I sat up in time to catch one of the rags, but my left leg was now bare, its wrapping tumbling upwards before falling down upon the rocks, then lifting and blowing still further away. I pulled my clothes even tighter and lay down again, dismayed at losing such a valuable piece of fabric.

The gust of wind passed, but then another came, and then another, and each time the wind grew stronger, until one gust rolled into the next and what had now become a storm began to howl around me.

Tiny pieces of grit were caught up in the wind and started pelting my face, growing ever more aggressive. After a while, the grit began to cut into my skin, like tiny, sharp blades. I shifted closer into the jagged cleft, securing cloth around my mouth and cheeks to stop myself from breathing in the grit. As the vicious little shards rained down, I tugged the wrapping up over my stinging eyes and sat, blindly huddled, making myself as small as I could get.

I had never known such a violent storm, and still the winds increased. I had to let go of the wrapping around my face, hoping that I had tied it well enough, and hold fast to the ridges, digging my feet into the stone to stop myself being thrown over the ledge. My fingers screamed in agony as my fingertips dug further into the shallow grooves. The wind tugged and pushed, trying its best to pry me from the shallow crevasse. I could not let go to secure my loose clothing: the fabric flapped with the wind, beating me along with the constant barrage of grit. The skies I had thanked earlier were now throwing everything they could at me.

The storm raged on; it seemed as though it would never end. I grew tired, and my stiff limbs became deadened with tension. One hand lost its grip, only to find it again just as the other hand could no longer carry my weight.

I knew I could not hold on for much longer. This had to stop – if only I could stop it. But I knew I could not affect the storm: the elements were mindless, and I could not influence them. But *he* could make it stop, I was sure of it.

"Help me," I panted above the noise.

You wish to join me now? His voice was smooth and calm through the noise.

"Not me," I gasped, "This wind. End this wind."

He did not reply.

"Please," I screamed in my mind.

Although I called him again and again, the howling storm raged on, and he did not answer.

Although my cloth-covered eyes were blind, I could sense night come on, but the winds still blew.

Surely, this cannot continue forever, I thought. But every time the wind retreated for a few moments and I loosened my grasp, another gust blew as if trying to trick me from my hold.

Finally, while the night was still in its prime, the gusts started to lighten until they were no more than a strong irregular breeze. I was spent and exhausted. With my fingers still buried in the fissure in the rock, I collapsed.

I don't know how long I lay unconscious. When I awoke, my skin was a mass of red blisters and tiny cuts. Each little wound was embedded with dirt and weeping. It looked horrible, and it felt worse. There was nothing I could do to make my wounds better except to leave them alone. I told myself that at least the pain would take my mind off my hunger and thirst. I was even thirstier now, and in a strange way, I welcomed having something different to focus on.

I knew I was weak. The mountain top looked even further away than ever, but I had to carry on. The thought of carrying myself, yet alone my bundle, seemed too much, so I took my bundle and carefully selected anything that I didn't think was a necessity: my spare sharpening stone, a piece of twine, two pots that were cracked, and, reluctantly, the last of my precious carvings. I sadly put them on the rock; I would leave these things here. At this point, I knew I could not carry anything that wouldn't help me live.

I pushed myself to my knees and looked to the top of the mountain. Yes, it was far, but it was not as far as the foot of the mountain that lay below me. I tried to stand, but my legs shook so dangerously that I sat back down. But I would not get this far only to have my own legs drop me to my death, I decided. So, I pushed myself on, crawling awkwardly on my hands and knees, my near-empty bundle tied around my neck and dragging behind me. I aimed for the top, imagining the sights that would greet me when I could see the other side. There had to be water, food and shelter there. I didn't think I could go on for much longer.

I crawled, strangely grateful for the throbbing in my knees when they became raw; it kept me awake, and if I was awake, I could move. And if I moved, I could find water. I couldn't stop thinking of water, and me drinking it, and drinking more water – so much of it that I could swim in it and drink and drink and drink as I swam.

I passed a small tree devoid of leaves; its stunted growth all twisted and grey, protruding at a strange angle from the craggy rocks. I found it strangely beautiful. It survived without enough water either, and had done so for a long time: it was dry, almost fossilized. The storm had knocked off most of its dead branches and a few lay scattered around. I crawled over to one. It was about my height, with a gnarled lump part of the way down, just below where I could hold it. I picked it up, wedged it into the rock, slowly pulled myself to stand, and hobbled on.

My thirst intensified to the point that my lips started sticking to my teeth. At first I was able to push them off with my tongue, but moments later, they would stick again, so I just left them. I resented the burden of carrying the empty water pots that reminded me of my thirst, but I stubbornly refused to abandon them. I occasionally passed tufts of wiry grass, looking at them grudgingly. I'd tried eating grasses, days ago, but it had only made me vomit up the last of my water, thus losing even more liquid from my ravaged body, and so I knew not to try it again. Everything reminded me of how parched I was.

The following day I slowly stumbled on, resting more and more regularly, even though I couldn't find sleep. At one point, I had to stop; a stinking liquid kept trickling down my face, making me retch so violently that I almost fell down the craggy slopes. It was oozing from the gash on my head, the only bit of my body that seemed to stay warm. I'd left its rancid bandage on the crags after the dirt storm, and now the liquid had nothing to soak into, so I grudgingly ripped another length from my skirt and bound it around my head to soak up the putrid drips.

I kept on through the night, wanting to rest, but my body hurt so much that keeping still was unbearable. I made little progress; my pace having declined to nothing more than a slow, staggering gait. I could barely move and I couldn't sleep. It seemed as if every passing moment had become a trial to overcome.

The following evening the winds grew again, but less fierce this time, so I hunched in once more, staying as close to the mountain as the jagged rocks allowed, and waited for them to pass. I covered my face in anticipation of the oncoming barrage of grit, but it wasn't grit that fell. Instead, the black skies opened with rolls of thunder and large beads of rain descended hard and fast.

I wrenched down my face covering and opened my mouth. Water! Water was touching my lips, my face, my hair – fresh, clean water!

I quickly groped in my bundle and found my empty water pots. I pulled them out, popping out the stoppers and, while I wedged my feet against the rocks to hold me firm, pointed them towards the onslaught of rain. It was blissful. I let the rain wash my face, and opened my mouth to take in every droplet that I could.

The rains came and went with disappointing speed. The rumbles of thunder passed over the mountain, leaving my tongue stuck to the top of my mouth trying to savour the moistness.

I checked my two pots to find that there was little more than an inch of water between them. I held it up to drink, and then stopped. Puddles of rain must have collected, I thought. If I hurried, I could drink them.

Next to me, the shallow ridges held tiny pools of water that were gradually draining away. I quickly put down my pots and bent, lapping the water with my tongue. Once I had gathered all I could from one tiny fissure I moved around until I found another, and then another, and kept on until I had licked the surrounding stone of all its streaming water.

I moved along to find more from the next protruding rock, but the wind had already worked its torment and driven the little currents away. I knew there was no point looking for more. What I had drunk was hardly enough to satiate my thirst; I thought I could drink a river, but I told myself it was better than nothing at all.

I tenderly poured the meagre contents of both water pots into one and stoppered it tightly, making sure the pot had no hidden cracks. Then, I gathered my stick and bundle and continued towards the peak. As I struggled on, I hoped for more rain, but it didn't come, and as much as I wanted to keep my prize of water, it was drunk by the end of the day.

As I neared the summit, wearily dragging my feet from one rock to the next, the way grew steeper. The walking stick helped, but the rough wood bit through the flesh of my hand, making it weep and bleed. It concerned me that it did not hurt, as I knew it should, but either way it didn't seem to matter anymore.

At last, I trod the final section of rocks leading to the highest point of the mountain. I gathered momentum, staggering as fast as I could, my enthusiasm giving me strength, and knowing that when I got to the summit it would provide panoramic views of landscape below. My daydreams were filled with visions of fat, fruit-filled trees and rushing clean water, and my spirits lifted to a high I'd forgotten I could feel.

It was the last few steps, I was nearly there; soon I would see, and everything would be all right.

One more step and then my line of sight will pass the peak.

I pulled my weight up that last step.

I dropped my stick.

There was nothing. No verdant landscape, no fruit-filled garden of delights, no pleasant land with gentle streams. There was nothing but more of the scrubby, craggy declines I had just climbed.

I squinted, my blurred, sticky eyes refusing to accept the despair that I felt looking down on the landscape below me. But my senses did not lie. There was nothing but a wasteland of pale rocks interspersed with tufts of brown-green grasses sprouting from sparse patches of hard soil. It was barren, untouched by the vivid growth I had hoped for; there was nothing but more of the same landscape that I had just struggled through.

In the extreme distance I could just about make out patches of darker green that I thought might indicate thick forests, but I knew they were too far away to offer any hope. I could faintly sense water, but even further away than the patches of green, and so far away that it was hidden from sight. Here, now, and in my path there was no food, no water, no warmth, and no shelter. These inhospitable spartan hills provided only disillusionment and desolation.

I thought of Threetops, and it seemed like a life lived by some other girl. But that life had been mine once; a life of ease, separated from the here and now by a towering monument of disappointment. And to think that I'd been so naïve as to presume that wherever I went, everywhere would provide for me like the land around my old village. I had taken so much for granted. Threetops, with its rolling valleys that always seemed warm, its plump fruit trees and vegetables that wanted to grow even where we hadn't planted them, the cosy beds with mattresses stuffed with softened grasses, I now missed them all. And fire, that precious flame that lived constantly, giving warmth even though we knew not how to make it. *Just to have fire alone*, I thought – that would be something. I was so cold.

My heart sank. My weight felt tiresome. I wanted to sleep forever.

I slumped down on the surprisingly welcoming stone and closed my eyes.

Oh, just to stop, to cease now, my thoughts taunted me. Look at you: you're a pile of bones and skin held together by nothing but cuts and bruises. There's nothing out there for you, no answers. There is no point to this, no point at all. Just choose to cease and leave this disappointment and pain. There is nothing in this world for you, nothing, so you may as well just cease. There's no food and water, so you're going to cease anyway.

Ceasing would not be so bad, I thought, and with that thought I felt my mind drifting into a calm warmth. *Yes, perhaps it is time to cease.*

For the first time in a long time, I felt peace.

I didn't think I was sleeping, but I saw the black-eyed one from my dreams. He was in my head, holding out his hand as he always did. But I didn't try to reach him this time. There wasn't any point, I never reached him. And so I just watched his image as he kept his hand outstretched. But then he moved to one side, indicating behind him, and through the darkness beyond his figure I saw images from my own memory. They were terrible images of Rew the orcharder, lying motionless in the grass as his last life energy dripped from his flesh, and of Wirrel, blackening in the flames until he was nothing but dust.

The black-eyed one fixed his gaze on me and spoke.

"Live," I heard him say.

Then he was gone.

Don't go, I wanted to say, come back. But my mouth refused to move and he didn't come back.

He had said, 'Live'.

No, I thought, *please don't give me a reason to go on, I think I've accepted that I'm ceasing.*

I felt compelled to open my sticky eyes and stare up at the sky.

Wirrel had ceased, I thought, and Rew too. After Rew fell from a tree, they had placed his empty body in the forest to be forgotten. I'd sneaked to look at him two nights later and he hadn't looked or smelled like the Rew I remembered anymore. He had looked like a seething pile of maggots on a very rotten fruit. My body would look like that if I ceased. I knew I would cease. I could feel the inevitability of it; it had been following me for days. But, I didn't want to cease, not up here, alone, without any answers to the things I'd travelled for. When Rew ceased, at least he'd had a full belly, a clean robe and contentment with his lot. When Wirrel had ceased, though the flames took his body, he had his fire for Soul to keep him strong. I didn't want it to finish here, not like this. I had nothing.

Nothing? I thought. I have nothing. Therefore I have something, even if it is merely nothing. This nothing can mean my ending, or I could choose nothing as my reason to go on.

I would not choose to cease while I could still go on. Surely, I thought, all I had to do for now was walk; all it takes is putting one foot in front of another. If I could walk, I could find food and water to make my body go on, to live.

I slowly sat, groped for my stick and scooped it up, and then stubbornly propped myself up to stand. Two deep breaths and I placed a foot heavily on the first ledge below me. Slowly, I lowered my body, dragging my next foot after it. Then to the next rock, then the next.

Yes, I could do this, I thought. I can keep living.

A single, dark motivation now kept me moving: the desire not to cease.

I tried picking out what I thought was the quickest and most direct route down the other side of the mountain. The downward sloping proved more arduous than the inclines preceding them, and I fell with increasing regularity, gashing, bruising, and scraping every part of my body as I did so. I left splatters of blood in my path. Perhaps I would not simply cease, I thought bitterly. Perhaps I would slowly leave little bits of myself on these rocks until there was nothing left of me. With each fall, I pushed myself to rise again with a smile; at least every tumble is a dozen steps that I do not have to take, I told myself.

My eyes remained focussed on the tiny patch of green in the distance, and I hoped that my intuition was not failing like my body. The nights slowly came and went, and, bit by bit, I covered ground. I could not stop to rest for the fear that I might never wake, so my mind took solace by counting every footstep and tumble that I took.

After a while, I forgot about counting my footsteps and had lost all feeling in my hands and face. I couldn't even think anymore.

I know more rains came and went, always with disappointing speed, but every drop that hit my mouth and found my water carriers was most precious. The word 'water' revolved constantly in my head, forming its own tune to my steps. At least, I think it was in my head; I might have been humming it aloud. I could hardly tell what was real and what was imaginary.

After some time, I noticed that I hadn't fallen down for several steps. I wondered if the rocks around me were beginning to level. It didn't matter; the nearing sense of water compelled me forward as if it was something that mattered to me. I had the vague thought that I had to keep walking, perhaps it was to reach the trees ahead, or perhaps I didn't know how to stop anymore.

It seemed as if it was almost high noon. The faint sun tried in vain to warm me.

It must be moving to autumn, I thought vaguely. *I should get home now and help father with the crops. I'm so thirsty. Didn't I bring water? I must have left it on the table. Mother will be cross. I hope she's making berry pie for supper. Didn't I leave some Kathi berries somewhere? I hope mother's using them, Soul will like them too. Where is Soul? Isn't she coming out to help today?*

No, Soul doesn't help with the crops, I thought. *That's not right. Who's Soul?*

Suddenly, some reality came painfully flooding back. I wasn't going home; I didn't have a home any more.

I didn't know how long I'd been walking; time seemed to have vanished, but at least I'd left the rocky mountain behind. Somehow, I'd made it down and had travelled a fair distance.

I strained my eyes to observe the approaching patch of green. It was a forest and, as the woodland grew closer, my heart jumped. I could make out familiar shapes. Huge Pine and Gera trees soared to the sky, their trunks entwined with the dead carcasses of rough Lewey Vines. Yes, I knew these trees; knew as well that their tall trunks and heavy canopies ensured that no edible vegetation could grow in their shadows.

My heart should have sunk, as I knew there would be no food, but I could only think of water, and I was sure that it lay ahead. The forest was thick with trees growing close together, making the soil seem black from their shadows. I stumbled around the outskirts of the wood, oblivious to the stark sunlight, pulled by the now-audible sound of moving water.

As the far edge of the wood loomed closer, the ground became dotted with clumps of shrubs and the sound of water rushed so loudly that I could almost taste it. The forest began to bend and I moved into its shadows. Suddenly, I saw a glimmer of a fast but tiny stream, vigorously spurting from a worn, rocky hole between the boughs of the trees. There was water! Lots and lots of wonderful water!

I clumsily ran, fell, and ran again until I lay by the water, drinking as much as I could. Then I was sick, and drank some more.

In numb exhaustion, I lay by the erupting jet, falling into a slumber only to keep awakening from nightmares of thirst. Comforted by my realisation that it was merely a dream, I would drink more water before drifting into sleep again.

I don't know how long I lingered by my new-found treasure, but I eventually awoke to daylight, feeling a grogginess heavier than I could ever remember. I clumsily filled my two dry water pots and staggered on to follow the incline along the forest edge, making sure I didn't stray too far from the stream.

The stream wove in and out of the trees, tumbling downwards; it often disappeared underground, but I could always hear it resurfacing not too far ahead, and that comforted me. The heady, sweet scent from the Pine and Gera trees mingled with those of many strange plants, wafting past me on warm currents. If the signs were true, the air was becoming warmer and moister, suggesting that somewhere before me was a valley.

The trees ended abruptly, from a shield of darkness rising up beside me to nothing. When the trees stopped, so did I. The view beyond warmed me more than the sun ever could.

Where the rushing stream emerged from the trees it opened up, running into a lake in the middle of a small, deep valley, the walls of which were covered in a rich array of growths. Where the trees curved around the valley, I could see clusters of tall purple flowers, the likes of which I had never seen before, standing proud in the trees' shadows, hugging their trunks. To my left, and sloping downwards, the thick green grass looked luscious, with sporadic clusters of colour burst from a myriad of tiny flowers that were catching the last hours of sunlight. The area directly ahead, beyond the lake, was mainly littered with small, heavily stocked bushes. The bushes looked familiar. They looked very similar to Punni bushes. They were! There was food! Edible and ripe Punni berries.

I clasped my stick tightly and hobbled as fast as I could towards the Punni berries. I wanted to gorge myself, to stuff as many of those tiny plump berries into my mouth as possible. But, I remembered how sick I had been from drinking so quickly after such a thirst, so as soon as I reached the first bush I picked a single fat berry and popped it into my mouth. I slowly rolled it around with my tongue, piercing the skin and letting the insides slowly dissolve. Punni berries had never tasted so good. I spat out the seed and took another, performing the same ritual. Fourteen berries later and I thought I'd eaten a feast.

I gathered a baleful of the fattest fruits into my skirt and traipsed wearily to the edge of the lake to where the grass looked soft and inviting. I could have easily slept there and then, but lying back on the slope, covetously munching through my stockpile, felt too good to sleep. There was no wind here, only a warm, damp current slowly drifting around the sheltered valley, and the last of the sun that could now warm my skin. The intoxicating scent from the trees washed through my body like an internal scented bath, covering my own foul smell. While thinking dreamily of a cool refreshing bathe, and relishing the sweet remains of Punni berry in my mouth, my eyelids drooped and I drifted into a deep dreamless sleep.

I awoke woozily as the sun was high, surprised that without anything covering my eyes I had slept for so long. I pushed myself to rise but could not move. I pushed again, but no, I still couldn't move.

Panic hit me; I was paralysed, unable to do so much as wiggle my arms.

No, I thought, *this cannot be!* How could I finally have reached this place to find food and water and then not be able to move? It was like a terrible nightmare.

I concentrated, and eventually, little by little, I managed to make my fingers wiggle. And then, with equally strenuous effort, I moved my arms. The movement was accompanied by a horrendous cracking sensation. It sounded like I was breaking, but I didn't feel any pain. Could my body be that damaged?

A part of me just wanted to keep lying in the grass, just in case any movement would break a bit more of me, but I knew I couldn't stay prostrate on the ground forever. So, with more moving and louder cracking, eventually, and with much noise, I managed to sit up.

I looked down, scared of the injuries I'd find after hearing such awful noises, but I couldn't *see* any injuries. In fact, I couldn't see any part of my body. I was caked in dried clay. The thick layers of dirt, dust and sand must have accumulated all over me, been softened by the damp dew, and then baked onto my body by the drying sun. I was not broken. I was encased in my own, thick, me-shaped pot. The relief made me fall back in laughter. If I pulled it off carefully, I could probably make a statue.

I eventually pulled myself up and lumbered down towards the lake, popping Punni berries into my mouth as I walked. I couldn't see my remaining foot covering. If it was still on my feet, then it was caked with so many layers of filth that it was invisible. I found a traversable sloping bank down to the water and tried wriggling out of my skirt, but it was rock-hard against my body, and so I gave up and waded into the water, still fully clothed. As the lake rose around me and the clothes softened enough to make them movable, I dispensed of the raggedy items, throwing them onto the bank.

The lake turned out to be surprisingly warm, and so I waded a little further out and took in my surroundings.

It hadn't occurred to me when I'd first seen the valley that the water, which had been my path and guide for so long, stopped here with this lake. This was where the river finally ended. If it plummeted into the earth, the re-emergence was so far away I could not sense it.

But, I wondered, if the river had continued, would I eventually choose to walk on? Surely not. I would not have to go anywhere. I had everything here I could need. But more than that, I had survived.

"*Live*," the black-eyed one had said. Just that one word. And I had.

ELEVEN

Orion was lost.

Chia had entered Orion's mind to try to find him, and now he was lost too.

Orion, Chia struggled to think. *Who is Orion? Where is he? Did it matter?* He vaguely saw a path; beyond it was something he felt he wanted to reach. There was light, or was it darkness, or was it nothing?

"Chia?" a smooth voice called. Smooth like . . . like something. "Chia, walk to me," the voice coaxed, "Listen and walk."

Oh, what a voice, what a song. All he could think was: *yes, I'll walk, just keep singing.*

"Walk to me, listen to me, walk to me."

So he walked, enchanted by the voice of smoothness.

But then the voice changed, "I have him!" it shouted.

The peacefulness evaporated and Chia felt himself suddenly caught up, trapped, as if his thoughts were being crushed into a tiny space. He fought back, trying to break free from the confinement, but every door was closed. He had to go in.

Chia came to. A strange kutu hovered over him. Slowly, he recognised the face; it was Jychanumun.

"Do not let him sleep yet," Chia heard Jychanumun instruct.

Chia watched dazedly as Jychanumun moved to lean over Orion, placing a single finger between his brows.

"Orion! Orion! Come, walk, find your way home," the black-eyed kutu sang.

"What is happening?" Chia stammered, trying to push himself to sit.

"I'm not sure," Stanze sighed, helping him. "You and Orion had stopped, just stopped. Never seen anything like it. When I found Jychanumun, he kept repeating that he had Orion, that he could not hold him for long. When we returned, Kraniel was trying to revive you both. Then this. That is all I know."

Chia wanted to ask more, but his mind and body felt numb, so he lay propped in Stanze's grasp, covered by a healing sheet, watching the white-skinned creature chanting songs to Orion's motionless body.

Jychanumun's voice had deepened to a husky growl.

"Stay," he kept chanting, "You have found yourself. Stay."

Suddenly, he let out a yell and shot back from Orion's body.

"He's found his flesh," Jychanumun whispered, staggering backwards. "But it is weak."

Orion's skin had already lost some of its bluish hue, but still he didn't move. Then Chia noticed his eyes moving rapidly behind his eyelids.

"He has readings again," Kraniel sighed with relief as he covered Orion in healing sheets. "Not strong, but they are increasing."

Jychanumun slowly teetered toward the nearest recliner, holding onto its side to steady himself.

"Is Orion alright?" Chia asked.

Jychanumun held up his hand. "Yes," he replied simply. "Rest."

Stanze helped Chia to a recliner and covered him in more healing sheets. As much as Chia felt drained to exhaustion, he did not want to rest. He strained to keep his eyes open; wanting to make certain that all remained well.

"What happened?" he asked again.

"You walked to the death paths," Jychanumun whispered. "I brought you back. You are well, Orion is well; rest."

With that, Jychanumun wearily staggered to the farthest recliner in the shade, unwilling to accept help from Stanze or Kraniel, and sank down, pulling a large cushion over his face.

"Are you alright?" the other kutu asked in concern.

"I need silence and darkness."

And although Chia did not want to rest, in no time, sleep soon overcame his aching flesh.

Chia awoke to a sore body and a foggy mind, with the sun penetrating his eyelids. He was so exhausted that he couldn't think clearly at all. How did he get to his recliner? Everything was a blur. Realising he held something in his left hand; he unfurled his fingers to look at a tiny communications module. He instantly recognised the little object; it was the very same communications module that had gone missing from the port in his chambers on the substation XLS. But hadn't this been hidden inside his Orb? He rubbed his thumb over the module, which sent the protective nanos on his body armour into a state of frenzied activity. The module was contaminated with tracking nanos!

Suddenly, the previous day's events came flooding back to Chia. He shot up, took a containment sphere from his flight case, activated it around the suspicious module and looked around.

Orion was no longer on his recliner, so he headed towards the sound of Stanze's voice, carrying the module in the containment sphere with him.

Stanze was by the large table, stirring a steaming vase of Ochrah, while Kraniel sat looking perplexed.

"Where's Orion?" Chia asked, concerned for his well-being.

"I'm here," Orion replied. He walked into the area, towelling his hair with a lumi cloth and looking surprisingly well. "Are you well, Chia?"

"Well enough," Chia nodded, relieved to see Orion up and about, "thanks to Jychanumun. Where is he?"

"He's out cold," Orion replied, taking a seat at the table and pouring them all goblets of Ochrah. "I want to ask him what happened yesterday, but whatever it was seems to have taken a great deal from him."

"Are you well enough to talk?" Chia asked.

"Yes, look at me," Orion shrugged. "Whatever Jychanumun did has restored me. As soon as he is well enough, I wish to discuss a new strategy with you all. I have found one, at last. Until then, talk to me, Chia."

Chia placed the small module, now confined in its containment sphere, on the table.

"That was in my Orb. It's a communication module – the very same one that went missing from my port on the substation. It's been modified. I've put it in a sphere because it's now teeming with tracking nanos. Because the module was already tuned to my chi, someone has heard every word we've said since I had the Orb. And the tracking nanos would have spread to everything it touched."

Orion stared at the module in the sphere, clearly dumbfounded. "And how, by Eskah, could that happen?"

"Only on purpose, by someone with the intent of tracking us and secretly observing this mission," Chia frowned. "Somebody has been spying on us."

"That's unheard of," Stanze said in horror.

Chia nodded. "Well, these tracking nanos did not get there accidentally. The Orb was a dud. This was purposely put inside it instead: I've put it in the sphere to blank its signals. It should stay there. We have been tracked and listened to since we left the substation."

"Spying is not the way kutu work," Stanze objected.

"Can we be sure?" Chia frowned.

"No, Stanze is right," Orion intercepted. "I was on the council for a long time; I would know. Privacy is respected and each kutu is allowed to make the right decisions. There's no need for spying. I have never heard of such a thing."

"Then explain that," Chia indicated to the containment sphere.

"Where has the Uana gone?" Chia asked, but did not wait for a response, beginning to search around the clearing. "The outer fragments of Uana? I would like to see them."

Kraniel rose and emptied one of the cleaning units, passing the dusty fragments of the Orb's outer shell to Chia.

Chia sat holding them for a few moments. "These are nothing – just pieces of Uana. I sense the residue of thousands of kutu, as I would expect. So at some point this Orb was indeed filled with kutu essence."

"If you can still sense kutu residue at all, then it must have been broken recently. Or else the residue would have completely dispersed," Orion pointed out.

Chia agreed. "But I can't pinpoint who modified it, or used its power, as there are too many essences present."

Kraniel arose, putting a large case on the table. He opened it to reveal a meticulously organised array of ornate apparatus. He indicated towards the containment sphere that now housed the spy module.

"I would like to examine it. Stay quiet while it is out of its container. I will put it back before I say anything more."

Chia took the module from the sphere and handed it to Kraniel, who put it in a magnifying box, studied it, and then quietly placed it back into the sphere.

"When you work with all the newest prototype equipment, you start to recognise the craftsmanship of an individual," Kraniel stated. "This I recognise; it's Anara's. Before we left he was working for Shursa."

"Shursa gave me the Orb," Chia added.

"He probably assumed you'd never use it to discover its sabotage; Orbs are too highly treasured."

"Why? What is to be gained from this?"

Orion had been deep in thought. He began pacing the length of the table. "By means of this Orb, Shursa would get to know our progress before anyone else, which would allow him to ensure that he could control information. And if you aren't sure it's him, remember that he did specifically request the chance to oversee the substation dealing with the Earth project. I've spoken with you, Chia, about my theories; if you've been monitored, he'd know those theories."

"And perhaps he was monitoring me when I was here the first time. Perhaps he saw what happened, and knows more about this place than he's saying. Perhaps he thinks he knows what's here and, whatever it is, he wants to be in control of it," Chia added.

"No, that would never happen," Orion frowned. "Kutu share. No kutu would grant Shursa control outside of authorised methods, especially Una the Supreme. Still, I must consider what I am going to tell Una; he will not be happy."

Stanze stood, looking around the 7A and its force field. "We must cleanse the area and look for more unwanted devices that could track us before we do anything else. We may still be being monitored."

The thought filled them all with alarm, and quickly they began searching for more tracking devices. Once a manual check had been done, Chia set the 7A to search itself, and then carried out a thorough chi sweep of the entire area. Once satisfied that there were no other unwelcome devices present, Chia set the 7A to thoroughly cleanse everything, including themselves, within its field.

As they waited for the 7A to finish, Jychanumun walked through the containment field. He looked terrible. His fine face was gaunt and grey, with darker shadows ringing his eyes. He stopped to observe the crystal in the sphere.

"I overheard you talking," he stated bluntly, before anyone could speak. "I must leave here."

He picked up a goblet of Ochrah, downed the liquid, and then walked up into the 7A.

Chia glanced at Orion questioningly, but Orion seemed to have no idea about what Jychanumun was planning. From within the 7A they could hear Jychanumun gathering his few personal items. It seemed he really was leaving.

Orion got up and went to him.

"You cannot just leave," Chia overheard Orion say. "Where are you going?"

"I can leave and I am leaving. Where, I have not decided."

"Why? What has happened?"

"Much. You are in danger. If I leave, you'll no longer be in danger."

"Why?"

"That's all you need to know."

Jychanumun walked back out of the 7A carrying a small satchel.

"No!" Orion cried. His voice rose as he followed Jychanumun. "That's not all I need to know. I've come to call you my friend. You know you can feel my thoughts, so trust me."

Jychanumun stopped, turning to face Orion.

Orion put up his palms, beseeching. "Please, just speak to me."

"You would not want to know. You would not believe me."

"I do want to know. You know I do," Orion replied. "It is my choice. I want to know."

"Very well," Jychanumun said, shaking his head. "Your choice."

He took a step forward so that he directly faced Orion, and put his hands either side of Orion's head.

Orion's eyes glazed over and his mouth went slack. Slowly his expression changed from blankness to one of horror. The two kutu seemed to stand there for an eternity, although in reality it was only a few moments, until Jychanumun dropped his hands. He dextrously moved forward, catching Orion as he staggered backwards and nearly fell.

Jychanumun manoeuvred Orion onto the bench and handed him a goblet of Ochrah.

Orion, his face still in shock, took several large gulps, considered the remaining liquid, and then downed it in one draught. He sat for a moment, clutching the goblet as if it were something precious, and then looked up at Jychanumun.

"You believe this to be true?" he asked.

Jychanumun nodded.

Orion considered this a moment. "Do you not think that maybe, just maybe, it was all either a hallucination or a dream-state. Perhaps from spending so much time in isolation? I know, and Chia knows, such mind tricks are possible."

Jychanumun shook his head. "I warned you that you would not believe me."

Orion rubbed his brow.

"Then for argument's sake it will be considered correct. I must share your beliefs with Chia, Kraniel and Stanze here. Do not leave yet, Jychanumun. Give me a few moments to speak with them."

"A few moments," Jychanumun nodded, and folded his arms, staring at the ground.

"Jychanumun has shown me something," Orion told the assembled companions. "I'll summarize: interrupt me if what I say becomes unclear."He took a deep breath.

"Jychanumun believes that there are many more of *his* kind; all black-winged and black-eyed, existing so far away that we do not know about them. They are like us, but live very differently. They apparently know how to cause death. To them, death is voluntary, but requires a guide to navigate the death paths. Any kutu can find their way onto the death paths, but without a guide to direct them, they would wander for eternity. There was only one kutu known who could navigate the paths; only one who embraced equal amounts of both black and white energy: Jychanumun."

"I did not enjoy what I had to do, but death was their choice," Jychanumun said bitterly, as if trying to justify his actions. "It was better than letting them wander the paths eternally." Then he fell silent again.

"One day, Jychanumun was told to bring death to one who did not choose it." Orion's voice became grave. "Their leader ordered Jychanumun to kill. Although he would not do it, he knew to refuse would have severe repercussions. So Jychanumun stole a ship and left without word, vowing never to use his skill again. Untold millenniums later, he joined us. But . . ." Orion paused, "Jychanumun believes that last night Chia and I entered the death paths, and he retrieved us. If someone has been spying on us, Jychanumun's skill will now be known to whoever tracks us. And Jychanumun is concerned that our kind would want his knowledge once they learn of it, and that it would be the start of terrible things."

Orion fell silent, awaiting a response.

Chia could see the predicament: Orion obviously thought the story was nothing more than a series of hallucinatory memories. And indeed, Jychanumun's imagery did have similarities to Chia's own experiences. But Jychanumun had spent thousands of years in isolation, without help or friends in order to recover – what Jychanumun believed was, to him, real, and therefore needed to be treated with seriousness.

"It is kutu principle never to demand knowledge, or use it for personal advantage," Chia stated. "None of us would demand your skills."

"How can you be sure?" Jychanumun's voice was stern. "My kind vowed the same in ancient times. The easy opportunity to gain power can change that."

"No-one would ever get that far. If necessary, we will deny everything," Orion rebutted him coolly.

The others looked at him, surprised.

"Yes, I know truth is the first law," he went on, "and we'll probably not ever need to lie. But think about it . . . If we don't speak of the incident, and if we erase any related data, nobody will ask us of it, because nobody would know. Except, that is, the one who has been spying on us. Our spy can never openly ask us about it, or they'll have to admit to spying. And then we would deny all knowledge of what Jychanumun has done."

"But you must not tarnish your integrity to protect me!" Jychanumun insisted. "That is how it starts."

"I see it as a justified action to protect all kutu."

"You do not believe me."

"I believe that these thoughts are in your head," Orion replied, "and I believe that something untoward happened last evening and that you helped us. I believe you have skills that surpass our understanding."

"But you don't believe what I say about of my kind, the nigh-kutu? You don't believe what I have told you about death, or of the facts I have shown you of my past?"

Orion just looked at him.

"You do not believe me," Jychanumun shook his head.

"Perhaps I am too focussed on the issues of here and now, which are many. You have my greatest respect, my friend. So may we just agree to treat your account as if it were true?"

Jychanumun looked stonily at Orion. "Regardless of whether you believe me or not, I still must leave."

"You may leave, but we will still hold the knowledge, and we would still need to hide it."

"The situation may have already gone beyond that."

"How?"

Jychanumun clearly no longer wished to talk, but Orion insisted. Jychanumun stepped forward, ready to pass his knowledge through mind-touch again.

"Please Jychanumun, speak," Orion said, rubbing his brow. "Your thoughts are so strong that I could barely hold them before. I know you don't like speaking, but please, just this time, tell us what we need to know."

Jychanumun stepped back, crossing his arms again.

"Initiating death, even by simply entering the death paths, is like lighting a beacon in all worlds. It is not just your kind to consider. My kind may have sensed that beacon. I do not think they did, but it's not a chance I'm willing to take."

"So?" Orion asked. "Your kind, these so-called nigh-kutu, can take a leap into Eskah's oblivion."

"Do you not think they would want me back?" Jychanumun asked, looking straight at Orion, "At any cost?"

"You would not have to go," Orion replied.

"I would not have a choice," Jychanumun said coldly.

"Then if they have sensed you, it's already too late. Your leaving would make no difference."

Jychanumun shook his head. "Then understand this, Orion. I go to protect you. It is not for me. Do you think they would leave any alone who knew of my abilities? No."

There was a long pause.

"Then we would be already involved," Orion sighed, "whether you left or not. And, if they did come looking for you, they would come here, and the rest of us would be easy to trace. You would be the only kutu who could possibly help."

Jychanumun stared at Orion, his face set in stern deliberation.

"What are the chances that we were sensed?" Orion asked.

"Small. But even a small chance is not good."

Orion nodded. "Stay, Jychanumun, and let's take that small chance together. You are needed here and now, on this team."

"Very well, I will stay," Jychanumun finally stated. "To protect you all. But if you enter death's paths again, its strength will be ten-fold, and we can be certain that they will notice. You would not want that."

"We all hear your words," Orion sighed, "We understand your beliefs. But I still have the imminent issue of this tracking module. I must speak to the Supreme."

Chia had sat listening with the rest of the team in silence. Nobody wished to contradict Jychanumun; he was a talented but clearly troubled kutu who had spent aeons alone in contemplation. But his words made no sense to Chia. Kutu did not die. No record of any kutu dying existed anywhere. Kutu *were*, and always would be. Of course they forget much: small incidents that were thousands of years old were insignificant to them. They existed within change. Moving towards an improved tomorrow was their principle for existence.

The team remained silent while Orion activated the communication port. Almost instantly, the transmission was connected. But it wasn't the Supreme looking back at Orion, it was Shursa. Shursa appeared to be in the Supreme's private chambers, looking radiant and relaxed.

"Shursa," Orion said, obviously taken aback. "I thought this was the Supreme's private channel."

"Una is busy," Shursa replied. "He's passed communication authority to me. It's a pleasure to see you, Orion. How can I help?"

"It's fine; it can wait," Orion said. "Could you ask Una to contact me?"

"Certainly," Shursa said. "So, how are you? And how is the mission progressing? Do you have anything to report yet?" His eyes narrowed as he spoke.

Chia noticed Orion make a discreet adjustment to the commport setting so it showed the image of Shursa with a stronger energy display. Shursa's image shifted. Now it showed the change in Shursa with great clarity. Not only did he flicker with his usual yellow hue, now he was a translucent shape shimmering with all colours. Shursa's energy had been changed.

"The mission is on track, thank you," Orion replied guardedly, "Although there is no specific news outside of our regular reports. I was simply hoping to speak to Una."

"I want to be the first to know when there's news of Factor X," Shursa stated abruptly. "The Supreme would want that, as he's preoccupied with other matters. You can come directly to me, Orion, even though I'm busy. I'll make time for you."

Orion nodded his agreement. In the background of Shursa's transmission, several communication signals were audible. Shursa was ignoring them.

"Is there anything else, Orion?" Shursa asked unhurriedly.

"No, you've told me all I need to know," Orion bowed. He then waved his hand over the port, terminating the transmission.

Orion turned to the team, his calm façade replaced with alarm and anger.

"Shursa has used the power of an Orb!" he fumed. "Did you see his colours? They've changed! Shursa is a pure yellow; he now has the temporary essence of every colour. The only possible place to find every kutu colour in one place is in an Orb. And only the power of an Orb is strong enough to temporarily change a kutu. Shursa's never been awarded an Orb, so it *must* have been him who infiltrated Chia's Orb. I have overlooked many wrongs from that kutu; but this time, he has gone too far!"

"There is even more going on than I can sense," Chia added. "Yet my chi is not telling me exactly what."

"And I must still speak with Una. Eskah knows why he's allowing Shursa to intercept his communications."

"I doubt Shursa will pass on your message."

"Perhaps I should return to Eden."

"No, not yet," Chia disagreed. "If you leave, who will be sent to replace you? Most likely it would be someone Shursa chooses. We may end up with no control in the situation at all. I believe Shursa wants whatever energy lays hidden here. We must ensure that we find it first and deliver it directly to Una."

"True," Orion frowned, rubbing his brow.

"You could send Una a message via Nirrious," Chia continued, "Perhaps in a crystal, as we don't know whose communications are being monitored. None of us has to leave here; the 7A can get to the substation alone, to be officially restocked, which is Nirrious's job. You can embed a message for Nirrious to find in the stock list. He can pass the message to Una."

"But surely even a stock list would be perused by others. I cannot see how we could embed anything."

"Did you know Nirrious' hobbies include studying the old arts of strategy . . . ?"

"Are you thinking the Transmeba codes?"

Chia smiled.

"But he would never know to look for it."

"Well, my friend," Chia was still smiling. "Maybe we have had just one lucky break today. As you have wisely selected Nirrious to head our substation team, and Nirrious was my captain for quite some time, we have an alert word. Use that and he will know something more is concealed within the data. He has the tenacity to decipher what we have used." He paused, "Unfortunately though, the word is 'Sauropsida.' You'll have to figure out an adroit way of getting that word on a shopping list."

"I think I can manage that," Orion replied. He immediately headed into the 7A to prepare the message for Nirrious, while Chia made a hasty list of necessary provisions for the stock list and primed the ship.

Once Orion had finished writing a message to the Supreme, Chia encoded the text into the stock list, knowing that Nirrious had the skill to work it out and start preparing the base. The 7A was programmed to reach the substation and return as soon as its stock quota was on board.

"What are you doing?" Orion asked, as Chia placed large discs in each corner of the force field.

"These," Chia huffed, directing Stanze to help him, "will temporarily maintain our force field while the 7A is gone. We could do with retrieving any portable equipment we may require too. Healing rods particularly."

Orion came back moments later, with an assortment of apparatus from the 7A's crew provisions all neatly packed into a small case: two hand-held scanners, four healing rods, a small pile of energy healing sheets, five detuners, and a flexible containment sphere.

"That'll do," Chia approved. "The 7A should only be away for half a day, or a day at the most."

"There is all my apparatus over there too," Kraniel added. "I'm sure I could put the basics together if we need something."

Orion agreed. "Are we done?" He was clearly anxious for his message to reach the Supreme.

"All done," Chia confirmed as he calibrated the last force-field anchor point.

He walked to the side of the craft, putting his hands over an area that appeared no different from any other part of the outer shell. The gleaming bio-mechanical mass responded, closing its hatches.

"Fly well," Chia said aloud as the 7A pulled away from the force field, rose silently and swiftly departed from the plateau in the direction of their the substation.

The team re-gathered around the conference table. Their concern was obvious.

"There's much to digest," Orion stated. "But we must stay focussed; our mission has not changed. We must find Factor X."

"We've scanned and searched repeatedly, but found nothing," Chia stated firmly. "Unless you have a new means of locating the source, we're at a standstill."

"My meditations were fruitful in providing direction," Orion nodded. "I've come to believe that the energy fluctuations came from a human."

Chia looked at him in bemusement. "If it was from a human, wouldn't the automated sweeps have picked it up? Wouldn't my scans of the continent, including their colonies, have picked it up? And anyway, if we can't absorb this energy; how could a human, a mere bios harvester who functions at only ten percent of kutu potential, possibly succeed? It doesn't make sense."

"I know," Orion shrugged, "But towards the end of my meditations I sensed the residue of the energy waves. There were specific locations. Within those locations I sensed human every time." He tutted to himself, as if struggling to get his point across. "Where are the continental maps?" he asked. "I'll show you."

Chia found a map and illuminated it, spreading it out over the length of the table.

"Around here, and somewhere around here," Orion pointed to two places. "But I can't be too sure, as it was so hazy. And I also sensed something here."

"But they're too far apart to come from a human source, let alone one solitary one," Chia objected.

The rest of the group sat silently, clearly sceptical too.

"I'm sure it is coming from a human," Orion said decidedly. "Somehow the automated harvesting hasn't detected it. Perhaps I've been foolish not to consider it as a possibility before, but humans are not just made from kutu genetics, they're made from Earth matter. And if they're made from Earth matter, and we don't fully understand all the energies present on Earth, surely there's a possibility of unforeseen developments in humans, including the ability to absorb Factor X. What I do know, no matter how implausible it sounds, is that one human is the link to these surges of Factor X."

Chia still felt sceptical. The areas Orion had pointed to on the continent maps, and the distance between them ... they just didn't seem consistent with a bios' capabilities. Chia noticed Jychanumun watching him.

"Orion's right," Jychanumun suddenly spoke, holding his gaze on Chia. "And she is hurt."

"She?" Orion cried out. "You think it's a she? What have you felt?"

"Her pain," Jychanumun stated simply.

"Do you know where she is?" Orion asked.

"I would not be standing here if I did," Jychanumun replied.

"Then how do you know it's a she? I don't doubt you, but there must be something else that could help our search," Orion quizzed. "Something, anything?"

Jychanumun shook his head. "The human is female. She is in pain. She is alone. That's all."

Orion studied Jychanumun for a moment, watching his unchanged expression.

"Very well," Orion eventually sighed, obviously realising that he was not going to gain any more information from Jychanumun. "We will find this female human. Humans were made for us to harvest, so once we've found her we should be able to harvest Factor X. Hopefully that part will be easy."

"I don't wish to be disparaging here," Chia interrupted, "but, as I have explained before, we have not found anything unique from humans or their settlements. Our equipment is useless for locating Factor X, no matter what form it takes. So how do you suggest we determine which human we're looking for?"

Orion shrugged. "We can only hope our instincts will guide us; either that, or your chi, Kraniel's analyses, or Stanze's sheer will. And we'll scour every human encampment in person until we find her, or a sign of her past presence."

Chia still was not convinced.

"Yes, it's a hopeful plan; but it's the right plan," Orion added.

Orion's unruffled conviction was all that Chia needed. He had seen it many times before, and Orion was always proved right. It was as if something in Orion would click into place, telling him that the situation was just the way it was: nothing to do with his opinion, it was pure fact.

"Then I suggest we get started; our situation has advanced to a matter of severe urgency," Chia stated.

"If we have to scour every human encampment, could we re-tune? Even just for short periods?" Stanze asked. "I'm aware of the potential dangers of high energy configurations in the presence of unknown energies, but wings would be faster."

"That would be wise," Orion agreed. "Use the portable re-tuners and re-tune just for travelling if you wish. If you re-tune just for short periods, when you return to flesh again it won't be too uncomfortable."

The team nodded in agreement, although Chia decided to remain cautious and opted not to re-tune. As much as the flesh was cumbersome and slow, it was safe.

"There must be nearly 100 colonies in the target area, so we have much to do," Orion told them. "Kraniel, organize the containment area for a more in-depth analysis of humans. Chia, get an update on all new human colonies within our parameters. Meanwhile, Jychanumun and Stanze, we'll visit some settlements and start looking immediately."

While he was talking, Orion had opened the case he had just packed and pulled out the two portable scanners.

"There are only two," he shrugged.

Jychanumun responded quickly: "I do not want one."

But Jychanumun did accept a re-tuner. Everyone took one. Without a further word, Orion positioned a re-tuner between his eyes and stood erect as the converter activated.

Chia knew that, just as tuning from energy to flesh was unpleasant, retuning from flesh back to energy was extremely satisfying; it meant returning to their natural state. He watched Orion smile as the retuning took effect. The weight lifted from his flesh, his luminescence increased and the hard lines of matter blurred as his body lost substance, while the crimson energy began surging through him. His hair began moving around his head, and his long, red energy-wings formed behind him. As soon as his wings had finished forming, he re-stabilized, relaxed, and smiled.

Behind Orion, Stanze seemed to grow in stature as he too re-tuned. Gold now shimmered around him, extending out to a huge set of wings. And Jychanumun's wings also unfurled. It was the first time Chia had seen this kutu's wings. They were long and pure black, shimmering with an energy that cast dark rays, like glowing shadows. If they had not reminded Chia of his past hallucinations, they may have even been beautiful.

"We'll be back before nightfall," Orion asserted.

Without a further word, Orion, Jychanumun and Stanze opened their energy-wings and soared into the sky for the first time on this planet. Within seconds, they were gone from view.

By nightfall, Chia had gathered the data he needed and had returned to the base, opting to help Kraniel in constructing the containment field. It wasn't long before he sensed his team-mates approaching. He looked up just as a dot of light appeared in the sky, which divided into three as the companions moved nearer.

Gradually, Orion, Jychanumun, and Stanze took shape, each one seemingly carrying something. Sure enough, as they descended the final section, it was clear that each of them clutched two limp humans, one under each arm.

They landed with a controlled thump. Orion and Stanze were arguing.

"We leave them out here," Orion insisted.

"But they may expire from the cold," Stanze argued. "Even if that doesn't perturb you, I don't want to drag another load here tomorrow just because you didn't agree to minor provisions."

"Point taken," Orion conceded. "Then we'll put them in the containment field. Is it finished, Kraniel?"

Kraniel nodded, and stepped back as he activated the containment field to show them. The corner points hummed, and then a shimmering wall rose from the ground, making a sizeable enclosed square. "You can pass through the containment field, but the bios cannot," he stated.

"Good. This will alert us if there are any problems. I just don't want them to access our living area. Agreed, Stanze?"

Stanze grunted acceptance, and waited while Kraniel deactivated the shields. Then he lifted the two larger bios, while Orion and Jychanumun took the smaller ones; together they placed them within the area. Once this was done, Kraniel reset the containment field, enclosing the six humans safely. Stanze then walked back into the enclosure, the invisible wall flickering as he passed through, and carefully moved the larger female, who had slumped onto the smallest one.

Jychanumun crouched, watching the bios with fascination.

"They're still functioning; we just made them sleep," Orion commented.

"Have you found Factor X in them?" Chia asked, even though he did not sense anything unusual from them.

"Unfortunately not. I'd have let you know straight away if we'd been that lucky," Orion replied. "These are just samples for comparison. We also need to analyse them for any generational changes that may help in our search. The two larger ones are third generation. The small ones are fourth generation."

"Fourth generation already? How quickly are they reproducing?"

"Very quickly, and in quantity too, which doesn't help our search. Their original numbers have increased over a hundred-fold."

"I'm keen to hear of your findings," Chia said, as he, Stanze and Kraniel joined the conversation.

"No sign of the one we're seeking yet," Orion began, "We initially tried communicating with them. Amazingly, they've already developed a basic structure of noises for communication.

I used their words and spoke to one; unfortunately, I temporarily deafened it. So, please make a note not to use the mind-voice, just use your mouth for sounds. I asked the first human I spoke to, a female, if she knew who we were. She replied, 'bird-men'."

Chia burst into laughter.

"You've got to give it credit," Orion smiled, "we still had our wings; it wasn't a bad answer. We entered the hut of this family unit. The female offered us food. I handed it to the male and the female rushed over, grabbed it, and took it away. She thought we'd found it offensive."

"Interesting," Kraniel considered. "Could they be trained to perform tasks?"

"Definitely," Orion replied, "Although you wouldn't want to conflict with their programming. They've also developed strong identities. One of the offspring even told me its name was Har, son of Barah and Sur."

"They all had names," Stanze added. "Anything that has developed enough to give itself a name deserves some respect."

"They are just bios, Stanze," Kraniel commented. "No different to the plant specimens that made up part of you supper last night."

"I could not consume anything that could give itself a name," Stanze quickly defended himself.

"They may taste good," Kraniel goaded.

"They're ten percent kutu – would you like me to tune to one-hundred percent physical so you can dine on me?" Stanze was clearly annoyed.

"Now that is a thought," Kraniel laughed. "But Stanze, I am teasing you. You really are too easy, you know."

"Even if you were serious, we can easily repair humans," Orion intercepted. "We'll return the specimens once we've finished with them, undamaged. They'll know no different. There's no point harming them. One bios pair generates twelve or so more; as the generations pass they become thousands. Regardless of Factor X, this planet has many resources to harvest."

"Good," Stanze nodded, "And Kraniel, once you've observed them I think you'll feel differently. You helped to design them to look like us; you might just find they act like us a bit more than you'd anticipated."

"We must understand these bios," Orion added. "Yes, we made them, but it seems as though the high mix of kutu genes, along with the unknown energies from this planet, has helped them to develop in unforeseen ways. Until now, they've just been one of many harvesting bios, a disposable commodity. Now we must view them with fresh eyes, without prejudice, because one of these humans is the link that we seek. We must understand more now, in order to help us find the one we're after."

"That'll take some time," Chia stated. "Today's sweep showed 134 colonies in the target area. I do not think she is in a colony any longer; the points of the surges suggest movement. And Jychanumun said she was in pain and alone."

"She must have been born in a colony. Even if we just find her lineage, we'll have a lead," Orion said. "We just need that first lead. Let's get to the conference table. Chia, we'll need the latest mappings of this continent, plus mappings of the human settlements."

Moments later, the team had regrouped around the table inside their force field. It felt oddly empty without the presence of the 7A craft.

Chia activated the results of their latest mappings, stretching them out in light-layers over the table so that they overlaid each other.

"Now," Orion began, "Human colonies have grown – there are many new ones. We'll discount the newest, as the one we're looking for must be adult, from her estimated speed. And these," he took a pointer and circled the areas that Chia had sensed the energy had come from, "are where we should start. If we work backwards through the timeline of surges . . ."

He pointed out on the map where Chia had sensed the minor surges from, finishing with an area that touched the outskirts of several small colonies. "One of these is where she was most likely born or originated from, or at least passed through. There may be a trace for you to sense, Chia, if we are close enough. Or she may have blood relatives there."

Kraniel drummed his fingers on the table, making the maps ripple. "Assuming that it did originate from one of these places, if humans now have names and can communicate we can ask specific questions of them, to discover who is missing. If we work backwards and find its lineage, we would have a genetic print that could be traceable through our equipment."

"Yes. We may even find that this link to Factor X runs in the same family line. There are three colonies to scour. We'll start at first light, at their waking time, and take one colony at a time. We've several portable sensor devices that will be useful." Orion paused. "I wish I could notify Una. When are we expecting the 7A's return?"

"It should have been back by now," Chia frowned. "Perhaps I didn't convey a strong enough sense of urgency to the ship to hasten its return."

"I'll find out its position," Orion replied, immediately walking away to contact Nirrious.

While they waited, Stanze unloaded supplies from their limited stores. Soon the table filled with an unglamorous, but adequate, assortment of dishes.

Orion returned with a look of concern on his face. "I've contacted Nirrious, but he could not talk back. I think the 7A is still in port at the substation. It seems we'll not have it back tonight. Can we manage the force fields without it?"

Chia nodded, "I can recalibrate so that we have enough energy for a few more days."

"Good," Orion pondered. "But I'm concerned. I sensed distress in Nirrious's voice, although he told me all was well."

"I know my captain well, and Nirrious is a very capable kutu," Chia reassured. "The 7A is in good hands. Do not concern yourself about him."

"Yes, I must keep my focus," Orion nodded, as though disciplining himself. "We must all eat and then rest. At first light we leave; we have three colonies to work through and a human to locate."

He glanced at the maps that were still spread out on the table. "They have even given the colonies names," he mused. "Perhaps we should use them. Tomorrow we visit Longplain, Whitehill and Threetops."

TWELVE

I had survived.

I had lived to find food, water, and everything I needed in this wonderful valley, and I didn't have to walk anywhere else if I didn't want to. I'd slept with a full belly for the first time in I didn't know how long. Then, after the shock of thinking I had been paralysed, only to realise I was merely baked in dirt, I had taken my stinking body to the lake for a much-needed wash.

Feeling hopeful at the very thought of not having to travel anywhere else, I swam in the lake, having just enough energy to keep myself afloat. It was beautiful and cool, but the warmth in the valley stopped me feeling cold. The lake's reflective surface distorted into ripples around me; gazing down, the clear water made the lake appear shallow, but it took only a quick dive to the bottom to find out that it was at least five times my height. A fat, lazy fish shimmered past, curious about the source of the ripples, and I tried chasing it, only to discover that it was surprisingly agile and easily slipped away from my grasp.

I wanted to stay longer in the lake, but my worn-out body was quickly exhausted, and so I paddled towards a low bank where I could sit without making any effort.

Pulling myself from the water, my emerging clean flesh shocked me. The dried mud had been concealing an array of sores, bashes, cuts and bruises. One foot was swollen to twice its normal size, and my legs were a colourful assortment of wounds, with flaps of skin hanging down from them in tiny rags. My torso was the same and my hands were even worse, but peering into the water to inspect my face gave the greatest shock. Amongst the blisters and cuts, a long, angry looking scar ran from my temple to below my eyebrow. I warily prodded it: the puffiness gave way under my fingers. It was mending, but only just.

The sight of my flesh made me realise that I would not be going anywhere for a while, even if I had wanted to. I would have to stay in this place until my body had a chance to mend the damage it had endured.

Over the following days I concentrated on rest, allowing my body to heal. But once I relaxed and did nothing, my injuries seemed to hurt even more. And despite how hungry I was, my stomach could not bear much food, although I ate what I could manage, instinctively knowing that it would aid the healing. It was bathing in the lake that brought the quickest improvements to my flesh, and so I spent as much time swimming as my arms allowed, and each day I swam for longer.

The warmth of the valley made it unnecessary to wear my ragged clothes, and the sun was a soothing tonic, so I lazed naked in the grasses most of the time, only covering myself with the remnants of my rags during the cooler nights. I could do little with my hands, as the healing progressed to puffiness and deep scabs, but I didn't care; there was nothing I had to do. The days were slow, and I pushed aside all thought of the life I had left behind.

After a few days, I forced myself to hobble towards that part of the forest where flowers grew on the woodland edge, on the opposite side of the valley. I sensed that many small animals were hiding amongst the dense trees, all as curious about me as I was about them. They mostly stayed away from my sight, but a few left their hiding places to take a peek at me. I don't think they'd seen anything quite like me, and I certainly had not seen the likes of many of them. I kept my distance, letting them know that this place was as much theirs as mine.

I found a new type of food in the forest; small round things covered in a hard brown casing. I'd seen some of the animals eat them, although the shells were harder for me to get through than the animals seemed to find them. I had to pound them with a stone to get to the edible centre, which meant that I squashed more than I ate, but they were worth the effort. They tasted like a vegetable, though they grew on trees, and I savoured every one that I could find.

I lost all sense of time as I gained strength; it meant nothing to me in this place.

I changed a great deal; physically I grew taller, although perhaps it was my rags shrinking from their regular dunkings in the lake, and I could feel how lean my body had become. My hands and feet recovered well, their skin hardening to my needs, but I'd given up trying to keep my hair orderly; it seemed to flourish in my new environment.

Yet of all the changes, it was my face that changed the most. My reflection in the lake was a chiselled structure with bruised eyes that changed from green to black and always gazed back at me as if they were not my own. The long scar above my eyebrow did not fade, and still seemed alien to me. Sometimes, I did not look like me at all.

Although I had changed so much, I felt free. Nothing stopped me from doing what I wanted to do except my own basic bodily needs. I still dreamt of the black-eyed one, although he'd not spoken since that single command: 'live'. Well, I had lived, and I had found this place. It had saved me, and now it sustained me. I loved my valley.

Sometimes I just watched the valley changing: changing with the night, or with the weather; it was a fascinating to watch the movement of everything. Sometimes I sat for days, contemplating the life that slept in the earth. Sometimes I just danced under the stars. I did many things and nothing. I just *was*.

I think it had been early summer when I arrived at the valley. Now the season grew cooler again, although the iciness of the mountains seemed far away. I moved from the lake-side to sleep in the forest, scooping out an area just big enough to lie in and filling it with dried grasses and leaves. When I wanted to sleep, I would lie on top of the crunchy mound and wiggle until submerged in a warm grass cocoon. It was even better than my old bed in Threetops.

In preparation for the possibility of the oncoming cold, when I suspected that finding anything edible would be a task, I had, after several attempts, successfully managed to store food that didn't rot. I'd hidden some in tree hollows, and blocked the entrance from foraging animals. I also fashioned a small wooden needle, and repaired some of my rags to make a badly fitting, but warm, tunic. When the rains fell, I thanked the forest for keeping its ample foliage and providing shelter. I seemed to need nothing that the valley couldn't provide.

The last two nights had been dry, so I'd chosen to sleep out by the lake. I missed the family of wild cats who had taken to visiting me in the forest, sometimes curling up with me for a while before taking to the branches to sleep. I'd observed quite a few new animals recently that were obviously breeding and expanding their living area. I liked them all, although it had initially shocked me to discover that they lived off each other as well as fruits and vegetables - something I'd not previously considered. And so I gave this matter much thought, placing myself in the overall scheme of things. Did nothing wish to consume me? True, the men of my village had hunted on the eve of a choosing, but I'd thought it was more about catching the animal than eating it. The eating of it was done out of respect for the hunt, a celebration of life, or so they said.

My contemplations moved to the nights that I'd seen the blue light. Did it feed on something that came from the people while they slept? I had seen light escape from Rew when he ceased, and so perhaps all people were made of light as well as flesh, and perhaps that light was edible. It didn't make sense, but I couldn't stop thinking about it. I battled with myself, thinking that, as I had no issue with the animals living off each other, surely I should have no issue if people were also within this food hierarchy. But I could not contemplate eating an animal; it didn't feel right, and to eat people, or somehow take from them? Ah, even the thought of it was too much.

A rapid succession of small plaintive sounds interrupted my thoughts.

I looked around. The two wildcat cubs stood at the edge of the trees, crying out. As soon as I sat, they bounded over, hesitating when they realised that they were moving from their terrain, and so I called to them, coaxing them, trying to communicate that it was all right. I tussled with them for a moment, before the mother called them back to the forest and they left me, happy that they now knew where I was. Mah and Meah I called them. Meah was the bossier one and Mah was quiet but sneaky, sporadically leaping on her sister as they both rejoined their mother. The charade was a pleasure to watch.

I lay back again, popping a handful of berries into my mouth. I'd lost my train of thought: ah yes, the blue light feeding on people. But this was my valley and I'd seen no blue light here, so did it really matter anymore? I popped another Punni berry in my mouth. Surely not, I thought.

I propped one arm behind my head and watched the clouds drift past as the sky darkened, filling with bright dots. I hoped for a sound night's sleep.

My recent slumbers had been riddled with unsettling images. I shut my eyes, purposely conjuring images of the things I liked and wanted to dream of. I knew I should be happy: all was so good here, and I loved my valley. But every time I settled down to sleep, restlessness seemed to grow quicker than my happiness, and I continuously battled against it.

Suddenly, from within my contemplations, I sensed movement around my face.

I came to with a start, shaking my head, thinking that a curious spider could be investigating my ears or nose. I briskly rubbed my face until I was satisfied I wasn't about to breath in an insect.

Perhaps I'm lying on an ants' nest, my tired thoughts cruelly suggested.

My whole body tickled in response, so I jumped up, shaking myself vigorously. Looking down to brush my legs, I reeled back with surprise. Were my sleepy eyes playing tricks? I rubbed them and looked again, but the image remained. I was looking at myself, asleep, lying on my back, my head resting on the bale of spare clothes, in exactly the same position I'd assumed that evening to watch the sky.

I shook my head and pummelled my face, but the image still would not go. I must be dreaming again.

It was the first time I'd seen myself in a dream, and it was indeed strange. Curiously, I peered closer. I looked different from how I thought I would, with my hair matted into clumps, fanning out scraggily across the ground and still glistening with the lake's moisture. I reminded myself of a dishevelled wild animal.

I reached down to push the hair from my sleeping face, but my hand moved through my flesh like liquid. I could feel something, but not the solidity I expected, and I didn't like it.

I should wake up now, I thought. *But how do I make myself wake from a dream?*

And then, distracting me from my absorption, I heard a faint, shrill pulse over the night's silence.

I quietened my breathing, trying to identify the sound. It was like cries – far off, indistinct cries that were pulsing in waves through my head, and they were growing louder. The hairs on the back of my neck prickled with unease.

Standing up cautiously, I sensed motion stirring around me.

What should have been a clear, bright night view around me now seemed blurred, as if my eyes would not focus. Everything around me seemed to be vibrating. Even the ground beneath my feet shuddered, yet I remained motionless.

"Is this you?" I called out.

There was no reply from the Earth-voice. I didn't even feel his presence.

"If it's you, please stop," I called again.

Again nothing. No, I could not feel him. This was not him. This was my dream; it was coming from me.

I held up my hands, comparing the dancing disc of the moon to the stillness of my fingers. The longer I watched my surroundings, the more violent the movement grew, until the vibrating trees oscillated wildly, the lake spun without making a wave, and even the dark sky shook, causing the silver white dots to become indistinct blurs. The cries now spiralled, wailing around me as if everything were saturated with the terrible sound. Shadows and shapes moulded into each other until I could no longer define any one thing: there was just one mass of moving darkness. I shut my eyes to stop the queasiness in my stomach.

"It's just a dream," I repeated out loud, "It's just a dream. Wake up!"

I opened my eyes, but I had not woken. The dancing, indistinct mass greeted me once again with a vengeance and the piercing screams spun directionless around me.

Covering my ears and straining to find anything to focus on, a shape began manifesting within the moving chaos. The dark blur that should have been the forest was fading and giving way to something luminous from the depths of its shadows. My eyes were drawn to it, the only still thing around me.

Gradually edges formed and the static shape became the image of a monstrous, golden structure now forming in place of the trees.

I was rooted with awe. I had never seen anything like it, standing ablaze against its dark backdrop, radiant in pale, shining gold stone. Its lustrous walls sloped upwards, interwoven with intricate carvings, the height of a hundred huts. Its mass then rose more jaggedly with thousands of steps, topped by a central domed tower. Above the tower was a huge core of spiralling light that raged like an angry bolt of lightning. Directly before me stood a gaping entrance, at least the height of ten men, framed by tall, carved columns.

I took a cautious step towards the magnificent structure, dropping my hands from my ears. The loud cries appeared to becoming from inside the building. I tried focussing on the inside, through the open doorway, and thought I saw movement, shadow on shadow. I didn't want to move closer – the cries were conveying a sense of dismay that threatened to overwhelm me – but I was compelled to do so.

Moving slowly towards the building's entrance, the screams rose in volume, coursing through my head. I stared up at the columns framing the doorway and reeled backwards. I could see now that the columns were statues of creatures, their huge pointed wings and chiselled, snarling faces looking down at me threateningly.

All my senses drove me to aid the one responsible for those terrible cries, but I could not move any closer. I was repelled by something dreadful and unknown. The fear overwhelmed me. I turned on my heel and fled.

I ran as fast as I could. I ran and ran until my legs were numb, my ears were away from the sound, and I could run no more. Finally, unable to continue, and convinced that I had escaped the spectre, I collapsed to my knees.

I stayed there, with my head in my hands, until everything grew silent and I dared to look up. I expected to see familiar trees or hills, but instead a new apparition grimly greeted me. A group of doors encircled me in darkness – there was just the darkness and the doors, forming one unbroken circle around me. Would this dream never end?

Cautiously I turned, looking at the doors that now surrounded me. I felt no dread, just emptiness and static silence. I stood and walked to one of the doors, my footsteps not making a sound.

The doors were plain, standing over twice my height, and each one had only a single, circular knob. They were black, yet somehow they leaked a dim light that defined their forms. There were no frames or walls in between them – there was just blackness. The ground was as black as the doors and there were no bright dots in the sky, just a continuing empty void.

I slowly leaned in to open one of the doors, but before I had a chance to grasp the handle it melted away from my fingers, and the door silently glided open.

I stared down a long, dark corridor filled with silence. Like the doors, the corridor seemed to be lit by a faint glow that came from nowhere. As my eyes became accustomed to the gloom, I saw that the glow emanated from the joins and corners of the corridor, highlighting an apparently negotiable passageway. Knowing that I wanted to be free of the dream, and not knowing what else I could do, I stepped inside.

I had expected the stale smell of mustiness usually found in such shadowy places, but the corridor didn't smell of anything. The total absence of anything to sense was even worse than the mass of spinning shapes. I turned to leave. But behind me, where the doorway had once been, there was now a mirror image of the corridor in front of me. I could see no way out.

I walked soundlessly, turning numerous corners. As I walked, I thought I saw somebody, but each time I turned a corner and tried to catch sight of them, they were gone. I kept walking; each passage looking identical, and the corridor went on and on. I thought it was endless, but then, thankfully, another door came into view.

I touched the shimmering handle, pushing through as the door began opening, and then stopped. I seemed to be in the same place I had started, encircled by blackness and doors.

I chose another door and touched the handle, and again it glided open. I entered the passage, and this time I started running. Now I definitely saw someone at the end of the corridor, and so I ran faster to catch them, but no matter how quickly I ran they were never any more than a distant outline. I kept running, turning corner after corner, until another door was before me. Breathlessly, I opened it. Again, I was right where I had started. I chose another door. Yet more corridors, the same blurred figure, and more doors – I just kept running.

I continued for what seemed the whole night and more,

passing through doors and running through corridors, finding no way out and never catching up with the distant figure. I was sure I'd tried every option several times, although I was confused with so many twists and turns, never sure which door I had entered last or its position relative to any of the other doors. Anger began welling in me.

Bursting through another door, only to be confronted with the sight of more doors surrounding me yet again, I felt I could not move. I *would* not move!

I gathered breath and screamed with frustration.

And with my scream, the apparition shattered.

I sat bolt upright, my damp hair sticking to my wet face, my body clammy and cold. I touched my face for reassurance that this was now reality, and I looked around, searching for more visions. To my relief, the world was real again. Around me, the tips of the trees swayed in the night's breeze and the dots filled the dark sky with a bright clarity over my valley. It was a beautiful evening, yet I felt cold.

Slumping back into the grass, and, holding my shoulders to stop myself shivering, I thought I would not return to sleep. I had no desire to. Neither did I have any desire to move. So I wrapped my spare clothes around me and watched the moon's reflection shimmer on the lake. I wished these dreams would leave me in peace.

Surprisingly, sleep did eventually find me, and I awoke very early the following day, feeling bad-tempered and irritable. The sun had only just entered the sky, and was now casting long, stark shadows across the dew-soaked grass. The lucky flowers were still lazily asleep, and the birds sang a noisy morning chorus above my head.

Eventually I sat up, still swaddled in my grubby clothes, and I rummaged for a comb among my meagre possessions. I took my foul mood out on my hair, tugging it violently, cursing the knots and the general impracticality of its length and thickness. My knife protruded from the ground beside me, glinting suggestively. I picked it up and hacked off a bunch of the troublesome knots.

I was still annoyed, and so I gorged on a large portion of my food, scoffing it thoughtlessly until I felt sick. Feeling sick made me even more annoyed with myself. Grumbling at my own greed, I arose and wandered the slopes, gathering the longest grasses to dry out for a bed.

"So, where are you?" I called out.

No answer.

"Well, I shall talk to myself and you'll just have to listen, because I know you can hear me. I dreamt last night. It was not good a good dream. It seemed real, but how could a dream be real?"

A familiar tingling rippled under my skin, and a warm sense of knowing washed over me. So, I was right, he was listening.

Dreams are reality. Non-linear, timeless.

"I have never seen a building like the one from my dream, so it cannot be real," I protested.

Silence.

"But I have not," I insisted.

There was silence again, the all-too familiar silence that told me: You already know these things, so you figure them out. Bring that knowledge to the front of your mind and embrace it.

"Very well," I eventually admitted with resignation.

I let my mind empty itself of thought, while some other part of my subconscious skimmed through everything I'd come to try to understand.

"Dreams are real, and you said they are timeless. But," I reasoned aloud, "this body that I walk in is not timeless. You've also once said that dreams put the substance of a life's fragmented knowledge together into a story. So, if this body lives according to a linear time, but my memories or dreams do not, I can, in theory, remember tomorrow as well as yesterday. So, if I know for sure that I've never seen these things before my dream occurred, the only explanation is that I will see them in the future," I concluded.

As I said this, it seemed plausible. But considering the previous night's dreams, it also seemed horrible. Nevertheless, I couldn't fully deny that this represented some vision of the future. I should have felt pleased with myself, because I had at last come to terms with my inner knowledge. But I didn't feel pleased; the implications of what I had learnt were not good.

"But that's terrible!" I exclaimed belligerently. "If I ever see anything like that, I'll know to steer well clear of it. Why dream anyway? Sleep should rest the body, not disturb the mind."

Your consciousness moves through time whenever you choose, sleeping or awake, he replied, unexpectedly.

"I did not choose it," I protested, but I knew I was just being disagreeable. Had my dreams conjured up this possible future? I didn't much like the idea of that.

I continued to talk, mostly to myself, trying to remember older dreams to determine whether or not they had significance for the past or the present. Part of me felt pleased at this new knowledge. Perhaps one day I would meet the black-eyed one from my dreams. And when I mentally queried if I could remember tomorrow's dream when in a wakeful state, he said that I knew I could. I had no idea how. The only experience so far had seemed involuntary, and had invoked something I'd rather not remember.

"Perhaps this is just a dream, and you're just a dream." I threw the idea to the wind. "Perhaps I am asleep in a corn field, and my father will wonder why I've been delayed in fulfilling my picking quota. Perhaps I'm still a baby in my cradle, dreaming of a tomorrow. Perhaps I'm just a part of your dream, which is why I never see you and why I feel so helpless. How can I be sure of anything, if time and my thoughts are not linear and my dreams feel so real?" I clasped my temples with my hands as if I could squeeze out the thoughts.

"I have so much to understand." I gritted my teeth. "And why am I talking to you? You understand everything, and yet you never say anything useful. You make me feel stupid. I don't feel as if I know anything, and I just seem to be getting more confused."

I was so agitated; I was angry at everything. I knew I should be silent – my exasperation was making my words disjointed. I sank down in the grass, as if even my own legs were refusing to help me.

You do understand, but you continue to insist that your needs are my needs, he said, and then paused. *Embrace it, little one. Words from me: you would not hear them if you could not understand them. Why do you allow your body to convince you that what it experiences is all that there is? Your physical presence is the smallest and most changeable part of you, yet you think it is the greatest part. Do not let your ideas about limits limit your ideas.*

I was silenced. It was the most he had said since I'd first heard him talk. I felt on the edge of some profound understanding.

I closed my mind and lay back on the grass, letting the warmth of the rising sun take the chill off my body. I wanted to relieve the tension; I wanted time alone, with no thoughts and no dreams.

At some point I must have risen and moved from my position, because a good deal of the day had passed when I found myself at the top of the valley, crumpled against a small rock, clutching an armful of long grasses and with a fresh gash on my knee. A quick inspection proved that the cut was superficial, and that it had already formed a dark, dirt-embedded crust. I stumbled down to the lake to cleanse it.

As I sat, swinging my legs in the water, I began braiding my newly cut hair. I felt a strange harmony performing the ritual. The water washed away my anxieties as well as cleansing my skin, letting my mind to flow freely. I halted in my work, looking at the lake as if with new eyes. Water was not just a physical substance, I thought. It had many properties, all interlinked yet changeable, depending on its surroundings. It was as if the lake shimmered with its true properties in colour and depth, far greater than simply reflecting the sun.

I stood up and looked around the valley. Yes, I understood. Everything had unique properties, but everything blended and complemented everything else.

The forest looked like a shimmering mass. I made my way towards it, and it only took a few steps into the trees for the world around me to change. The bright day was the outside world now. It was as night here, with only occasional glimpses of flickering light to brighten the gloom. The darkness and smell of damp earth made me feel at home.

I came across a tiny clearing and lay on the ground, closing my eyes and thinking of nothing. I could feel the hairs on my arms responding to the dampness of the soil and the beating of my heart. Then I sensed the blood pulsing through me in spirals, filled with life. I went deeper into my blood; within the spirals, there was light. I was filled with light.

I opened my eyes and held up my hands. Instead of flesh, I saw long strands of glowing violet swaying in front of my face. When I closed my eyes, I could still see them.

I craned my neck to see that my torso had become an intense fusion of colours beyond anything that my eyes had ever seen. The colours spun out beyond the boundaries of my flesh; I could feel them. I was not just this body, this mass of tissue, bone and blood, I was more. And if I thought about it, I knew that I could move the light around.

I pushed out from within my body, and light spilled from my belly, oozing through my fingers to weave an intricate pattern in the air. I was hypnotised by the residue it left as I traced patterns with it, and I started to laugh. Laughing made golden light gush from my mouth: some shot into the air, whilst some formed tiny crystalline pieces that fell around me like rain.

Then I realised that the containing form of my body had been part of my self-illusion, an aspect of my desire for uniqueness. I could let go of it completely. I could just be this essence, devoid of space and time. Was that what *he* was?

I looked around me with this new sight, my surroundings now only vaguely resembling the place I remembered. Now everything was so much *more*. The trees glowed with a noble and gentle essence. I could hear them singing in low, mute fluctuations, merging their songs with one another. I knew that each tree held a relationship with the next, and that together they were part of the whole. Other forms around me had a presence where I knew no physical object existed. Lines criss-crossed randomly above my head, pillars rose from beneath the ground to far above the trees, and pools shimmered in mid air.

I trailed my hand through one of the puddles of silver that hovered above the ground like suspended water. As I touched the puddle, its silver glow flowed through my arm and down my body until I complemented it, lying as I did like a form of molten metal. The essence of the silver puddle was quiet and shy, yet resolute as an aeon-old rock. Momentarily I had merged with it without losing myself.

I am part of the air, and light, and dark, I thought. *I am they as they are me. I do not need to understand, I know.*

Whether I floated or walked I am not sure, but I moved through the forest, touching and knowing the essences all around me. The moments seemed to stretch on forever. Waves of bliss and serenity filled me. It was as if everything I perceived released understanding. Nothing was wrong anymore.

So it seemed as though I could see the world in two different ways. I could see with my eyes, which was the only way I had known until this day. With my eyes, I determined form and structure from an object's physical mass. Or, I could see with my mind, a vision that felt like true vision. With this true vision, I saw energy, movement, meaning, and relativity. The true vision had been available to me all along; I had just been blind to it. Perhaps I could learn to use both, although my eyes fought to dominate my inner sight.

I walked slowly through the forest, back towards the valley, practising my new found ability and trying to merge the true vision with the physical vision. It didn't come easily. My eyes, the instruments of physical vision, won out every time. But by the time I had reached the cusp of the trees I had managed it: I could now bring the true vision into line with the sight in my eyes, and the valley shone in a glorious fusion of sunlight and true light.

The light dappled on my arms as I held them out.

"Speak with me," I called to the wind.

The response was immediate: the world rippled and I saw *him*, my Earth-voice.

He was beautiful – delightfully beautiful, hideously beautiful. And he was everywhere, yet without shape or form. He was the light and the shadow, and every substance in between. It filled me with dread, awe, enlightenment and joy. He had no face and no body, but his fingers wove through everything there was. I felt him. I saw him. At last.

I wandered towards the lake. It shimmered reflections of the sky and blossomed in response to his radiant beauty of silver and green. Tiny specks fizzed above its physical surface, emphasizing the perilous shadows below.

You are beautiful.

I heard him laugh.

You can hear my thoughts? I asked him with my mind.

Always, he replied. *And beauty, little one? If I had form, that form would not fit your dreams of beauty.*

I felt myself blush. He knew of my dreams of the black-eyed one.

Come, he said, as slivers of light snaked through the ground towards me. *For I am the last. I am the Old One. Now share a timeless dream of mine with me.*

I stood under the bright sky, embracing my new vision as he curled his thoughts around me and took me into his dreaming.

I know not where I went, in fact I do not think I went anywhere, but I travelled and I saw as he saw, and what I saw I came to know, for it seemed I dreamt his dreams for eternity. It was terrible and it was wonderful. I saw the truth of his energies, all energies, consciousness and existence, and I came to understand. But what I saw I could never say, for only he can truly know it. And I, if I so chose it, could stay with him and know it too.

And time passed in that dream state, where time was nothing.

It seemed I lived a thousand lives in his dreaming in what was, to the flesh, a mere moment.

I awoke, reborn.

I understood.

I knew myself.

Every dormant sense in me was alive.

I had become whole.

At last, I had seen *him*. And I had not just seen him, I'd felt him, known him, and dreamed his dreams. He was the Old One. And I had touched a sacred fact. He had a name.

I know your name, I thought.

Yes, little one, he replied. *And that is the one thing that you must never speak aloud. It is memory, and you stir my awareness enough.*

Then it is forgotten, I avowed.

Was I a fool not to stay with him in endless dreaming? Probably.

I felt the Old One retreat from my thoughts, and with my mind's true vision I watched him recoil through the land. Yet he was still everywhere, dormant, but dreaming in timelessness, until we next spoke.

Now alone again, I pushed my newly awakened senses out far and wide. My journey to this place had been the beginning of something new, not a simple walking away from all that I had known.

I had spent what seemed like eternity in his dreaming with his true vision, and now my flesh seemed foreign to me. Struggling to familiarize myself with my body one again, I started walking. This time I walked with both visions: the vision of my eyes and the vision of my mind, the true vision.

I stumbled clumsily as I grew accustomed to the mixed senses, and headed away from the valley, towards the rocky regions I had not traversed before. I followed my nose, revelling in my newfound vision, feeling at peace with the world around me.

I sensed the sun declining past the horizon and ignored the chilling of my skin as the sky opened and heavy rains drenched me. The shadows had shadows, making finding my footing on the mass of small rocks arduous. But every time I dropped my true vision to make out my footing, the world seemed flat and empty. Suddenly, my ankle bent sharply to one side and I fell. I hit something. Everything went black.

I must have lain there for quite a while, because when I awoke sunlight beat down upon me. It was already the start of a new day.

A warm glow emanated from my stomach. I strained to lift my leaden head and open my eyes, focussing on the physical world. Lying on my belly, watching me sleepily, was Meah. She was half curled, with her legs hanging over my side and her head flat on my chest.

Strangely, I was not surprised to see Meah here. I moved an arm and stroked her thick, tufted coat, which had dried into spikes. She must have laid on me while it was raining. Then I realised that she had slept on me to keep me warm. She stretched lazily as if to confirm my thoughts and sat on my belly, staring down at me as her paws dug her weight into my stomach. I propped myself up and she got off me, sauntering over the rocks and back towards the valley.

I inspected my leg. It was nastily bruised and swollen, but I had suffered far worse in the past. I rose on my one working foot. The swollen ankle refused to hold my weight and I cursed that I had left my stick in the valley. I was now surrounded by a sea of useless rocks. I began a strange but effective gait of a hop then a swing, hop then a swing, keeping the weight off my swollen ankle until I could bind it. I would have looked ridiculous to a casual observer; if it didn't hurt so much, I would have found it funny.

A journey that should have taken a few hours saw me hopping late into the night. When I reached the lip of the valley, I hopped a little too quickly down the slopes, aiming towards my bundle of scrap fabrics, and dropped down breathlessly. Hopping certainly was hard work. I pulled out strips of previously used but clean fabric and bound my ankle.

I am such a fool, I thought, *I should have learnt the limitations of the flesh*. But although the true vision is life itself, I had chosen to stay in this flesh. I had a body and I could not do without my eyes. I had a choice: either see with one vision, or learn to merge the two together. Merging was more accurate, but caused problems, as I'd just discovered. Also, it seemed that now that I'd awoken to the true vision, I could not entirely switch it off. So, I concluded, they had to live side by side, in harmony.

I decided on a harsh yet appropriate solution to make both visions work in harmony: I turned to the lake. With my true sight the lake had no defined edges: its mass spread out, far up the valley walls. With my eyes, of course, I could see the boundary between land and water. I set my true vision at a point in the centre of the lake and ran, trying to stop at the water's edge by quickly adapting my eyes to physical sight. At first, I inevitably found myself sprawled and flapping in the water. So I tried again and again, stopping more and more often at the lake's edge.

Over the following days, I disciplined my eyesight to conform to my will, learning to switch both visions on and off and merging them together. My valley was even more beautiful with both visions together, and my link to *him,* the Old One, had grown stronger. During this time, I spent more moments with him in his dreams, learning many things. His knowledge gave me peace. I also spent much time in my own dreams. My own flesh dreams did not give me as much peace. My dreams of the black-eyed male returned, but frustratingly, I always awoke before I reached his outstretched hand. And the dreams of the huge golden building with its fearful wails always left me with feelings of dread and dismay.

Regardless of my often restless sleeping, the days were warm, and the smells of budding growth filled me with vigour. I'd grown confident with my body as well as my mind, and now ran with the animals and swam with the fishes almost as naturally as they did.

I learnt to use the Old One's energy to be at one with all creatures, and found I could link my consciousness with animals and birds, threading my energy through their minds. With this, I could hold onto their essence as they moved, becoming at one with them. I learnt to see through their eyes, feel what they felt, and sense their surroundings as if they were my own.

Fishes were nearly impossible to form any connection with

at all, so I only tried it a few times – each time, it left me feeling quite numb. Birds felt very fragmented, especially the smaller ones, and becoming one with them produced an strange and unsettling queasiness. Land animals were easier. Even so, putting my own consciousness inside that of another felt very dislocated, and so it wasn't something I kept doing, but I came to understand the creatures around me with greater empathy.

It was my bond with Meah that grew the most, until she could read my every move and I hers. Sometimes we would play together as flesh, and sometimes we would join minds so that I could run with her. She loved that game. She would run and climb the trees, leaping like a cub again, and I experienced her world through her senses.

My life before this place had faded into memory. I had made peace with the fact I'd left my parents. I felt at one with life and all that was around me. I was at one with the Old One. I had become whole.

THIRTEEN

With their minds troubled by the day's events, the 7A's delayed return, and the need to focus on their new strategy as soon as the sun rose, none of the team slept well.

Eventually, the rising sun heralded the new day. Chia took a brisk walk around the plateau to stretch his stiff limbs, and purposely diverted his walk towards the humans in the enclosure. Kraniel was watching them intently, and the bios were awake and active. The smaller ones sat on the grass, pulling and prodding an assortment of small, deactivated kutu devices. One female stood over them protectively and a male stood further back, his eyes scanning the area.

As Chia approached, the female stared at him, her bright eyes analyzing him as much as he was her. He found it disquieting.

"They have a look about them that's far too questioning for bios," Chia said.

"They're developing very quickly," Kraniel replied. "Too quickly. On reflection, I think ten percent kutu was too much to give them. Once I've more data I'll send it to Eden and request that further units be produced with less. Our fellow kutus still intend to populate other continents here."

Chia nodded towards the fourth-generation humans sitting on the grass. "It is strange to see something made in our likeness, yet made to reproduce. It's . . ." he pondered for a moment, "it's inelegant."

"It's a perfect system," Kraniel said defensively. "It's a self-sufficient method of keeping the harvesting units toxin free, without us having to make more or cleanse them. You know, theoretically, we could still reproduce with the humans," he laughed to himself. "It's a technicality I never pointed out to the council when I presented the new design; I thought it might disgust them."

"It *is* disgusting," Chia frowned.

"Oh, the bios seem to find sexual contact quite pleasant," Kraniel mused. "Their programming ensures that. And I think the fact that they are ten-percent kutu gives them plenty of scope for the emotion of pleasure."

"Kraniel, that's quite enough," Chia chided. "Just tell me if you've discovered anything that may be of use to us."

Kraniel smiled, his bright eyes flashed as he activated his HOTS so that all could hear

"Kraniel here . . ." he paused, "I have the first analyses of these humans, and some pointers that may be of assistance today. The humans reveal far more than they're aware of. At first, they have a fear of us, which confuses their responses, but we can partially soothe this through mind-to-mind reassurance. If you need to ask them specific questions, soothe their fear first, and then imprint appropriate images into their minds. They seem to understand images particularly easily, and then they respond with mind images of their own that we can translate, as well as responding with verbal answers. You can also clear their minds and empty them of anything you've asked them. Or, you can simply touch their temporal lobe, locate the memory store and remove all recent additions, so they don't remember anything about you. That's about it for now."

"Well done, Kraniel," Orion replied over the HOTS. "The information will help us immensely. Is everyone ready to leave?"

Kraniel quickly packed away his apparatus, checked that the human's containment field was secure and, once done, walked with Chia to join Orion.

Orion handed out the two portable scanners to Stanze and Kraniel. He and Chia had to make do with an odd looking assortment of wires attached to a readout panel, which Kraniel had concocted. They really could have benefitted from more adept scanning equipment, but they would have to make do with what they had.

"We want listings of the human bios according to their reproductive lineage and family names," Orion directed. "Map them out so we know who are missing, noting their gender, age, where and when they were last seen, and where they may be now. Search for any residue of Factor X, and keep a look out for anything unusual."

The team left the plateau, with all except Chia using their wings. Chia raced ahead in the pod, and when the first colony came into view he nestled the craft amidst some dense bushes on the outskirts of the settlement. After activating the pod's camouflage, he walked the short distance to meet his team.

It was still early light and the humans were just starting to rouse. The kutu split up, immediately entering the nearest huts.

They made excellent progress in the first few hours; entering each hut, calming the resident bios and questioning them, meticulously noting the information gathered. But as the humans began their daily chores, and many moved away from their huts to farm the surrounding vegetation, the work of locating them and gathering information from them became more and more protracted. Chia caught up with Kraniel, who seemed very exasperated.

"This is called Longplain. A most appropriate name: their fields stretch far beyond that forest. But locating each human is most time-consuming," Kraniel grumbled. "According to my information, this hut should have twelve inhabitants. All bar two have gone to the fields to work. I'm fed up with traipsing around to find them. I would have designed the bios differently if I'd known we were going to have to do this."

"Perhaps they'd be vulnerable to a mind-command," Chia pondered. "We could try summoning them to their huts."

"It may hurt them; their minds are not developed enough."

"What are the odds?"

"Low enough that it's worth trying," Kraniel nodded in agreement.

Chia quickly passed the suggestion to the others, and when they tried it, they found that the mind command worked – the bios came streaming back from the fields to their huts. The kutus were now able to continue their search using this much-improved method. They would enter a dwelling, scan it to identify who lived there, and then broadcast a mind command to bring any missing bios back to the dwelling. While they waited for these new arrivals, they collected genetic data on the inhabitants. One by one, the humans returned to be put into a trace-like state to keep them calm and then questioned. The facts were logged, and then the bios' minds were erased of the experience. It was much quicker, and certainly less exhausting.

Even with their improved method of information gathering, however, the process of listing every detail on each family line was far more time-consuming than the team had expected. Eventually they met up at the back of the village, having passed through over 700 dwellings. Twilight had darkened the surrounding area and they were spent with weariness.

Kraniel collected their data, concentrating as he examined the contents. "There are no bios missing from this colony, other than standard pairings to neighbouring colonies. I have confirmed bio readings of those said to have died."

"And I sensed no abnormal levels of Factor X," Chia added.

"We may need to return for specimens once we know the genetic line we're after, but we're finished here for now," Orion concluded. "Do not be disheartened. There are still two more colonies to analyze on our list: the ones they call Whitehill and Threetops."

It was late, and there was no more they could do in this human colony, so the team returned to the plateau. They had a long day ahead if they were going to try to scan both remaining colonies.

None of them could rest. Chia in particular kept rousing himself, thinking he'd heard the return of the 7A, but the craft was nowhere in sight. He repeatedly tried to raise a communication link with the ship, but got zero response. The ships lateness, the lack of contact with Nirrious, the unavailability of Una, the Supreme, and his sabotaged Orb, all made him too apprehensive to sleep deeply.

Stanze refused to attempt sleep, pacing the plateau in full battle dress while the others tossed and turned or made regular excursions to stretch their limbs.

Eventually, the light of the rising sun, the bustle of movement, and a foul smell that Chia did not recognise, all served to nudge him fully awake and prompt him to rise.

"You've been very restless, my friend," Orion said, offering Chia a goblet of potent-smelling liquid, the source of that foul smell. "Drink this, it'll help wake you. Earth product: coffee."

"I didn't think I'd manage to sleep," Chia replied groggily.

He took the goblet and swallowed the bitter stimulant. It nearly made him retch, but it did indeed rouse his body.

"Any news from Nirrious?" he asked.

"None," Orion replied. "I regularly try contacting him. He just cuts me off and bars me from his mind. I also keep trying Una, but Shursa always collects. Shursa will not directly answer any of my questions, yet he is the only outward communication I can raise."

"It will be fine," Chia said, not convincing anyone. "Regardless, we must keep with your strategy. What else can we do?"

"I am waiting for inspiration," Orion smiled.

Chia readied himself swiftly. Today's destinations were Whitehill, then Threetops. Both were considerably smaller than Longplain. It would be possible, albeit difficult, to scan through them both in one day.

By high-noon, the team had swept through Whitehill. The task was finished rather faster than they had anticipated, due to the high number of deaths of newborns that the colony had suffered, and thus the reduced numbers of offspring there. Many of Whitehill's newer inhabitants had relocated to Longplain, a seemingly more fertile region. Kraniel had adeptly skimmed through the collected data and confirmed that there were no humans unaccounted for before the team moved on. The next colony to scan was Threetops, which was an even smaller colony. Chia silenced his own disquiet that they ought to have provided some sort of result by now, if they were on the right track.

Approaching Threetops, the pod gave Chia a clear birds-eye view of the sprawling huts and well-cultivated land, spreading far around the dwellings. He concealed the craft on the outskirts and walked to where the rest of the team congregated, now re-tuned to the flesh once again.

As before, the team split up to cover as many dwellings as

quickly as they could. Chia was sure he could sense something extra here. He instinctively walked to the farthest group of huts, which were nestled into a row of three small hills.

Chia stood before the first hut, rolled his shoulders and cleared his mind. Inside should be descendants of the bios known as L1 and M1.

He pushed the hut's rickety door open, stooped so he could fit through, and entered.

Inside the hut, several small humans sat around a grubby table, eating rapidly. A depleted looking female bent over them, placing more nourishment in their bowls. She stopped, looked at Chia, and then straightened, her wide eyes staring in fright.

Chia quickly sent a soothing mind message to placate them. Then he pressed on with his thought demand: *I call all who live here yet are not present, to return to this abode.*

He turned his attention to the only adult present.

"I am Chia, of those who made you. Who are you?" he asked the female, sending soothing images into her mind.

The female was younger than he'd first assumed, and her eyes glinted as she understood the gist of his words and images.

"I am Mele, youngest of Linn and Mina," she replied.

Chia sensed the confirmation that she was telling the truth from the images that came from her mind. This made sense: Linn and Mina were L1 and M1 of the first generation, parents of this female.

"And where is your male?" Chia asked; his equipment was giving fluctuating readings on the adult male.

"Rew is ceased," she replied.

Ceased must mean expired, Chia thought, which explained the unusual readings from his makeshift portable scanner. He picked up imagery from her mind of her dead mate. There had been an accident. Much hard work had followed, with crops to tend and young bios to feed. No wonder the female had weathered rapidly.

"How many offspring?" Chia asked. He could easily pick up how many children this bios had, by performing a straightforward mind scan, but the simple questions allowed him to ascertain her level of understanding.

The female looked confused, until he implanted visions of young ones in her mind. The female indicated she'd had eight offspring, seeming ashamed that there would be no more now that her mate had died.

Chia only counted three children in attendance. It would still be a few moments until the others arrived from his earlier calling, so he made those present sleep, making sure they did not damage themselves as they slumped down.

Scans of the hut confirmed that no adult male had been living there for many months: the traces of the missing man were scarce and weak. Eight small rickety beds and one larger one gave readings of one human per bed, corresponding to the number now living in the dwelling. The oldest five offspring were not present. Chia logged the codes of all the inhabitants, and, satisfied that there was nothing remarkable in the hut, returned to the main room. By now, the missing offspring had arrived and were dazedly staring at their motionless family. Chia confirmed their codes and sent them to sleep.

The data gave no sign of concentrated Factor X in this hut, but Chia was sure that there was something, somewhere in this village. He woke the parent female.

"Have you seen any unusual-looking humans?" he asked, wondering if a human containing Factor X would look different to the others.

The female stared at him, an image of himself coming into her mind.

"Any others?" he continued, concealing his amusement at how the bios saw him. "Female?"

She stood blankly while her mind raced through the possibilities of the faces she had seen, but none occurred to her to be in any way different. Chia didn't wait for her response as she struggled to find an answer to please him. "Clear," he ordered, penetrating her mind, making her immediately forget the question.

"Do you know of a missing human?" Chia asked, implanting the idea of a length of time in the female's mind that roughly matched the first readings of the energy anomaly. "A missing female, not ceased, just gone?"

An image of a young female came into her mind.

Chia probed for further details. The female bios had no option but to respond.

"Tachra," the female eventually said, mentally imagining a direction away from the village. Then a stronger image, of a young, pale-skinned female, entered her mind. The female she pictured, Tachra, had lived in the neighbouring hut, and an image of that place also entered her mind.

Chia knew he was onto something. The knowledge instinctively tingled through him, the same way it used to when he was trailblazing and was pulled towards a certain planet or galaxy. He immediately woke the family from their telepathically induced slumber, blanked their minds so that they would forget he'd ever been there, and promptly left.

The neighbouring hut lay on the far side of a large, newly ploughed field. When he saw it, he knew that it was the right place; it exactly resembled the image from the female's mind. He checked his data. In this hut should be the bios D1 and E1, or their descendants. Not wanting to waste a moment, he mind-called the inhabitants as he approached, and then entered.

As soon as Chia walked over the threshold of the hut's door, the emanations of Factor X were so strong that he reeled backwards. Two first-generation bios, a paired male and female, entered from an adjoining room and watched cautiously while he collected himself.

Chia quickly soothed and scanned the two bios. These were the original bios, certainly: D1 and E1, now past reproductive age and well into the degenerative stages. He still felt the presence of Factor X intensely, even though his equipment indicated nothing. It clung to their flesh and permeated the dwelling, but they were not the source; the source of the essence, he sensed, was no longer here.

"Where are your offspring?" Chia asked the human pair.

"Paired," the male bios replied.

Chia mind-scanned the male. Images of pairings and feastings for many offspring flashed through the male's mind. Then the image that he had already seen in the neighbour's mind formed once more: the dark-haired, pale girl, but this time accompanied by a strong sense of grief. The man's feelings were beyond any that a first generation bios should feel. From the image, Chia knew, this was undoubtedly the same girl that the previous female had called Tachra.

"Where is Tachra?" Chia asked.

The male visibly shook on the spot. "Gone," he stated.

Chia sensed that Tachra had indeed left this hut and that there was little more these bios could tell him. He made them sleep and called to his team

"Everyone," Chia announced through the HOTS. "Come to my position. I have found something."

Not waiting for a reply, Chia climbed a set of narrow, rickety wooden stairs to a low-roofed upper area. Instinctively, he walked towards the small room at the far end.

Chia went to walk through the doorway into the room, but as he tried to enter, something stopped him, as if he'd walked into a solid wall. He pushed out his hand towards the invisible shield. It repelled him, but he held his hand against it, bearing the discomfort it caused for as long as he could. It was a barrier, both invisible and firm. He scanned his data: the harvesting ships had never detected a human in this room. Yet he undoubtedly detected a past bios' presence, and the small bed inside the room confirmed his convictions.

This, Chia had no doubt, had been the dwelling place of the one they sought, Tachra, and somehow Tachra had made a barrier around her room that their sensors could not pass through.

Chia guardedly opened his mind to the properties of the barrier. It was still strong. He knew he could probably find a way to analyse and penetrate the barrier, if he had the time and resources, but with little time available he looked for a quicker way to enter the room. He sent his mind along the unseen mass, scanning for imperfections or the presence of known substances that he could manipulate. But what he found was even better than that. Moving his mind around the perimeter of the barrier, he found, on the far side of the room, a small area where the barrier gave way. The spot coincided with where a window overlooked the colony.

Quickly exiting the hut, Chia went outside, stopping under the window to Tachra's room, just as Orion, Kraniel, Jychanumun and Stanze arrived to join him. He explained his findings about Tachra, and then about the barrier around the room, hence the necessity for making such an unconventional entrance. He insisted to Stanze that, as a Sensitive, he was the best kutu for checking the room for energy anomalies before anyone else entered. And then, using the natural indents of the wooden exterior, he nimbly eased up to the opening.

Chia cautiously put his hand through the window and into the room. Nothing repelled him; he was right, there was no barrier. He climbed in.

Tachra's old room smelt stale. Only an empty bed, a wooden trunk and a water barrel filled the space. Walking towards the doorway, Chia cautiously extended his hand towards the invisible barrier. His hand passed through, the energy pulling him, as if expelling him from the room. He quickly snatched his hand back. This barrier was a one-way energy field; he could leave without any problems, but could not enter. And the existence of the exposed hole around the window made Chia suspect that Tachra probably didn't realise that she had put these barriers in place. In all likelihood, Tachra was unaware that she had the ability to manipulate energies.

"This is indeed Tachra's room. It's safe for you all to enter," Chia announced to his team.

As the others entered, Chia swept his gaze around the room, but there was nothing unusual. He pulled back the rough bed coverings and looked under the bed, but there was nothing but a build up of dust from the crude grass mattress. The water barrel beside the bed was empty, and from the moisture level in the wood he ascertained that it had not held water for almost a year. He shifted the large trunk away from the wall, to open the heavy lid, and stood, staring in amazement, at the portion of exposed floor.

"I think you should see this," Chia stated.

There, etched into the section of the wooden planks that had been concealed by the trunk, was an array of tiny carvings.

Chia pulled the trunk further out, exposing the entire floor it had rested on, revealing hundreds, probably thousands, of symbols; symbols that looked like writing, engraved in the floor. Not just any writing, but writing that resembled kutu language.

And yet, despite the similarity to the many scripts Chia knew, he could not read it.

"Eskah!" Orion exclaimed, as they all stood staring at the carvings. "She has learned how to write."

Jychanumun bent down, running his fingers over the marks in fascination.

"Tachra must have written it," Chia remarked. "I can't read it, although it looks similar to our scripts. You know many scripts; can you read it, Orion?"

Orion studied it for a moment. "No, but I feel as if I should; it looks familiar."

"Perhaps the parent bios can read it," Chia decided.

His eyes hazed over as he concentrated. "I've called them to this room," he said.

A moment later, the parents entered the room; Chia noted with some surprise that they had no trouble passing through the invisible barrier.

"Read it," Chia instructed to the humans, pointing towards the floor.

They both looked down, their faces full of blank uncertainty.

"Tachra wrote this. Read it," Chia instructed again, putting images into their minds as he spoke.

"Tachra wrote this?" the male asked, seemingly surprised. He dropped to his knees and ran his hands over the carvings, as if treasuring them.

Chia sensed another wave of grief from the male, and he spoke to the others urgently. "They cannot read it. The male is upset; they should be taken away before they're damaged."

Orion nodded, "We want them healthy. If we're fortunate, the ability to harvest Factor X may run in the same genetic line. Stanze, take these two bios to our base; we'll want to analyze them. Look after them well. Kraniel, get back to base and start analyzing the humans as they arrive. Chia, Jychanumun, we'll try to find anything more here."

Stanze made the two parent bios sleep, tucked one under each arm, and then departed through the doorway, grunting as the barrier unexpectedly propelled him forward. Kraniel carefully slipped through the doorway after him.

While Orion made notes on the carvings, Chia sat on the dusty floor and began emptying the contents of the large trunk. It held an assortment of items: they were mainly basic pieces of a bios' existence, although there was nothing remarkable that might aid their search. He leaned forward to shut the trunk's lid, but then stopped, noticing an assortment of pebbles at the bottom of the trunk, among the dust and woollen fibres. He scooped the pebbles up. They were too light to be stones. He blew off the dust, revealing intricate engravings around the outside in tiny script, much like the engravings in the floor.

A scan of the pebbles revealed, to Chia's surprise, that they were carved from a rare type of wood. He turned to show them to Jychanumun.

Jychanumun sat on the window's edge, looking out over the colony. Chia sensed that he was troubled.

"What concerns you, black-eyed one?" Chia asked.

Jychanumun didn't move, keeping his gaze out of the window, "I sense her. Tachra: I know her name now. I did not know how I would feel when you found out who you were looking for."

"What can I do to help?" Chia asked.

Jychanumun looked at him thoughtfully, and then shook his head. "Nothing. But I will show *you* something that might help in your search."

He jumped down from the window sill and sat in front of the carvings on the floor, radiating energy out through his fingers until they formed thin, reflective sheets, which he then formed into a mirror around the carvings.

"Now read the language of the stones," he said.

Chia squinted, trying to interpret the images now reflected in the force field. He managed to recognize the tail of letter and part of a word. "It seems even more like our language now, but I still can't read it; it's too fragmented."

"It is an ancient script," Jychanumun quietly stated.

"I recognise some of it!" Orion's voice quivered with excitement. "I can make out a few familiar words: water, one, dream, and water again, but I do not understand it all enough for me to read it. Can you read it, Jychanumun?"

"Yes," Jychanumun said, drawing back the energy field and standing up. "But it is personal to her."

"Jychanumun, read it," Orion insisted. "It may help us to find her."

Jychanumun shook his head, "It'll not help you find her. It is her private thoughts. But I wanted you to see: Tachra is more than just a bios for harvesting Factor X."

"Are you sure that what is written here would not aid us?" Orion asked, exasperated.

Jychanumun nodded.

"And these?" Chia queried, handing Jychanumun the small wooden pebbles.

Jychanumun examined them with intensity while Orion waited.

Finally, Jychanumun handed them back. "They are private too, although there are gaps in her story. Some of the carvings are missing. At least two, maybe three."

"Two missing?" Chia stated, his mind racing. "But there are no more here. They're carved from Tachra wood. We only manufactured a few Tachra trees, but then went on to a more advanced species."

He thrust out his hand towards Orion, indicating that he wanted to use the portable scanner, not the makeshift one, and then started looking up data and entering queries.

"We're in luck, of the four manufactured trees, one survives. It's at the centre of this colony; the hills must have protected it. With only one tree remaining, there can't be much Tachra wood around on the continent. So perhaps if we find the missing carvings . . ."

"Then we find Tachra," Orion finished. "We'll search for any trace of Tachra wood."

Although there was only one surviving Tachra tree, there was an abundance of Tachra-tree debris. The pod sensors indicated numerous Tachra-wood readings as soon as Chia took off. Some of the fragments turned out to be leaves that had blown into crevices, and others turned out to be partial fragments. But, as small and insignificant as they were, they all showed up on the sensor as potential results, and they all had to be inspected. Once they had been inspected, Chia ensured that they were vaporized to clear the area, allowing him to continue.

Chia had just finished inspecting another cluster of rotting leaves when someone finally announced that they had found something. It was Orion. Chia immediately sped towards his position, and the pod soon descended into the gloom of dense woodlands. The wide trees, tightly packed on an almost vertical drop, meant that Chia had to leave the pod hovering and navigate the final steep area by foot.

Orion and Jychanumun stood in a small clearing overlooking a wide, partially concealed river. A tall old tree bore more of the now-familiar symbols engraved into its trunk, and around the tree was an assortment of items, randomly scattered on a patch of well-trodden moss. Embedded in the moss was a short crude knife, surrounded by old stripped branches covered in yet more familiar symbols. One of the carved branches, it transpired, was Tachra wood.

"She has been here many times," Orion stated, "But although we have found Tachra wood, we have found no more of the beads."

Chia walked around the area. He felt a surge of contentment, and knew the feeling was not his own. He sensed that Tachra had enjoyed this place.

"We must analyse these," Orion stated, "and get data from Tachra's genetic line as soon as Kraniel analyses it. I suggest we take this lot back to base and compile our findings before continuing."

The three gathered up Tachra's abandoned possessions and headed back to base as the sun set and darkness covered the land.

Once back at their base, it was clear that Stanze had been busy. The six original specimens were gone from the enclosure to be replaced by over two hundred humans from Tachra's family line. They slept, levitated horizontally above one another.

Kraniel had set up another small force field, filled with apparatus, and was intensely working over one of the full-grown bios. Chia tried desperately not to think of all the energy the additional force fields were draining from their limited supplies.

With such a heavy workload, Chia immediately began helping Kraniel. Their equipment registered no trace of Factor X from the bios, and so Chia utilized his abilities to examine the humans one by one. He sensed a residue of the energy on several of them, but none of them was a source. It was bitter news, and the bitter news did not stop there.

"I've analysed Tachra's genetic lineage," Kraniel said. "I've gone through all data, and she has never shown up on any of our scans or harvesting schedules. It's as if she's invisible to us."

"That makes searching difficult," Orion stated. He looked towards the human enclosure. "We may as well return the humans to their dwellings."

"We should keep the father a while longer," Chia added. "I sensed a strong emotional tie between the male bios and Tachra. And some of the family line bore residual traces of Factor X. We should study them further. I'd like to know if they have a stronger emotional link, too. There might be something, somewhere, I can work with to help trace her."

"Let it be done," Orion nodded.

Chia arose and beckoned to Kraniel, "I'll need them roused one by one to filter out those to keep. I'm afraid your night's work has not quite finished, my friend."

Kraniel directed Chia into the small force field rather than the main enclosure, and stood taking notes while Chia worked his way through two hundred and twenty one humans. For each analysis the human would be roused, and then Chia would imprint their newly awake minds with various images of Tachra and gauge their response. By the time he had gone through them all, the night had waned and he'd whittled the selection down to eighteen. Exhausted, he left Kraniel reorganizing the humans' enclosure and went to the closest recliner, sinking down for some much-needed sleep.

When he awoke from his deep, and mercifully undisturbed, sleep, Chia ached, having forgotten to remove his protective body-suit. He stretched, running nano cleansers through the suit, and noticed a fresh goblet of stimulating fluid and a small goblet of Ochrah by his recliner. He downed the coffee stimulant and carried the Ochrah through to join the others.

Chia found the rest of the team not only rested and roused, but having finished their analyses of Tachra's possessions. He grumbled that they should have woken him earlier.

"There wasn't any point waking you until we were ready to leave; you needed rest," Orion smiled, clearly pleased about something. "Kraniel has found a definite genetic imprint for Tachra. There was blood residue on the knife we retrieved."

Chia took a sip of Ochrah, savouring the taste. "I don't want to dampen your enthusiasm, but how will that help?" he asked. "Even if we do know her genetic code, she's undetectable to our equipment."

"But blood on the knife *was* detected by the equipment," Orion answered. "It seems as though inert organic material is detectable; only the living organism is invisible to us. If the blood has left her body, and not returned to the elements, it registers on our sensors. There may be more blood residue in her trail, helping us to find her."

"That also suggests that we need to capture Tachra alive in order to gain Factor X," Chia pondered. "I suspect that it's Factor X that makes Tachra undetectable; if she dies, the link to Factor X will most likely die too."

"Agreed," Orion nodded. "At least we have two things to look for now that could lead us to her: blood and Tachra wood. Are we ready to go?"

The team all assented, although Kraniel and Stanze were not happy that they had the cumbersome task of returning the unwanted humans before continuing the search. They all gathered the day's necessities, and Orion and Jychanumun swiftly left the plateau using their wings while Chia mounted one of the pods. He entered the co-ordinates from their previous evening's findings to run alongside the locations of previously detected energy surges; these then became his main target areas. He sat in the cockpit, looking at the map on the display panel.

With the addition of a third coordinate, something suddenly became very clear. Chia could barely contain the enthusiasm as he raised the others through their HOTS.

"Team: update," he announced. "Listen, we have a common denominator. We have a path! All registered locations for Tachra are very close to the same river. It appears as though Tachra has followed this river. I'm now updating tracking to follow this course."

"That's excellent news!" Orion exclaimed breathlessly. "We're rerouting."

Chia reset the pod's coordinates. *I knew it*, he thought to himself. *Tachra has kept close to the water even after leaving her colony.*

The sensors swept the area more quickly than the portable versions the others used, and so while the team trailed the river, Chia raced ahead in their search for Tachra wood and Tachra's blood. Tracking Tachra had not been straightforward so far, and so Chia was pleasantly surprised when the sensors let out a bleep of confirmation early in the day.

The area was a parched scrubland; the air was dry and brisk and filled with grit that kept the pod's force-field busy as it descended. It had a stark beauty from a distance, with tones of merging gold and beige, but up close it was unattractive and bleak. The region was well beyond the kutus' original development areas, and so was yet to flourish with plant bios; even so, a sizeable human encampment had sprung up in the distance.

The pod landed in a desolate area, where the sensors indicated, but there was nothing obvious in sight. And then there, heaped behind a large protruding rock was what looked like a smaller rock. The disturbance caused by the pod landing had blown away its covering of sand and underneath was a pile of sun-faded, coarse red fabric.

Chia picked up the fabric and shook it, making sand and grit billow into a dust cloud. He was left holding a red rag. From its condition, it had been buried for many months. Dirty dark marks streaked one side, and the marks were blood. He had a match: Tachra's blood.

Noting that he was quite a distance from the river, and that Tachra would undoubtedly have needed water, he tucked the fabric into the back of the pod and headed for the nearby colony.

The colony was a stark array of small dwellings, packed closely together, and as unattractive as the surrounding wasteland. As Chia hovered over the dwellings, a single confirmation flashed on his screen; there was Tachra wood below him, coming from one of the small grey huts. He hastily departed from the pod, set his HOTS onto constant transmission to his team mates, and then cautiously approached the hut's door.

Chia entered the hut, where an adult female stood leaning over a crying baby.

"Sleep," Chia projected.

The female succumbed to the sleep command and Chia lunged forward to catch her. The infant remained awake and continued crying. This time he directed the sleep command directly at the child, which immediately lulled into silent slumber.

Chia quickly scanned the area. Although this female was not the one they sought, and wasn't from the same lineage as Tachra, she had a lingering trace of Factor X. The entire hut had a lingering trace of Factor X. Tachra had been here, and in close proximity to where he now stood.

The portable scanners also directed Chia to the female. Around her neck was another carved Tachra-wood bead.

He pulled the bead from her neck and commanded her to wake.

The female rubbed her head groggily, and then leapt towards her child. Seeing that the child was safe, she grasped it in her arms and took a step back from the apparent stranger.

"I mean you no harm," Chia soothed. "I am Chia, of those who made you. And you are?"

"Soul," the female replied.

Chia was surprised at the speed of Soul's response, and the fact that she didn't give her heritage as humans usually did.

"Where did you find this?" he asked, holding up the necklace as he probed her mind.

"It is mine," Soul replied. She was clearly agitated that he held the bead; she considered it hers.

Chia sensed that Soul didn't want to tell him anything, but she couldn't help the barrage of images that flashed through her mind. The images were like points of time captured in pictures: Tachra with blood on her face, Tachra frowning, Tachra laughing, and then Tachra earnestly holding out the small round bead.

"What happened to Tachra?" Chia asked, broadening his awareness as he held out the bead towards her.

Soul's expression was indignant and unmoving, but her thoughts flowed like a gushing river. This time, the image of Tachra in her head moved. The image had sounds, fragmented as they were, but he heard them nonetheless.

Please take it, the image of Tachra said, holding out the bead. *If ever you need me . . . I will know.* Then Tachra moved forward with her arms outstretched, and the link broke. Chia shivered as if a shadow had passed over him.

Soul still held out her hand expectantly. Chia gave her the bead necklace, knowing he could retrieve it later, and then commanded her to sleep again, allowing him to peruse the surroundings unhindered.

The little dwelling was awash with strong energy. As well as the scattered remains of Factor X, the hut had an essence of strength and resolution radiating from everything. Soul had made this place her own and it was filled it with her essence. She was only third-generation bios, and although Chia accepted that his knowledge of humans was not absolute, Soul had developed a self-identity that in his opinion was too strong – stronger than he thought possible.

A dark stain on the wooden floor turned out to be Soul's blood, spilt many months ago. Not too far away was another dark patch, smeared in a fine line towards the door. The readout gave a completely different genetic code, matching neither Soul's nor Tachra's. Yet another dark stain, splattered around the floor by the small wooden table, was Tachra's. The splatters looked as if they'd dripped from a height.

Chia put his hand on the largest of Tachra's blood stains and a jolt rippled through him. Before he could pull his hand away, visions began bombarding his mind. It was as if he was there, pulled back in time, watching a large red drop of blood drip off the table, and through the space where he now held his hand. Chia moved with the vision and looked around. He was in the same hut, but many of the contents had moved, or were different now. Above where he knelt, the image of Soul silently moved.

Chia's mind saw Soul wearing a full red gown and tending a limp body on the table; by its size, a female, with blood dripping steadily from her. It had to be Tachra. The image of Soul carefully unwrapped a red cloth from Tachra's face, revealing pale skin covered in sticky dark blood. Tachra's eyes were closed; the wound on her head was deep and raw, and potentially fatal.

The images started to fade. Chia tried holding on to them, but the pictures dispersed. He was left staring at an empty table. He stood; feeling disorientated, and looked around. Orion and Jychanumun stood watching him intently.

"Didn't you hear us?" Orion asked anxiously as he walked forward.

Chia shook his head. "No. I had a vision; something strong happened here."

Orion reached out and touched him, verifying that he was

indeed well, and then stood back, looking concerned. "Your flesh flickered, as if it could not hold itself here."

"Something happened here that I've not experienced before. I have theories about what went on," Chia said, pulling his thoughts together: "Either Tachra died from the wounds that I saw she had sustained, or whatever happened here was traumatic enough for me to sense it. I don't think she died; I found a rag she'd been wearing which was discarded after receiving her injury."

"And her?" Orion indicated towards the sleeping Soul.

"Soul. I want to question her further. She has a bond with Tachra, and had one of the carved beads," Chia replied. "We'll need to take her offspring too; it's too young to leave and she'll be useless if she's concerned about it."

"Take them to the base, and question Soul before Kraniel analyzes her," Orion decided.

Chia nodded. "There was a third party involved here, the owner of that blood stain," he pointed to one of the marks on the floor. "I'll find that person too. We should know what happened here that was so disturbing."

"We'll continue searching," Orion nodded. "Come, Jychanumun, we still have at least one more carved bead to find."

Jychanumun was examining Tachra's bloodstains on the floor.

"I'll stay here for a moment," he said.

Orion nodded and left, followed by Chia, carrying Soul and her offspring. When Chia pulled the hut door shut, he saw Jychanumun kneel, placing both his hands flat on the blood stained floor.

Back at base, Stanze and Kraniel had finished returning the humans to their huts. Stanze had left to join Orion, while Kraniel sat observing the remaining bios. They were fully awake and huddled together at the far end of the enclosure, watching everything with frightened and wary eyes.

Chia had identified the third human, Huru, a bulky man, who now slept soundly with Soul and her child in the back of his pod. He stopped the pod beside the humans' enclosure, much to their awe, and swiftly lifted Soul and her child out, leaving Huru asleep.

"Oh good, you have more," Kraniel said sarcastically. "But if they need to be taken back, you can take them. Air-lifting a couple of hundred humans is not my idea of fun."

"We'll be keeping this one, for now," Chia said. "I need to question her."

"Be my guest," Kraniel indicated. "But I've had to detune the force field around my work area, there's not enough energy left to feed it."

"Then I'll work here," Chia replied. "There's nowhere for her to run to anyway."

Chia carefully put the female down, and handed Kraniel the bundle from her sleeping arms.

"Her offspring," Chia indicated, pulling the swaddle from the child's face.

"Oh no," Kraniel groaned. "The younger ones just excrete liquid everywhere. Just wake the parent and give it back." He put the child at Soul's side.

"Wake," Chia commanded.

As Soul came to, a look of panic came over her face as she observed her surroundings. Her panic increased even more when she noticed the humans huddled in the enclosure. She cautiously picked up her child, took two steps back, turned, and then started running away from Chia with a surprising speed.

In the enclosure, Tachra's father started making a strange noise. He stood with his hands on his hips and his head thrown back, laughing.

Chia was quite impressed with Soul's efforts to find a way off the plateau, but it took little effort for him to catch up with her, as there was no safe way down. She stood at the edge of the plateau, looking over the side at the long drop down.

"I mean you no harm," Chia said softly, sending soothing thoughts to her.

Soul looked at the drop below her, then Chia, and then her child. She sank to her knees, realising that she was trapped, and began sobbing.

Chia felt a pang of guilt, which surprised him, and he slowly walked up to Soul, who was still clasping the small carved bead in one hand and whispering Tachra's name over and over as tears streamed down her face. This time Chia did not make her sleep, but gently collected her and her child, carrying them towards the containment field, thinking that perhaps being with others of her kind might soothe her more.

He placed Soul and her child in the enclosure. And, once Chia had left, the humans sprang into action and moved towards them. It looked as though they were consoling her.

Chia gave Soul time to stabilize, before making the entire selection of humans sleep except her and her child, just so he could question her in peace.

Hopefully, Chia considered, this bios will give us some information, any information, that will help in our search to find Tachra.

FOURTEEN

I had found peace. I had embraced my flesh and I had let my mind dream the dreams of endlessness. I had learnt to unite both sides of my existence.

I came to know many things, but I never discovered the origin of humans. When I asked the Old One, he directed the questions back at me. Yet whenever I looked inside me for the knowledge, it was as if I came to a wall, beyond which was nothing.

But this absence didn't really matter. I thought that I would never see another person again, and for now, the only human I encountered was my own reflection. Once or twice I contemplated walking back over the mountain, but then I would look around at my valley, at its beauty, and I knew that I did not want to leave.

Then one day something happened, and I knew that I had no choice but to leave.

I'd had a restless, dream-filled sleep, and so roused myself early and played with Meah. We played one of our regular games of hide and seek, which was actually less than a game because we always knew where each other was hiding. She was now almost fully grown; she only stood as high as my knees, but her strength was immense and her vigour even greater – she always exhausted me first.

Once the game had ended and she had left with her sister, I lay back in the grass, recovering from her limitless energy, soaking up the hot sun. It was almost too hot, but I was too contentedly lazy to swim, so I absently watched the drifting clouds. I pushed my thoughts upwards, finding myself floating high in the misty coolness, looking down on myself lying in the grass. I wasn't concentrating, I was just drifting with the air, my mind blank, vaguely taking in whatever was around me.

Suddenly, I realised that something was bothering me. I was so comfortable lying in the grass that my irritation surprised me.

I focussed on the irritation, and immediately became aware of a presence. I instinctively recoiled, but then I pushed my mind out to try to pinpoint its source. To no avail: it was like seeing a shadow in the corner of your eye, and then, when you look directly at it, there's nothing there. I started to refocus my mind on the shadow's source, and then it hit me straight between the eyes, as if it had been magnified a thousand times. A girl's voice.

Tachra! Please come! Tachra! Tachra!

I pulled myself back abruptly, and then cautiously threaded my thoughts out again. The same message: *Tachra! Please come! Tachra!*

The voice was only in my mind, but it was as loud as if the girl were beside me. It was Soul, I knew it. Soul was calling for help.

I tried focussing, to try to sense what was wrong, using the same skills I had learnt when joining the minds of animals. But I found myself thwarted by the chaos of her mind, which now was disordered by her overwhelming desperation. She didn't know where she was, and clearly she was terrified. I tried looking through her eyes, and this time I had some success, although I could see only her hand, clenching and unclenching around the carved bead I had given her. And as much as I pushed at her thoughts, I could not make her hear me.

All I knew was that Soul was in trouble and that she wasn't in Hollow. I had no idea where she was.

I jumped back into myself, letting my thoughts race. I had a vague sense of Soul's direction from where I stood, but she seemed far away, beyond the other side of my valley, in the opposite direction to the route I had travelled and far from her village. I took a long, deep breath. Previously I had not sensed people to the west, but now I did. They were only a few, though, and they were too far away for me to know how many there were, and exactly where they might be.

I had to locate Soul, but I didn't know how. My eyes instinctively roved the skies as I strove for a solution, and one immediately occurred to me. It might just work.

Up by the hills was a large black bird, circling intently and patiently near one area where I assumed it had found some food. Although I didn't like maintaining a connection with birds, I reached out with my mind and approached it, easing slowly into its mind and taking a passive role there. I saw through its eyes its fragmented view of its prey: a furry, warm thing, probably a shrew, unaware and scurrying between stones on its own mission. The bird glided gracefully in circles, observing, patiently waiting for the easiest moment to catch the animal.

I knew that this dance conducted between birds and their prey could take a long time, so I stealthily leapt out of the bird's mind and into the mind of the animal, letting it understand that a predator was close. The little creature didn't hesitate. It pricked up its ears and ran quickly towards a safe hole, not far off in the rocks, and darted in.

The bird knew that it had missed its meal, and swooped out

of its circling flight to perch in a nearby tree, continuing to watch the hole just to be sure. Giving the tiny shrew a last warning, I rejoined the bird's mind.

Connecting with animals could be done in two ways: either I could take a completely passive role, choosing to experience things as the creature did, or I could link with the creature's mind, making my thought processes like those of the creature, a process that felt very disjointed. I decided to take a passive role with the bird, guiding it with hints rather than occupying its mind.

The bird actually wasn't hungry; it was just taking advantage of an easy target. It now sat eyeing the hole to see if the rodent would resurface. It was a patient beast, and would have sat for hours had I not conjured up images of many small, edible creatures rooting around, *just over there*, and imagined for the bird that these animals were very slow, very tasty, and very, very easy prey. I pointed my thoughts towards the direction I had sensed Soul calling from. The bird launched from its perch in search of the even easier lunch I'd suggested, and now I could ride with it, linked to it mentally.

As the bird flew, I could now guide it; it rose higher on the warm valley currents and soared in the direction of Soul. It flew further than any of the places that I'd seen from the top of the valley, and headed into unknown territories. I constantly fed it images of easy food, enticing it beyond its usual boundaries, and the bird flew willingly. When it started tiring from its extended flight, I fed it my strength and it pushed on.

We eventually approached a valley lined almost entirely with a carpet of bright yellow flowers. Straight ahead, just above the height of our flight path, was the lip of a sheer drop into the valley that stretched up higher and straighter than any I had ever seen. I sensed Soul was there somewhere.

There, I indicated to the bird, *is where lunch is.*

The bird struggled to rise to the lip of the plateau, so I fed it more strength until I could see over the lip to a domed mass that shimmered with all colours. I could not tell what it was, but it was the size of several huts, set amidst an expanse of green grass. From the bird's perspective, the object was simply not a good place to land: it was too smooth and exposed. Nearby was a small, heavily wooded area, so I directed the bird there. It landed atop the highest, leafiest tree I could find. I knew this was the right area: Soul was here. I now started to observe the area along with the bird.

At first, I could not clearly make out what I was seeing. I'd never seen anything like it, and seeing through the eyes of a bird made it even more difficult to determine. I could tell that the shimmering mass was partially transparent, and that inside it were many things of vibrant colours. I thought I sensed movement, but the bird stubbornly refused to move its line of sight; it had become mesmerised by a tiny, bright object sparkling inside the dome. Its thoughts of food were gone, transfixed as it was by the glinting of this thing. It eyed it greedily, wanting it more than food. Soul was here, somewhere, I could feel her. I tried convincing the bird to fly around, but it was too fixated on its glittering treasure.

The bird sensed no threat from its surroundings, and so it gradually flew from tree to tree, drawing nearer to the edge of the wood, its sights ever-fixed on the small shining thing. It spotted a way into the transparent dome and gracefully swooped inside the opening, taking a perch high up, with a good view of the sparkling object. The bird jumped forward until it was looking directly at its desire. Then it hopped down to a flat surface and up to the bright thing. It took one more hop, quickly grabbed the object in its beak, and then bent to take flight.

But suddenly, the bird was struggling frantically. It couldn't launch. Someone was holding it from behind, and the tight grasp around its body restricted it from opening its wings. I knew it was not Soul; it was someone intent on trapping the creature.

I felt the bird panic, and in my thoughts I willed it to wriggle and thrash as much as it could. It tried, putting its strength into pushing its wings free, but there was no hope of release. Its wings were too firmly held. It squawked and pecked at its captor while its body writhed, and I felt the clasp around its body as if it was I who was being restrained.

I released my thoughts from the bird and raced up the long pair of arms to the one who held the bird captive.

Let go! I screamed in the captor's head, as a rush of dizziness overcame me. *Let me go! Now!*

FIFTEEN

Once the full team were back at the base, Chia filled them in on the memory data he'd retrieved from Soul and Huru. It was gruesomely fascinating, as well as useful. They saw all that the two bios knew of Tachra's life: they knew that she had witnessed the burning of a human and had tried to make the flames stop, and in so doing, she had injured her head. They learnt that Huru had attacked her, that she'd stabbed him and that he'd succumbed to her use of a voice of command. Finally, they learnt that she had left Soul to travel once again, although Soul didn't know where. The dates of the burning and subsequent voice command exactly matched the dates of the surges of energy.

As the team discussed the implications of this new information, Jychanumun slowly stood, his eyes focused upwards, motioning his hand for silence. Above them wheeled a sleek black bird.

The bird boldly entered their force field and stealthily hopped from one hanging to the next. It seemed unperturbed by their presence, and although its head darted from side to side, its gaze remained fixed on the small glittering object suspended in the centre of the table.

"What a fine example of animal life," Kraniel whispered. "Catch it for my specimens."

Jychanumun nodded, and quietly moved towards the bird.

The bird paused above the end of the table and decided that Jychanumun's movement was not a threat. It swooped down to the table's surface and gingerly hopped towards the crystal, its head twitching. It reached its target, and then with a quick jerk poked its head forward and aimed its beak inside the containment field and towards the sparkling object.

Jychanumun pounced forward, seizing the bird with both hands.

"Well done!" Kraniel laughed aloud. "I'll get a specimen field."

The captured creature wriggled frantically to release its wings, but Jychanumun had a good hold. It continued struggling, fruitlessly writhing its body to find a way out of its grasp, as Kraniel moved forward with a containment jar.

Suddenly, Jychanumun twitched, let out a painful howl, stumbled forward, tried to regain his footing and then fell, releasing the bird and hitting his head against the table. The bird launched towards the force field entrance and, with a few flaps of its wings, took to the skies.

Chia leapt towards Jychanumun, who was bent double, retching violently.

"Don't touch me!" Jychanumun yelled, shaking Chia off.

Chia backed off as Jychanumun gained control of his retching and straightened, leaning heavily on the table. "Are you all right?" he asked.

"I'm fine." Jychanumun shook his head. "When someone touches me I hear them as well as feel them: it's too loud, like they're shouting."

"Sorry," Chia frowned, holding up his hands to indicate that he wouldn't touch him again. He pointed towards a large gash, welling with fresh red liquid, on Jychanumun's forehead, in the same place where he'd previously sustained an injury.

Jychanumun looked perplexed and rubbed his forehead, smearing the blood.

"It was not you that shouted," he said to Chia. "It was the bird. The bird demanded that I let it go."

SIXTEEN

I was stuck inside the bird's mind, seeing only the fingers wrapped around the bird's body, holding it tightly. I had shouted at the bird's captor in attempt to break it free; there was a jerk of movement and the bird had freed first one wing, and then the other, and launched towards the opening.

The bird flew upwards, with me still inside its mind, rose into the sky, and then dived down over the lip of the cliff in an adrenaline-filled swoop, flying as fast as it could back towards familiar land. My head reeled with vertiginous flight, and I flung my thoughts away from the bird and back into myself.

I came back, relieved to return to my own flesh and feeling sick from the sudden jump. I expected my heart to be racing, but I felt surprisingly calm. I shook my head to clear my thoughts.

I knew the bird could easily find its way back to its usual hunting ground. The poor creature would quite likely be shocked for a while, but I was jubilant for it. It had felt vindicated in its freedom flight, and I knew that it had succeeded in snatching the glittering object of its desire.

I had not seen Soul, but I had sensed her presence strongly on that flat mountain, even through the bird. Her calls for help still occupied the back of my mind.

I would go to Soul, I decided. I would go to the flat mountain and help her. I had promised.

I wasted no time, completing the preparations for my journey far more efficiently than I had on my previous travels. I already had a good imprint of the direction I needed to take, although I knew that the bird's flight had given the illusion that the route was easy. I had noted many valleys en route that would undoubtedly yield food, so I'd concentrated on collecting everything that could contain water.

Along with my last intact bottles, I gathered the strange looking assortment of hollowed out fruit husks I had made that I could plug with reasonable effect; I filled them all and wrapped them in my bundle. I added my knife, a fresh sharpening flint, and a bundle of twine that was one of my better efforts at rope making. I'd also retrieved my stick. Although there were many better pieces of wood available, this gnarled branch had accompanied me before and I'd grown oddly fond of it.

It didn't take long until I was ready to leave. I looked down, feeling that something was amiss. It then dawned on me that if I was to encounter other people, even if it was only Soul, I could not travel naked.

My skin had become my only clothes, and my old garments were now a threadbare pile that had long been reconstructed into useful tools. The exception was the last dress that mother had made for me, my choosing dress. The dress had functioned as a head covering when traversing the mountain, and had survived better than any other garment. Its fabric had been too delicate to serve any purpose since. In truth, I had thought it too fine to rip up. I retrieved the garment from the forest and put it on, fondly touching the weave and pushing aside the surfacing thoughts of my parents.

After wrapping extra fabric around my feet and hands, I tied up my bundle and placed the remaining rags in the hollowed-out sleeping area for the cats, who would be reassured by my scent. My quiet rustling in the forest alerted Meah's curiosity and she padded over to investigate. After a few sniffs of my clothes, she sat watching me expectantly.

I'll be back and you are not to follow, I told her.

She looked at me in her superior way, and I knew that the tone of my thought would make her understand, even if the words did not. I ruffled her fur, and then sensed another cat watching close by: a male, young. She followed my gaze towards the male. She liked him, I thought.

"Well go on then. When I return you can introduce us."

Meah trotted off, making a wide arc around the male so that she could casually stroll past him, and looked back at me once before disappearing from view. I could see she was content.

I picked up my stick and slung my bundle over my shoulder, grimacing at the familiarity of the action. Would there be no end to my travels? Would I spend my days in an endless cycle of walking and resting?

Perhaps, I thought. But for now, one more journey beckons.

SEVENTEEN

Jychanumun stood holding his forehead. Streaks of red trickled between his fingers.

"It shouted at me," Jychanumun repeated.

"Birds cannot shout," Kraniel stated matter-of-factly. He still held the empty containment sphere he'd picked up, ready to hold the creature. "And that was a bird, of the family Corvidae to be more exact."

"It *made* me let it go," Jychanumun scowled.

Kraniel considered this. "I'm not ignorant of the touch-understand abilities, but that was one of the Corvidae. Birds don't have enough kutu genetics to communicate with us, let alone make us do anything."

"What do you think happened?" Orion asked Jychanumun, stepping forward.

Jychanumun shook his head and walked off, fetching a healing rod as he went. The team were left staring at each other uncertainly.

"It isn't possible," Kraniel grumbled. "There's absolutely no way a bird could do that."

"We know that," Orion nodded. "Perhaps Jychanumun was mistaken." He paused and added, "The energy on this planet seems to have had many odd effects on us."

It was obvious that Orion's words were a diplomatic way of saying that Jychanumun must have been mistaken, but that they shouldn't make an issue out of it. Chia had never doubted the black-eyed kutu's sanity, but none of them could know what his past had done to his mind. Anyway, it was only a bird. Kraniel had enough for his collection, and the creature had managed to take something from them.

"Did you realise," Chia said, purposely lightening the mood, "That the bird made off with the tracking module from my Orb? Shursa will end up knowing the habits of a Corvidae very well."

The tension broke immediately, with small chuckles growing into laughter. It would be quite some time before Shursa realised that the movements he was tracking through the module were not theirs, and they all derived great satisfaction from this.

"Well," Orion eventually declared, "We still need to find the human, Tachra. I don't know about the rest of you, but I'm too anxious to sleep."

"I am too," Chia agreed. "However, as we still don't have the 7A, we must conserve energy. We should deactivate all the force fields."

"But working without energy will hinder us," Kraniel pointed out. "And we need energy both for our equipment and for the containment field when we find Tachra. And that's just the start of it. There must be a better solution."

"I don't know how to get more energy," Chia replied. "I only know that there's not enough. Eskah knows I've tried summoning the 7A umpteen times. I've tried summoning every damn ship that I know. Nirrious won't respond, Shursa speaks in lies, and the Supreme still hasn't contacted us."

He set up the communication port to try to raise communications again, while the others watched. The 7A didn't respond; Nirrious – still nothing; his old flight team – nothing. And then, one by one, he tried contacting every ship on the substation. Nothing and nobody could, or would, collect his attempted communications. Finally, he contacted the Supreme, knowing Shursa would collect.

The port connected and Shursa's irritated face stared back at him.

"Una, what a surprise; you look just like Shursa," Chia said sarcastically.

"What do you want?" Shursa replied brusquely.

"To speak with the Supreme, immediately. Not later. Now."

"He's indisposed," Shursa smiled unpleasantly.

"Then you'd better sort it out," Chia ordered him adamantly. "Una assigned me as head pilot and you've taken away my ship. If the 7A is not returned soon, I'll have to find a way to commandeer one of the harvesting ships and come and get the 7A myself. I want my ship back and I want to speak to the Supreme."

Chia knew that commandeering a harvesting ship would be impossible, but Shursa was neither a pilot nor a sensitive, so it was likely that he didn't and wouldn't know. Chia played on Shursa's ignorance a little more.

"We are short of supplies. We need food now. Commandeering a harvesting ship from the closest colony can be done tonight. If you can assure us that the 7A is immediately dispatched I will wait until morning, but no longer."

"I'll see what I can do," Shursa said, clearly irritated. "Now go away and stop interrupting me, or I'll have your position downgraded."

"There are other issues too," Chia replied forcefully, leaning towards the port, "I wish Una to know that the Orb I was awarded had been tampered with – a deception as unsubtle as the one who perpetrated it, Shursa. Does the Supreme know about this?"

Shursa's eyes narrowed, his dislike for Chia surfacing. "Only a fool would accuse me of things they know nothing about. The Supreme is aware of everything. More than you would ever know."

"Be calm, Shursa," Orion interjected, standing up next to Chia. "Chia requires a meeting with the Supreme, and I would like to talk to Una as my old friend. I'll take responsibility for you having to disturb him. There's no problem with that, is there?"

Shursa's façade changed instantly upon seeing Orion.

"I don't see that disturbing either the harvesting ships or Una is necessary," Shursa replied, adopting a calmer tone. "I can arrange the return of the 7A. There must have been a problem with it, but I'll ensure that it is dispatched immediately. You'll have it before the close of the day. And I'll request that the Supreme contacts you before the end of the day too."

Shursa broke into a false smile with his last words, and then closed the connection before any more could be said.

"Why were you so reasonable with him?" Chia asked Orion, still annoyed with Shursa. "He was lying."

"I know," Orion replied, "But his tone told me that he would not back down, no matter what. Our best course was to close the conversation. Do you recall those small bios that you had such trouble with after disturbing them?"

"Wasps – vicious little attackers," Chia replied, getting the gist of Orion's question. "So, you think I've just put my hands firmly in the metaphorical hive again."

"We both have," Orion agreed. "I have had enough of dealing with Shursa. Right now, I'll just be glad to complete this mission, return to Eden, and see the Supreme. On the bright side, you've successfully negotiated the return of the 7A. I feel better knowing that you could commandeer a harvesting ship if necessary."

Chia raised an eyebrow and smiled.

"Ah, I see," Orion nodded, realising that Chia had been bluffing. "Then we shall not dwell on that."

Regardless of Shursa's unpleasantness, the team readied for the day in an optimistic mood. They would have their ship back before the end of the day. They knew who they were looking for, and they had agreed on a good plan to locate her. Today, they were determined to find her.

They continued their search for Tachra by starting from her last known location, just outside the settlement called Hollow. They soon reached the river, but found no further trace of her, even though they trailed the course of the water and even followed each tributary as it appeared.

Chia zigzagged the length of the river, travelling as far from the water as he thought a human could survive. As he travelled further from the colonies, the land grew rockier, the vegetation sparser, and the river shrank until it was no more than a trickle. The altitude of the land increased, and the tiny stream began dipping in and out of rocks, resurfacing for shorter periods each time. Then the water suddenly stopped, dipping into the rocks and showing no signs of resurfacing. In the distance, a range of tall mountains spanned the horizon. They appeared impassable for any creature without wings, and the sensors confirmed that they were beyond human reach without a water supply.

Logic told Chia that he should turn around and start tracking a new route, but he pushed ahead, following an almost overpowering intuition. Still the bare land revealed nothing, but Chia kept on until he skirted the lower faces of the mountains. After several zigzags, each time increasing in altitude, he was finally ready to turn back. It was time to pick another tributary; this route was a dead end. His hunch had obviously been wrong.

Chia slowed down, instructing the pod to follow a new course. The craft rose and spun in response. But as it moved, something blinked momentarily on the readout panel.

Chia reversed his trajectory until the readout blinked once more. There were two dots – one indicating fragments of Tachra's blood, and the other indicating Tachra wood. Both were further up the mountain and well beyond the point that any human should have been able to reach. He communicated his findings to the others and bolted towards the co-ordinates.

There was nowhere to land near the first destination, which turned out to be a wall of vertical grey rocks with remnants of dead bracken poking out from shallow cracks. Directly ahead, a long dirty rag hung by a few threads from a protruding twig. That was it – the source of Tachra's blood. He slowed the pod, deactivated the shields, and plucked the rag from its hold.

Moving further up the mountain, Chia located the position of the second reading. There was a small recess, too narrow to land on and barely wide enough to stride across. Whatever he was looking for wasn't immediately visible, so he left the pod hovering, got out, and climbed onto the weather-beaten stone.

At first there was nothing obvious, but then Chia noticed a crack in the corner, just large enough to get his arm in. It was the only possible place where something could be concealed. He kneeled down and slid his hand into the crevice, immediately feeling something lodged there. He pulled out an empty container, badly damaged and made of hardened mud. Putting the pot to one side, he thrust his arm back into the gap and, one by one, pulled out more objects: another damaged container, a sharpened stone, and grass strands woven into twine, but nothing of wood. He pushed his arm as far as it would reach and searched carefully with his fingers. As soon as he touched it, he knew he'd found another carved pebble.

As Chia examined this latest find, a flurry of wings loomed closer. Orion, Stanze and Kraniel joined him on the cramped ledge.

Chia showed his team mates what he had found, and took the rag from his pod, confirming that it was stained with remnants of Tachra blood. Orion stared at the blood-splattered rag in Chia's hands, and then down at the broken items littering the ground, his face becoming increasingly troubled.

"We must search for the remains of her body," Orion said quietly, shaking his head.

"Body?" Chia asked.

"Look where we are. Look at these," Orion waved his hand over the objects. "Do they not tell a story of their own? These are fragile remnants of a long journey. She would not choose to leave these things behind, and she would have been too far from sustenance to survive. We have our discoveries and they show that Tachra has died."

"There is more," said Kraniel. He had taken the rag from Chia, and now examined it further. "This is covered with Tachra's blood, and the blood shows high levels of contamination. We know that the damage she sustained to her head was severe. It seems her wound was badly infected. No human could survive such toxins."

"We will search for her remains," Orion acknowledged sadly. He glanced down at the broken objects by his feet, shook his head, and then took to the sky.

Kraniel and Stanze silently followed Orion, leaving Chia on the small ledge. He looked around for something, anything, to give them hope that Tachra still lived, but his heart felt heavy. Orion's logic seemed correct; no creature would get this far only to leave everything behind. And the toxins in her blood surely confirmed their fears.

What a terrible waste, Chia thought, feeling an odd compassion for Tachra. To have travelled so far, for reasons they would never know, and to die in this unpleasant, scrubby place.

Climbing back into the pod, Chia began the horrible task of looking for Tachra's remains.

The pod was a good, agile craft, well-suited for searching the mountain face, and Chia started at the bottom of the cliff, directly below the ledge. The entire cliff was cluttered with narrow ledges and cracks, and each one had to be searched, regardless of whether or not the sensors detected anything.

Chia cursed the fact that humans were so much smaller than kutu, but he was also glad that he didn't have Stanze's bulk, as he was forced to squeeze into umpteen splits in the rock whenever he left the pod, only to find nothing of significance. One fissure opened up to become a small cave that was inhabited by a pair of wolves. Chia made the animals sleep and scanned their lair, quite relieved that the human's remains weren't present and that Tachra's end had not been in the belly of such creatures.

As Chia searched, he passed his team-mates many times, each of them investigating yet more crevices and recesses. No communication passed between them, but although nobody announced that Tachra's remains had been found, they all seemed to feel the same unanticipated sense of sorrow and compassion.

As time wore on and the night's gloom sank into the day, as well as into their hearts, they made their way back to the base, deciding to search again the following day.

"So, we've no body yet," Orion pondered over a large goblet of the last of their strongest drink. He was noticeably deflated.

"There may not be anything left of it," Chia said. "I detected hunting bios in the area."

"That's true," Orion agreed with a sigh. "Finding a pile of bones would be useless to us. I've notified Jychanumun, but he didn't respond; I think he's as dumbfounded as we are. Perhaps we should all just go home now. Tachra's dead flesh cannot contain Factor X. Perhaps we should just leave her remains in peace, wherever they fell."

There was a long pause while the group dwelled on the thought. Chia searched for a good argument to refute the composer, but he could find none; perhaps it was just time to go home.

And then a small bleeping sound echoed in the background.

Chia's heart lurched; he knew that sound immediately. He had heard it so many times. It was the 7A's communication call.

Rushing towards the port, Chia placed his hand over the confirmation panel, and a few moments later Nirrious's voice crackled through.

"Chia," Nirrious' voice echoed oddly. "Must keep this brief."

Chia started to speak, but Nirrious allowed him no time. "Shursa has given the instruction that the 7A is to depart from the XLS, Earth-bound, tomorrow morning," he stated flatly.

"That's good news," Chia confirmed, relieved. "How are you, Nirrious?"

"That's all. I'll forward the ETA shortly," Nirrious ignored his question and closed the connection.

Chia frowned, turning away from the blank port.

"Why is there a growing habit of people cutting me off before I've finished?"

"Perhaps he'll send a communication in the 7A, as we did," Orion suggested. "Perhaps now Una will contact us too. Although I do wish we could give him better news of our findings. Even Una believed this new energy could be our next evolution."

"We've worked diligently and hard," Chia stated. "There is no shame in that. This human is the link to the Factor X; there's still the energy source itself."

"That could take millennia to find, if we could find it at all," Orion shrugged. "I would like to stay here and search for it, but I feel an urgency to return to Eden to speak with the Supreme. Matters at home are disquieting."

"At least we now have a ship to get home." Chia pointed out.

"Yes, come," Orion decided, standing up and stretching. "None of you have taken sustenance today. You must eat. We don't know what lies ahead that we may need our strength for."

"The food rations are finished," Stanze sighed dejectedly.

Orion started laughing. "I'm sorry, I don't know why I'm laughing," he said, shaking his head. "This situation is extreme. I came here thinking I would find answers to our legends, but all I've found is anxiety and an empty belly. Come, it's our last night and we're hungry; we'll cook with Earth matter. I'll cook. You all need nourishment."

They built a small fire on the plateau and gathered an array of the foods they'd kept for the bios. Chia prepared the force field for the 7A's return, in anticipation of their inevitable departure, and then joined Orion, who was dishing up plates of unappealing-looking lumps of food.

Jychanumun still hadn't returned, so Chia contacted him to let him know that the meal was waiting for him. Jychanumun said that he didn't want anything.

"What are you doing?" Chia asked.

"Waiting," Jychanumun eventually responded enigmatically.

"What for?"

"Tachra."

"Have you not heard? We're preparing to leave. Tachra has died, Jychanumun."

"No, she is alive, I have found her home."

Chia glanced at Orion, who nodded, indicating that he'd heard the exchange.

"We're coming," Orion quickly added. "Send us your co-ordinates."

They left the half-eaten food, agreeing that the pods would be quicker than winged flight, and crammed into one, with Chia as the pilot. The co-ordinates were inputted, and within moments, they'd departed from the plateau.

It didn't take long to reach Jychanumun. He sat at the outskirts of a forest, beyond the mountain ranges they'd searched earlier. He stood up when he saw them, and waited for them to join him before indicating that they should follow him.

Jychanumun walked along the border of the forest until the trees stopped and they overlooked a deep valley with a large lake at its centre. He paused for a moment, and then continued down into the valley, silently indicating towards signs of human occupation as he went: footprints in the damp soil by the lake; grasses carefully arranged in a mound; a small length of twine woven from bark – these things and more suggested that a human had lived here.

Chia scanned the objects they passed, but none registered a strong enough trace to suggest that a human bios was close. And the whole area was awash with Factor X, but it felt slightly different to his previous sensing: it was calmer, more serene.

Jychanumun kept walking, slowly making his way into the shadow of the trees. Once he was in the darkness he knelt, pointing towards a patch of leaf-strewn soil. The patch looked like any other part of the forest floor until Jychanumun swept the leaves aside with his hand, revealing a length of cloth neatly spread out over an excavated, long, shallow hole full of grasses. It was an improvised bed, and clearly had been slept in very recently. Jychanumun covered the cloth back over with leaves and stood again, walking a few paces and picking up a handful of recently dried fruits that had been placed inside a tree hollow. He showed them to the team, carefully returned them, and then walked back into the sunlight and stood gazing over the lake.

"This is where she lives. It is beautiful," Jychanumun said.

"It is," Chia agreed. "I can feel it too. Eskah knows how she made it this far. I'd say she's been here very recently."

"Tachra made it here!" Orion exclaimed. "Oh joy; she didn't die on the mountain. She made it." He smiled to himself and sat down on the grass, shaking his head as the news sunk in. "Beyond the scope of what we thought a human could survive, she made it here – Tachra is alive! What a creature of perseverance she must be. What a remarkable human."

"Perhaps she is not only human," Jychanumun remarked.

"It is only through absorbing Factor X that she is able to endure more. Factor X is significant: She is still human." Chia noticed Kraniel nodding in agreement.

"We'll see," Jychanumun stated.

"Do you know where she is now?" Orion asked.

Jychanumun shook his head.

"Well, there's no point searching for her," Orion stated. "We'd have to fly at too low an altitude and we want her contained before she's aware of us; we still do not know the extent of her capabilities. She lives here. She'll be back soon. We'll wait, unseen, for her return. Then we'll contain her."

"I'll find the vantage points," Stanze nodded, leaving immediately.

There was a rustle in the trees behind them and Chia turned just in time to catch a glimpse of a cat withdrawing into the forest.

"That's still further evidence that she was here," Jychanumun paused, noting Chia's glance. "But if I tell you about it, it must be left alone."

"But of course, if you wish. You have my word," Orion replied.

"It's a wild cat. It has a bond with her."

"A bond with a cat? We should really analyse that."

"Remember your word," insisted Jychanumun.

Orion went to speak again, and then shook his head and dropped the subject. He had given his word that the cat would be left alone, and he would honour it.

Stanze silently reappeared beside Orion, having finished scoping the area. "There are many places of concealment, but I can easily keep watch alone," he asserted.

"Excellent," Orion nodded his approval. "We have her now. All we have to do is wait."

The team entrusted Stanze, with his Anumi training, with the task. Stanze decided that he should hide in a suitable position and enclose Tachra on her return, using the modified containment field. After that, they'd use any means necessary to make her sleep, ready to take her to Eden.

Stanze positioned himself out of sight, surprisingly managing to conceal his large bulk behind a small run of bushes, and then instructed the others to leave so that his concealment could be effective.

As the others returned to the pod, and Jychanumun walked on ahead, Chia pondered an obvious subject.

"Something is troubling all of us; about this mission, about Tachra," he murmured.

Orion nodded his agreement.

"I've heard Stanze's comforting words to the humans when he thinks we can't hear," Chia went on. "I feel Jychanumun's acknowledgement of the bond between Tachra and the cat, and you have developed an admiration for this human. Even Kraniel has expressed concern about the humans' increased emotional development. We've made humans in the likeness of ourselves, and found that they can think, feel, and – Eskah forbid – even bond. Tachra knows choice. Choice is sacred to us. Would we deny her choice? Whatever the outcome of this mission, I will be troubled."

"Humans are made to be our tools," Kraniel argued, pushing aside his own rising feelings of compassion, "and the female, Tachra, is still just a bios. She is obviously an anomaly, and malformed bios usually do not last long beyond manufacture."

"I suspect Jychanumun does not agree with you," Orion replied, in a tone that stopped any further conversation.

They reached the pod, but Jychanumun wasn't there and so they climbed in, thinking that he had probably already returned to the base. They piloted the craft back to the base without him, and once they had landed, Chia went straight to the human enclosure.

No one had yet fed the humans that evening, and they huddled together in one corner. The bios Soul, who had seemed so relaxed with Stanze, didn't seem to like Chia at all. She stood as far away from him as possible, glaring at him while he handed out fruit. She would not take any food, and so he held out a particularly good-looking apple. Her expression took him by surprise: it could only be described as wariness. It was yet another emotion that they had not expected the humans to develop. He left extra fruits for her and returned to the force field, nestling down on his recliner, taking solace in the knowledge that they would soon have their ship again.

Chia had just fallen into a reasonably comfortable slumber when he was shaken awake. He automatically leapt to his feet, taking a defensive stance.

"It's only me," Orion whispered.

It was dark outside, but Kraniel was sitting at the table. Jychanumun was in his bunk, and as Orion moved to awaken him, Jychanumun turned, nodded, and rose.

"The 7A will be here any moment. Not tomorrow as we

expected. Nirrious has sent a message," Orion explained. "We can't be in the force field when it returns, as I want to sweep for more nano-trackers."

Chia nodded. From his newly wakened senses he sensed something familiar: his ship.

A tiny silver star in the distance grew in the night's sky until it dwarfed all others, and then the 7A burst into view. A fraction of a moment later, the gleaming giant craft manoeuvred stealthily over its landing spot, connecting with its force field.

Chia ran to the 7A, placing a sweeper crystal on the craft.

Use the HOTS, he announced telepathically. *Let's not speak until we know we're not being monitored.*

The 7A opened its hatch, and a shadow seemed to hover in the light of the doorway. Chia took a step back: *no one should be onboard!* As he moved, so did the shadow, resolving itself into a figure that stumbled forwards and collapsed.

It was Nirrious.

Chia lurched forward to his aid. He looked terrible, and barely conscious.

"Get me a re-tuner," Chia shouted, immediately forgetting that he should use the HOTS.

Orion pulled his own re-tuner from his mouldings and placed it on Nirrious' forehead.

Chia scooped Nirrious up, laid him on a recliner and covered him in healing sheets, leaning over him, studying him intensely. He recognized many of the symptoms that Nirrious was displaying only too well.

"He hasn't properly been acclimatized for travel or this planet, but he will be fine," Chia stated, relieved. "He's been re-tuned to physical too quickly, on a ship that was going too fast."

He inspected Nirrious further, finding that there were several large patches of blood over his tunic.

"He also has wounds to the flesh, although that's nothing to do with re-tuning. The healing sheets will repair them."

Nirrious was stirring: the re-tuning was slowly balancing his body. Suddenly, he bolted upright, his eyes wide.

"I made it," he rasped, trying to swing his legs off the recliner.

"Be still," Chia stated. "You haven't re-tuned properly. We have to reverse it a little bit. The feeling will pass soon enough. We should use the HOTS for communication."

"It doesn't matter if we speak aloud," Nirrious replied. "No one can hear us."

Nirrious opened his clasped fist. Over a dozen tiny listening probes and tracking modules sat de-activated in his palm.

EIGHTEEN

Soul's requests for help came and went involuntarily through my mind, raising my concern for her welfare. I could think of little else while I walked. I hadn't expected that there would ever have been a reason to leave my valley: I'd had enough of walking, and had finally found a place that felt like home. But Soul's need for help was one of the few things that could have made me leave my home. I knew that I'd be back, though, and perhaps this time Soul would be returning with me.

Experience made me set a steady pace, and I hoped that the journey would take no more than eight days. More realistically, I knew that it would take eight days just to reach the mountain of stone, which seemed to go on forever. Somehow, Soul had found herself up there, on top of that lofty plateau, and I hoped that my perception of the height of the mountain had been exaggerated by seeing it through the eyes of the bird.

I tried not to dwell on the seemingly impossible climb, knowing that I would figure out how to overcome it when the problem was in front of me. If Soul had found her way up there, then surely I could too.

I'd started the journey at night, meticulously traversing the sea of rocks beyond the valley. I chose my route carefully, following a winding path through the safest areas, and I eventually navigated the region without mishaps. It was a relief to feel the dry, sandy soil under my feet. I walked through the following day and into early the next night, when common sense told me to stop, rest and refresh myself.

A great sense of unease accompanied this travelling, although I knew not why, so I made small detours to stay undercover, protected by whatever vegetation the land had to offer, whilst not delaying my passage. With this, I used my knowledge of the Old One to blend invisibly with the earth. It made me feel safe.

As I tried sleeping on that second night, I noticed a change in Soul's calls. At first, her pleas for help became more sporadic. This didn't perturb me, because I presumed that she merely rested or slept. But then I sensed a change in her that did perplex me. She no longer called to me for help; instead, she repeated the word 'no,' as if trying to repel me. No matter how much I tried reading more of her thoughts, I could only sense the strongest of them, that single new word, accompanied by feelings of trepidation. I increased my tempo with an even stronger resolve, knowing that her need must be great.

By pacing myself well and resting for short intervals, I passed through the arid ground after two more days, and soon the land started to show signs of healthy greenery, nourished by the water that I could sense beneath the land. I'd not encumbered myself with food for the journey, knowing I could survive eight days without it, and so I was glad to find bushes heavily laden with edible fruits. And I carefully rationed my water, remembering how unpleasant thirst could be.

I reached the valley of yellow flowers that preceded the cliff in less than seven days: I'd made even better time than I'd estimated. I waded through the sweet-smelling blooms that grew knee-high until I stood in the flowerless shadow of the vast rock face. My destination towered far above me. The bird had made relatively easy work of this obstacle, and now I realised that its eyes had made it seem shorter, rather than taller as I had hoped.

I was at an apparent dead end.

To climb to the top of this mountain would be impossible, I realised, scanning the expanse of rock, which stretched as far to my left, and right as my eyes could see, and which seemed to reach to the skies – far higher than any mountain I had seen. Its walls were sheer in places, with ragged sections and large overhangs, so that the summit loomed far above and over my head. Other areas were lengthy, sheer drops that were many times higher than my reach. And towards the top, the highest ledge jutted out, protruding like a great barrier. There was not even a tuft of grass or loose vine to offer a hand-hold.

I couldn't see any way that I could climb even the first fraction of this mountain, yet alone get to the top. It looked impassable.

I camped there that night, refusing to accept defeat, disciplining myself to think hard and use my senses to find a path. If I kept both my eyes and my true vision open, I thought, a course would become apparent.

I lay down with my head on the grass and forced my thoughts to become still, and then I sank deep into my sub-consciousness, opening my true vision and becoming at one with the soil beneath me. I pushed out, spreading my senses wider.

The solid cliff that I wanted to overcome went far below the surface of the earth, its vertical walls leading up to a large flattened top. As I curved my senses around the rock, I became aware of a narrow, more sloping area on the opposite side of the plateau. It had partially collapsed a long time ago, and it was now a steep stony mass, littered with the occasional sparse bushes and tufts of grasses in the layers of soil that had accumulated over the seasons. I felt its instability; it was still settling and its energy was a frenzy of activity within the deceptively motionless stone. But it was also the only possible route to get my body upwards. I had found my path.

I pushed my mind in a different direction, following the rocky slope to the plateau, and tried to sense Soul. Immediately I was bombarded with a chaotic mass of movement that I didn't recognise. I tried to weave through the chaos to sense her, but it seemed impenetrable. I would need to get closer; I did not yet recognise everything that I felt.

I threaded my thoughts back through the land and returned my consciousness to my flesh. The route to the plateau would certainly be extremely difficult, I thought, and if I was to face those inevitable difficulties, I knew I had to rest.

I slept lightly, awoken as usual by dreams, all of my which had been overlaid with Soul's repeated 'no,' as if she sat beside me, chanting. I had dreamt of the black-eyed one, but this time he did not hold out his hand to me.

I awoke, keeping my eyes closed while trying to quell the churning sensation that my dreams had left.

All of a sudden, my nerves jolted. I opened my eyes and instinctively looked up. At the top of the mountain something moved. It shot into the distance, too quick for me to see, leaving a trail of dissipating blue light. Oh, I knew that light only too well! But this was much smaller, and moved so much faster. Then, without warning, another bolt of blue sped from the mountain top, leaving another fading trail.

I kept immobile for a moment, waiting to see if any more passed over me. None did. I got up, silently gathered my items, and started walking. I had been concealed under the ledge of the plateau, and now my true vision was alert, ensuring that I blended with the land. My objective was still to find and help Soul, but it seemed there might be more at the top of this mountain than I'd expected.

I made good progress, but when I finally saw my path upwards, my stomach turned: it looked impossible. I could not imagine how Soul had managed to get to the top. She would have had her child by now, and it looked an impossible climb for any one person, yet alone for someone with an infant. But she was up there somehow, and I was going to get up there too.

I stood for a moment, and used both my true vision and eyes to map out my path. My worst fears were confirmed: it was a mass of unstable areas to be avoided. Huge, sturdy looking rocks were often delicately balanced, and a good wind might send them tumbling. The long stretches of pebbles could give way under foot with the slightest wrong move. The few solid ledges hovered in unreachable places, and even if they were reachable, they were cluttered with shingle and dead trees that had fallen from above. Despite the obvious difficulty of the climb, I had to try.

I started the lower slopes, leaping from stone to stone. This brisk momentum didn't last long, however, as a boulder that should have taken my walking weight dislodged and shifted, making a tumble of gravel slide down the slope and almost taking me with it. I stilled while the land settled. From that point forward, I controlled my pace without letting my concentration slip.

Frustratingly, I could not climb in the dark: my true vision told me the rigidity of things, but I needed my eyes to find holds for my hands and feet. The first evening set in quickly, so I found a firm recess and tried to sleep.

I made good, steady progress on the second day and, when darkness set in again I kept going for a little while longer, having pre-mapped the next section of my path. When I knew I could go no further, I settled in a niche in one boulder and slept.

As I slept, nestled in stone, I dreamt the strangest dream: of a world so full of people that the land was almost barren. The people were full of suffering and hopelessness and an overwhelming sense of lethargy, and they inflicted their pain on all else around them. I dreamt that I wanted to help them. I didn't run away, I didn't scream, I stood tall and determined. It was singularly the most terrible dream I'd ever had, yet in it I saw a side of myself I'd never seen before.

I awoke, shivering in the crevice. If these things were to be, I would help, I thought, because that world was a terrible place.

It was still night, and in the sky above me what looked like a star appeared, seeming to dwarf all others. The star grew larger. It moved at a ferocious speed, falling downwards, seemingly aiming at me. And then, as it grew closer, I saw it properly: something huge, silver and smooth. It slowed just before hitting the mountain top and disappeared from sight. My heart jumped. What if it had fallen onto Soul? I pushed out my mind and was thankful that I could still sense her.

Although it was still night, I gathered my bundle and cautiously began climbing again. This time I kept my mind open, constantly aware of Soul and ensuring she came to no harm.

I climbed for a further day and, although the way was fraught with calamities, I kept my senses alert, and they all served me well. After a stretch of complex navigation around wide patches of shingle and unstable rocks, my path showed signs of healthy plant life in a section that had not shifted for years. The boulders decreased in size, and were now submerged amidst patches of deep-rooted shrubs. The ascent became easier and

I made better speed. By late afternoon, I was scaling the last patch of freshly tumbled grey stones.

I pulled myself up a ledge, and at last, my eyes saw the green plateau.

A large patch of trees stretched before me. I knew these trees from when the bird had landed here; they spanned half the perimeter. The smell of burnt timber tainted the air; there was a fire in the centre somewhere. The vegetation obscured my view, but I clearly sensed Soul's presence and knew she was close.

A part of me wanted to run, but prudence had taught me to tread with caution. I darted from bracken to bush, keeping low until I reached the safety of the woodland, and then crept forward, through the trees and into the prickling bushes that thrived at the outskirts of the forest.

I now had a clear view of a huge, silver-coloured dome. It was not a natural formation – that much was obvious – and I could not imagine how anyone could construct such a perfectly smooth thing. Its size was immense, taking up a good portion of the open land, and its surface reflected distorted images of its surroundings, making it almost invisible.

To one side of the dome several large horses stood grazing. Seeing the horses reassured me; I had an affinity with horses and knew that they would not graze if they sensed danger. Still, I remained cautious and moved slowly forward, choosing to remain obscured by the edges of the woodland.

To the front of the main dome, I saw another, smaller one from which light was emitting; this dome seemed to be attached to the larger one, but it was almost translucent. Inside it was awash with colour in patterns that could rival the very flowers of spring. The structure of a table the length of a hut took up a good portion of what I could see through the shimmer, and lengths of luminescent fabric hung in strips, obscuring the bulk of the remaining space. The fabric astounded me; our old village weaver could never have produced anything like it, even if he had years to work on it. But this place had obviously been constructed, and someone seemed to inhabit it, even though I sensed a great deal of things that I had no name for.

Intrigue and unease battled for supremacy within me. How had Soul come to be here, so far away from her home? How had she made the climb here? And surely, neither she nor anybody else could have built such a place. But I did sense Soul, although she was nowhere in sight. I had to find a better view to try to locate her.

I continued through the woods towards the lip of the plateau, and then I crawled forward, out of the cover of the trees, until I had nothing but a rangy Hawthorn bush concealing me. Through the fluttering breaks in the vibrant hanging fabric, I caught glimpses into the transparent dome of light. Then I saw something.

By the skies!

No, Tachra, stay as quiet as a mouse. Be still. Be invisible.

My breathing became thunderous to my ears, so I covered my mouth with my hand.

The thumping of my heart was so fierce I felt anxious that they might hear. From my crouched prime position, I watched.

What were these things?

They were not human!

There were creatures, several of them. They had the basic similarities of people; head, arms, legs, but they were more, much more. Other than *him*, the Old One, they were the most amazing things I had ever seen.

NINETEEN

"The 7A is clean now," Nirrious said, putting the neutralized tracking devices on the recliner beside him. "Similar devices keep turning up all over the substation. I've found many in my rooms; I'm getting to be quite an expert in finding and deactivating them."

"The council should never permit such widespread intrusion," Orion replied angrily.

"The council has changed," Nirrious frowned. "Much has changed since you've been gone. Shursa now speaks for Una, and most of the councillors have been replaced with his supporters."

"What?" Orion exclaimed. "But it takes millennia to appoint even one new councillor. I knew things were not right, but I did not expect to this extent. I must return to Eden immediately."

"At first, that is what I came to ask of you, and why I chose to arrive in secrecy. I thought you could stand up to Shursa better than anyone," Nirrious began.

"That's not what I meant . . ." Orion interjected.

"But," Nirrious interrupted, "What I've since learnt leads me to fear that if you return without completing this mission, vengeance will be upon you." He sighed, shaking his head. "I came anyway; so you'll know what to expect. Much has changed and much continues to change. The new councillors, including Shursa, say that Factor X is our step to enlightenment. He is obsessed with your mission and its success. Many terrible things are surfacing on Eden and the substations as a consequence of this obsession."

Nirrious pulled down his tunic and to reveal his shoulder, where a deep, raw wound was unsuccessfully trying to close as his body rebalanced.

"Do you have any healing rods?" he asked. "I don't want to lie under a healing sheet."

"How did that happen?" Orion asked on seeing the terrible wound, and Chia quickly fetched a healing rod.

"I found another tracer embedded in my shoulder when I was on the 7A en route here," Nirrious said. "I had already taken to flesh, or tried to, and only had my knives to remove it with. I must admit I did it in haste and I started slipping into unconsciousness before I could heal it."

The team looked on in horror, hardly able to believe what Nirrious was saying.

Nirrious indicated towards the recliner opposite him. "I'll explain from the beginning. Perhaps you should sit down."

But none of the team wanted to sit; they were all far too agitated. Chia went to Nirrious' side and began ministering to his wound as Nirrious continued speaking.

"When the 7A docked, I retrieved your message, in private, and readied to leave for Eden to locate Una. However, just before I left, four kutu came to my chambers, and I was promptly escorted to Shursa. I don't remember what happened after that, but I found myself back in my own chambers, feeling ill; over a day had passed and I'd been temporarily relieved of all duties. The following day, I discovered the first tracer embedded in the back of my neck – I removed that one and healed the area. But . . ." Nirrious paused anxiously, "I have had nightmares. I cannot confirm what I suspect they did to me, for no one would speak of it, but I think they tortured me. I only hope I didn't tell them about your hidden message to Una, but I fear that if I cannot remember, then I might have."

"Torture?" Orion gasped. "How could things change so much?"

"Shursa twists the minds of many kutu. I do not know what has happened to him, but I have heard things," Nirrious paused, glancing at Orion.

"Go on," Orion urged.

"I heard that you snubbed him; that you told him he was not a visionary. He desires success. He wants Factor X under his command so that he can control all others, especially you."

"I did tell him he was not a forward thinker," Orion admitted. "Perhaps I even snubbed him. Could my words really be the cause of such things?"

"Orion, you would only have told the truth," Chia intervened. "You cannot be held responsible for another's deeds. And Shursa? I sensed discord in him long before we came here."

"Then if Shursa wants Factor X, and me, so strongly, perhaps he should come here and get them for himself!" Orion's voice was vehement.

"Perhaps he will," Nirrious stated. "But I've sensed a fear in him; either he fears this place, or losing control of the council, or both. His grip on the council is firm, but it's not total. He desires the human link to Factor X. He says that Factor X is the key to the growth of all things. Most believe him, and so willingly let him lead. They choose to not see that his only interest is in his own growth."

"It's not just his chosen councillors that believe him, then?" Orion asked.

"Most kutu believe him," Nirrious nodded. "Even I nearly did. Then Peniva took me aside and clarified things in a way that only the Anumi can. Many of the Anumi are not persuaded."

"That is good," Orion stated. "But has this poison spread so far that only the Anumi are spared? Nevertheless," he pondered, "whether Shursa is right or wrong is immaterial; it is not his place to make decisions for all. He doesn't have Supreme balance. Una is the Supreme; he could and should be controlling this. Did you contact him?"

"No. I tried, but I couldn't gain access to him," Nirrious replied. "Una's presence is little felt now anyway. It's clear that there's something grossly wrong with the Supreme, but I've not isolated the problem because he's barely seen in public. In his rare appearances, he is always accompanied by Shursa, and even then, he never speaks. Now most kutu are so driven to obtain Factor X that they want to listen to Shursa, and of course he says that he speaks on behalf of Una."

"We've also had problems communicating with Una. Shursa intercepts all his communications," Orion said, before pondering for a moment. "We could attempt a mind probe. Una once said I had the balance to create one."

"A mind probe is not only dangerous, it would be unsuccessful," Chia intervened. "Even if we didn't get 'lost' along the way, even if we located Una without damaging ourselves permanently, we could not get into his mind – we wouldn't be touching him. We'd need direct access to him, kutu to kutu, to use the mind-touch abilities, and for that we must get past Shursa."

"I know," Orion shook his head. "And to get to Shursa we need Factor X. We almost have Tachra; we just need a little more time, that's all."

He slammed his fist down hard on the table. "Time! Time! Eskah knows we need it on our side, yet everything goes against us!"

He immediately contacted Stanze through the HOTS, who confirmed that he'd had no sighting of Tachra in the valley. They had all expected that Tachra would have returned and been contained by now. Stanze told him that he was not unduly fatigued, and so Orion told him that the 7A, and Nirrious, had returned and that their problems were greater than they'd anticipated. He didn't go into details, but Stanze didn't seem to need them; he was Anumi: he was trained to expect the worst.

"Do not take it all upon yourself, Orion," Nirrious stressed. Chia had finished with the healing rod, and Nirrious inspected his shoulder and smoothed his tunic over the scar. "I came so that you would know what you would be returning to on Eden, and I wanted to help where I can. Shursa will not know I'm missing; the Anumi have helped to arrange a good cover-up. I've trained Peniva in 'old style' communications; just enough to allow him to keep me, and us, fully informed."

Orion paused. "That's good," he said finally. "I want to return to Eden now, yet it seems more prudent to wait until we have Tachra as bargaining power. And this troublesome female is invisible to us. All we can do is wait."

Chia watched Jychanumun walk away from the group and lie on a recliner. At first Chia assumed that he was resting, even though his timing seemed inappropriate. But instead, Jychanumun lay on his back with his hands behind his head, staring up at nothing. He sensed that Chia was observing him, glanced over, and then rose again.

"I must speak with you, Orion," Jychanumun said abruptly.

Orion looked at him expectantly. "Speak, my friend."

"What do you know of Tachra?"

"We know what she looks like, her bloodline, and that she's a harvestable link to Factor X," Orion responded. "Other than that, we know little of her."

"Exactly," Jychanumun replied. "What do we know of her will? Her choices? Her wishes?"

"What are you implying? Even if she does have a will and does know choice, what would you propose?" Orion asked, seeming a little annoyed.

"I propose that you decide your actions after you have all the facts. It seems you've already decided to take her to Eden," Jychanumun retorted.

Orion was about to argue, clearly exasperated, but then Kraniel intervened. "Jychanumun's got a point – maybe Tachra's link with Factor X would be broken if we removed her from the planet. We should utilize our expertise once we have her, and then decide on our next step."

"Yes, of course we will!" Orion snapped. "Although there's more at stake now than simply one harvesting bios."

Jychanumun did not reply, turning his back on the group and walking from the force field. Without a word, he re-tuned and launched into the sky, diving down over the ledge of the plateau and out of sight.

Jychanumun returned within the hour to find that the team hadn't moved from around the table. He nodded to the group as he approached, and helped himself to a goblet of newly stocked Ochrah. Moisture glistened on his skin and his breathing was heavy. He still frowned, but he'd clearly eradicated many of his frustrations by flying.

"A decision must be made," Orion stated to the group, while looking at Jychanumun. "By all of us."

He proceeded to call Stanze through their HOTS, requesting that he leave Tachra's valley temporarily unattended to join them.

While they waited for Stanze's return, Orion set out goblets for them all and piled up a plate of nutrition for Stanze, knowing he would be hungry.

"We must come to a decision," Orion said solemnly, once Stanze had joined them. "We rely on our eyes and ears to sense Tachra, and still we have not found her. We could be here for months, even years, before we find her, and that's if we do find her at all. We have no guarantee that she will return to the valley we've been watching. Her trail so far indicates that she travels regularly. She may have left that place permanently."

The team nodded their agreement. They had all expected that Tachra would have returned to her valley by now if she had made it her permanent home.

"Time is of the essence," Orion continued. "The situation on Eden is growing worse every day. We must decide whether to return to Eden empty handed, without Factor X as a bargaining tool, and so aim to rectify matters, or wait, thus taking a chance that we might locate Tachra, and accepting that it may take a long time, while matters at home grow rapidly worse."

The group sat discussing the two options. Neither was ideal, and the conversation grew heated; several of them paced around the perimeter of the force field to ease their frustrations. Only Jychanumun seemed not to find Orion's options a quandary, but sat quietly watching them as they argued.

Finally, Orion decided that their arguing was getting them nowhere, insisting that they should vote on the matter. The majority would decide. And after a brief period of calming down, the voting started.

Stanze went first, voting to leave. "I can rally the Anumi from

Eden," he insisted, "We could correct matters. Here I can do nothing."

Kraniel was next. At first, he was indecisive, verbally weighing up the odds of the resources from a prospective new energy against helping the Anumi on Eden. But finally he came to a decision. "Oh, leave," he said. "All this fuss about Factor X; we're not even sure if we'd be able to utilize it anyway. We should get back home."

Chia also opted to leave; they had already been on the planet a long time and could not be sure if they would find Tachra any time soon. They had given the mission their best efforts, and were still empty handed.

Nirrious opted to abstain from voting, stating that he did not have enough information to make a fair judgement. Orion nodded, accepting the decision.

Jychanumun was last, although the outcome of the decision was now already set. The majority had already voted to leave.

"We should stay," Jychanumun said.

Orion looked at him steadily. "I've already explained that time is of the essence; the situation is dire. We must make a move now, not wait," he said, as if hoping Jychanumun would change his vote. "Tachra may have left her valley for good; no amount of waiting will help that. Are you sure of your vote?"

Jychanumun nodded. "She will come here soon," he said.

Orion stood impatiently waiting for him to go on, but it seemed that that was all Jychanumun had to say.

"Jychanumun, my friend," Orion stated, "We have a majority vote to leave without the human. If you know any good reason for us to stay, I suggest you tell us."

"Tachra has sensed that Soul is here," Jychanumun eventually said. "I felt Soul call out to her. Tachra will come here: to Soul, to us, to me."

"Are you sure?" Orion queried, "Why did you not tell us sooner?"

"I was not sure before. Her absence from her valley has confirmed my belief that she is moving closer – I can feel her."

"How long would we have to wait?"

"Two nights, probably less."

"Really?" Orion frowned. "Two nights or less?"

Jychanumun nodded.

"Then it is settled. The majority has voted to leave, so we will leave. But we will wait two nights to give your conviction a fair chance. We'll leave at dawn on the third day." Orion rubbed his brow. "This is a troubling mission, in troubling times. I need a good goblet of Ochrah."

Stanze was already pulling out further supplies, and poured them all a goblet full. He took a long draught of his own, drinking it in one go.

"If Eskah smiles upon us, I drink to the human Tachra coming to us," Orion stated.

He lifted his drink towards the others. Stanze looked down at his empty goblet sheepishly. Orion laughed.

"To us," the others replied in unison.

Jychanumun didn't lift his goblet: he seemed too deep in thought, gazing through the force field to the trees beyond, frowning as if he could see something. Chia followed his stare, but there was nothing there, just trees and bushes.

Jychanumun shook his head to himself and finally lifted his goblet with the others.

None of them sensed that they already had an audience.

TWENTY

I crouched, concealed by the prickling bush, watching the amazing creatures with awe. They did look human in some ways. If it were not for my true vision I might have thought that they were, but they were too tall, too strong, too beautiful, too *everything*.

Their eyes shone, their skin glittered, and their hair curled in thick radiant strands. Each creature seemed to have a different hue, and that was just what I saw with my physical eyes. My true vision saw much more: emanating, swirling masses of light filled with vigour, adventure, change, and greatness. And their auras were full of colour, so many colours.

There were three of these beings that I could see, but I sensed there were more concealed by the hanging fabric. The three that I could see were the same as each other, yet so very different, shimmering with tones of red, gold and violet.

The creatures seemed to be having a heated discussion, a process that made more colour flow between them, hard and fast, as if their words held substance. I could just about hear the noises that came from their mouths, but I couldn't understand them. Their voices sounded like a chorus of many layers, each layer saying something different. Then one of them laughed, and it sounded like a full laugh that encompassed its being and lifted the atmosphere. I couldn't remember ever having seen anything looking so alive.

I quickly flicked to my true vision, and the sight of them assaulted my senses once again; they were so complex. The one who had laughed had sprinkles of brilliant red light streaming from his mouth; the others spoke a short phrase in unison and the rainbows of colour danced together and around them, as if they were temporarily interwoven by their communication.

I tore my gaze from the creatures' spectacular interactions and observed their surroundings. The three stood by intricate sloping chairs, or beds, which seemed to be suspended in the air with lights shining below them, inundating my senses with even more brightness.

The closest creature had a mass of red hair that moved around his head as if it had a life of its own. His vibrant, crimson clothes shimmered when he talked, and seemed to reflect in his eyes. I strained my own vision, convinced that I wasn't seeing correctly, but I was right, he had the strangest eyes. The red wasn't a reflection – they were that colour, all red, with no whiteness, and flickering like a flame.

My heart leapt. The only place I had seen similar eyes of all one colour was in my dreams, but his were black. My black-eyed one was not one of these three figures, but perhaps, just perhaps, he was here.

Standing close to the red-haired one was another, standing with his back to me. He was huge and beautiful and radiated a mixture of gold and a colour I have no name for. It was the colour that looked like a smile. He wore a short skirt with a wide belt, with many strange things hanging from it. His top half was clad in what looked like a sleeveless golden metal plate, yet it didn't have any shoulders, as if it was glued to his body. More metal covered his lower and upper arms, leaving his joints exposed. Like all of them, he was holding a large container and drinking something that smoked with a multicoloured haze.

The third I could see was moving his arms as he talked. What long hands he had! Unlike the others, he had no hair, but his features seemed even sharper and more angular, and his piercing violet eyes illuminated the skin around them. He was dressed in the oddest attire; black matt fabric all over that was so close to his body that it looked like skin. As I watched him waving his arms, I sensed movement; a fourth, a fifth, and then a sixth figure moved in the background, obscured by the hangings.

I could only see the feet of these three others; one went barefooted, and two wore heavy-looking boots.

My eyes were drawn to the one with bare feet. He started walking, still concealed, and I caught his movement flicker past the hangings. Then the dome quivered and a gaping archway opened up.

He walked to the entrance and stood still.

I caught my breath again. It was, without a doubt, the black-eyed one.

I could see him clearly from head to foot, exactly as he'd appeared in my sleeping dreams.

He stood, solitary and striking. His long, gleaming, straight black hair and familiar black, pit-like eyes shone out against his pale skin. His clothes – black like his hair, with a long skirt and cladding on his arms – was exactly as I'd dreamt too. When I switched to my true vision, I saw the potential of a mass of colours contained within a barrier of shadow and light. Yes, I knew this one. I recognized not just his face from my dreams, but also his black and white colours.

I kept my true vision and looked at him more deeply. There was something else, right at his core — something even more familiar, yet obscured. I tried to sense it fully, going deeper into my subconscious and letting my instincts take over, but it was as if he were guarding it tightly. Before I could probe any deeper, I suddenly snapped from my thoughts. I sensed I was being watched.

I closed my true vision and used only my eyes. Even though I was well concealed by bushes, the black-eyed one was staring in my direction. Then he held out his hand towards me.

It was the image straight from my dream. A part of me wanted to run to him and finally reach his outstretched hand. But he was with these creatures and I didn't know if I could trust them; in truth, for all his radiant beauty, I didn't know if I could trust him. Soul was here somewhere and had cried out for help. I had to be cautious until I found her and knew what was going on.

I kept perfectly still, but his gaze remained fixed in my direction. He seemed to be aware of my presence even though I knew he couldn't see me through the bushes. I had to do something.

I dug my clasped hand into the sharp, thorny bush, ignoring the pain of the spikes, allowing my flesh to absorb its essence. The wiry green strands wove through my skin until I felt the entirety of the plant. I *became* the plant. The black-eyed one should no longer sense me; now he should feel only the thorny bushes. Then I kept still and waited.

The black-eyed one's gaze moved, scanning the area as if searching for something. He waited a moment, and then shook his head, turned, and walked back into the dome. The archway closed behind him.

I kept still for as long as I could manage, which wasn't long, and then silently released my grasp on the Hawthorn and drew back into the woodland. It was a perfect place to hide; the trees were dense, with a strong essence that was easily absorbed. I could return to conceal myself here, if necessary. I let my instincts guide me while my head reeled with what I'd seen.

I tuned into the essence of the land around me, absorbing the energy from the plants and soil so that I could not be so readily detected. And then I stealthily walked back to the margin of the trees to watch, as activity was stirring in the dome.

The entrance was open again, and now the creature with violet eyes ventured out, walking with long, graceful, almost catlike strides. The huge golden one walked to join him.

I let out a gasp; attached to his back were what looked like wings; twice his height, yet not made of feathers, but of a myriad fine interwoven lines of light. Or rather, to my outer eyes they seemed to be made of light, whereas through my inner eyes, my true vision, I saw them as a continuation of his energy. No wonder they lived in such a high place, I thought: they could probably fly like birds too.

The golden one had a long rod with a glowing tip protruding from his back, set between his light-wings. He started conversing with the violet-eyed one, but I could not understand their words. Moments later, another emerged; he too had light-wings.

If I had ever doubted it, I didn't now: these were definitely not at all human.

As mesmerised and entranced as I was, the need to find Soul still pulsed through my mind. I could not see her, but I knew she was close. I merged with the land and trailed my awareness around the edge of the plateau, following my sense of her. Then I had her. I could feel her clearly, sleeping lightly with dreams that were a turmoil of colours and sounds. She had her child with her and both seemed healthy; they were positioned somewhere at the other side of the dome, obscured from my view.

Then I sensed something else around Soul – something familiar. There were more people there. I felt a jolt as if my insides had been grabbed. Wasn't the familiarity I sensed the presence of my own family? No, I told myself, it could not be, because Soul had no knowledge of who my family was. I ignored the sensation, telling myself that adrenaline was probably altering my perceptions, and pulled my consciousness back into my body.

Knowing that Soul was not in any immediate danger, I decided to watch the creatures and wait for an opportunity to go to her. I would have to walk over exposed ground to reach her, and so I had to be vigilant.

The creatures had emerged from the dome and settled around a pile of wood, which began to blaze with no apparent effort. There were six in total, including my black-eyed one. Their every move portrayed their immense strength of mind, body, and spirit, and they were all magnificently beautiful. Then I perceived another creature, whom I had not noticed before. He was clad in white, with long white hair, and was lurking silently in the background, not interacting with the others. He didn't seem to do anything other than watch them. My outer eyes did not seen this one at all, but my true vision saw him with as much clarity as the others.

Tuning into the land meant that these winged creatures could not sense me, although the black-eyed one kept glancing towards the Hawthorn bush where I'd previously hidden. He was not just the one from my dreams; he was somehow different from the others.

The creature's expressions indicated that they were discussing something serious – their words flowed together into a stream of sombre but engaging music. The one with red hair spoke the most, although it seemed more from necessity than because he enjoyed the sound of his own voice. I wished I could understand their words.

The colours and sounds poured from their mouths. I opened my emotions to the pitch and vibrations of their voices, and my true vision to the meaning and truth of their sounds. I began picking out repeated phrases, which became tied both to emotions and to other phrases. Some phrases conveyed feelings similar to those that I knew, but there were many more unfamiliar ones, with deeper and wider implications. Very slowly, the sounds started to take form and I could piece several together to form the meaning of a word, although nothing yet made sense. Perhaps I could understand them if I tried.

Summoning all my resources, I pushed every sense and emotion, every aspect of my reason and judgement, to try to understand.

Very slowly, the pattern and structure of their words took form in my mind. I silently mimicked their lip movements and awkwardly twisted my tongue as if repeating the sounds back to myself.

The first thing that I understood was their names, as they addressed each other frequently. Orion was the one who talked the most. But slowly, very slowly, other words pieced together and began to make sense. Their language was full, and far more complex than my human tongue, but gradually, yes! Gradually it seemed as though I could understand a little of what they were saying.

Their words were fragmentary to my ears at first, but then I started growing accustomed to their pace. They spoke very quickly and with a great passion for everything.

Then I had it, as if it had just been switched on in my brain; it hit me all of a sudden. From hearing only fractured unstructured words that I didn't understand, suddenly I was able to piece their sentences together and know what they were saying.

I was picking up the creatures' conversation.

"Una would make a balanced decision," the one they called Orion said.

"But he does nothing," Chia replied.

"Which is how I know something is wrong; it is not the way Una works."

"And if the council has changed . . ."

"Yes," Orion seemed anxious. "Although they would still need Una's energy to unite any council."

I kept my attention on their conversation on the subject of the one named Una. Their voices lowered with the seriousness of the topic, and I couldn't hear their words well enough to decipher them. As they spoke, the white-haired one who hovered in the background moved forward a little. He seemed agitated, but he still didn't join the others and he never spoke.

The conversation came to an abrupt end and they were very unhappy about something. The one they called Kraniel walked with Stanze and Chia onto the grass near the edge of the plateau. Chia stood and placed a small round object on his forehead.

Thankfully, I was only relying on a small part of my true sight, because if I had been watching them with that alone I'm sure I would have been blinded. Suddenly, a dazzling flash of light shot forth from Chia's head. He seemed to grow, though his stature never changed, and his body shimmered with even more rolling streaks of luminous violet. Slowly, a large pair of violet wings formed behind him.

"That's better," he remarked, flexing his back. "And Kraniel, can you feed the humans? I can't have them ravenous; their minds won't function properly."

Kraniel shook his head. "There's no food stores left for them. Just make them go to sleep."

My heart jumped at their mention of people. I was right, Soul was not alone. And it made me uncomfortable that their tone suggested that they had little consideration for the humans – it was as if they were a burden to feed.

"But I need them awake," Chia objected.

"Then give them a mind command so that they're not hungry."

Chia tutted. "Yes, and they would still be hungry and not functioning properly, they just wouldn't know it."

"Well then, as my tactics are not satisfactory, you can go and get them food."

"Very well. And Kraniel," Chia frowned, "next time you design bios, make their intake requirements less."

My thoughts suddenly halted. Make their requirements less? Bios design?

These creatures – whatever they were – did not see humans as individuals, but as commodities. And the terms they used to describe people were terms of ownership and control. You only truly own what is yours, what you made.

Could these creatures possibly be the makers of humans?

Suddenly, interrupting my deep thoughts, Chia part ran, part flew past the remaining group and towards the edge of the cliff. He leapt off the edge. Moments later he soared back into sight, far in the distance, with his wings open like a large beautiful bird. Behind him, he left a trail of dissipating blue light.

Blue light!

I heard and saw nothing for the next few moments – suddenly it was all adding up. Creatures that can alter their appearance and can fly? How far could their abilities go? They were, without a doubt, beings with many more skills than humans. And what of the blue light, which had hovered over the encampments on my travels, and I had searched for? This same blue light now trailed from these winged beings as they flew. These creatures spoke of humans in a manner that showed ownership. These creatures – whatever they were – must indeed the makers of humans.

I had found the blue light. It came from them.

The makers of humans, I pondered repeatedly.

The thought felt oddly calming.

I think I liked these makers of humans. I definitely found them fascinating. But I did not like the tone they used when they spoke of people – the term they used, 'bios' – and I knew that Soul was held by them. As much as I wanted to stay observing these creatures, I knew I had to get Soul away from here.

I had a rough sense of where Soul was on the plateau, and that she was with other people. They were all on the far side of the great domes, concealed from my sight. I tore my gaze away from the makers of humans, retreated into the trees, and picked through the vegetation so I could view the rear of the larger silver dome.

My view of the back of the dome revealed nothing except its own vast mass. I could hear Kraniel and Stanze out of my line of sight on the other side of the dome, arguing about which food would be most suitable to give the humans from their own provisions. They were close to the people, and thus to Soul. Frustratingly, Soul's position was one of the few places I couldn't get to whilst remaining hidden by the trees.

Kraniel and Stanze continued their dispute, but their volume decreased as they took their argument back to the remainder of their group. Without thinking, I seized the opportunity and ran as fast as I could towards the back of the dome.

As I got closer, my proximity to the dome made my skin tingle; this big, metal, smooth thing was alive. Its presence filled me with sadness, and the surprise I felt at this made my step falter, but I had no time to dwell on it. I skirted around the object. I was sure I heard the faint whispering of people talking.

Keeping as close to the living dome as my frayed senses allowed, I crept nearer until I caught sight of a slim pillar of light, then another pillar. My true vision saw that the pillars formed some type of enclosure without walls. I flinched when I realised there were beings inside the enclosure, but my senses told me they were all human, so I peeked around the corner.

I didn't see Soul straight away, because my sights were fixed on another. It was my father!

He stood, whereas the others sat. He looked tired and grey, but his eyes were alert. A new silvery white streak ran through his hair. What had they done to him?

In panic, I scanned and took in the other faces around him: my oldest sister Gem, my third and favourite brother Marl, and his oldest girl Ila. Then I saw Soul; she also sat, clutching a young babe. There were more people, all familiar faces from the life I thought I'd left behind. I counted nineteen, excluding Soul's child, and I knew of and cared for every one of them. They were trapped between walls of light that were visible only to my outer eyes, my true sight. The people all looked exhausted and scared.

Suddenly, I did not care for my caution anymore. I would not have this. I would not have anyone held captive if I could do something about it, especially ones I cared for. I braced myself and walked towards the enclosure.

Father spotted me immediately and jumped towards me, his face a mixture of dismay and relief. His sudden movement made the others look up. Soul put her hand to her mouth, and a look of horror washed over her. Father put his fingers to his lips to silence me. If it had been anybody else, I would have yelled, but this was my beloved father.

Forgetting what I had seen of the barrier, I ran towards him with my arms outstretched, and was immediately flung back with a vicious force. Something sparked, and I caught a better glimpse of the invisible wall. This wasn't just a wall, it could push me back. I opened my true vision to see walls of energy around them, holding them captive.

"Father?" I whispered as I crawled back towards him. I stretched out my hand slowly until I encountered something that felt solid, although my eyes could not see it, my true sense could. I wanted to hold him, to tell him how sorry I was, but the unseen division kept us apart.

"Tachra my child, you are safe," father breathed quietly as he hunched down the other side of the barrier.

Tears rolled down his cheeks. I had never seen him cry. I hated myself for the fact that I could bring this strong, courageous man to tears. He lifted his hand as if to touch the scar on my face, and then his stance changed and his eyes filled with great concern.

"You must leave, my child. These creatures . . . we believe it is you that they are looking for."

I tried to interrupt him, but he silenced me with a look.

"No, child. We are all well. They treat us well. They will no doubt take us back to our homes soon. You must leave this place."

Soul came forward and sat by father as the others quietly crowded behind them.

"You must listen to your father, Tachra. You must go," Soul implored me. "These creatures made people – they will not make us cease. They have held all your family here at one time, even Huru, and have taken most back home. But," she paused, "although I do not understand their search for you, I know enough to think that their attention is not good. They speak our tongue when they wish and they ask us nothing else but of you."

"Of me?" I stated in astonishment. "But why?" I shook my head, it didn't matter. My friend and family mattered.

"How long have you been here?" I asked. "And why do they keep you?"

"We do not know," father answered. "They can make us sleep, and time passes so that I know not how long this has been. But we are fine. They keep us to ask questions about you; it is you they seek," he repeated. "Please, leave here now, while they are occupied – leave while you can. Do not let them find you; you cannot run from them, as they can do things to make you stop, to sleep – whatever they wish. Leave Tachra, my child. Leave now."

"I do not care for my leaving. I will get you all out of here." I said.

I looked down at Soul's young babe. "Oh Soul," I sighed.

Soul smiled and pulled down the cover of her child so I could see its sleeping face.

"Iris, she is Iris. And you . . . you must go," she stated. "I'm sorry I called you here. I was scared. I knew you would hear me. Then, when I realised they wanted you, I tried to tell you not to come. Did you not hear that? I tried so hard to tell you not to come."

"I heard you, but I do not break a promise," I replied. "And I promise you this now. I may not know what they want with me, but perhaps knowing that they do want me means that I have an advantage. And I promise that you will all get out of here, and very soon."

I stood and looked at father, knowing I must take this opportunity in case I did not get another chance.

"I'm sorry, father," I said. "I'm sorry that I left without word. I did not want to leave you; I just wanted to find myself. I'm sorry that because of me you are here. I didn't want to be a problem, but it seems I only succeeded in becoming a greater problem."

"Tachra, hush." Father smiled warmly. "If you are well, stay well. Please leave here now, and you will make me happy knowing that you are safe."

"I cannot," I replied. "I would do any other thing that you

asked of me, but not that. I must go, but I will be back very, very soon. I will find a way to get you out."

Then, before he could forbid me from anything else, I turned and quickly left.

As I walked away, a flash from the invisible wall behind me lit my path as father lurched forward.

"Don't!" I heard him shout. But I would not listen to his words and I would not turn around. It felt like my heart was bleeding.

I stood behind the metal dome; not wanting to touch its cold, conscious shell, and mustered my courage. So they were looking for me. Perhaps, I thought, I could present myself in such a way that would still not find me. Just as I could project myself as a tree or bush, perhaps I could make myself look like somebody else. Yes, I decided, and it would have to be someone who was here, so I could tap into their essence. Also, that way, they would not be suspicious. Ila, my oldest brother's daughter, was about my height, age and stature, although her face was very different to mine. She would be ideal.

I concentrated on Ila's face, pulling the Earth's energy up and around me like a fine sheath. Slowly, I brought Ila's features to myself: her light-brown, wavy hair, her wide, shallow-set blue eyes, her thinner lips and fuller face. I had never tried this before, and I did not know if the disguise would work on these unearthly creatures, but I would try to keep my advantage for now. I would not look like me; hopefully to them I would be Ila.

I strode from the shelter of the back of the dome and into view of the creatures' fire. Chia had returned, Kraniel and Stanze still argued, Orion, Nirrious and Jychanumun sat by the fire.

I took my shaking courage in both hands, embraced the anger at seeing my family and Soul in such fear, straightened, set my jaw, and then walked into their sight.

Chia noticed me first. The flash of his eyes made me stop immediately.

"Kraniel, one of them has escaped!" Chia called, getting up and regarding me with his chin up and hands on his hips.

Kraniel stopped his bickering with Stanze, looked at me, and walked over.

"Impossible," Kraniel replied. "I've just checked them. The bio-screens can't be breeched."

He stopped and stared at me. I looked back into his piercing green eyes.

"Well, one *has* got out," Chia confirmed. He moved closer towards me, the motion of his wings making my hair fall in front of my face. I kept perfectly still. Stanze had been staring; he walked over to stand by Kraniel.

"The bio screens must be resonating too slowly," Kraniel said.

I silently followed their foreign conversation, shifting my gaze from one to the next until they all stood around me, staring.

"Let the people go home, please," I said in my own human language, holding onto my anger for now. I had to give them the benefit of the doubt. I had to try asking first.

Kraniel looked at Orion and burst out laughing.

"Did you hear that? She asked us to let them go. The humans are demanding of us!" He continued laughing.

The others started laughing too, all except Jychanumun, who had a strange expression on his face. I knew Jychanumun recognised me, although I didn't know how.

Their laughter almost made me drop my guard. My anger welled inside me, yet I had it well controlled.

"Please," I said, keeping my composure, pointing in the direction of my friends and family in the enclosure. "They want to go home. Take them home."

Their laughter seemed only to increase. Kraniel eventually

gathered himself, leaned forward so that his eyes were directly in front of mine, and stared straight at me.

"No!" he said loudly, and they all laughed even more.

"Well, this is a fine thing," Orion said in his own language, still laughing. "She wants us to take the others home. But what of herself? She omitted herself. Perhaps she wishes to stay."

"Who knows?" Kraniel said. "But as she seems to have become adept at making demands, why don't we ask her?"

He leaned towards me again.

"Well, human, what would you like us to do with *you*?"

I looked towards the silent one, Jychanumun; his eyebrows were slightly raised. He certainly recognised me, as much as I had recognised him, even though my disguise was fooling the others. How could he have let these people, my people, stay cooped up in fear? Asking nicely obviously wasn't going to work. And they were laughing at my request. How dare they! I was so angry.

"What shall you do with me?" I fumed, just about controlling my voice enough not to shout. "Ask him," I brushed the hair from my face and pointed in Jychanumun's direction. "He knows exactly who I am."

They all suddenly went very quiet and looked at me in shock; I had used their tongue. Their language had formed surprisingly easily in my mouth and, although I stumbled on one or two sounds, they understood very clearly.

Then I let my disguise drop. I looked like me again.

Their mouths fell open.

"No, ask yourselves," I continued in their language. "It seems as though you have been looking for me, so surely you would know me and what to do with me."

Orion stepped forward, "Tachra?"

I looked back at Orion, the anger at the treatment of my friends and family making my vision redder than his hair. *I want*

372

to obliterate you all, I thought. I wanted to stay angry, but I sensed no malice in him and that subdued the agitation in my stomach.

"Yes, Orion, it is I, Tachra," I eventually replied.

I turned to Jychanumun, "Now I am here, you will let my friends go. It's not right to hold them here. You must take them back to their homes immediately, using those strong wings of yours."

"It will be done." Orion stated with a nod.

Wasn't that too easy? I wondered. Did he sense how much I seethed?

Kraniel went to object, but I threw him a stare that would silence thunder.

"I will take them," Stanze offered.

Orion nodded, but his crimson eyes never left my face as Stanze walked off.

"I will not move until I know them safe," I said, holding Orion's stare.

His eyes seemed to penetrate my mind, as if he was trying to get into my head. I threw barriers against him; the image of a broad wall of stone covering my thoughts.

Orion smiled. "And how will you know they are safe?"

I could tell from his changed expression that he sensed I was putting barriers in front of my thoughts. I could feel him trying to penetrate them.

"Oh do not be concerned with that," I retorted sharply. "I will know."

Orion kept watching me, his face tightening. He was trying to breach my walls with a great deal of strength. He slid along the barriers in my mind, looking for a way in. I felt him push hard, and my barriers momentarily bent, but they did not break. He pushed harder with the force of strong intent. I thought of *him*, the Old One, of eon-aged rocks and the immovability of everything timeless. Still he tried.

"Stop!" I commanded without thinking. "Stop or I will show you things that will turn your mind."

Orion floundered and took a step backwards, immediately retreating from my mind.

Jychanumun put his hand on his arm to steady him.

"Listen to her. She can do it," Jychanumun insisted, and I felt as though he had spoken with his mind as well as his mouth.

I dropped my guard for a brief moment on hearing the black-eyed one speak. My threats had been merely words; words that I thought were empty of substance and generated from fury. But now, as I spoke, images of the Old One's slumbers filled my mind, and I knew that I could see beyond their boundaries. Through *him*, the Earth-voice, the Old One, I knew of places that these creatures could never reach, of times before even they existed, and of timelessness and concepts that would paralyse their minds.

"And you," I turned to Jychanumun. My heart wanted to embrace him, to talk, to touch, just to be with him. But I was too angry. "How did you recognise me?"

He pointed to the scar that ran down his forehead, almost identical to mine, and then indicated towards my own forehead.

It seemed my earlier disguise had not concealed my scar.

"Oh," I snorted, trying to sound as though I didn't care. I did care; this one seemed to see through me. I didn't want to feel vulnerable in front of any of them.

Orion swept a deep bow. "Then, little one, as you speak our tongue so eloquently, may we talk?"

"Do *not* call me 'little one,'" I frowned. How dare he use the name that the Old One calls me?

"Tachra,"

"Nor Tachra," I said. It did not seem right for these creatures to call me by the name my parents had given me. Tachra was my true name; the name that, when spoken aloud, would demand my attention. No, these creatures would have no power over me.

"Then perhaps we can begin with a name that you would like," Orion stated patiently.

"In your tongue, is there a word that means 'I am three?'"

"This would make little sense in our tongue," Orion considered. "But the word would be 'Ias-tha.'"

"Then to you I will be 'Iastha,'" I replied. It sounded right as I formed the word and spoke it aloud.

Orion's gaze flicked fleetingly from my face and I turned to see what had stolen his attention.

A large object hovered above the ground. My family sat inside the object as Stanze gently lifted Soul and her child to join them. I looked back at Orion dubiously.

"Stanze will return them safely to their homes," he stated. "They are in a pod. It flies."

I heard the truth in his voice, but glared at him anyway. I would not show them anything other than strength.

"Leave me to talk with them," I stated, and walked away before he could reply.

I approached the object they called a pod.

"You will not harm them," I scowled at Stanze. He was bigger and looked far more vicious than any of the others. I was not too happy that he was the one taking my loved ones to their homes.

"I would never harm them!" he replied with vehemence.

He carefully released Soul into her seat, pulling the baby's cover snug around its face, before leaping in one stride into the space in front of them. Soul seemed comfortable with the big creature. *This one is fond of these people*, I observed, *and Soul is not afraid of him*. I felt a great deal better then; I knew he would not harm them.

I reached out for Soul's outstretched hand. "I will see you soon," I whispered in our tongue.

"Are you not coming?" Soul asked desperately.

"Not yet, but soon," I replied with conviction. "All is well – do not be concerned. Huru was a greater worry than this!"

That made her smile.

"Tachra, be careful," she said. "They seem to know so much about you."

She tried to hide her concern, but it was clear on her face. The others looked relieved, knowing they were going home – all except Soul and my father. Father looked grim, and his jaw flexed as I'd only ever seen it do when he was thinking very deeply.

I took a step forward so that I was leaning on the pod, and I put my hand to his face.

"I will see you soon, father, if you and mother will see me," I said.

"Of course I will see you, my child." His voice faltered, and then he went silent for a moment. "Your mother misses you greatly." He paused. "*I* miss you. Come home, Tachra, whenever you can. We want you home. There you can do whatever you wish."

I would not show him my distress and guilt; he had been through enough. Soul put her hand on his shoulder reassuringly.

"I am sorry, father," I sighed, "I will come home, I promise." Then a fleeting thought passed through me. "Father," I urged, "could you take Soul and her child under your roof if she would have it? She is in a terrible place," I pleaded.

"It has been offered, and accepted, already, my child," he managed to smile as he patted Soul's hand. "We will all look forward to your return."

I smiled, and Stanze glanced at me. I could tell he was waiting for me to finish so that he could take my family and Soul home.

As much as I wanted to stay with them, I nodded to Stanze and pulled back my hand.

"Be still," Stanze said gently to his passengers as a fine shield of light glided into place around them.

The floating pod lifted and smoothly surged forward, with nineteen pairs of worried eyes watching me. Soul's babe was blissfully asleep. I held up my hand, and then they were gone. Only a long streak of light fading into the distance left any sign that they had been here.

I stood watching the fading glow, and then turned. I felt someone standing behind me. It was Jychanumun, my black-eyed one.

"I think you know how I feel." I scowled at him. "You knew those people were terrified and anxious, but you did nothing. I had hoped for so much from you, yet you are the worst of them all, because you knew."

The hurt at my accusations shone from Jychanumun and he turned to leave. My stomach jerked at the vehemence of my own words and I knew it had not been his fault. I caught his arm. A shiver of light rippled to my shoulders. For a short moment, I knew him. I saw his colours. In that brief moment, I understood a life filled with guilt for many things that had no foundation other than the false expectancy of others. He knew too well the disappointment he caused, because he could not be who they wanted him to be. He wanted only truth and peace; it should be so simple, but for him it had caused an endless internal war.

"Do not look!" Jychanumun growled, in the deepest voice I had ever heard.

But my heart went out to him; I empathized with him. I could not blind myself to that knowledge.

"I cannot close myself to you," I replied and he did not pull from my hold. "We are different, but our paths lead us to the same place. There is something in you that I recognise."

Jychanumun opened his mouth as if to speak, but then he nodded his head and fell silent as Orion and Kraniel walked up behind him. He had sensed them approaching.

"Iastha," Orion motioned towards the dome of light. "We have done as you asked. Now, we must talk."

Although I didn't like the way Orion had used the word 'must,' I let him direct me towards the transparent dome filled with coloured opalescent cloths and ornate seats, trying not to appear awed by the beauty of their objects. I took a seat beside a huge table. It was too big and my feet didn't touch the ground. I disliked that it made me feel childish.

"What do you want of me?" I asked, before the others had finished taking their seats.

"First, we wish to understand you," Orion replied. "We wish to understand how, and why, you are different."

I didn't answer. My attention was pulled towards Kraniel. He was smiling while fondling something around his neck. I could sense that he had intentions, but I couldn't tell what they were.

"What are you doing?" I asked him.

Kraniel stopped moving and dropped his hand, revealing a small object hanging from a cord. He didn't answer.

"It is a containment field, for you," Jychanumun replied.

Kraniel shot him a glance.

"She senses truth," Jychanumun said to Kraniel. "There is no point in lying."

I didn't fully understand what a containment field was, but presumed it was similar to the invisible barrier that my family had been held in – it was not something pleasant. Was this black-eyed one being protective? I looked at him, and then slowly looked at the others, scanning to read their intentions.

There was much I could sense, and my senses were straining to understand them all.

"You would like to understand me," I said. "And I would like to understand you. I believe you made humans. I'd like to know why and how."

Suddenly, the sound stopped coming from my mouth and my limbs felt restricted, I could hardly move. Everything around me was now suffused with a pale blue hue and rippled with distortion.

As if in slow motion, I watched Kraniel jump up and Orion stand. I could not hear them, but I could see their lips slowly move. From the expressions on their faces, it seemed as if they were shouting. Kraniel held the cord around his neck with one hand, but now the small crystal had gone. In its place, a thin line of blue light ran from the cord to me.

I am contained, I thought, detached and calm. This is their containment field; they wish to capture me.

From my strange distorted view, I watched as Kraniel tried telling me something. I think he was telling me to sleep. I watched his lips move, and then moments later the thought came into my head with his voice. *Sleep*, it said. I did not feel sleepy at all, but I did feel very numb.

Jychanumun had stood up and was staring with a look of horror on his face. He started waving his arms. He looked angry, but the others were ignoring him.

Then Orion came closer. He seemed to be swaying back and forth, but then I realised it was me who was swaying.

Orion's lips moved silently; moments later, I heard his voice in my head. He too was telling me to sleep. But I didn't want to sleep. My mind was alert and I was getting the profound sense that I had been through a similar experience before. Hadn't the Old One wanted me to sleep, to sleep and join him in his endless dreams? And his offer of sleep had felt much more all-embracing and true than this. Still, I had said no then, and I still didn't want to sleep, no matter who offered.

I tried telling them no, I didn't want to sleep, but I don't think they heard. Why were they doing this? I had done nothing to them. I had been prepared to talk, as they wished.

It seemed as though I would have to do this the hard way, I realised. I would have to throw out my senses and feel the barrier so I could break it. I ignored their commands and gathered my senses, but I was not able to comprehend the barrier as quickly as I could the plants and animals. I felt I could do it, but it would take time.

Suddenly, something hurt my leg and broke my concentration. It felt rather like a wasp sting, but through the distortion of blue I could see Kraniel holding a long pointed object against my skin. No, not again my skin; it was going deep into my flesh, and fluid was being pushed into me through a thin hollow tube.

A numb sickness started to fill me, moving from the point on my leg and working through the rest of my body. I didn't like it at all. It felt as if I was losing control of every nerve and muscle. It was terrible. I felt the liquid moving through my body, making everything cold and dead as it touched it. I thought I was about to cease. I was sure they were making me cease.

The numbness was growing. Soon I knew it would reach my head, and then I'd feel nothing at all. Panic surged through me. If I did not stop this, I would cease. They would take away everything I was.

Then I realised that this flesh of mine had not served me well. Even if I could stop what was happening, what would be the point? Throughout my journey, this flesh had only caused trouble and pain. My hopes of understanding these makers of flesh must've been misguided, because these creatures just wanted to take away my choices. No, this flesh had not served me well; only *he*, the Old One, had been true to me. With him, I could be whole in his timelessness, without the cumbersome flesh.

I was about to cease. I knew it. I accepted it. The time had come to join him.

Where are you? I called, earnestly pushing out my thoughts before it was too late.

I am here, little one, came the immediate reply, and I knew that he was truly there.

I'm coming now, I called. *I'm coming to you.*

I didn't wait for a reply. I stepped out of the body, my body, before it ceased, and walked into the timeless dreams of the Old One.

TWENTY-ONE

"I think we've finished her," Chia stated bluntly, staring at Tachra's body.

Tachra seemed to have been aware of what was going on. She hadn't slept as they'd commanded, and she had watched Kraniel administering the sleep potion into her leg. She had then slumped forward. Now it didn't look as if she was breathing.

"Nonsense," Kraniel shrugged, "This is a basic bios sleep inducer; it's harmless. Where the sleep command fails, the sleep inducer is useful. We can easily reactivate her."

He took the containment field activator from around his neck and deactivated the shield. The blue haze around Tachra disappeared, and she fell forward onto the ground. Kraniel turned her around so that she lay straight, on her back. There was no colour in her face, and her lips had paled.

He kneeled, pressing various points of her flesh, and then looked towards Chia.

"Can you see if there are any activator wraps left?" he said calmly. "She has stopped breathing."

Chia quickly retrieved an activator sheet from Kraniel's work area and handed it over. Kraniel was holding his hand over Tachra's heart. A thin line of energy streamed from his palm, disappearing into her flesh, as he tried using his energy to start her heart pumping again.

"Is this supposed to happen?" Orion asked, looking distressed.

"No," Kraniel replied, "Maybe she was sensitive to the inducer."

"She has gone," Jychanumun stated, glaring at them angrily.

"Then I'll just bring her back again," Kraniel replied, draping the activator wrap over her body.

Moments later, Tachra's chest began to rise and fall. Kraniel shot Jychanumun a triumphant glance.

"It is only mechanics, empty flesh," Jychanumun bristled. "There is no hope anymore. She has left her body. You made death her only choice."

Jychanumun couldn't contain his anger. His eyes flashed as he clasped and unclasped his fists in agitation.

"You have destroyed the very thing I've sought for, you fools, and ruined the one thing that could help you," he continued. "I cannot even walk the death paths to find her, as doing so would put everything in danger. My heart knows I want to, but the price you'd all pay would be too high. She was willing to communicate. There would have been another way. You have listened to nothing!" And with that, he stormed away, as if the situation was too much to bear.

Nobody went after Jychanumun; everyone was too busy watching the shroud-covered Tachra.

An activator wrap always rectified the bodily mechanisms of a human who was not faring well – they'd used them hundreds of times before. Soon Tachra would regain consciousness and then, as her body stabilized, she would sit up and would not remember anything about the experience.

But the moments passed and Tachra didn't stir, let alone sit. Only the continuous rise and fall of her now-automated breathing indicated that there was a body underneath the wrap.

Kraniel pulled away the cover, revealing Tachra's pallid flesh. As soon as the activator wrap was no longer over her, she stopped breathing.

Orion stood over her, pouring his energy into her, trying to activate her heart, while Chia ran to get another wrap. She was covered once again, but still there was no change. Over the following moments, they tried every approach to reanimate her. Nothing seemed to be working.

"Jychanumun is right," Orion stated flatly. "She has left her body."

"I think we may have just lost our only chance," Chia replied. He too thought Jychanumun was right, and from the way the others looked at him, it was clear that they all now thought the same.

"I had no idea. I did as we'd arranged," Kraniel looked quite shaken. "It was just a standard sleep potion."

"I agreed to her being contained and put to sleep," Orion said, "It is not your fault, Kraniel. I am the overseer of this team, it's my responsibility. But, I have no idea what to do now."

Orion stood, looking stunned, unable to offer thoughts or suggestions.

"What have I done?" he whispered. "I made death her best choice."

He looked imploringly at Chia. "Do you think that the death paths that Jychanumun speaks of are truly real? Perhaps they could be. And if they are, perhaps she follows those paths."

Even if there was such a thing as a death path, how could a human bios know of it? Chia thought.

He was about to say this to Orion. He opened his mouth to speak. His heart lurched as he watched Orion's eyes grow blank. *Is he? Yes he is! He is going into her flesh to see if there is a death path! He goes to see if he can bring her back!*

"Orion!" Chia shouted and grasped his friend's arms as he slumped to the ground. This was too dangerous. If Jychanumun had really been correct with his description of the death paths, Orion could die there. And hadn't Jychanumun warned of even greater dire consequences?

Chia shook Orion to bring him around and to give warning through a mind-touch.

It was too late. Orion was gone.

Chia let go of everything he knew, held tight to Orion, and leapt into his mind.

Orion's thoughts were already racing ahead down a dark path, racing to find Tachra. Chia ran to catch up with him, and soon had him. He wrapped his thoughts around what there was of Orion's, and held them so tightly that neither of them could go any further.

You must come back. This is dangerous! Chia shouted with his mind. *Human flesh cannot hold a kutu's chi!*

Orion's strength was forceful, repelling Chia with all its might. *No, let me go*, Orion struggled. *I must retrieve the female. I must undo what I have done.*

Chia could barely hold Orion, his motivation was so strong, and so he focussed on one thought: if Orion went too far, he might never return as the same kutu Chia had grown to love as a friend. That thought kept him holding on and attempting to stop Orion from going any further. But Orion's will was great, and Chia knew that he could not hold on for much longer. Suddenly, a stronger force of will swept into the area, encompassing them both, and rooted them to the spot. Neither of them could go anywhere.

You should not use these paths, Jychanumun's voice told them.

Tachra must return, Orion argued, as his mind struggled to be free.

You do not have the knowledge of these paths; you cannot find her, Jychanumun replied. *Come back, or be lost forever.*

But Orion's mind remained, stubbornly refusing to move.

The paths of the dead are for the dead only, Jychanumun commanded. *I know you do not choose death, and so you do not belong here. I do not want to have to force you back, but I will and I can. Every moment you stay here is perilous for many. Return now!*

Orion's mind loosened a little. He seemed to comprehend the truth of Jychanumun's words. Then he stopped fighting completely. Chia kept hold of him, until he felt his submission and retreat. Only then, once Chia felt his friend's absence in that dark place, did he allow Jychanumun to guide his own mind back into his flesh.

This time, Chia hurt when he returned to his body. He hurt with a pain he didn't know he could feel. He had gone deep into an unknown place of dark paths, almost too deep to return. He found himself slumped on the grass, still holding onto Orion, finding it difficult to think straight.

Orion was stirring too. He opened his eyes and looked up. Chia followed his gaze. Jychanumun stood over them both, his arms folded over his chest, looking furious.

It was the first time that Chia had seen Jychanumun angry, but this was more than anger; he was enraged – his black eyes glistened and his face was contorted with fury.

"You gave your word!" he raged, as vibrant energy spooled from his mouth.

Orion and Chia were too shocked to speak.

Jychanumun lifted his hands to the sky and his wings formed, huge and black behind him, bristling with energy the likes of which Chia had never seen before.

Jychanumun lifted his head to the sky and howled.

The earth trembled beneath their feet, and the sky darkened as the cloud cover thickened. Chia turned his head away, expecting a flash of light or wave of energy that would send him flying. Instead, sheets of icy rain came down thick and fast. After a few moments of silence, he looked back at Jychanumun, but now the anger was gone. The kutu stood, looking crestfallen.

"You know not what has been done," Jychanumun said sadly. "But I do. You lit that beacon, I felt it. You were prepared to die for your cause. You entered the death paths with intent, which made a ripple in the energy of my kind. They would have sensed you there. By your actions we have been heard."

"Heard? By whom, your kind?" Orion gasped.

Jychanumun looked towards Orion, nodding slowly. "Yes, my friend," he said. "I told you, yet you did not believe me. I showed you, yet you did not believe me. You walked the death paths. You have left your mark this time. Prepare for a new and terrible world!"

Orion went to speak, but Jychanumun spoke first. "I will try to undo those things. For all that has happened, it has been good to have accompanied you."

Jychanumun sank to his knees and bowed his head, the hard rain making his hair stick to his glistening skin.

"I may not be back," he said quietly.

He shut his eyes, and as he did so, he smiled.

Slowly, all light and shadow drained from his body. The rain stopped. He sat hunched, as empty and motionless as a burnt out star.

TWENTY-TWO

I walked towards the Old One. I had taken my essence away from my body and now went to join him. There was nothing left for the flesh anymore. All my choices had been taken away, except one. So I had made that final choice and left the body that had carried me through life so far, to be with him in eternal dreaming.

Each mental step took me closer to the heart of the Old One. Wafts of his dreams tinged me with wonder. I was going to join him now. I was ready.

This would be the last time I walked any path, for where I was going was everywhere and every time. It felt as if I had flesh, yet I knew I had left it behind. The motion of walking, the awareness of having form, these were things I knew I would come to forget.

I gradually discarded a little more of myself. The coverings fell from my feet; one by one they dropped discarded on my path. The wrappings on my hands peeled away and silently fell. I did not look back. The tie to my gown unwound. The necklace I had made was released from my throat. My gown peeled away;

the fabric I had considered so fine was now just a fragment of nothingness. These things meant nothing to me. They were irrelevant. I walked naked and ready to leave the last piece of my earthly life; the form that held me.

For a brief moment, something disturbed the serenity around me. I thought I heard someone calling something familiar. Yes, I remembered, it was my old name from when I had flesh, Tachra. And I knew the voice too; it belonged to the red-haired one they called Orion.

Remembering made me stop.

I turned and looked, thinking I saw Orion, but all of a sudden he was gone again, so I kept walking. I felt a hint of sadness, because I also remembered that I'd met the makers of flesh, yet would never know their ways or reasons. But I knew this would not matter soon – that too would be forgotten.

I became aware of another call, and then another, and these calls had a pull. Whoever made these calls used many names, and I knew them all. I stopped and looked back again.

The one they called Jychanumun was a long way away, standing at the entrance to my path. He called to me, entwining the words around a tune. I knew that tune, as my fleshly lips had hummed it many times. That was my song that he sung, the song that I had heard back in the Jute fields with my father. That same song that had awoken so many dormant things within me, and the Old One too.

I sensed desperation behind Jychanumun's call, and could not close the tune from my mind. It made me remember curiosity, and it drew me towards him until I stood at the cusp of the place I'd left behind.

Jychanumun stood at the other side of my path, between gateways. He looked different without his flesh; he now radiated a vibrant array of energy that swirled around him, like a shadow that attracted light. He was quite beautiful. I walked up to him until I stood a fraction away, but he didn't seem to be able to see me.

How do you know my song? I asked.

Jychanumun stopped singing and looked around, trying to see me.

I have always known it, he eventually replied. *I heard it before you were born into flesh, yet you sung it even then. I heard it in the death paths, many millennia ago, for it seems time has no weight there. And more recently, I heard it when Orion wrote it; he named it the Summoning Song. Yet it has always been your song.*

Yes, I thought, I had been aware of him in my song, and I had seen something in Jychanumun's core that looked familiar. He'd walked the paths towards *him* many times, yet he'd never embraced him. He could never embrace him, not as I could.

This is my path; a path of joining and life, not one of death. It is closed to all except me, I said. *Why do you come here?*

I had to come; this was my last chance, he answered. *I wish to understand you, and myself. You have always been part of my existence. For once, I wanted that to be more.*

I don't remember if I like you, or dislike you, I said, struggling to remember Tachra's thoughts.

I do not know if I like myself, Jychanumun replied.

I smiled. Yes, I did like him, I knew that I did.

I looked at Jychanumun and could see he was suffering discomfort from standing so close to the Old One, but he stood there nonetheless.

Go somewhere without discomfort and I will follow. But just for a short while, I insisted. *All paths are mine now, but not all are yours.*

I would go with Jychanumun for a while. I was in no hurry; where I was going was timeless.

I crossed the boundary of my path to stand beside him, allowing my form to show as Tachra.

Now able to see me, Jychanumun swung around, smiled, and held out his hand. For the first time in a thousand dreams, I took that hand.

As I took Jychanumun's hand, the nothingness around me changed: no longer a peaceful emptiness, I found myself surrounded by familiar black doors, each with its single, circular knob. Tachra's memories surfaced, and I nearly recoiled. Then I remembered that I had left Tachra behind, and that nothing could harm me anymore.

I have seen this place before; in my sleeping dreams, I told Jychanumun.

I have often seen you, Jychanumun replied, *but never managed to catch up with you. This place is in my mind. It is where I choose a path.*

But I have only seen the doors lead back to themselves.

They lead wherever I wish, he answered. *My paths are not literal paths; like yours they are perceptions stemmed from knowledge and understanding. I create doors as defences to my knowledge.*

Then I understood the doors from my dreams, Jychanumun's doors. The Old One was the link: Jychanumun could see paths that led to *him*, and had created these doors to be portals in his mind, to segregate and direct his knowledge. Jychanumun understood the notion of beginnings and endings, he understood death and timelessness, which created a link to the Old One.

It seems you can see the ways to the Old One, I commented, and then looked at him. *Yet you do not understand it, or him, as I do.*

I leaned forward, lightly touching his chest. *You are not whole.* I said, sadly. *You say you would like to understand me. I would like to understand you.*

Where would you like me to begin?

At the beginning.

Jychanumun began talking of his world and of the ones called kutu, the makers of humans. He had so much passion in his words, yet frustration that he couldn't communicate every thought and sensation. But he tried; he tried with fervour to explain worlds I had not seen.

If only I could show you, he said, shaking his head in exasperation.

You could show me. I know of a way, if you wish, I suggested.

Jychanumun nodded, not even questioning me. Strange as it felt, he trusted me.

Gradually, I dropped the façade of the girl Tachra, until my energy swirled around in the vague shape of a body – it was looser now, and wilder; it was *more* me, not less. I saw him with my true vision; saw his light of black and white, interwoven without the slightest tinge of grey. I stretched out my consciousness, brushing him with my energy, and then pulled back quickly. It was just enough to give him an indication of what it would feel like to share, not just thought, but understanding.

I was aware that I could harm him with the wholeness of who I was, and I wished him no harm. Would he want to understand so much? Would he want to give so much of his own understanding? I didn't have to ask; his energy and thoughts surged forward until he encompassed me.

Jychanumun was so thirsty to show me what had made him the way he was, and to develop his own understanding, that I felt as if I was drowning in his memories. For those moments, I knew some of his existence as if it was my own. He showed me some of the occurrences that had made him that way, and I felt them as if they had happened to me. He showed me his knowledge of humans, and how the Shaa-kutu had made them to harvest resources from this planet. I learnt how they made humans to reproduce, refine harvestable energies, and then finally to die, taking the toxins of their refining back to dust once their bodies were too contaminated. I understood the place of my parents in the scheme of things: they had been made, and their children, and their children's children, were merely units to work for them. I also understood that I had surprised them by forging a link to something they didn't understand; the Old One.

Just as I understood Jychanumun, he understood Tachra, both her short human life and her extended existence through the Old One. I took Jychanumun down paths that knew no end and he clung to me at first, I sensed pain from him, but he wanted to go on, and the further we went, the more he understood.

I could travel this path for eternity, I thought, but I sensed his time limitations. *But you cannot. You must go now.*

I uncoiled my energy from around him and returned to the form of Tachra. We had not moved, and still stood in the dark place, surrounded by doors.

I looked down at my form, my swirling energy now tinted with specks of purest black and sharpest white, and then at Jychanumun, whose energy now flickered with threads of colour.

Understanding has changed us, I observed. *And I can feel your thoughts.*

And I yours. He too was looking at the new colours weaving through him. *It cannot be undone.*

This was true, although I did not want it undone. By understanding him, I now recognized the part of me made from Shaa-kutu. My knowledge felt whole.

You would not have chosen to die, would you? he asked.

No. I still had much to understand of that flesh. But it does not matter now.

It matters! Live! Take back your flesh. You can walk your path to him at any time, but the girl Tachra – she is only once.

Live? I thought. *I think I have heard you tell me that before.*

Jychanumun looked at me and I felt his urging as if it were my own emotion. He flickered before me as if he could not hold himself within the paths any more.

My time is running out, he admitted sadly. *Please, return to flesh, and I will too. I have seen things that have not come to pass, and they include you.*

I have seen a world of humans and kutu embracing life, knowledge, and love, and embracing them in peace. I have also seen a later world of pain and suffering, a world where the Old One cannot rest for the suffering he senses. I have seen you, Tachra, Iastha, bring peace back to that world and peace to the Old One. I do not know when, or how, but I see you in flesh, not in the death paths.

I have seen that world too, in my dreams, I considered.

But Jychanumun's thoughts had told me something that I had not dreamt before: that the Old One could not rest in the world of suffering, and if I was bound to him, then neither could I. The Old One would not tolerate his dreams becoming nightmares. He would snuff out the cause in an instant. If I could prevent that, then I must: for humans, for kutu, and for the Old One himself. But for all the knowledge I had gained, I didn't know how. I looked at Jychanumun, and although I saw his strength and resolve, I realised that he didn't know how either.

I will stand with you, Jychanumun motioned. *But if I am to return to life, I must go now. I will not go without you, Tachra. If you walk to him, I will choose the death paths for eternity and wait for you.*

I cannot return to my flesh. It is too late. I have made my choice.

It's not too late, he implored. *Not all choices are ultimate. They keep your flesh active. I can show you how to return. You will remember from my memories.*

I had no time to make a decision, but I did not need to. I held out my hand. *Then guide me.*

He took my hand, led me towards one of the doors, and opened it. Beyond I saw a mound of shimmering cloth, surrounded by kutu. I knew that my body was under the cloth. Jychanumun guided me towards it.

Do not mind them; they will not harm you, he instructed.

And then, as if the memories were my own, I remembered how to re-enter a body.

Slowly and effortlessly, I stepped over the threshold and pushed my thoughts back into my flesh. Then I wanted to sleep, but not the kutu sleep and not the sleep of the Old One, just the sleep of my flesh; healing, restful, and dreamless.

TWENTY-THREE

The rains had stopped as fast as they had started, and Chia's stunned gaze moved from Tachra to Jychanumun and back to Tachra again.

Tachra's body was motionless except for the robotic rise and fall of her chest, stimulated by the activator wrap. Their attempts to reanimate her had failed. They had killed her. Now Jychanumun had also gone, his static body kneeling beside Tachra's with his head hung low and his lifeless hair clinging to his face, still wet from the rain. He too showed no signs of returning.

The situation had rapidly deteriorated until it was now shockingly critical.

Chia shakily helped Orion stand up. "Do you think Jychanumun will come back?" he asked.

Orion didn't reply. From Jychanumun's words, it didn't seem as if he had intended to.

Orion, Chia, Kraniel, Stanze and Nirrious all stood staring at Jychanumun's drained and slumped body, and at the cloth-covered mound that enclosed Tachra's empty flesh. They waited in anticipation for anything to change.

After a seemingly eternity of silence, Orion pulled away, touching Chia's arm.

"I should have believed him about the death paths."

"We all should have believed him."

"But I knew him. Of all of us, I should have known his truth."

"It did not seem plausible."

"He has been away for too long. I don't think he'll be back."

"You don't know that. Give him time."

"He has had too much time," Orion frowned. "From what he revealed to me, there's a limit to how long you can be away from the body, after which the forgetfulness of the paths take over. Should I venture to search for him?"

"Absolutely not!" Chia said sharply. "If anyone can return, Jychanumun can. If he can't, none of us stand a chance."

"I think he intended to leave for good," Kraniel added flatly.

"I agree," Orion stated. "I think he wanted to join Tachra. We had already done the damage. He knew the consequences of what had happened. I don't think he meant to return."

"It did sound like it," Kraniel agreed.

"I don't know. I just don't think so," Chia responded. "I have sensed a great strength in Jychanumun. He will be back. Surely we are just being overly concerned."

"Overly concerned? Look at this situation, look at *us*," Orion replied. "What have we done? Of course I am more than concerned."

"Do not be."

From his kneeling position, Jychanumun slowly raised his head.

Chia gasped, taking a step back as Jychanumun's hair fell away from his face. With a shock, Chia realised that Jychanumun *looked* different. His pure black eyes now had flecks of bright colour that shone from within the darkness. As his body reanimated, his hair and wings moved, tinged with colour, rippling like the feathers of ravens.

"You have colour!" Orion said, his eyes wide in amazement. They all knew that no kutu should be able to change their colour: colour defined who they were.

"I always have had," Jychanumun smiled.

He stood and stretched, pushing his long wings behind him and flexing his torso as if his body was new to him. As he stretched, blocks of shadow fell from him, revealing a radiance that shone out over them all.

"I understand now, and I am free," he said. He looked towards Tachra. "She merely sleeps. She will awaken soon. You will not harm her."

"We didn't . . ." Kraniel started.

"You did," Jychanumun interrupted. "But it does not matter now. It is past. Today is the beginning."

Jychanumun bent towards the mound on the ground that was Tachra, gently pulling away the wrap that covered her. To the relief of the others, she continued breathing. Jychanumun discarded the wrap, carefully picked Tachra up and carried her to one of the recliners, putting pillows beneath her head. When he touched her, ripples of light passed between them.

"What has happened to you?" Chia asked, as Jychanumun turned back to them.

"I am still me," Jychanumun replied. "I accept who I am now, and have seen far beyond my boundaries." He looked towards Tachra's sleeping body. "We are all the sum of what we know. I have known her, she has known me; we are now aligned. But we are not the same."

"And the girl, Tachra, or rather Iastha?" All the kutu were focussed on Jychanumun.

"There is none other like her," Jychanumun replied. "Even I will never comprehend the source of what we have called 'Factor X,' the source that she calls the Old One, for I am not part of him as she is. But she could teach us. You lit the beacon of the death paths again. She may help, if she chooses."

"I don't understand," Orion stated. "For once I do not even know what questions to ask in order to help me understand. Where do I start?"

"At the beginning." Jychanumun beckoned, holding out his hand. "I will show you."

Orion walked forward.

"All of you," Jychanumun nodded to the group.

Chia approached cautiously; he'd never been keen to communicate through mind-touch, it always seemed to engulf him entirely. Nevertheless, he walked forward, and he and the others all placed their hands between Jychanumun's.

Suddenly, Chia's mind was bombarded, becoming awash with images from a time before time, when there was no such thing as time, and there was no such thing as right or wrong. Everything was nothing, and nothing was everything. All universes had timeless consciousness. Consciousness expanded, and universes enveloped each other, one rolling into another, one consciousness merging into the next. Growing and merging. Growing and merging. It was a natural fusion, until in the end the last two consciousnesses remained. These two kept growing, and at the moment they touched, realisation was born.

Realisation created time. The two consciousnesses realised that this was not what they wanted, and so choice was born. The smaller of the consciousnesses knew that its end was close and did not want to lose its self awareness, and the larger did not want to envelop it, but it was inevitable: what they were could not stop it from happening. In that split moment of newly created time, the smaller one fragmented, pulling itself into millions of pieces. The explosive fragmentation flung its pieces to distant galaxies; some pulled by the power of light, and some by the strength of darkness, each piece being too incomplete for the larger one to merge with, yet complete within itself. Feeling the fragmentation, the larger one discovered sadness, for it had realisation that it was now the last. It centred his consciousness, knowing that it now filled all universes and could touch all times. He, whom Tachra calls the Old One, centred itself here, in this planet, Earth, where he sleeps, because it is as good a place as any.

Chia felt himself fall to the floor as Jychanumun pulled his hands away.

The next thing Chia knew he was propped up, being handed a goblet of Ochrah.

The rest of the team were also sitting, close by. He looked to one side, to Orion, whose hands were shaking uncontrollably as he muttered to himself. Jychanumun bent towards Orion, lifting the goblet in his hands, encouraging him to drink.

"I think I understand. I do, I think I understand," Orion kept repeating, his teeth chattering as if he felt dire cold. Chia wasn't sure if he got anything.

Jychanumun sat on the floor in front of them. "Yes, you do understand," he said calmly, placing a hand consolingly on Orion's arm.

"We, the kutu, are all the fragmented remains of the penultimate Old One. The fragments that were pulled to the light are your kind; Shaa-kutu, and those to the darkness are my kind; Nigh-kutu. That is why we are attracted to this planet; here we can be close to the last Old One."

TWENTY-FOUR

Returning to my body was surprisingly easy, as if putting on a comfortable item of clothing. Once I returned, I think I slept, although I don't know how long for.

When I awoke, Jychanumun was the first thing I saw. I sat up quickly, looking for danger, but sensed none.

Jychanumun leaned down and asked if I felt well, reassuring me that his kutu friends meant me no harm. No sound left his lips. Even though I was back in my body and we were no longer merged, I could still hear his thoughts.

I silently told him I was well, and he heard me too, telling me I'd slept only a short time.

It was dark outside, and I'd been moved to one of the long beds inside the kutu's transparent dome. I could see the rest of the kutu sitting around their table. They sat in silence, looking most perplexed, and each drinking the same smoking liquid. They must have detected my sudden movement as they turned in unison, looking at me.

I frowned at them. The one who had tried to contain me, Kraniel, smiled self-consciously.

I quickly examined my body, but I didn't find any damage; even my old scars were gone. When I asked to see my reflection, Jychanumun found it funny, saying I was being vain. Nevertheless, I was glad to see that I still looked like me and that the scar on my forehead was still there; I had earned that scar. Jychanumun told me about the accident with a bird – now it was my turn to find something funny. I should have known it had been him.

See, he silently said, *our paths are more entwined than even we realise.*

It turned out that my healthy state was thanks to kutu flesh-healing tools. I immediately thought of Jan with his damaged legs, and I asked Jychanumun if their tools could mend them; when he replied that they could, I made him promise that it would be done. In fact, I sensed he would attend to it himself.

I realised that Jychanumun and I were being watched, and I turned to see Orion standing at the opening of the 7A. He nodded and walked towards us with a questioning look on his face, his demeanour uncertain, as if he was unsure how to approach. He had probably found it strange watching Jychanumun and I communicate without words, I considered. The only signs that anything was passing between us had been our hand and facial gestures.

Orion leaned forward and gently touched my arm. I let him, although I watched him with caution.

Welcome Tachra, or rather, Iastha, I heard Orion say, although his lips hadn't moved either.

"Can you all communicate by mind?" I asked aloud.

"No, not all of us," Orion replied, after taking his hand from my arm. "We are all composed of different energies; some are more adept at mind-speak than others. And even those who can mind-speak can only do so when actually touching the one they wish to speak to."

None can hear our thoughts, Jychanumun said with his mind.

I smiled at Jychanumun and turned to Orion. "Thank you for your welcome, Orion. I trust there are no more containment fields lurking to trap me."

Orion smiled. "Not this time," he said good-humouredly, although I sensed him tense up. "I apologise for that. We did not mean to harm you. We tried to contain you because we were not sure of your abilities. Nothing like that will happen again; you have my word of honour. Jychanumun has explained a few things. You have our respect."

He looked over at the others. "Please excuse their anxious appearance. We live in troubled times. Nevertheless, they would all like the opportunity to meet you properly. If you are ready, would you like to be more appropriately introduced?"

"Yes," I said, genuinely glad of his openness. "I would like that."

Merging with Jychanumun had already told me much about these kutu. They were already personalities in my mind and I felt as if I knew them. But all I knew was a mosaic of Jychanumun's opinions, not my own. Jychanumun liked these kutu, and I felt a new keenness to meet them. So, as Orion introduced 'his team' one by one, I greeted them with caution, remaining aware of their intentions through my own senses, while embracing Jychanumun's knowledge of them. I think I wanted to find something about each one to dislike, but as I met them, I liked them all. I even liked Kraniel, despite the fact that he had attempted to capture me; in fact, I thought Kraniel was remarkable.

I sensed tension in all of them, but I also sensed that they were relieved that I had not ceased; clearly, my ceasing had not been their objective. But there was one kutu to whom I was not introduced: the white haired one. He sat silently in the distance, just watching.

Before I could question why I had not been introduced to the white haired one, Stanze asked if I would like refreshments. My mouth drooled at the thought of food. I had to admit I was ravenous.

"Do you eat the same as normal humans?" Stanze asked, rather self-consciously.

"I believe so," I replied, amused at the question. Although I was curious as to what foods they ate, because Jychanumun's memories were full of experiences that transcended mere taste sensations, I did not think their provisions would suit the needs of my flesh.

But then Stanze brought forth an abundance of fruits and vegetables, enough to feed a small village for a week. I smiled when I saw a large bowl of Kathi berries, but I could not bring myself to eat my favourite fruit as they reminded me of my father and of all the trouble that I had brought him.

"Did you return my family?" I suddenly asked.

"Of course," Stanze smiled, with a mouth full of Kathi berries, which had made his teeth go blue. "Look, I can show you."

He got up and came to stand beside me, putting a thin grey sheet in front of me.

"You gave them a port?" Orion asked with disapproval.

"Yes. It was the very least we could do."

Stanze touched the port. Immediately the inert grey sheet became a moving image. It was the front of my parents hut, a scene from just outside the front door. The door was open. I could see father and mother sitting at the table. I could hear too; this port also showed sound. My parents were talking, but to someone else. Then Soul walked into view and joined them, smiling, holding her child. Father took the child from Soul while she sat and started eating her food.

I smiled to myself; they looked content, all of them, and I bet

Soul enjoyed the food from Threetops far more than those awful sour fruits of Hollow.

"You can speak to them," Stanze said. "I've shown Soul how to use the port; it's just outside the dwelling. I wanted to put it in their kitchen, but they wouldn't have it indoors. Would you like to speak to them?"

"Next time," I replied. "I just wanted to be sure that they were well."

Yes, I thought, they did look content; that was enough for me for now. I would only speak to them once I was more certain of their safety and mine. I had seen as much as I needed.

Stanze nodded, returning the port to its holding place. "Whenever you want. I'll show you how to use the port too, if you wish."

Around their table, with Jychanumun beside me, I could feel that the others were unsure of what to say, so I started asking questions – about them, about why they were here, why they made humans, and why they had been looking for me.

Although I knew much of Jychanumun's past, the others had led a very different existence, and this fascinated me. I learnt how they utilised apparently useless energies and elements, making an existence of joy and exploration. I learnt about their ability to transcend from matter to energy and back to matter again. I learned of their love of the arts and sciences. They spoke with great joy about things I knew I could never do, and I listened with wonder, as if I was doing those things myself.

They told me of how they had initially thought this planet was just another place to harvest energy, and how they had made bios to harvest it. They had developed plants, animals, and humans, taking Earth matter and adding kutu genetics. Apparently, humans were the most advanced model they'd ever made, existing at the top of an energy-refining chain. The energy that the humans refined was utilized by them and then collected by harvesting ships during the night, while people slept.

And those harvesting ships, which located humans to sift off the refined energies? They, I discovered, were what I saw as the blue light.

I was deep in thought for a moment. I had found so many answers in just one day. Answers I had searched for, as well as answers that I had never realised that I sought.

I glanced around the table at the amazing creatures. Jychanumun caught my eye.

Do you prefer the ways of these kind to those of yours? I silently asked.

They are just different, he silently replied. *My kind were glorious beings once; less contained. But they consumed their good with their greed. These Shaa-kutu have kept honour – at least, most of them.*

I smiled, rejoining the conversation with all the kutu. They were busy explaining how, after placing bios here, they sensed an unknown and powerful energy. They had called it Factor X. At first they'd thought it was another energy to harvest, but more recently they'd found out what it really was – the Old One. They had wanted to harvest *him*. I couldn't help laughing.

As the moments wore on, I grew to know and like all the kutu team. Oh, there were hiccups, many of them, mainly revolving around their attempts to discuss 'bios' and 'harvesting' in ways that they hoped would not be offensive. In truth, I found none of their discussions offensive, but occasionally pretended that I did, and they soon grew aware of my teasing and stopped delicately tiptoeing around me.

Yet, regardless of their laughter and conversation, I still felt their anxiety. It had not lessened and I knew it was not directly linked to me.

I felt Jychanumun's mind. *What troubles them?* I asked. *They do not say, but they all have undercurrents of tension.*

Yes, and for good reason.

The white kutu, who remained unknown to me, moved a little and caught my eye. Something about him bothered me. It also bothered me that we hadn't been introduced.

"Who is the one who never speaks?" I asked aloud. "Is he a guard?"

"You have met us all," Orion answered, perplexed, and I saw a great look of concern on his face.

I passed Jychanumun an image of the one I kept seeing.

"She sees Una," Jychanumun said flatly.

"She does?" Orion gasped, shocked.

I could tell from their expressions that they didn't know he was there.

"Can you tell us more?" Orion quickly asked.

"He's over there, now, by the side of your ship. He's been there since I got here," I replied. "He just watches you all. I assumed you were aware of him."

Orion immediately arose and asked me to show him where I sensed Una.

I walked over to the white one, but, even though we all stood immediately in front of him, the others still couldn't see him.

When I touched the spectre they called Una I felt his presence only vaguely – it was as if he was not wholly there.

Orion began speaking very quickly, and I found the words of his newly learnt language hard to follow at such a speed, but it was clear that what I'd said had disturbed them all. They were arguing, and kept mentioning someone named Shursa as well as Factor X.

"Perhaps Una is just participating in regular mind-probes to the planet; that's why he's inaccessible. But to probe alone would be very dangerous," Orion suggested.

"No," Chia replied. "I would sense him if it was a mind-probe. Una's consciousness must be stuck here."

Orion disagreed, saying, "But it would take the power of thousands of kutu to dislodge one as balanced and strong as Una."

"The power of thousands, such as could only be found in an Orb," Chia added. "An Orb like the one that Shursa utilized. The same Shursa who has conveniently taken Una's place."

"He has the opportunity and the motive," Kraniel nodded.

I touched Jychanumun's arm. Jychanumun stopped listening to the others and looked at me. I was staring at the white-haired one.

"I think Una can hear you all talking," I told him.

Jychanumun looked at me expectantly, waiting for me to go on.

"It's as if he's trying to tell me something," I added. "He knows I can see him. But because he's not all here, I can't understand what he's trying to say."

Orion looked around as if trying to see Una. "Una?" He asked, "Can you hear us?"

The spectre that was Una slowly nodded his head.

"He can!" I exclaimed. "He nodded. He can see and hear you."

"Una, are you dislodged here?" Orion asked.

"Yes," I told them, after Una had nodded again.

Orion tried asking several more questions. Una kept trying to speak and I was frustrated that I couldn't understand his silent words. All I could see was the obvious shake or nod of his head. I think Orion was even more frustrated. Eventually they managed to ascertain that someone called Shursa was indeed responsible and that Una most certainly needed their help.

Orion started talking hurriedly to the others again. It was obvious that they weren't sure what to do to rectify the situation.

"Try using the truth," Jychanumun said amidst their debate. It was the first time he'd offered any opinion during the whole event.

Orion went silent for a moment.

"You're right," he sighed. "Although my knowledge of Shursa and his recent actions have led me to believe it wouldn't be successful, it must be tried."

I wasn't sure quite what their intention was, but they left Una hovering at the side of their ship and walked into their dome. I followed, feeling bad at leaving the white one alone when he seemed so lost. Orion headed towards what I had learnt was a communication port and made a motion with his hand.

"Contact Una, the Supreme," Orion commanded.

A sharp-featured, yellow-haired kutu, sitting in an empty white room, appeared on the screen. It wasn't Una.

"Shursa," Orion introduced. "I have much news, but it must be discussed before the entire council."

"Have you found Factor X?"

Orion nodded, "It is news that must be heard by all the council. Could you arrange a time when I could speak to them all, at the earliest opportunity?"

Shursa thought about this for a moment.

"You are in luck. I was in the middle of holding a meeting. One moment . . ."

The screen went blank. Orion looked around uncertainly, unsure if Shursa had switched the machine off. Then, a moment later, Shursa's face appeared again. He was surrounded by other kutu, all sitting around a huge, glistening, black table. It seemed that Shursa had moved in to a different room.

"Councillors," Orion greeted. "We have uncovered Factor X . . ."

A burst of questions, laughter and congratulations interrupted his words. He waited a moment for them to quieten enough for him to be heard.

"But," he continued, "we cannot harvest Factor X."

That silenced them completely.

"The link to Factor X is a human, but the two cannot be separated. Factor X is not an energy to be utilized by us. It's the presence of a life form far older and greater than time itself. We will never be able to possess it. In our search for this, we've discovered our forgotten identities; we originate from an Old One too. This knowledge is the step to enlightenment that we seek, not Factor X." He smiled, "There's nothing here we can forcefully extract, but much that can willingly be learnt. Only Una has the balance necessary to unite us to move forward with this new information. Whatever has been making him inaccessible must be rectified."

Orion stopped, as though waiting for a response. The councillors were stunned into silence. Shursa stood up, moving towards the communication port.

"Una will undoubtedly speak to you regarding this. Expect communication from him before the close of day. Meanwhile, we, the council, must discuss this immediately."

The screen went blank.

Orion turned back to his friends. "Well, I have told them the reality of our situation. I just hope they comprehend the potential enormity of the news."

"Remembering our origins and discovering an ancient being are things we should be celebrating. We should not have to vex about whether or not our findings are believed," Chia interposed.

"Did you sense if Shursa understood?" Orion asked.

Chia frowned, but before he could reply, the communication port made a sharp humming sound.

Orion turned, waving his hand over the screen, and Shursa's face appeared once again. He wasn't with the councillors around the large black table anymore, he'd returned to the white room, apparently on his own.

"I want the human brought here," Shursa announced abruptly, "and I want Chia to come off the Earth project and return to the substation."

"Why?" Chia demanded, standing up and moving to Orion's side.

"Get him out of my sight!" Shursa exclaimed angrily.

Chia felt Orion motioning him aside, and although he seemed ready to take on any fight with Shursa, he backed away.

"You, Orion, are to bring the human here to Eden." Shursa repeated, once Chia had withdrawn from view. "And Chia is to leave Earth. Understood?"

"I see no reason for Chia to leave here, and you heard my earlier words: Factor X cannot be harvested. It's the knowledge it brings that will enlighten us," Orion replied, frowning. "The female would choose to die if we removed her. That would prevent us from understanding Factor X fully."

Shursa made a scoffing sound. "I don't believe you, and so I'll take that chance. I want you to personally bring the human to Eden."

"I cannot," Orion replied. "What I said was true – there's no point. Our path should be one of learning now. You must see that."

Shursa leaned towards the screen, so that his face took up all the space. "Do not think that you'll reap this glory for yourself, Orion," he growled under his breath. "I spotted the original anomaly, I kept the project together; Factor X is mine. I may share it with you if you are good to me, but it is mine."

Orion took a step backwards, as if distancing himself from Shursa's vehement words. "I do not want any glory," he replied, keeping his voice level. "I strive for the good of all."

"You cannot fool me, Orion," Shursa laughed. "I know you've had your sights on this; you and your so-called friend

Chia, who so conveniently plays dumb about what he knows. You see I am a forward thinker. I know you better than you think. And I know that you would fill Una's seat at the first given opportunity."

"That's not so! Una is Supreme and I love him greatly for that. Shursa, understand that Factor X is not an energy source; it's a being greater than we could ever be. The human link could help us understand. We cannot bring her to Eden, or she will choose to die. If she dies, she is nothing but empty flesh. It is her understanding that could help us, not her flesh."

"You lie!" Shursa exclaimed, raising his arms and leaning back. "Your temperamental and petty deceit will not fool me anymore. You will not keep Factor X for yourself."

"Shursa," Orion replied slowly. He was keeping control of his emotions, although it was clear that he was exasperated. "I am not lying to you. I have no reason to lie to you. I do not want Factor X. I do not want Supremacy. Right now, I just want you to understand the truth. Factor X is a conscious being, and one that will probably obliterate us like a breath of air blowing out a candle if we disturb it. It can never belong to any of us."

"More lies," Shursa frowned. "I see straight through you. Bring me Factor X and be rewarded, or do not and suffer the consequences. It's not too late to make amends, Orion." A small smile touched his lips.

I could see Orion was becoming angry. My true vision showed his energy swirling around him, as if desperate to break free.

"I cannot remember when I ever took orders from you," Orion fumed, "and I cannot imagine that I ever will."

"My appointment as Supreme is merely a formality now," Shursa replied smugly, leaning back and crossing his arms. "As Supreme, you will have to take orders from me. I'm giving you the choice now; either come willingly with Factor X, or I will

414

come and get Factor X anyway. Once I'm Supreme you'll have no choice but to do as I say."

"No!" Orion protested. "You are not Supreme material and never will be."

"Watch your words!" Shursa scowled. "Or you may lose what little favour you do hold. The council and Una all agree that I am to be appointed. With their support, your opinion doesn't matter. Or if you'd prefer . . ." he drawled, savouring his own words, "Una, while he is still Supreme, could command you. After all, I did promise that he would speak with you. Come Una, give Orion his orders."

Shursa leaned forward and spun the port around to point to a kutu beside him. It was Una.

Una barely resembled the spectre I'd seen on the plateau, although I could tell it was the same being. He looked older, so much so that he was barely recognisable. He sat slumped but awake, and his thinning hair hung around his gaunt, haggard face in dull grey clumps. His eyes looked grey and hollow, flickering as if trying to hold any colour at all.

"Una, what have they done to you, my friend?" Orion whispered, leaning towards the port.

"Bring Factor X," Una grunted flatly, without the slightest sign that he had recognized Orion.

Shursa spun the port back around to face himself once again. He sat there, smiling, leaning back in his big white chair, and drumming his fingers together. I decided that I really did not like this being.

"What have you done to him?" Orion shouted, his energy moving around him like flickering flames.

"He did it to himself, the fool: he was blind," Shursa replied with a shrug. "Don't you be a fool too. You see, Orion, I'm to be appointed as Supreme in eighteen days, after ten days of glorious celebrations, and so I have much to arrange; consequently, I don't have time to chat, I'm afraid. I want you to personally deliver the female link to Factor X here on Eden in time for my appointment and before the feasting has finished, or . . ."

"Or what?" Orion interrupted, crossing his arms as he tried to contain his fury.

"Or, you'll wish you had, it's as simple as that. I've made many new friends, Orion, more than you could imagine, and from places that you could never dream of. And my new friends can be very persuasive indeed."

Jychanumun stood up, and I felt his horror. I picked up images in his mind of many beings that looked like him; they were his kind: the Nigh-kutu, black-winged and black-eyed, but lacking his compassion or understanding. They felt like nothing I'd encountered before, and their energy bristled with aggression.

I felt Jychanumun block his thoughts from me; these were clearly beings he didn't like to bring to mind. These were Shursa's new friends, and they were Jychanumun's own people. He stood beside Orion in view of the port.

"Do not trust the black-eyed ones," Jychanumun told Shursa gravely. "They would not contact you unless they had a greater reward for themselves."

"Ah Jychanumun," Shursa stated arrogantly, "So you do talk after all. I've heard so much about you from your kind; it seems you're a traitor and deserter to them. I do believe they'll want a talk with you when they arrive here. Anyway," he shrugged. "I was speaking to Orion. Orion? Arrange Chia's departure and bring Factor X to me. Leave tonight. Tonight." With this, he ended their communication, leaving them with just a blank white screen.

Orion turned to his team, shaking with anger. Energy spat from him in jagged bursts.

Jychanumun grabbed onto Orion's arm, holding him as he whispered something in his ear. They seemed to be standing in that position for a long time, with Jychanumun whispering quietly, and then he pulled back, still holding onto Orion, and looked at him steadily.

Orion seemed to have calmed. He looked at Jychanumun and nodded.

"We must find new options," Orion stated to the others. "I now know what use Shursa made of the power in the Orb. When Una was in a mind probe to this place, Shursa used the power to cut the connection. Una's consciousness is now lost in that probe, somewhere here. Una is all but useless. His thoughts cannot be heard and his body is just a malleable substance. It seems as though Shursa really is giving the orders now. We must find a way to do something. Shursa will be made Supreme in eighteen days. So we have less time than that."

Orion paused; he seemed to be calculating. He looked at Chia. "There is something in you that Shursa fears or dislikes, and it is more than just his obsession with me. What is it?"

"I don't know," Chia shook his head. "It started after I discovered this planet, when I lost all sense of time."

Orion frowned. He knew Chia could not recall what had happened then; they had spent months, years even, working together to heal the damage that had been done. It was not something that could be solved in mere days. Whatever it was, Shursa seemed to know something about it.

"How much time do we have?" Orion asked. "If I left tonight, when would they expect me on Eden?"

"Nine days," Chia replied, "if the 7A flew at maximum speed."

"Then we have a maximum of nine days before I'm missed on Eden, and nine days before any suspicions are aroused from your still being here," Orion replied. "Nine days to find a solution."

"You do not want me to leave?" Chia asked. "I don't want my presence to cause greater problems."

"Of course you're not leaving. None of us will be obliging Shursa's petty requests. Anyway, we need you."

I had been listening to their conversation, disturbed by their troubles. There seemed to be so much deceit around these immensely powerful creatures. And it sounded as if I, or rather my connection to *him*, was one of the causes of the problems.

"Is this because of me?" I asked anxiously.

"No," Orion smiled. "I am sorry you are involved. The issue started long before you were born. It is not usual."

"But it seems as though I am involved, whether I like it or not."

Jychanumun turned and caught a hold of my hand. "I must speak with her . . ." he said to the others.

"We all must speak with her," Orion interrupted him.

"Alone." Jychanumun finished.

Jychanumun turned to me and held out his hand. I knew that he wanted to take me somewhere private, and I sensed that he was worried that something terrible was brewing. Despite my fears, I took his hand and together we walked away from the force field perimeter. I expected he would just go somewhere out of earshot on the plateau; instead, he wrapped one arm around my waist, opened his wings, and leapt into the sky with me held against his chest.

My head was spinning with thoughts, but when Jychanumun and I climbed through the air my anxieties momentarily silenced. Flying was amazing, breathtakingly so, and so much better than when I'd connected with any bird. He held me tightly and I knew I would not fall. It was as if his wings were my own, and I felt the wind rush against my skin as we flew high up to where the air smelt of sweet metal. I watched the valleys below us roll together.

We were travelling a path that I recognised – the one I'd walked to the plateau. I could have stayed up there forever.

It seemed no time at all until we started to descend. We were heading down to a very familiar place: my valley.

Jychanumun landed by the edge of the forest overlooking the lake and let me go. I sensed Meah close by, but she retreated further into the trees, initially unaware that the stranger was me.

"It's beautiful here," Jychanumun stated.

"Yes, it is," I smiled, walking to a patch of sun-dappled grass. "Come speak to me. I know much about you, but something new troubles you."

"These new troubles involve us both."

"Then show me."

I opened my eyes to the true vision, reaching out and brushing his swirling raven energy with my own colourful aura. Within moments, Jychanumun had shown me Shursa's and Una's part in a scheming plot that put him, me, and all of Orion's team in grave danger. In fact, all Shaa-kutu were in dire trouble; his kind – the Nigh-kutu – were now involved too. To help me understand, he showed me more of the black-winged ones and I understood the lengths that the Nigh-kutu would go to in order to get what they wanted. It was grim.

I pulled away, my mind gasping as if needing breath, and dropped my true vision like an unwanted stone.

"Can kutu really be that evil?"

"The potential of greatness can be tipped either way," Jychanumun sighed. "This is not what I hoped for us. But I have seen a world of peace as well as strife; there must be a solution."

"There has to be," I considered. "No-one can just take *his* energy. It's impossible. And if they disturb him, he'll simply eliminate the source of the disturbance. This could be catastrophic; humans and kutu could be ceased in a moment as if they were nothing.

He's not prone to anger, but to prod him in his slumbers is asking for devastation."

"I understand," Jychanumun nodded.

"And if these black-winged ones come here, there are no good outcomes. From what you've shown me, they won't want to listen to reason."

I fell silent, realising that I was saying things that Jychanumun already knew.

"I have not found a solution yet," Jychanumun eventually said. "But I must."

He looked at me and smiled. "I have known you for only a short while, yet I have shared my existence with you; what you are has given me greater understanding, and who you are has given me hope. That I would willingly die for."

"I will not let that happen," I said, moved by his sincerity. "I know that neither of us fears our own ceasing, but these events are more important than my life; you know this flesh is only temporary. What if I was to cease? You could take my body to Shursa, he would realise he couldn't extract Factor X and he would leave this planet and you alone. I must cease sometime; surely it is better to make use of that fact."

"Although it would pain me, I have certainly considered it. But it could not work."

"Why not?"

"They would still come here, to the source."

"Then my death would buy time; time to leave this place, taking as many humans as possible and getting as far away as possible. Then if the Old One retaliates, perhaps you will not be harmed."

"Humans could not exist elsewhere for long periods. Even if they could, we would still not be helping Una, or any other under Shursa's sway."

"Well, that squashes that idea," I frowned. "I don't want to cease yet, anyway. I've put enough effort into living. I was just trying the simplest ideas. It seems that this Shursa must be stopped or made aware of his consequences, and somehow you must reinstate Una."

Jychanumun nodded. "Yes," he agreed. "Una is balanced. But he was defenceless against treachery, as it did not exist with his people."

"Except for Shursa," I pointed out. "And it seems as though only a few can see that."

Perhaps, I thought, there is another way.

"Jychanumun, you know: to run with a cat you must think and act like a cat."

He looked at me questioningly.

"You have shown me some of the capabilities of kutu. Through your life, I have witnessed some of the skills that you all have. We just need to use those and beat Shursa by his rules; through lying, deceit, and treachery. We just need to find out what he wants the most."

I spoke quickly; ideas were forming with every word. There were a few things that I could do that the kutu could not, and many things that they could do that I could not. Perhaps, I suggested, I could connect to Shursa enough to listen to his mind. He was too guarded for Jychanumun to hear, but my ways were different; he might not be guarded against them. If I could connect to Shursa, I could find his desires; we could lure him with whatever he wanted, and then catch him and reinstate Una. It seemed rather simplified, but I thought of the way that cats stalked their prey. Their prey would never know of the cat's intentions until it was too late.

"Also," I said, "if Shursa can break the connection between Una's consciousness and his body, then they can be reconnected.

Orion said that with a mind probe he could do it, but that he needed to be touching him for it to work. But I don't need to touch flesh to feel minds. There must be a way to work together. And if we could get Una here, somehow, then if it didn't work he would be accessible for Orion."

Jychanumun explained more about a mind probe and how it worked. I didn't completely understand the principles, but it sounded like a precarious, though possible, task.

I looked at Jychanumun. "Then it's quite simple. Either we go to where Shursa and Una are, or we get them to come to us. Here would be better, so that we would have Earth skills to call upon."

We both sat in silence for several moments, looking out over the lake. He clearly didn't much like the idea, and admittedly, it was a very loose idea with umpteen flaws, but neither of us could find a better suggestion.

"I don't want you in such danger," Jychanumun said, finally.

I touched his face, making energy dance from my fingers to his skin, and smiled.

"What's the worst they can do, my black-eyed one? Make me cease? If we don't do something, we'll all cease anyway. I'm more concerned about Orion: you say he has not attempted a mind probe, yet can do it. I'd be relying on him while I'm doing something I've never tried before; goodness knows what could happen."

"I can help Orion," Jychanumun replied. "We would all willingly die to rectify matters."

Now I felt uncertain, but I couldn't object.

"I'll be back in a few moments," I said, getting up. "If you cannot think of a better idea by the time I return, we must discuss our options with the others."

Jychanumun nodded and I left him thinking quietly while I walked into the forest. Once I had entered the thickness of the trees, I called to Meah.

Meah must have been close already; she was probably watching me all along, because as soon as I called to her she stalked out from between the trees and cautiously approached, her nose flaring at the strange scents that covered me. She knew it was me and was very pleased to see me, but she didn't think I smelt right anymore. I bent to ruffle her fur, and as soon as I touched her she dropped her guard and became the young cub I remembered. She tussled with me, trying to wrestle me to the ground. My, she had grown strong. I let her win the tussle and sat with her, trying to tell her that I would come back, but that I might be some time. She had no sense of time, it was only ever now, but she let me go away again after I told her I had to hunt. She approved of that.

When I walked back out to Jychanumun, he was standing waiting for me.

"I cannot think of a better solution," he said.

I didn't need to say anything. I walked to him; he put his arm around my waist, opened his wings and took me to the sky once again.

It was early evening, and we travelled so quickly above the land that I wondered why humans had not been made with wings. In no time the domes of light high on the plateau shimmered like a guiding beacon. As soon as our feet touched the ground, Jychanumun and I joined Orion's team at their table and told them our idea.

At first they seemed surprised at my willingness to help. I don't know why; to me it was obvious. I was already involved, whether I liked it or not. And it was not just me; the implications extended to my family, my friends and everything that I loved on this planet, as well as these kutu whom I'd quickly grown fond of.

"So," I concluded, "We will get Shursa here."

"Spoken like a true warrior," Stanze said approvingly.

"If you and Jychanumun are right, this may be our only chance to reinstate Una and rectify matters," Orion added.

"But if we are wrong, terrible things could happen," I said.

"And terrible things will happen if we do not try," Orion replied. "Our attempts will not make matters worse."

"Then you must work swiftly and act before the black-winged ones get to Shursa," I said, surprised at my own forthrightness.

They all agreed.

"I will offer myself to him, to Shursa."

Jychanumun went to object, but I threw him a look that Soul would have been proud of.

"I must make a link to Shursa." I insisted. "But I'll need to see him or speak to him in order to connect at such a great distance. Can you set up your communication device so that I can speak to him – but not with an image? I don't want him to see that I know your language. Make it sound as if my words are running through one of your word translators."

"The human language hasn't developed enough to run through a translator," Chia remarked.

"Shursa doesn't know that," Orion stepped in. "Our reports have only shown that humans have developed language."

"No, Shursa doesn't know," Chia smiled. "We may get away with it. I'll have to do a few adjustments."

Jychanumun had already set up their port. His dislike for Shursa was obvious. I didn't like the sensation of any being disliking another with such intensity. I desperately hoped that if I linked to Shursa I would find something hopeful and positive in him to build on.

Once Chia had finished adjusting their port, I confirmed that I was ready and stood in front of it, waiting.

Suddenly Shursa's face popped up, staring at me. I looked at Jychanumun and he assured me that the image was only one way:

Shursa could not see me. But I found this off-putting, so Chia stilled the image so that I could only hear Shursa's voice.

"Shursa?" I said, trying not to let my voice waver with the nerves I was suppressing.

"Who's this?" he replied. "Address me properly and make sure you give your introduction formally next time."

"Shursa, it is me, the female you've been looking for," I stated. Shursa didn't reply.

I felt a vague inkling of his utter astonishment.

I started talking. I just had to talk about anything – I was prolonging time. I chattered on, telling him, in an over-simplified manner, what Factor X was and why they would never be able to harvest it. It seemed as though he had heard this before, and I sensed that he thought I was mistaken.

I changed my tactic slightly and lied by suggesting that perhaps I could filter the energy for them. Yes, I felt he wanted that.

Good, I thought, I can sense him pushing out his own senses. I was starting to feel Shursa strongly now, not just hear him. Just a little bit more then perhaps I could read him.

"I have been told that you want to see me," I said. "How would you like me to present myself? I have never met my creator; you must be a great and noble being." I was thinking of Soul, and of how she had so charmingly spoken to Huru. It seemed to be working; Shursa was flattered by my words and was opening himself up. Yes, I definitely could see him, even though the screen before me was blank.

I then opened my true vision as wide as I could and pointed it towards my mind-image of Shursa. I could see, feel and sense him. What I saw filled me with such horror that I almost faltered. I concentrated on finding the traits that drove him. It was not easy. This one had a twisted mind. And then I found it - Shursa

425

wanted power, control and adoration more than anything, and was prepared to go to any lengths to get it.

"I have a humble suggestion, great one," I stammered. He interpreted my stammering for awe.

"I am told you are to have a great ritual. If you held it here on Earth, I will give you Factor X. It runs through me, but only here on Earth. I can't do it when I'm not here. If you were to come to this place, I could make you even stronger, even greater, with more power – so much that it would be a great spectacle for everyone to see how great you are. I can make you move through time, allow you to know everything, and so much more. But it is too much for me. I do not understand it all. You would, though, I am sure of it."

There was a pause. Had I been too elaborate? I hoped the translator was making my words sound human enough.

"And why would you do those things for me?" he asked. His suspicion was roused.

I scanned quickly. This one knew only selfishness. I had to address him in a different manner.

"Because you can do much for me," I replied. "I would like a big building to live in that is always warm, with lots of foods that I do not have to pick myself, and a bed like they have here that is very soft, and to be able fly when I want to," I replied, trying to sound greedy, yet simple. "And lots of Punni berries all the time, and Kathi berries; they're my favourite. If you're in charge, you can do those things, cant you?"

I sensed he was amused. Yes, he accepted the personality I was showing him.

"Or," I added as an afterthought, "I could start now and show your workers here what I can do. I am feeling much better already. I do not have to wait unless you ask me to."

"No, wait," Shursa said, a little too quickly.

Then I knew I had him; he was convinced.

"Wait and I will give you anything you want," Shursa hurriedly added.

"Really?" I said, trying to sound pleased, "Anything?"

"Oh yes, anything," he answered, talking to me as if I was a child. "But you must wait for me. Do you understand that? Wait for me."

"Yes," I said, "Wait. Will you be long?"

"Oh no, not long," he replied. "I'll be there in eighteen days. Can you count to eighteen?"

"One, two three, four, five . . ." I said slowly. In any other circumstance, it would have been embarrassing.

"Very good," he drawled. "Do you know Orion?"

"The red-haired one?" I asked,

"Yes," Shursa replied. "Can you go and get him for me? Get Orion."

Orion was standing by me. I touched his arm, indicating that he should be silent for a moment longer. I stood up, making a point to be noisy, and muttered 'Ri-on' under my breath, but loud enough for Shursa to think I was looking for him, while Chia removed the translator from the port. He nodded to Orion once he had finished.

"I'm here," Orion said into the communicator. "Now you have proof that we have the female. It took a short while to repair her, but she is now ready to go to Eden. As per your last request, I'll be ready to depart for Eden before the close of the day, and the 7A can drop off Chia at the substation on route."

I quickly looked at Orion, and touched his arm in order to speak directly to his mind again. *Give him conditions; do not be too willing*, I silently, and hurriedly, told him.

"But," Orion quickly added. I could see his thoughts racing, "in honour of our great efforts, I have a request: twenty clicks of leave for me and my team once this is complete."

I held my hands up, indicating that he should show more self-interest.

"Twenty clicks for my team, one hundred for me," he added. "And assurances that I can select my role on Eden once we return, and the opportunity for me to play regularly in the great arena whenever I wish."

I nodded to Orion. Good, that was enough.

Shursa laughed.

"So, you're starting to show your true colours, Orion," Shursa replied, smiling. "I like that. Very well, I understand a kutu of your nature, even if you do push my patience. However, my wishes have changed. It seems as though I will have the greatest anointment of any Supreme ever. I will bring my entourage to Earth for my ceremony and take on Factor X for myself. Then you will see my true colours and my power, and witness my forward thinking."

"Of course," Orion smiled through gritted teeth. "Would you like me to prepare a ceremonial area?"

"Yes," Shursa replied. "Make it the greatest sight on the planet, the greatest in all the universes, and you will be duly rewarded."

"I will hold you to that," Orion replied. "For this I will need to use the 7A's facilities. Chia's departure will be delayed."

Shursa hesitated and frowned, clearly unhappy with the suggestion.

"Oh, very well, I suppose a few days will make no difference."

"How long do I have?"

"As I said to the girl, it should be eighteen days," he decided. "But I think I will bring the ceremony forward to twelve days. There will not be as much feasting, but it will be worth it." He laughed again, seemingly ecstatic with himself. "Twelve days, Orion. And you will be one of the first to witness the beginning of our enlightenment. I will be a god. And you, you can take the seat to my right at council. You will be my chosen one; we will build a new home-world. How do you feel about that? Is that not a great reward indeed?"

"I am truly honoured," Orion replied, though it obviously pained him to say the words.

"Indeed you are. I must go. I have many preparations, and so do you. Keep the female safe. I do not want anything happening to her. I'll be there twelve days from now."

He cut the transmission.

I looked at Jychanumun. *Can Shursa hear us now if we speak?* I asked with my mind.

"No," he replied aloud.

"I feel dirty," Orion shuddered.

But even before Orion had spoken, I had got up, run out of the dome and thrown up the contents of my stomach.

I rinsed my mouth with water, splashing some on my face, composed myself, and then went back into the dome to face the others.

"I did connect to Shursa," I told them. "He does not believe that Factor X cannot be harvested. He intends to destroy you all, with the exception of Orion, whom he wants for himself, and Jychanumun, whom he intends to hand over to the black-winged ones, having already made an arrangement with them. He has some particularly sinister thoughts about Chia, and wants to inflict as much pain on him as possible. He also intends on destroying all humans once he has what he wants, lest another like me happens to come about who might try to take Factor X from him."

As I spoke, the things I had sensed in Shursa turned my stomach again. He was not balanced, and his intentions stemmed from wrongness, a terrible distortion in his spirit. I had omitted telling Orion's team about the thoughts I had picked up, detailing exactly how he was going to maim and cause pain to these kutu. I stood up, ran outside, and retched violently again.

TWENTY-FIVE

I had seen inside Shursa's mind, and what I'd seen had made me sick. Nevertheless, I gathered myself together and walked back to join the kutu, feeling rather humiliated by my body's weakness.

"Sorry," I said. "I do not know if our ideas will be enough to stop what Shursa has started."

"We must try," Orion insisted. "We will begin preparations." He handed me a clean gown – it seemed exactly my size. "The 7A has a materializer," he smiled. "It makes things very quickly. Come, we all have much work to do."

We had twelve days: twelve days before Shursa arrived here on Earth. Twelve days to make a ceremonial area fitting for one as pompous and self-regarding as Shursa. And twelve days to re-connect Una's consciousness to his body. Twelve days sounded like a long enough time, but once we got started, I knew it would go too quickly.

I had many concerns about our plan: there was too much we were assuming and too much that counted on those assumptions.

Una, as the resigning Supreme, would need to be present at the ceremony. Shursa and his entourage would arrive and need to be at least partially re-tuned to flesh. The ceremony would have to be contained in an area no greater than eight hundred metres in diameter; the maximum that the 7A could project its field. Shursa could not suspect anything. Our plan was even based on the assumption that they would not just arrive and contain us first. So many things could go wrong.

The objective was to unite Una with his lost mind, contain Shursa and his entourage using the 7A, and then reinstate Una as Supreme. Through Nirrious' communications, we hoped that some Anumi might help. But with events changing rapidly, we knew we could not rely on them.

And I was the bait.

Chia was working with Kraniel to modify the 7A. While Kraniel adjusted the facilities, Chia connected to the craft, talking to it like an old friend. The kutu knew that the 7A was both alive and powerful, as, apparently, all their piloted ships were, but they had not realised just how strong the bond was between Chia and his craft. I had seen it immediately. Now they were utilizing it. I felt as though I was betraying the ship, but they reassured me that I just didn't understand their bio-mechanics. I still wasn't convinced.

Chia had selected a place for Shursa's ceremony. At its centre, they had excavated an area exactly the right size to eventually bury and conceal the 7A. Then they'd returned to the plateau with a problem.

"If we are using the 7A's resources for a containment field, how are we going to adorn the ceremony area?" Chia asked.

That had stumped them all for a moment. If Shursa arrived and the area wasn't the extraordinary spectacle that he wished for, he'd want to know why not, and also want to know where

432

the 7A was. Of course he would be suspicious; even I would be suspicious in such circumstances. We had to make the area a fitting enough spectacle to lure him down and suspect nothing.

They started talking of possible ways to convert energy for illumination, but it sounded like a lot of effort for very little effect.

"Why not just use what is already here?" I asked. I was thinking of the effectiveness of people all wearing the same red outfits in Hollow. To me the solution was obvious. "If Shursa wants pomp and adoration from the multitudes, we can ask people to stand around the outside of the ceremony area. If that materializer can make enough clothes, then dress them all in one colour with Shursa's stamp marked on their clothes. I'll wear the same."

"And with people arranged around the outside, there'd be natural barriers for the containment area, ensuring that kutu were not beyond that point," Orion nodded in agreement.

"And in the centre, use flowers – thousands of them – all arranged in Shursa's colours and marks," I continued. "And add trees made into archways, yet still growing, to make tree-lined pathways. And right in the middle should be stones, huge ones, arranged in the pattern of his mark. Is that possible?"

Chia just looked at me with his head tilted back. "You do not demand much, do you?" he said, and then laughed. "But it is a very good idea. I will arrange it."

There was so much to do that twelve days seemed as if it could never be enough. There was little unnecessary talk between the kutu, as none seemed to have time. Both the base and the ceremonial area heaved with activity. They worked so fast, sometimes it seemed there were hundreds of them, not the paltry few that they were.

The time went quickly – too quickly. The allotted twelve days had almost passed, and we were still barely finishing the final

433

arrangements, when Orion received news that Shursa and his party would be arriving just before sunrise the following day. We had less than half a day to go, and he was arriving half a day earlier than expected. Orion had assumed that the ceremony would be in the evening, as was apparently customary, but this ceremony would be at sunrise. This caused a few problems.

The kutu had been taking turns to call humans to the prepared area. They had started with those living furthest away, but who were within walking distance, and the people had already begun arriving in droves. The closest humans were going to be called at first light, but now they all had to be in position before first light. All efforts were put into either calling them or gathering them in the pods, and there was nothing more I could do to help.

I stood at a distance, overlooking the hastily prepared ceremony area. I had watched the kutu work with such speed that my eyes could barely keep up with them.

From appearances alone, I would not have guessed that underneath the mass of colour and stone that made up the ceremony area, now lay the 7A. Chia had only buried it the previous day, hiding it with earth so that it did not rouse suspicions and yet could project a containment field at an allotted time during the ceremony. I could feel its presence, a fact that concerned me, but the others had said that the pull of the Earth drowned out their own sensing of it. I sent it my soothing thoughts, and it felt me.

People lined up, standing on the upper steps around the large circular clearing. There were already thousands of them, all dressed in deep yellow tunics with Shursa's emblem glistening on their chests. The kutu had commanded them to stand still, and they did, so that the only movement came from the occasional flutter of hair in the breeze. Stanze had organized Nirrious and Kraniel at points around the circumference to direct the humans. As the humans arrived, the kutu put them into the trance-like state, gave them their yellow robes, and then instructed them where to stand. I was not keen that my fellow humans had been manipulated in this way, but I had to keep focussed: they would come to no harm from their stupor, and what we were doing would hopefully save their existence. Nevertheless, I had requested that any human who might find standing for long periods difficult be omitted. The kutu had obliged.

Orion had made the decision not to include any of my family or friends. *You cannot be distracted*, he had pointed out. I understood. Selfishly, I was glad, but a part of me did want them here. Here the people would witness their makers, even if they were in a trance-like state. Maybe something inside them would remember. Perhaps, in the future, others would ask questions about their origins, and perhaps someone, somewhere, would remember and be able to answer them.

The rows of yellow-clad people were only the beginning of the spectacle, and I marvelled at Chia's interpretation of my idea. The floor of the arena was a gloriously colourful mass of flowers, and every flower had been meticulously arranged by hue and height, woven in intricate three-dimensional symbols of kutu importance. Right at the centre was a raised podium constructed from huge slabs of stone, with further stones all around it as if guarding the centrepiece. On the central podium were three heavy wooden stools, which Nirrious had carved and adorned.

The lower steps of the arena were prepared for Shursa's entourage. The closer they were to their new Supreme, the more important they would be deemed to be. Chia had covered the steps in thick grasses, and somehow had pressed the greenery down in various directions, making further complex patterns. It truly was amazing.

We can do beautiful things when we wish, I heard in my head.

It was Jychanumun. He had silently landed behind me.

435

Indeed, I replied, without turning around. *Such beauty is worth seeing, even if for a few moments in time.*

We are almost finished. We have one last thing to do, and then we must rest, especially you.

Yes, it is time. I sense that Una's consciousness is present today. I turned around and looked at him.

"If this does not work; if we fail . . ." I began speaking aloud. I was scared.

"Hush," he said. "We will not fail."

I wanted to tell him I was sorry, but I didn't know what I was sorry about. He put his arm around my waist and took me back, through the air, back to the plateau.

The base still looked the same, even with the 7A gone. Now, instead of the large ship, an identical visual interpretation of the craft shimmered in its place. I could only tell that it was not the 7A with my true vision; all my other senses told me that it was.

Orion and Chia were already on the plateau. They'd arrived just before Jychanumun and me, and now stood waiting for us. I knew that Jychanumun could do the next, vital, thing without Orion and Chia, but Orion could do it as well, and so Jychanumun insisted that he bind me, to keep me safe. I had agreed. They'd talked about the mind-probe with trepidation, which made me even more anxious. We were all apprehensive. We had wanted to start the mind probe sooner, but Una's appearances on the plateau had become more sporadic and vague. I was relieved that I could sense him at all; I had worried that he might not appear before the ceremony.

"We're ready to create the mind-link," Orion said as we joined him. "Shursa has reached the substation. He'll take a short break while he gathers the rest of his entourage and will leave shortly. It is a small window of opportunity."

He looked at me. "Do you sense Una?" he asked.

"I do," I said, opening up my true vision and tracing my senses around the plateau.

Una stood silent and white, transparent, like a shadow made of light.

I walked over and stood in the middle of where I perceived him. I felt a ripple pass through me. Yes, this was the right spot. I sat down, right where I sensed he stood, and Jychanumun, Orion and Chia followed, sitting around me to form a triangle with the hope that their positions would prevent Una from moving.

"Does he sense you?" Orion asked.

"No," I replied. "He is too weak."

Chia took a fine cord from around his neck, grasped Orion's hand and bound their wrists together. "So I cannot let go, no matter what," he smiled. "Do not worry, I will keep you rooted."

Jychanumun flicked a knife from an invisible closure in his shin moulding and cut off a length of his hair. He caught my hand and bound our wrists together. "And I will stop you from being rooted," he said.

The thought of it made my stomach turn upside down.

"I have not done a probe before," Orion stated, matter-of-factly, "and so I apologise in advance if this is a rocky ride."

I nodded and watched as he clasped his hands and bowed his head. His body began shimmering. The shimmering increased until he was a bright light, and then the light vanished and he was gone. Only a vague red haze lingered, a silhouette of where his body had just been.

Suddenly Chia screamed and thrashed his bound arm, as if trying to rid himself of the red haze attached to his wrist, but the red moved with him. I went to jump up, but Jychanumun held me back. Then Chia calmed and slumped forward, making painful whimpering noises.

Are you ready? Jychanumun asked with his mind.

I nodded, resolute but apprehensive.

He gripped my hand tightly and I emptied my mind. *Follow me,* he said, *And do not let go under any circumstances.*

Then something happened, and I knew pain unlike anything my body had ever made, pain that ripped through my head as if my thoughts were being extracted from me, pain as though every sense in my body was fighting with me. In agony, I tried to pull back.

Don't let go! I heard. It was Jychanumun; his voice surrounded me like a balm. *It's all right, I have you. I have your mind. I'll keep it safe. I'm keeping you connected to your body now. You're safe.*

I felt him tugging me forward, and the pain stopped. I felt my mind moving away from my body, but this was nothing like the soothing walk through *his* energy. My thoughts felt disjointed and fragmented, as if they had been split into a thousand pieces. I could hear Jychanumun talking. Slowly his words took form.

Orion is creating a path to the substation. We are following that path before it closes. Not far now, we are close, Jychanumun said.

I knew he was talking in order to make me focus.

I cannot see anything, I replied.

It doesn't matter; I can see, Jychanumun said. *Use your senses to locate Una's body. We're close to the substation. Tell us where we need to go.*

I thought of Una and how he had felt when I had brushed his essence, and how he still felt around the flesh that I'd left behind. I kept my senses touching my body, touching his essence, and stretched them far beyond my mind, pushing outwards through the empty space between Earth and the kutus' far-away home. I wove strands of myself through the darkness, searching, seeking the one thing that would feel the same to my senses, trying to locate a hint of the essence that Una's body still might contain. Then I sensed it. I had it. I could feel something else, far in the distance. It was Una.

I have him!

Directions? Jychanumun asked. *We need directions. We cannot sense as you do.*

I made myself aware of where Jychanumun was holding my mind and began directing, pushing forward to where my senses were pulling me.

I felt my mind move forward, allowing Jychanumun to lead as I gave him further directions. All the time we were drawing closer to Una and I felt his presence grow stronger.

Stop! I suddenly called. *He is here.*

We stopped immediately. I sensed the presence of both Orion and Jychanumun, and I also sensed Una. I knew there might be others around him, but I could not sense any too close by. Good, I thought, this was how we had hoped it would be.

I was now in control, as I was the only creature who could take on the essence of another. I had to do this on my own. I knew I would not have much time, because Orion could not hold his mind open for long, so I moved forward a fraction, sensed Una's essence, and threw my mind into his body.

As soon as my thoughts entered Una's body, I felt him twitching. I soothed his nerves and made him still. His mind was not completely empty - in fact his thoughts were all there, just jumbled, going round and round in an infinite loop. I settled into his body, allowing myself to become him.

Are you ready? I asked Jychanumun, or I think I did. I was feeling as if I was in so many different places at once.

Yes, I heard him reply, *I'm with Orion. He is ready.*

I studied the looping of Una's mind, and then caught the loop and made it still. With all my might, I then imprinted the exact position of where my body was, tracing back the location, the images, and the sensations. I imprinted the thoughts as if Una had made them himself. All Una would know was that this was where his consciousness was, where he should go to get it, and that there was already an opening made for him to travel through to get there.

It was done.

Go! I cried out to Jychanumun in my mind.

I let go of the loop in Una's mind and it rapidly started uncoiling; Una knew where he was. He was no longer lost. I felt him surging forward.

I had to hurry. I must move my body from that place, sitting on the earth, touching Una's consciousness; if I didn't we could be forever entwined.

Go! I shouted out again.

Then Jychanumun was pulling me with all his might. We were rushing back to where he had me routed, following Orion as he paved the way. We had to return to our bodies before Una located his consciousness and reached the same place. I too was sitting where Una's consciousness waited; the consequences for me would be dire if I did not move my body.

I knew Jychanumun was pulling with a speed and force that touched the limits of his endurance; it was so fast that I sensed nothing, and felt only a numb dizziness. Then I felt pain, and knew we were next to our bodies. I used every memory of Jychanumun's and slammed my mind back into my flesh. But, I was too disorientated; my body felt like stone, and I couldn't move it.

Move, I thought. *I must move.* But I could not.

Suddenly I felt myself thrown forward. The abrupt force made me regain my senses and I found myself ungraciously sprawled across Chia, with Jychanumun squashing the air from my lungs. Jychanumun must have lunged forward and pushed me from the place where I was sitting. He stood up, pulling me to my feet and dragging me further from the area where we had been.

Chia stayed where he was, and Orion was still only a shimmering mass.

I sat, too numb to move, just staring at Orion and Chia. Jychanumun bent down so that his face was close to mine. He looked very concerned.

Are you there? he asked silently with his mind.

I blinked and shook my head, as if to say no.

That's not funny, Jychanumun said sternly, but he smiled too.

"Yes, I'm all here," I said aloud, "but why have they not returned?" I was alarmed that Orion still shimmered without his body. I think my words came out quite muddled.

"Orion goes again to imprint a message with Una while the way is still open. If we have succeeded, Una must know that he must pretend that nothing has changed until tomorrow," Jychanumun replied as he unbound our wrists. "Una is still only one kutu. He cannot take on Shursa, his followers, and a new council on his own."

"I think we have succeeded," I said as I studied the area I'd just been sitting in. "I did sense Una detecting his mind, and his presence is no longer here. But," I hesitated, "it could just be that we have dislodged him to another place."

"Would you sense him if he had?" Jychanumun asked.

"If I had time, yes," I replied. "If I had time I could trace the universe for him. But we do not have time, do we?"

"No, but I think we may have succeeded," Jychanumun smiled. "Come, sit with me. I do not have to ask what you think of kutu mind travel; the look of disgust is on your face."

"It's not for me," I said as I sat down next to him.

He pulled me to lean against him to keep me warm. It made me sleepy, but we sat and waited edgily for Orion's return.

I felt great relief when Orion began solidifying. Chia's face smoothed from the tightened façade of discomfort he'd been wearing and he relaxed, opening his eyes.

"Orion," Chia called to the returned kutu, who slumped forward, still attached to his wrist.

Orion looked up and nodded. "I've done all I can," he said, as he slowly straightened, untying himself from Chia. "I can only hope that Una heard me."

"Your first leading of a probe and we live to tell the tale," Chia smiled wearily. It was clear that he was exhausted.

Orion put a hand on the back of Chia's neck and started giving him some of his energy.

"No," Chia replied, pulling away. "You are too weak."

"Come," Jychanumun said. "We must all rest before tomorrow unfolds."

I collapsed, worn out, onto one of their recliners, and slept straight away.

It seemed as if I had only rested for a blink of an eye when Jychanumun roused me. It was still dark outside and I groaned as I climbed down from the recliner. My body felt fine, but my mind felt quite sore. Unfortunately, none of the flesh-healers they used for human mending could work on my mind.

Jychanumun handed me cup of bitter-smelling liquid. I took a sip and wrinkled my nose in disgust, took another sip, and decided I rather liked it.

"Coffee," he explained.

A loud yellow tunic – so bright that made my eyes hurt – was draped across the end of my sleeping place. I slipped it on. The large mark of Shursa splayed across my chest made me feel like an owned object, but I didn't have time to worry about it. The others were ready, and stood dressed in a glorious array of garments that made them shimmer with even more beauty, and made me feel like the afterthought. Without talking, we all walked out into the open and silently took to the dark sky.

Held by Jychanumun and soaring swiftly through the air, I

saw Shursa's ceremonial area from a long way off. The kutu had embedded light-emitting crystals within the arena, illuminating it like a bright marker. It looked even more spectacular now it was finished.

We landed on the lower steps, straight ahead of the raised podium. Directly behind me was the only space left among the humans. I walked up to the top steps and stood in the gap between two other women.

We are here; this is it, I thought. *Our plans are no longer distant and detached arrangements. It is going to happen now.* My heart beat heavily in my chest and I felt sick. I was nervous. I'd never felt this nervous about anything before.

Do not fret, Jychanumun told me with his mind, as he too took his place further down. *You have done your part, now Una will do his and we kutu will do ours. All you need to do is stand there for a while and tell me what you sense.*

Jychanumun was right, I had done my part. Convincing Shursa to come here and reuniting Una with his lost consciousness was my part. But still I felt nervous. What if Una hadn't fully grasped his mind co-ordination? What if the 7A's containment field did not work? What if? What if? The questions raced through my mind.

In no time, the pre-dawn sky became filled with a mass of tiny dots, making my stomach churn with anxiety. The dots grew larger, taking form as huge ships, and the ships came closer until I could pick out the intricate details in their shimmering surfaces. Then the ships stopped, remaining suspended over us. The undersides of the crafts opened up, flooding the area with light, and then from within the light myriads of winged kutu began descending.

Without a word, the kutu gracefully descended into the arena, landing and taking positions on the upper steps, below the humans. There were hundreds, no thousands, of them, descending to stand side-by-side on each step, and then the next step, and the next. If my senses hadn't been so alert for trouble, I would have been able to marvel at the radiant beauty of each and every one of these creatures.

As the kutu continued descending, taking their places, I thought they would never fit into the arena, but Stanze's calculations had been perfect; when it seemed as if no more could be accommodated, they stopped arriving.

Thousands of kutu now stood with their chins high and wings upright, turned to a point surrounding the vacant podium. All was silent.

The beams of lights dimmed as one by one, the ships closed their hatches. Only one light was left, shining directly over the central podium. A small formation of around thirty kutu emerged from within the light, hovering in a circle. Two kutu seemed to be supporting another between them. My heart jumped; my senses told me it was Una, but he didn't look in control of himself.

It is Una, I silently told Jychanumun. *But I cannot tell his mind state.*

Keep observing, but do NOT let anyone sense it, Jychanumun instructed.

I wanted to reach out to Una with my senses, to ensure that his consciousness and body were reunited. But I dared not, just in case another might sense me or that I might startle Una. I could only hope that his appearance meant that he was good at pretending.

While the thirty kutu hovered above me, another slowly descended into the middle of their circle. This, I knew, was Shursa. I tried not to make it obvious I was looking at him, as all the other humans stood with their eyes lowered, but his gaudy brightness drew my eye. His yellow attire was cluttered with glittering stones, and he was adorned with too many jewels. Everything he wore was embossed with his yellow crest, as if to ensure that everyone knew exactly who he was, and the effect was discordant and garish.

The circle of kutu, with Shursa at its centre, very slowly descended. Shursa landed on the podium, and another landed to his right. Una was placed on the stool to his left, slumped down, with his chin touching his chest and his matted hair concealing his face. The remainder of the thirty kutu took positions around the podium, facing outwards as if guarding Shursa.

Once all the kutu had taken their positions and Shursa had taken a seat on the podium, the light dimmed, as the last ship closed its hatch, leaving the arena lit only by the crystals.

The kutu to Shursa's right then stood and began chanting a deep, melodious tune. The chanting lasted a long time, and occasionally he would stop and mumble something before continuing with his chanting. At other times, he would wave a ball that he held on a long chain, making smoke waft around the podium. The sun started to rise and morning lit the arena. Still he sang on.

Suddenly, the chanting kutu stopped, looked at Orion and said, "Present her ready for the new Supreme," and then began singing again.

My heart jumped; he was referring to me, asking Orion to bring me forth. This was not what I, or we, expected.

It's fine, Jychanumun silently told me, sensing my apprehension. *Go with Orion, nothing will happen.*

Orion looked around and beckoned to me. I walked down the steps and Orion caught my arm and led me towards the podium. The chanting one and Shursa looked down at me as I walked across the arena towards them, but Una did not move.

Show that you are submissive, Jychanumun quickly told me as I reached the podium.

I fell to my knees and lowered my head, enough to look submissive, while keeping my true vision alert so that I could sense what was happening.

The chanting one lifted up the smoking ball and looked around. "Do all kutu nominate Shursa the Knowing as their Supre-e-eme," he sung loudly and melodically, drawing out some of the words while his pitch went from high to low. "To guide and to rule for the good of all? Say yes or no-o-o."

Shut your ears! Jychanumun commanded.

I didn't think twice, and imagined that my ears were like rocks.

"YES!" came a loud roar from all around.

It seemed as though the kutu had all shouted as loudly as they could. If Jychanumun hadn't warned me, the sound would surely have deafened me.

It's all right now, Jychanumun said soothingly, although I could feel his tension.

Above me, Shursa was looking smug. The chanting one beside him was still singing and muttering, nodding satisfactorily as if pleased by the response. He moved to stand behind Shursa.

"Do you, Shursa the Knowing, Shursa the Thinker, Shursa the Mighty, accept their wo-o-ords?" He sang.

"Yes," Shursa stated boldly, unable to suppress a wide smile.

I managed to glance up a little while still keeping my position. Una was still slumped on the stool beside Shursa. Shouldn't he have done something by now? I was worried. Surely he would not be permitting this charade to go this far if he could do something to stop it. I tried quelling my anxieties, but they were growing with every passing moment. And feeling so vulnerable, on my knees in the middle of the arena, was not helping my anxiety at all.

"Do we of the council," the chanting one sang louder again,

elongating the words, "Do we of the council, the wise kutu council, nominate Shursa the Knowing, Shursa the Thinker, Shursa the Mighty, as Supre-e-eme?" As he sang, he walked around the elevated podium, around Shursa and Una, wafting his smoke-filled globe. He stopped, looking down towards one of the guarding kutu who stood at the bottom of the podium.

"Do we, do you?" he sang.

The kutu standing on the ground directly in front of me turned around and looked at the chanting one. "Yes," he declared loudly, lowering himself onto one knee.

So, I deliberated, the ones around the podium, whom I had thought were guards, were actually the council members, even though they did look more like guards, with their strange-looking weapons hanging from their hips and behind their backs.

Still Una did nothing.

Jychanumun? I pushed out desperately with my mind.

Patience he quickly responded. *It's not time yet.*

I suppressed my fretting, but it was still there.

The chanting one was still singing. He had moved a little so that he was now standing above the next councillor, and he sang the same words as before. "Yes," that one also replied, again lowering himself to one knee.

One by one, the chanting kutu addressed the kutu council standing around the podium. They all in turn said yes. The chanting one walked around the podium several times, swinging the smoke so that it went over the kneeling council. Some of the smoke wafted over me, making me feel woozy. I battled against the sensation, trying to concentrate on the activities, and thankfully the giddiness passed as the smoke dispersed.

The chanting one had moved to stand behind Shursa again. "Do you, Shursa the Knowing, Shursa the Thinker, Shursa the Mighty, accept their wo-o-ords?" he sang.

"Yes," Shursa loudly declared. The smile hadn't left his face. I didn't like his expression; it made me think of what I had seen in Shursa. I closed off the thoughts before my stomach heaved.

The chanting one took a step to one side, so that he now stood behind Una.

"Do you, Una," he sang, raising his voice again, "Shaa-kutu Una, relinquish, surrender, renounce and resign all rights of supremacy to Shursa the Knowing, Shursa the Thinker, Shursa the Mi-igh-ty?" He wafted the smoke over Una's head, until the Supreme sat shrouded in mist and I could barely make out his form.

This was the moment. I could feel it through Jychanumun. If Una were going to do something, if anything was going to happen, it would have to be now.

Una didn't move, or say a word. Then, within the dispersing smoke, I saw him slowly lift his head. He straightened himself, and looked directly at Shursa. I could see his eyes flashing as his hair fell back from his face.

"No," Una stated.

For a moment, none of the kutu around the podium knew what to do.

Shursa refused to look at Una and kept his eyes fixed firmly ahead, sitting proudly on his stool and smiling, but I sensed him tense. "You do, Una," he muttered under his breath, trying to keep smiling. "Remember, you do!"

Slowly, Shursa turned to look at Una. As soon as he saw him, he knew that Una was no longer the mindless one.

"No, Shursa, I do not!" Una repeated even louder. He pushed himself upright and stood, allowing his flaccid wings to rise. His eyes flashed and a brilliant white energy flooded from him, illuminating the area.

"I am Supreme and I say NO!" Una bellowed.

TWENTY-SIX

In my heart, I felt like cheering.

Una, the kutu Supreme, had stood tall, proud and powerful, defending his Supremacy. His radiating light was bright and strong, and I felt its balance. He was beautiful inside and out, full of wisdom and truth. He was whole again and I could see why he was their Supreme.

"You cannot go against the council," Shursa hissed, quickly gathering himself. He looked towards the now silent chanting one.

"Seize Una," Shursa ordered. "He goes against the council and all kutu. None may do that."

The chanting one went to grasp Una, but Una pushed him away with a flick of his hand, without so much as touching him, sending him flying off the podium and sprawling amidst the flowers below. Then all the council from around the podium leapt up to restrain Una. As they launched towards him, he threw them aside with flashes of white energy from his fingers. One by one the councillors landed, picked themselves up and hurled themselves at Una again. Sparks flew, but they kept coming back. Una made it look easy, but I could see that with each rebuff his energy declined; he could not continuously fight off the attacks of so many. I didn't know what to do. I was right in the middle of it.

Una cannot take them all on, I silently called out to Jychanumun.

I noticed Jychanumun nod to Stanze. Stanze looked to one side and made a discreet signal.

"You will *not* restrain Una," I heard from amongst the kutu lined up behind me.

Run back here, now, Jychanumun shouted silently to me. *We must initiate the containment field. NOW!*

I jumped up, pivoted on my heel and started running from the arena. As I ran, a huge kutu wearing a golden head covering stepped forward from the masses and down to the arena floor.

"Do not touch the Supreme!" he boomed. It was Stanze.

Another stepped forward, one even taller, wearing a similar golden head covering. "We of the Anumi say release Una, he is the true Supreme," he bellowed.

It was the cue the kutu had been waiting for. As soon as the massive kutu had spoken, others stepped forward, then more, all similarly huge like Stanze and adorned with elaborate golden headdresses.

It's the Anumi, I heard Jychanumun call with his mind as I reached the edge of the arena. *It's the cue to activate the shield. Get out. Now!*

I leapt the last section from the arena and Jychanumun launched forward and grabbed me, pushing me up to the higher steps with the humans. He turned back, lunging forward to get back into the enclosure. However, at that moment a wall of light rose up from the ground and formed a dome, trapping all the kutu inside, and Jychanumun was stuck on the outside with me and the other humans.

Jychanumun thumped the barrier in frustration. His fist bounced off the force field, creating a small wave of light. "No!" he shouted.

He was too late; Jychanumun couldn't get in to help. There was nothing he or I could do.

From our excluded position, we watched as the Anumi stormed into the councillors' fracas. The councillors saw their approach and started aiming their attacks towards them, as well as the Supreme, and Shursa joined in, hurling his energy at all who opposed him. I knew little of the Anumi; apart from they were of Orion's kind, ones who had chosen to devote their energy to the art of protection. Their art made them strong and agile, and now I saw them in action I was relieved that Shursa had not poisoned their minds.

The council fought hard, throwing their might in long jagged shards at the approaching Anumi. The Anumi, for their part, used the mouldings on their forearms to deflect the barrage of attacks, redirecting the energy back to the councillors and knocking them off their feet. Occasionally, whenever there were many councillors aiming at one Anumi, shards of energy might get through, flinging the Anumi back to hit the barrier hard, causing deep ripples across the force field. But such attacks were what the Anumi were trained for, and Stanze and his companions led the huge kutus forward, taking blow after blow from the councillors and from Shursa, only to re-gather and keep advancing.

With some stealthy manoeuvring, the Anumi began separating the councillors, encircling them with small groups of warriors so that they could limit the damage. The attacking shafts of energy gradually lessened as one-by-one the council were contained.

Just when it seemed that the Anumi were gaining control, however, other kutu from the middle steps of the arena began surging forward from the masses, leaping upon the Anumi, trying to hold them back and release the captive councillors.

Orion and his team leapt forward to help the Anumi, beating off their fellow kutu with all their force, and then others joined in to help them. Some kutu remained standing around the outside; they appeared either too stunned to do anything, or not sure what they were fighting about, or who to fight with.

As more and more kutu surged forward to take sides and join the battle, the arena became a blurred mass of brutal activity. Their strength flashed and pounded within the containment area, making the containment walls a constant heaving mass.

Kutu were hurled in all directions, and long spears of light missed their targets to shatter against the 7A's force field, distorting its energy, making it impossible to see through. Occasionally a kutu landed against the barrier and I could see his distorted face or twisted limbs as he slid down and disappeared from sight.

I could feel the 7A struggling to keep the containment shield together, and I knew I could do something to help. As if the 7A was an animal, I reached my mind forward and gave it courage, strength, and perseverance. The 7A took my strength, almost grateful for the understanding, and as the warring raged inside its barriers it held true.

Slowly, the ripples in the containment shield declined, leaving just small pools of violence that occasionally disturbed the smoothness, as if a large stone had been thrown into water. The flares of light were dying down, and between the ripples and the flashes I could see what was happening inside.

Some kutu were backing off, as if retreating, standing at the edge of the force field, held back by lines of Anumi. I could make out other groups of Anumi in the centre, each surrounding a councillor who stood defeated. Only a few councillors still fought, but the Anumi were closing in on them too. Stanze and Orion stood with several Anumi; they also had Shursa, and Shursa wasn't fighting anymore.

I put my face close against the shield, and I could see Una standing on the podium, directing the Anumi. Then, within seconds, most of the battle stopped, leaving one solitary councillor throwing shards of energy at the approaching Anumi. He would not be fighting for much longer, I thought.

They had succeeded. It seemed the plan had worked. My heart leapt with joy.

I turned to embrace Jychanumun. For that moment, the world was perfect.

They have done it, I said in delight. I hugged him. *Against all odds, we have won.*

Jychanumun was smiling, and I laughed for the sheer relief that our plan had worked.

Then I saw Jychanumun's smile drop.

I froze. Then I turned to the direction of his stare, towards the hovering ships. I sensed his horror, but nothing looked any different. As if in slow motion Jychanumun's gaze moved down to Chia, who also stood looking up, his face frozen into an expression of terror. He turned, catching Jychanumun's stare, and then sprang into action.

"They come! Prepare yourselves! The black-eyed ones from my visions come!" Chia shouted. He swiftly bent and from his boots pulled out two concealed long daggers. He held them up, his wings immediately growing in stature, frantically signalling to all around him.

Then suddenly, in the distance, outside the force field, I sensed kutu, thousands of them. They had been concealed! Now I felt the presence of so many kutu that they drowned my senses.

From behind the hovering ships black-winged ones came swarming down like locusts, darkening the skies more than any storm I had ever seen. They made noises, like hissing, and as they grew closer it sounded fearsome. Every one had black eyes that radiated darkness, casting shadows with their stare. I knew this was something terrible.

The black-winged kutu swooped down with speed, the first batch landing crammed together on the top of the 7A's shield while the others hovered above them. The ones on the force field moved closer together until they looked like a wall of black, before they bent down and raised their fists. Then, in one unified motion, they punched the shield and yelled.

I tried reaching to the 7A to give it strength to hold on, but it was too late. I felt the 7A's pain, and then nothing. The containment shield collapsed and the black-winged ones leapt down, immediately pouncing on the Anumi, Orion, Una and everyone else I knew who was fighting to rectify things.

Hide amongst the humans, Jychanumun instructed me fiercely.

I sensed fear in him. His fear gave me fear, and made me leap up several steps to stand with a different group of people. Then, as if out of nowhere, a swarm of black-winged ones descended on Jychanumun. I tried to connect to his mind.

Disappear, he thought frantically, and then he closed himself to me and I could no longer see or sense him.

The black-winged ones had engulfed him, forcing him into the centre of the activity. I searched frantically for him, and although only a few seconds passed, it felt like an eternity. He had closed himself to me.

Not knowing what else to do, I touched the arms of the females either side of me and absorbed their characteristics until I knew that I could not be recognised, and then I willed the Anumi to fight back.

The black-winged ones outnumbered the Anumi greatly, and appeared to know of deceptive fighting ways that were strange to the Anumi. From what had seemed, only moments before, to be a successful plan was now falling to dust.

I knew I could not physically enter the fighting; my flesh would be no match for even their weakest attack and my strength was equally inferior, but I could use my senses. I kept my eyes open and watched while I opened my true vision and pushed out, winding my awareness through the land, feeling the activity. Immediately I found one of the Anumi down and hurt, and I pushed strength into him while trying to dull his agony.

I could make out Orion, his red hair blazing against the black that surrounded him. The long sword that he had worn at his hip was now in his hand, blazing with scarlet as if it was on fire. He moved in short, graceful strides, bringing his sword down from above his head, slicing through his closest black-winged attacker, and then he pivoted, plunging the blade behind him into another who approached.

I saw Orion hesitate, as a kutu, not a black-winged one, walked towards him. Orion nodded to him in recognition, but the advancing figure frowned and lunged forward, striking Orion in his side with a bolt of energy.

Orion fell back, holding his side in pain and astonishment. He had thought his attacker had been a friend. I directed my senses towards Orion and started feeding him strength. Several of the black-winged ones were advancing, but before they could get to Orion they fell, knocked down by a blaze of violet light.

Then the violet blaze stopped: it was Chia. He pulled Orion to his feet. They nodded to one another and Orion began wielding his sword again, bringing down his vehement anger on everyone who approached.

Chia fought beside Orion, but, seeing that Orion was holding his own, he took several jumps forward to help another who had fallen. He moved at a ferocious speed, his arms flailing around him, striking every black-winged one he could see. At first I thought he was just using his hands, and then when he paused, ready to strike, I could see the short gleaming blades protruding from his clasped fists.

I struggled to sense Jychanumun again, but his thoughts were still shut from me. My senses jumped around, giving strength both to my kutu friends and to the Anumi. My heart wanted to help everyone I found fallen, but I had to be selective, aiding only those I was sure were not fighting for Shursa. There were so many getting hurt I could not keep up with the injuries being suffered.

Una was still on the podium, using his vantage point not just to fend off his own attackers, but also to assault those who were attacking others. His face was set in stern concentration as he sent energy flying rapidly from his fingers in all directions, taking down one black-winged one after another.

A very large group of hundreds – perhaps as much as a thousand – black-winged ones swarmed beyond Una. I knew that someone was in their midst, as their formation kept heaving back as if suddenly pelted with ferocious force from inside. I fed strength to whoever was inside that centre, hoping it might aid them in their seemingly impossible struggle.

A huge wave of energy rocketed past me, over my head, so strong that it made my skin tingle. Then another passed, this time to one side and lower, hitting the upper rows of humans. Hundreds of humans just fell down, motionless, ceased. I followed the path of the energy to a group of hundreds of black-winged ones, all surrounding someone, flying up and then swooping down, trying to subdue them. Another wave of energy emitted from their midst, shooting into the air and sending dozens of them hurling back. The energy wave had created a gap, inside which I could see Stanze, kneeling, with the long golden rod in his hands. The rod was resting against his face as he concentrated his aim, but it seemed as though he could not produce the energy waves quick enough, as before he could get another launched a group of the black winged ones landed on him and began beating him viciously with their fists. I fed him strength too. My heart went into my mouth, but my eyes were torn to another: Kraniel.

Kraniel was also injured, not far away from Stanze. Black-winged kutu held his hands and feet, pinning him spread-eagled to the ground, and another stood over him, stamping his foot into Kraniel's head repeatedly. With each pounding, a bright light flashed and Kraniel jerked, but he couldn't do anything as the others held him firm.

Although Stanze hadn't had enough of my strength, I focussed my attentions onto Kraniel, but then I sensed Nirrious was in even more need, and then Chia; he was down now too, and then another, and another. Dozens, no, hundreds were terribly injured and needed strength, and their numbers were increasing. I could not work fast enough anymore, and most of my friends were badly injured.

I struggled to look for the Anumi to help, but to my dismay I realised that most of them were already badly injured. The ground was littered with writhing bodies, and only a few Anumi were still standing and fighting; many of them were also terribly hurt.

I saw Stanze. He had somehow rid himself of the swarming black-winged ones and was striding forward, his eyes set on reaching a fallen comrade. Black-winged ones dragged behind him, holding onto his legs and body, trying to make him stop by beating spikes into every part of him. I saw him falter from weakness and pain, and then push on again, each step getting slower and slower, as only his grim determination kept him going.

Suddenly, I heard a long, loud roar, which rattled the air and made my hair dance around my head. A shiver ran up my back and I felt dread in my heart.

Stanze suddenly halted and looked around. The black-winged ones continued beating their spikes into him and then stopped too, still holding Stanze firmly.

Suddenly, most of the fighting halted. Those who were still standing turned and looked towards the sound of the roar – towards the podium.

Lying crumpled and prostrate on the podium was Una. Over a dozen black-winged ones held him down and another stood on his back. Una's eyes were open, and I could see pain and anger in them.

"Stop, or your Supreme will be shown ways to make him wish he was dead," the black-winged one standing on Una's back called out.

It was the first words I had heard a black-winged one speak. Their language sounded similar to the kutu I knew, yet more guttural, less musical.

"You are outnumbered and failing. We have your Supreme. We have won," he continued.

A few scuffles began again, with kutu shouting 'no', refusing to accept defeat. Stanze was one of them, and I saw him try again to beat off the dozens that held him. But the Anumi, Orion, his team and their friends were not only outnumbered, most of them now lay fallen, and too injured to move. Black-winged ones quickly contained the few fighting ones that remained standing, until all in the arena was quiet and at a standstill.

From the layers upon layers of fallen kutu I saw Shursa pick himself up and limp towards the podium, straightening his gown and brushing the dirt from his arms. Some black-winged ones also bustled forward, stepping over fallen ones. In their midst was Orion and Jychanumun, badly injured and propped up on either side by their captors.

What shall I do? I asked desperately

Jychanumun had been keeping his mind closed from me. He opened his thoughts.

Stay hidden, keep safe, keep quiet unless they sense you, was all he said.

The black-winged ones made way for Shursa, who looked very angry. He stopped when he reached Orion and stared at him.

"You fool," he uttered into Orion's face, and then leapt onto the podium.

"You will all submit to me, or my new friends will make other uses of you," Shursa spoke. "Make your choice, pain or not, because today I *will* become the Supreme."

Nobody moved. Then, slowly, some of those who had fallen pulled themselves shakily to their feet, fighting against the injuries they had sustained to make the effort to move. I saw Chia, Stanze, Kraniel and Nirrious, and there were Anumi too, many of them. Jychanumun and Orion stood higher, shaking themselves from their captors' grasp. They knew that they could not win, but by standing tall they were showing Shursa that they would rather die than submit to him.

"As you wish," Shursa shrugged, making a hand signal that I didn't understand.

Some of Shursa's challengers were pushed into one area by the black-winged ones, who started whipping them violently. Stanze leapt forward, trying to stop them, successfully striking two of them with one double-handed blow of his weapon. A larger group of black-winged ones leapt on Stanze, pinning him to the ground. Shursa looked at the spectacle nonchalantly. He knew he had won.

"Submit to me, Orion, and bring me the human with Factor

X," Shursa said. His eyes scanned the arena, taking in the humans that stood around him.

Orion looked back at Shursa stonily. One of the black-winged ones thrust something into Orion's stomach, making him crumple down to the ground. Slowly he gathered himself and stood again.

"Do not hurt him yet," Shursa instructed. "Bring him closer,"

Orion was thrust forward so that he stood directly under the podium.

"Closer!" Shursa barked, pointing to the podium.

The black-winged ones around Orion picked him up by his clothes and threw him towards the podium. Orion landed awkwardly, sprawled at Shursa's feet. Slowly, he pulled himself up to a sitting position.

"Now, Orion, you thought I was not a forward thinker. You fool," Shursa drawled. "Now I give you one last chance. Bring me the human, and then beg me, beg me to forgive you, beg me not to despise you, beg me to desire you."

"And what possible benefit would my begging bring?" Orion asked, looking up at Shursa.

"That I might be lenient with your so-called friends," Shursa replied haughtily. "You will bring me the human and beg, because, as you can see, my new friends have had many millennia to discover ways of causing pain. I believe they are very effective. They will work through every one of your friends and every human here until either she comes forward, or you bring her to me. And that's only after you have begged to me not to punish you further. In fact, I think you should beg now."

Orion slowly stood to face Shursa. He put his hands on Shursa's arms, pulled him forward, and then embraced him, kissing him on each cheek.

"For any wrong I may have done you, I beg you to forgive me,"

Orion said with sincerity. "But I cannot beg you not to despise me, for that is your choice, and I cannot beg you to desire me, for I do not want your desire. You can stop this, Shursa, this is wrong, it does not have to be this way; that I would gladly beg of you."

"You refuse me even now!" Shursa yelled. He pushed Orion hard, sending him flying from the podium and back onto the ground. "Contain him," he instructed angrily. "I'll deal with him later."

Several black-winged ones advanced on Orion as he rose. They closed in on him, and although I did not see it, I knew they assaulted him. I fed him strength to numb the pain, but there was little more I could do. When the black-winged ones drew back, Orion was on the floor, unmoving.

"Jychanumun," Shursa smiled, turning his attention to him. "I want this energy now. Please bring me the female."

"I cannot," Jychanumun replied.

"Bring me the female; I order it!" Shursa shouted.

Jychanumun didn't reply, and immediately three black-winged ones simultaneously moved forward from behind him; they were holding long, thin spikes in their hands. Suddenly, they thrust the spikes into Jychanumun's back. Jychanumun fell to the ground. Through our connection I shared his pain, feeling it as if it were my own.

My mouth involuntarily screamed out and I fell down as my knees gave way.

"*No!*" I heard Jychanumun shout, and then they hurt him again, but I didn't feel it this time; he took the pain for us both. I felt my eyes clouding over as a line of black-winged ones launched towards me.

When I came to, I was laying prostrate on the podium with Shursa standing over me.

Shursa bent down and pulled me up by my hair, bringing my

face close to his. Of all the things I could have thought of, all I could think was that I should have cut off all my hair.

"So it seems I have her after all," Shursa said, smiling. "I am Shursa, your god," he continued in a simplified human tongue, "If you promise to filter the energy for me I will give you whatever you want."

"It is not mine to give," I replied in kutu tongue.

Shursa suddenly let go of my hair, dropping me. His face was full of uncertainty. Then he quickly recovered from the shock and regained his composure, looking down at me with anger and distaste.

"Do you not understand?" I said, again in kutu tongue. "The energy here is a life form far older and greater that anything you could imagine. It will retaliate if you disturb it."

"Now, we both know that is not true," Shursa drawled, while still smiling. "Now link me to that energy and you will have all that you could want."

I stood, embraced my courage, and looked him in the eyes. They were cruel eyes, but I held their stare anyway.

"What I want is for you to let my friends go, to let Una remain as Supreme, and to stop poisoning the minds of others," I replied. "But I cannot give you what is not mine to give. Even if I wanted to, I cannot."

"So, these traitors have washed your minds for their own benefit, and you call them your friends?" Shursa laughed. "We'll see." He made some gestures with his hands that I did not know.

Moments later, a group of black-winged ones forced Jychanumun, Orion, Chia, Stanze, Kraniel, and Nirrious to line up behind me on the churned up flowers. Two more black-winged ones flew up, grabbed my shoulders and pulled me down to the ground, forcing me to face my kutu friends.

Shursa jumped down to stand next to me. He took something from a black-winged kutu beside him and pointed a shining object towards Chia. Then I saw a light, then nothing, and Chia fell to the floor. Then came another light, and Kraniel fell to the floor.

Shursa looked at me. "How many do I have to harm?" he asked. "It's up to you. I'll stop when you give me what I want."

"Please," I whispered, "Do not do this. I cannot give you what is not mine to give; I do not know how. It is not mine. I am nothing."

Shursa glanced at me with disdain, and then launched several successive flashes into the bodies of my friends. I instinctively leapt forward to protect them. My mind told me it would not do any good, but I could not stop myself; if my words did not work, all I could do was shield them.

As I leapt forward, I felt a stinging pain in my torso.

Suddenly, my legs gave way as I looked down. A dot of red grew larger on my tunic and a warm fluid trickled down my back.

I have a hole straight through me, I though, as I sank to my knees.

I felt a commotion around me, but it felt surreal, as if it no longer mattered. The life of my flesh oozed out of me, dripping to the ground, and I watched it with a distant fascination. *I have not chosen this*, I thought.

Within my own dislocated numbness, I felt a stirring in my belly, an anger that wasn't mine. It was *his*. I did not fight that feeling, I embraced it. It was not me that was angry; all I felt was awareness of injustice. *He* was angry. He was angry because I had no choice. He was angry because the wrongness disturbed him. His anger welled through me, a sensation so intense – far more intense than ever before – that I felt as if I could catch fire. His awareness consumed me, filling me with purpose, yet I was in control. It was as if his power truly was mine.

I was summoning his strength, drawing it to me as a consequence of the wrongs around me. I felt the use of the voice gather in the pit of my stomach, I knew it was coming and I wanted it with my whole being.

As black-winged ones rained their spiked fists down on my friends' heads, I looked up, held my bloodied hands to the sky, and shrouded myself in images of the things I knew they feared. I felt light pouring from my body and directed it all around me.

"STOP!" I whispered, but it came out as a roar so loud it would silence thunder. "STOP! FEEL THE PAIN YOU CAUSE INFLICTED BACK A THOUSAND FOLD,"

I could hear the words as if I was detached from myself. They were deep and booming, making the ground vibrate. The sky above me blackened with thick, dark clouds; rumbles of thunder crashed around me and lightning flashed through the sky.

I looked around. The black-winged ones behind my kutu friends stood with their fists poised in the air, caught part way through their striking motion with a look of distress frozen on their faces. Orion's mouth was ajar, as if he had been caught just before calling out. Shursa stood with a wide, sickening smile on his face, part-contorted into one of pain. I had wanted and commanded it. They had stopped, and immediately their minds had filled with the injuries they had done, reflected back to them a thousand fold. Nothing moved. Everything was motionless; everything, except his planet and me.

I looked down at the blood oozing from my stomach to the ground and opened my true vision. He was all around me. He did not want me to join him like this. It was not my choice.

Heal, I heard him say, and I saw shivers of the lands light ripple through my body. I could feel the blood stop pouring as the flesh closed around itself. I slowly stood, feeling stronger than ever and more at one with him than I had ever been.

So the voice was your voice all along, I said to *him*. Now I knew that the power I wielded was linked to him.

Now it is also your voice, little one, he replied. *It seems at last you have understanding.*

Yes, I said, *I understand. I am three, but we are one and always will be.*

Yes, he said sleepily. *The little one understands. I will be with you always. Come to me when you choose. I will always be here.*

And always have been, I added.

I felt his peace, which came through my peace, because I understood existence and time, and knew that all other things were matters of choice. He did not need to walk with me; he was always there. I saw his light through the land. It was still there and always would be. He was beautiful and always would be. He had found peace enough to sleep again.

I would join him one day, but not yet, not today. I no longer needed answers because I embraced life for just that; the wonder of living. I smiled to myself as I looked at my flesh and the light that was his.

We will share many dreams, I thought. *I will teach you something; the love of life.*

I felt him smile, as much as an Old One could smile. Was he returning to his slumbers? Yes, it seemed as if he had found peace enough to sleep again, for now.

Good night, I said.

He didn't reply. He didn't need to.

I walked up to Jychanumun and gently stroked his face.

Not you, I said with my mind. *Awaken.*

Jychanumun slumped to the floor, letting out a gasp. The black-winged one who had been holding him still stood poised, with his hands now empty where Jychanumun had once been.

I bent to Jychanumun. *Come,* I said silently, as he recovered his senses, *you must show me who to awaken and who to leave sleeping. It seems a new plan has taken precedence.*

Jychanumun stood and looked around as the lightning flashes highlighted thousands of faces captured in stillness.

"Iastha! What have you done?" he gasped.

"Everything. Nothing. What was right," I calmly replied. "Now, you must help me choose who to help."

I knew immediately to awaken Orion and the rest of his team. Arousing Kraniel took a little more time, as a black-winged one had stopped with an instrument still embedded in Kraniel's head. Nevertheless, once he was roused he helped us, and made no complaint of the pain I knew he carried. It would heal.

Una awoke, thrashing and angry, but became immediately subdued when he looked around and began the task of rallying his newly wakened comrades. Once all the Anumi had been revived I walked with Una, rousing his kutu, and he filled them with his balance, cleansing them of the poison that Shursa had instilled in them.

The high sun came and went as I worked. Time was meaningless. The awoken kutu released the humans from their positions, sending back to their homes those that could walk. Many humans had died, and those who were wounded I insisted they healed. Still, by the close of the day, thousands of kutu stood motionless around us, many injured and desperately needing healing. Limited by my pace and the time it took to heal and rebalance, we continued on, walking around the arena through the night and well into the next day, until finally only black-winged ones and Shursa remained unmoving.

"You must decide what you wish to do with them," I said to Una and Jychanumun.

Una studied them. "Some are retrievable. Others are beyond my balancing abilities."

"Will they not inevitably walk the same cruel paths?" Jychanumun asked.

"It is their choice. We cannot remove choice," I replied. "But if they are awakened, I can implant a forgetfulness of this place so they will not remember for a long time, if ever."

"Then those who are retrievable will be rebalanced and given a choice as to where they go," Una decided. "Any who are left will be sent away on a craft, with forgetfulness in their minds."

"And Shursa?" I asked.

Una contemplated this for a while. "I must take him back to Eden with me," he decided. "He is a councillor, and my personal choice for a councillor at that. He was a good kutu once. I will take him in hand, and re-educate and rebalance him. I cannot believe that he is lost to us entirely."

"Very good," I smiled at Una. I did not like this Shursa, but I had not liked Huru either and I had not wanted to cease him. I could see why Una was Supreme. He endeavoured to be just and honourable whenever it was possible.

So it was decided, and after two more days, we were done. The arena was cleared of kutu and humans. Only broken remnants of the battle littered the floor, covering the still-buried ship.

I asked Chia what we were to do with the 7A, and told him that it was still alive, but badly hurt. Chia insisted on using a fleet of pods to uncover his ship himself. I did not interfere, but I fed energy to the craft and soothed its agony, letting it know that soon it would be free.

Then, feeling the entirety of my exhaustion, Jychanumun took me back to the plateau and I slept for a long time. I dreamt of strange things and familiar things, but I slept soundly. I felt at peace. The Earth felt at peace. *He* was sleeping again, and I knew the whole of myself.

TWENTY-SEVEN

When I awoke from my slumbers, Una, Supreme to the Shaa-kutu, was sitting by my recliner, waiting for me to wake. He greeted me as soon as I opened my eyes.

"Iastha," he smiled.

I quickly rubbed my eyes. "What's wrong?" I asked, sitting up immediately.

"Nothing is wrong; all is well, now," Una replied peacefully, and then waited while I composed myself. "Are you rested?" he asked.

"Yes, I think so," I replied, "Thank you; well rested."

"Good," he nodded.

I looked down and, seeing that I was dressed, got out of the recliner. Una held out his hand and helped me slide down.

"It makes me very happy to know you are well," I said, smiling at Una. "I see in you why your people love you so, and why you are Supreme."

Una smiled back and I felt the warmth of his smile. He took

my hand and tucked it into the crook of his arm, and together we slowly walked outside.

"And it seems that you, too, have caught the hearts of many," Una said as we strolled. "Orion's team all wish to stay here on Earth for a while. They would like to learn what they could of the Old One. And I do not think Jychanumun will be leaving at all. I have granted them leave to stay here for as long as they wish."

"And I will be pleased to teach them what I know," I replied, "and any others who come here with an open heart."

"It is as I hoped," Una replied. "And I myself: although I must return to Eden now, I will also return here soon; there is much that I too can discover. But for the immediate future I have to re-teach our kutu harmony and balance, so my load will be full for a while."

"I will always welcome you, whenever you can return," I said.

"Then I look forward to it," Una replied, smiling again.

"Thank you," I said, pausing to bow.

"Please, no formalities," he laughed, and then took both of my hands in his. "Let me thank you," he said.

Una let go of my hands, leaving a small object in my palm. It was a beautiful and intricately woven symbol, made from a piece of palest silver, hanging from a delicate cord. It gave off a soft blue hue that rippled in my hand.

"It means 'I am three,'" I said, holding up the symbol. I knew it instinctively. I put it around my neck.

"Yes," Una smiled. "And if ever you need me. I will know."

His words made me smile. He looked at me quizzically.

"It was those same words, but from my own mouth, that led me to the Shaa-kutu," I said. "When you next visit, I will tell you all about it."

"Very good," he smiled, taking my arm again. We headed

towards the edge of the plateau, where the others sat waiting with several of the Anumi clan.

"You will not harm any humans, will you?" I asked Una, before we reached them.

"No, of course not," he replied, "Although if we continue producing bios, they will be different. They certainly will not contain such a high percentage of kutu genes. But the humans here will continue to thrive, too; I acknowledge that they are capable of choice."

I nodded. It was a satisfactory compromise.

"Is there anything I can do for you, young Iastha?" Una asked.

"Not for me," I replied. "Unless . . . could you stop other humans from ceasing?"

Una stopped and thought for a moment. "I cannot," he said. "The combinations of what humans are made of and how they live – it is part of their make-up. But, I will look into ways of lengthening and improving their lifespan, and I will ask Orion and the others to pass on the knowledge of our ways of mending."

I thanked him as we reached the assembled group. These were all the kutu I had come to call friends, plus several I recognised as Anumi from their golden head-dresses. Jychanumun stood as we approached, and bowed to Una.

"Jychanumun," Una bowed back and smiled. "I had hoped that you were not lost. It is a pleasure to finally meet the real you." He turned to Orion and the others. "And all of you, I cannot repay your loyalty enough. You have a special place in my heart. Such things can never be forgotten."

Orion and his team stood and returned the courtesy. Una nodded to the Anumi and walked with them to the edge of the plateau, taking to the sky with the Anumi following close behind.

"Well," I said, watching Una fly towards the ship in the distance. "You probably have many questions, and there is much joy to be had, but first I would like to visit my parents, and Soul, just for a short while. I have some tales I would like to tell them; tales that should not be forgotten. In generations to come they must remember who they truly are, and who you truly are."

TWENTY-EIGHT

FINALLY . . .

Una breathed a long sigh of relief when he finally boarded his craft and sat down. He had just checked on Shursa in the rear of the craft to see that he was well, and the ex-councillor had greeted him with spits and cursing. It weighed heavy in Una's heart that one of their own could become so bitter inside, but he remained determined to help Shursa to overcome his problems in any way he could.

One of the Anumi, Peniva, handed him a long goblet as he settled into his seat. He savoured the first sip of Ochrah he had tasted in a long time, leaned back and closed his eyes. Peniva waited, seemingly wishing to ask something.

"Speak, my friend," Una said with his eyes closed. "Lest your anticipation become catching."

Peniva activated a long viewing table and implanted a small crystal. A three-dimensional image of a building sprang into view. Una opened his eyes and leaned forward.

"We of the Anumi wished to do something in Iastha's honour," Peniva said. "We were busy while she slept, building a tribute. A building in her name, surrounded on three sides by grassland and trees, overlooking the lake where she lived for a while; we understand she loved it there. We also heard that she wanted to learn and teach; we thought she could use this building as a gathering place for that purpose."

"This is splendid," Una agreed. "It's a wonderful idea and a fitting gesture. You have my full approval."

"Thank you," Peniva smiled. He clipped his heals and performed a shallow bow. "May I inform Stanze to go ahead with the finishing touches and then present it as a surprise gift to her?"

"Yes, yes," Una smiled. "And leave these plans with me for a while. I wish to study them. They really are most excellent; it seems you have many hidden talents."

Peniva beamed proudly and left, while Una poured over the designs.

The large golden building for Iastha stood facing a lake. The Anumi had made a huge doorway with tall pillars in the form of statues either side. The statues were representations of kutu, wearing the snarling headdresses they wore for ceremony, looking down as if guarding the entrance. The walls of the building stepped gradually upwards, carved from glossy golden Uana. In some segments of the stone, the Anumi had carved kutu tales of bravery, with Iastha's tale taking centre place. At the top of the building, a central domed tower made from transparent crystal would sparkle under the sun and reflect the water. It was stunning – a monumental golden building.

Yes, Una thought to himself, as he relaxed back, letting his wings trail to the floor with a smile. This is a spectacular creation, built by our Anumi and a fitting tribute from their bravest kutu to this astonishing young human; a towering monument of brilliantly gleaming gold stone. I think Iastha will enjoy living there. Yes, I think she will like it a great deal.

But that night, despite Tachra's inner peace, the nightmares of the golden building, with screams coming from inside the huge framed entrance, returned with a vengeance.

Order Form

As well as you local bookstore, you can order further copies of this book direct from Ruby Blaze Publishing.

To order further copies of *befφre the gφds*, please send a copy of the order form below to:

Ruby Blaze Publishing
Mews House, 13 Gloucester Street,
Taunton, Somerset, TA1 1TA

Or visit www.rubyblaze.com to download an order form or to order online.

- -

Please send me ____ copies of *befφre the gφds* at £9.99 each.

Please add UK postage/packaging at £1.00 per book.

☐ I enclose a UK bank cheque or postal order, payable to Ruby Blaze Publishing, for £ _____

Name:

Address:

Postcode:

Please allow 28 days for delivery. Please do not send cash.

☐ Tick if you would like further information on The Chronicles of Fate and Choice. Your E-mail: _____

We never share or sell our customer details

- -

The second novel in The Chronicles of Fate and Choice trilogy

The war begins . . .
The Nigh-kutu return with vengeance in their hearts and a
plan that cannot fail. Darkness flies with them, casting shadows
in the hearts of the weak.
Who will fall?

Release date Summer 2010
Available for pre-order:
Visit www.rubyblaze.com/tumultus

About the Author

K.S. Turner grew up in East Anglia,
studied Art and Design at Central Saint Martins
and Middlesex University in London, and now lives
in Somerset with a posse of fluffy animals.

befφre the gφds is the first book in
The Chronicles of Fate and Choice trilogy.

To find out more about Kate, visit www.rubyblaze.com